# TWICE

# SHY

ISBN 9798394135989

This is a work of fiction.
All characters are fictitious and any resemblance to real persons is
accidental and unintentional.

*For Mam*

# PART 1

# CHAPTER 1

It's one in the morning, and the seating area in the centre of the food service hall is virtually deserted, just three lost souls sitting far apart. A cleaner, gripping the handlebars of a humming mechanical floor washer, guides it in slow motion around the perimeter.

The stores are closed, shuttered up for the night, only two fast food outlets staying open: a coffee shop with over-priced snacks, and a burger bar manned by two staff in black tunics and baseball caps, one on the counter, another attending to the grills and fryers, a third, in short-sleeved shirt and tie, flicking through a sheaf of paperwork. I buy a bottle of water from the coffee shop and choose a seat with a clear view of the main entrance. If I'm right, he won't be long.

It's two minutes before the automatic doors at the end of the hall slide open and an unprepossessing figure lumbers in, arms hanging loose, gorilla-like. Beady eyes scan the sparsely populated room and for a second, meet mine. I ignore it and stare at the phone, swiping up and down a non-existent feed. It waddles over to the burger bar and within a minute, leaves clutching a brown paper bag. It makes a show of looking for a place to sit and though spoilt for choice, meanders towards me, choosing the next table but one. I can tell it's looking in my direction but avoid eye contact or even acknowledging its presence.

It unpacks the bag; twin burgers wrapped in paper, double fries in a box, extra-large coke. It unwraps one and begins to devour it with a visceral grunt, masticating audibly like a horse with a carrot.

"Alright?" it mumbles through a mouthful, stuffing it simultaneously with fries. I turn my head at the sound. He's big and bald and folds of loose flesh ripple down the back of his neck. Black tee-shirt of a death metal band, fleshy, muscular arms tattooed all the way to the wrist. I wince at the acrid stench of griddled meat and oil that competes with body odour, a pungent cocktail of sweat, urine and raw onions. *He smells.* The first impression, he's too distinctive, too easy to describe, too easy to pick up on CCTV, not the grey, innocuous type that merges with the background. There have been no witnesses, no leads, apart from one.

It's a plain, white carriage, she said, bearing a three-pointed star, she said. We all know the type. Invariably in the outside lane, fast enough to overtake anything, even fully laden. Can't be more than a few hundred thousand. There's something else, she said. Black wheels. I check images online. It narrows it down; smaller haystack, same needle. And he smells.

So I drive the motorways, day after day, calling at every services, concentrating on the ones he hasn't struck, cruising the lorry and van parks, seeking the needle. Twelve weeks of budget hotels, nights stretched out in the car, umpteen cartons of junk food. Ten thousand miles later, I'm heading north once again, tired, subdued and ready to crash for the night, when it passes me doing ninety. I feel a shiver and rush of adrenalin. I tap the dashcam to make sure it's recording.

The Mini-Motorway-Murders. Triple-Ms, as designated by the tabloids. Six disappeared women, their cars, all Minis, left abandoned at or nearby a motorway service station. Police have made no progress, are under intense pressure, and the papers love it. It's a story they can run and run as long as the perpetrator remains at large. It's exquisitely salacious and permits relentless pillorying of plod. They rage and grieve misty-eyed for victims and their families, but they don't want it to end.

I give chase but there's no need. The Sprinter pulls into the slow lane until I catch up and overtake, and a few minutes later it's passing me again, this time at a slower speed. I stare straight ahead but I sense he's having a good look. It pulls in behind me and follows at a discreet distance.

I exit the motorway the next services. Like many, South Alston has only one camera and that's at the car park entrance, its sole purpose to ensure visitors comply with the two-hours-free rule. I park in a secluded area behind the service building next to some industrial sized bins, away from the few cars clustered around the main entrance door. I switch off and wait for the Sprinter to coast in, slowly circumnavigate the car park and stop a few spaces away.

I check hair in the mirror and fasten jacket, securing the glass brooch on the lapel. I lock up the Mini and head for the entrance, pulling down the hem of my shorter than usual skirt, tottering carefully on my higher than usual heels, avoiding eye contact with van or driver.

\*\*\*

Three months ago and almost two years after Clare's accident, I reunited a daughter with her natural mother, forty years after they'd been separated. She'd found me by word of mouth, connections, seemingly obscure and irrelevant. You never can tell what's going to come up in this game. You do something good for someone, they tell someone else, either to express gratitude or to relive their own joy, and one thing leads to another. I don't do divorces; that's taking sides. I don't do family disputes of any sort, especially inheritance as there's no way of knowing who's deserving and who's not. I help people in any way I can, as long as their motives are honourable, they appear vulnerable, and have nowhere else to go. I never set out to be like this, but then I never expected to die, so figure I may as well make myself useful.

I'm bidding farewell to long lost mother and daughter when my phone rings unexpectedly; unexpectedly because I only have three contacts and haven't spoken to any of them for well over a year. Sue Jenkins is one of them.

"Kate! How are you?" she says effusively.

"I'm well Sue. It's been a while." Eighteen months to be exact, and over twelve since I left Oakdale.

"Where are you these days? I turned up at the cottage but the owners said you'd moved."

"Pastures new. You know what it's like."

"Certainly do. Best thing I ever did was leave." Former WPC Jenkins is referring to her previous life in the Dales Force.

"So what are you doing now?"

"I'm retraining as a psychotherapist. Family orientated. Mental health, eating disorders, marriage breakdown, anxiety, kids mainly."

"I guess your old job gave you an insight into personal trauma."

"Yeah. That's one good thing about being a copper. I got lots of first-hand experience, but the difference now is I have the power to help. What about you?"

"Still writing, but I'm doing investigative work more and more."

"Oh wow! You're a PI?"

"Hardly." *That's exactly what you are Kate.*

"Oh my God! Wait 'til I tell Dave."

She's willing me to ask. I must oblige. "Dave?"

"My fiancé," she says proudly, and I can sense the joy. "I'm getting married Kate, and I want you to come." She's bubbling with excitement, looking forward to the best day of her life and who would blame her? She's overflowing with love, intoxicated by the drug, kicking off a new, romantic chapter in the book of life. I strain every sinew to sound enthusiastic and happy for her, and deep down, I suppose I am.

"That's great! Of course I'll come."

"I'll text you the details. Can't wait to catch up on everything. Gotta go. Lots of calls to make. Love you."

I hardly know her, and if she hadn't contacted me about this, we would probably never have met again. Six weeks isn't long. Maybe they'd dispensed with the optional 'let's see how it goes' phase and gone straight for the finish line? Maybe they're simply head over heels and can't wait? Maybe they've been engaged for a while and she's trawling through her address book for people to make up the numbers? Who knows? I said I'd go.

So, I've dug out my best frock and best hat and smiled sweetly and chatted with complete strangers, glossing over my acquaintance with the bride and waiting for an opportunity to slope off, when she bounds across the dancefloor, hand in hand with the hapless Dave.

"Kate! This is my husband, Dave!" she says, giggling from the combined effects of champagne and euphoria. Dave is more than a foot taller and has a relaxed, confident smile. He's also fifteen years older.

"Sue told me all about you, Kate." *All she knows Dave, which isn't very much.* "Always pleased to meet someone in law enforcement, even those on the fringes." No handshake, just the put-down.

"I hope you'll be very happy." It's a feeble response that has a latent ambiguity, unintended but nevertheless true. I'm out of place, out of my comfort zone, watching actors in a play in which I'll never take part. But I note that despite her bad experience with erstwhile police colleagues, she obviously found one who was different from the rest.

"Guess what Dave does for a living," says Sue, swirling her lacy gown and tossing her head back.

*Can't guess.* I'm losing the will, and it's too early for a game of charades, especially when I'm sober. When the best man delivers a speech in native plod, regales us with tales of derring-do when he and groom were keeping the streets safe

11

for the public, *'those heroes',* and of the laddish pranks they got up to when off-duty, *'those rascals',* it was never in doubt.

"Copper?"

It's enough to make his lip curl, and I suppress the urge to laugh.

"Used to be," she gushes, snuggling up to him, bursting with pride. "Dave's a director in the National Crime Service!"

"Really! Where are you based?"

"East Midlands," announces Dave. He's superior to a regular copper, less stilted, more charming, more important than your bog-standard officer of the law. He's about to elucidate the scale of that importance when one of the two bridesmaids rushes up alongside and grabs his free arm. I'd wondered who they were. Nieces perhaps? This one's the older of the two, about fifteen I guess, and not yet blessed with the social graces.

"Dad?" *Make that daughter.*

"I'm talking sweetheart." She screws up her face and glowers at me. She has a serious matter that needs to be addressed and I'm holding things up. "Lily, this is Kate, one of Sue's friends."

"Hi," says Lily offhandedly, unimpressed.

"Go ahead Lily," I suggest. She doesn't hesitate.

"Justin wants to take me and Chloe for a run in his car."

Dave's forced smile evaporates and he raises himself up to his full height, towering over us all.

"When?"

"Now?" says Lily, flashing her eyes at him.

"No."

The switch is instant; feverish anticipation to frustration and contempt in one tenth of a second. "Why?"

"Because I say so." Lily lets out a furious gasp and stomps off. "Sorry about that."

"Not at all. I was like that once."

"Me too!" says Sue, mildly embarrassed, unlike Dave.

"I was married before," says Dave, needlessly.

"The girls are really lovely," says Sue, but it lacks conviction. "They've made me very welcome."

Two teenage daughters? I don't buy it. Getting adopted by a ready-made family is a leap of faith. I don't know if Dave is divorced or bereaved and I'm not about to ask, but whatever the circumstances, they're all going to have their work cut out. I wonder uncharitably whether her training in psychotherapy will stand her in good stead.

"So, you're a private investigator?" says Dave in a tone that's borderline pejorative. *Leave it to we professionals.*

"Not really. People ask me to find things out. Mundane stuff, nothing terribly onerous."

"Of course," says Dave with a condescending smile. I'm ready for a lecture, when the best man puts a hand on his shoulder. He looks serious.

"Sorry to interrupt, boss. Can I have a word?"

"Please excuse me," says Dave. "It was very nice to meet you."

I watch the two men go to a quiet corner and engage in muted discussion. The body language is telling; hunched stance, close-up, eye-to-eye, head movement signifying surprise and despair, hands in pockets, pensive, wondering what to do. Something bad has happened. I realise Sue has been talking at me.

"…but he's a lovely man, not like the idiots and creeps I used to work with. Generous too."

I give her a hug. "I wish you every happiness."

"Thanks Kate." She dabs at the corner of one eye. Despite confident assertions, she's not sure.

"I must be going."

"Already?"

"Got a long drive."

"We never had a chance to catch up."

"Another time. Enjoy the rest of your day. It's been lovely."

So I get into my Mini and set off on the two-hour trip back to the Wolds, thinking about Sue and Dave and Lily and Chloe, hoping they'll make a go of it, when the radio news bulletin grabs my attention. Another woman has gone missing. Carole Foster from the West Midlands has been missing for two days and her Mini found abandoned at services on the M6. Carole is the sixth in two years, missing, already presumed dead. Murders carried out by the same individual but in different parts of the country, each in a different police authority, each near motorway services, the cars they drove and to some extent their professions, the commonalities. Like three of the others, Carole was a sex-worker. The two that weren't looked the part, judging by the provocative images the tabloids plucked from social media.

Police have made every attempt to pool resources, but with no evidence and no witnesses, the only assumption they make is that the killer is male and will strike again in a different place. This would at least narrow down the search, if they had any idea who or what they were searching for. Consequently, the case was handed over to the National Crime Service. Dave Parker, regional chief of NCS East Midlands is the latest recipient of bad news.

As it happens, my great, great, grandmother Edith Hawley knows a lot about the sex trade and has a thing to say about men. When she's not ranting over her egregious treatment at the hands of her husband Jacob, she's fulminating over her exploitation in the fleshpots of early twentieth century London. In particular, she's wont to denounce the judge who sentenced her to hang for administering summary justice to an evil monster, just because he happened to be a peer of the realm and one of his mates. That I'm descended from said monster is something I'd like to forget, but despite her execution in 1912, Edith doesn't feel the need to keep quiet.

14

Edith is the reason I'm still here, and for the most part we rub along quite well, even though there are times I wish she hadn't intervened in the way she did, leaving me in this state of limbo. But when Edith has something to say she lets me know, usually in the middle of the night and often, but not always, while I'm asleep. On this occasion, however, she had something useful and original to impart.

One of Edith's best friends, someone who worked alongside her at Soho's infamous *Angel's Delight* was Annie, known to her clients as *Lara de la Mer*. Annie attended Edith's execution, waving a tearful goodbye to her friend before they were eventually reunited in October 1940 when Annie succumbed in the blitz. Carole Foster was Annie's great, great granddaughter, Annie has told Edith what happened and later that night at around two in the morning, Edith told me. She didn't suggest I do anything about it, she simply took the opportunity to articulate her eternal loathing of the male of the species, or at least, those who commit heinous crimes against women.

So I get in touch with Sue, express my sorrow when she tells me that, due to unforeseen circumstances, Dave has had to postpone their honeymoon, and tell her I have information that may help. But I will only talk to Dave.

"What information?" says Dave, when, a few days later we meet in a hotel reception in Lincoln.

"I know the make and model of the van and that the guy emits a pungent body odour."

"Go on."

"It's a white Sprinter with black alloys."

"Where did you get this?"

"Sources." It's pointless explaining. He would never believe me even though he'd be wrong not to. He turns pompous and officious.

"Miss Duvall, I should warn you it's a criminal offence to withhold information which may be of assistance to the police

15

either in preventing a serious offence or apprehending someone who has committed one." *To quote from the NCS handbook.*

"I've just given you information."

"It has no value if I don't know where it came from. Is it a witness?"

"Yes."

"Then we need to interview him, or her."

"You can't."

"Why not?"

"There's no point telling you because you'll laugh at me and do nothing about it."

"Let me be the judge of that."

"Sorry. The point is, I trust my source and I know you won't. With luck we have a few months before anyone else gets murdered and I have an idea, which is why I'm here."

He looks vaguely affronted. The upstart amateur PI standing her ground, calling the shots. The reality is, I'll do it without his help, it will just be a bit harder. And if he wants to tie me to a chair and shine a light in my eyes until I crack and tell him my source, then let him. He'll let me go as soon as he knows she's been dead for over a hundred years and it came to me in a dream.

"It's quite simple. I'll cruise the motorways and service stations in a Mini looking for a smelly guy in a white van until either I find him or he finds me."

"Human bait?"

"Sort of."

"Don't be ridiculous. That could take months, if not years."

"You have a quick fix?"

"Police all over the country are working on it. We'll get him. Leave it to the professionals." It's patronising but I'm not mad at him because he can't help it. He's just plod.

"How are you going to stop me?"

"I can't, unless I believe your actions are reckless, put other lives at risk and are prejudicing police enquiries."

"How can it? I'm just another pair of eyes. You lot are always asking for help from the public. What's the difference?"

"You lot?" I've struck a nerve. "Listen, I strongly urge you not…"

"But I need help." Parker sits back in his chair and shakes his head wearily. His face says it all. "When I find him…"

"If…"

"…when I find him, I'll need immediate backup from the boys in blue, wherever I am in the country."

"I only control East Midlands."

"But you have national cover which is why you need to brief your colleagues nationwide, especially those in areas he hasn't struck."

"Brief them? What do I say? Some half-witted PI wants to put her own life at risk and as soon as she gets herself into trouble and cries for help, you have to come running?"

"Do you want this guy or not?"

"And why immediate?" he says, ignoring the question. "Why can't you just get a license plate and call it in?"

"Because you need evidence. You have to catch him in the act."

"What? The act of murdering you? You're wasting my time. Do as I say and leave it alone," and with that, Parker storms off in a huff.

A couple of days later, he's back on the phone. His new wife has bent his ear, telling him I'm credible, and he needs to listen. He's still not convinced, obviously. He still thinks it's a waste of time and reckless of me even to consider it, but if I'm that determined and there's nothing he can do to stop me, he may as well help. We agree there will be no names, no money, no records and no publicity. It suits me just as much as him; he can't be seen to be courting the assistance of an

17

amateur nor putting her life at risk, and I want to remain under the radar. He will provide me with an emergency transponder and circulate the number to all regional forces with a code red response. If nothing happens, then nothing happens, but it's possible he'll wind up a hero for cracking the case. It's equally possible I wind up as victim number seven, but that's my lookout.

***

So that's how I ended up here at South Alston services at 1.30 in the morning, watching this snuffling warthog, still unsure whether he's a sad, lonely misfit or a serial killer. He's on the second burger now and glances across. He tilts his head to peek under my table, but my legs are securely crossed. I offer him two seconds of disdain before returning my attention to an inactive phone, continuing to flick through imaginary feeds.

"Hope that ain't porn you're watching," he says between mouthfuls, chuckling at his own wit and burping loudly.

I turn my head slowly and watch him chew, open mouthed, a human garbage disposal unit. "How did you know that?"

He sniffs and his face twitches. "I can tell you're a woman of the world." He's almost unintelligible, mumbling through a gob of pulverised pap.

"Really?"

"Yeah. Working late?"

"I'm not working."

"Finished for the day? Thought you girls were always open for business." I ignore it. "What is it then?"

"What's what?"

"What you're lookin' at?"

I stay focused on the screen for a few seconds and let out a sigh. "Dark web. Triple X, fetish."

"Nice."

"Just getting a few tips."

"Yeah?" He plucks a phone out of a pocket, swiping and stabbing the screen with podgy, greasy fingers. "I'm on it. What's the site?"

"Ugly, bald, tattooed tubs of lard, dot-com."

It takes a moment for the insult to sink in and the grin to dissolve. "Clever bitch." He puts the phone away and wipes a hand across his mouth, the mere raising of one arm propelling a nauseating waft of armpit odour in my direction. *He smells.*

I sense a tingle between shoulder blades and a rush of adrenalin. He's the one. He scrunches up the burger wrapping, drops it on the floor and pushes back his chair, the metal legs screeching on the tiles. He hikes his pants up and waddles over, placing two hands knuckles down, on my table. The stench intensifies. It's enough to make me faint. "My van's outside. Give you twenty for a blow."

I stay focused on the screen. "Go away."

"Thirty."

"Go away. Please."

"We can negotiate outside. Take your time."

He swaggers off towards the toilets, baggy cargo pants sagging to reveal the waistband of his grey, extra-large CKs. I'll give him ten minutes and then press the button. I have to time this right.

\*\*\*

There's been a heavy shower and the surface of the car park is glistening under the lights. The rain has stopped, the sound of motorway traffic behind the service yard amplified by the swoosh of tyres through standing water. The parking area is extensive but contains no more than twenty cars and a few vans, all the heavy trucks lined up for the night at the far end.

The Mini is the only car in the yard, the next nearest vehicle, a green Transit opposite fat boy's white Sprinter, all

19

largely out of sight of the main car park. I head for the car, put the phone away and blip the key from twenty feet. The Mini's lights beckon.

I take my time, deliberately. I know what's about to happen but not exactly when or how, so I need to stay alert. I reach for the door and wait a few moments, staring up at the sky, primed for an attack that doesn't come. The door handle invites my touch and I reach tentatively for the chrome as if it's electrified, but it gives up a familiar clunk and I slide inside, putting my bag on the passenger seat. *Stay calm Kate. This could be a false alarm.*

I wait, staring at the Sprinter, but see no movement. I slide the key into the ignition and the dashboard lights up. Immediately, there's a yellow warning light with a tyre graphic. *Nothing false about that.* I climb out and check the driver's side, then the other. The front nearside tyre is partially deflated. I'm still staring at it when the smell carries on the wind.

"Need a hand?" The sound startles me and I spin around. He's appeared from nowhere, standing between me and the two vans. *What did you expect Kate? He's done this before.*

"Go away."

"Only tryin' to be nice."

"I'm fine."

"Got a spare?"

"It's run-flat. It'll be okay for a while."

He sucks in his breath. "Wouldn't risk it if I were you. How far are you going? I'll give you a lift." He takes two steps towards me, his bulky frame rocking from side to side.

"Keep away," I say nervously, not meaning to deter him, but to spur him on. I slide both hands into jacket pockets and take a step back until my way is blocked by the Mini. It works. He steps forward again.

"C'mon sweetheart," he says, extending a hand. "Just bein' friendly. Let me take you home."

"Excuse me? Are you okay there?" Another voice. Measured, calm, authoritative. Fat boy grimaces and turns around to look. *No! The last thing I need right now is a knight in shining armour.*

"I'm fine thanks."

"You sure?" He's appeared from nowhere. He's late forties, good looking and casually dressed in white shirt and jeans, grey moustache, the streetlight picking up silvery flecks in otherwise dark, back-combed hair.

"You heard her pal. I got this covered."

"I suggest *you* move along, *pal*," he counters, the emphasis on two words, the challenge laid down.

"I was here first."

*This is all going wrong.*

I try again. "It's fine, thank you. I've got a dodgy tyre and this gentleman is offering to help."

"See?" says fat boy, turning back to look at me, grinning, encouraged by the apparent endorsement.

"No way," says the man in the nice shirt and jeans.

*You're about to ruin everything! Walk away!*

Fat boy's expression darkens and he clenches his fists. He turns around to face his rival and spreads his legs. "I won't tell you again." The hard-man act is short lived. He's facing an extended arm with a gun pointing down at his crotch. "Jesus!" His frame sags and his legs twitch, both arms stretching forward involuntarily, an instinctive, futile defence. I despair. I'm so close, but my plan's in tatters because of the actions of a misguided do-gooder.

But there is a problem. Handguns are illegal, which makes him either a special copper, a villain or a fool. No ordinary man in the street wanders around with a weapon, not in this country.

"Okay, okay. I'm outta here," says fat boy, raising both hands. Maintaining his distance, he sidles around the guy with the gun, the extended arm tracking his progress. And then, I'm

21

confused. I watch as he gets into the green Transit and roars off, tyres spinning on the wet tarmac. All I can do is clock the personal license plate; B16 MAN. We watch him go, but the gun remains in full view by his side. It's all wrong. A strong aroma of cheap cologne comes downwind, filling my nostrils. *He smells.*

"Who are you?" I already know who he is, but I was wrong before and I could be wrong again. Maybe the situation can be retrieved?

"You've got a flat tyre."

"I know."

"Need a lift?"

"No thanks."

The charm dissipates, the anxious passer-by act, over. He takes a few steps towards me. "Get in the van," he says calmly, waving the gun towards it.

He's made a mistake. Complacent perhaps, invincible, he assumes, but for the first time, there's a witness. When I'm eventually found, big man will see it on the front page of his favourite tabloid, and if there's anything in it for him, tell plod what he saw. Smart guy clearly believes it's a risk worth taking.

*Wrong again Kate.*

Big man may see the story and put two and two together but he'll keep his head down. He's already on CCTV inside the services making conversation with the victim. The ugly tattooed tub of lard won't come forward and point the finger at an imaginary smart guy in a nice shirt and jeans who he says has a gun. They'll take one look at the unprepossessing thug, slap on the cuffs and before they read him his rights, the red tops will have plastered his ugly mug on the front page. Game over for the obviously guilty-as-hell serial killer. It's no mistake and no risk. It may even be a stroke of luck.

"Get in the van," he says again.

"Why?"

22

"Because I say so."

"Otherwise what? You'll shoot me?"

He grins broadly. He's loving it. I show no fear, no panic, leaning casually against the car, hands in pockets, a challenge to be overcome. It heightens the thrill, and after all, isn't that what this is about? Number seven will be his favourite, the one he remembers for a while. He'll make this last.

"You may even enjoy it."

"Being murdered?"

"It's not mandatory, not if you promise not to scream."

"But I will scream."

He shakes his head. "No you won't."

I notice lack of movement on the motorway, traffic at a standstill. There's been an incident and it's bound to impede everyone's progress. I need to play for time.

"What's in the van?"

"Stuff. Tools, equipment."

"Everything a pervert could possibly need."

"Please," he says with mock indignation. "Pervert is so emotive and judgemental. I prefer dedicated and professional."

"You didn't mention the lashing straps."

"Know your vans then?"

"Well enough to track you down."

It's made an impression; small, but it's there. The flicker of doubt, the casual arrogance deflated, reappraisal necessary.

"Get… in… the… van."

"You'll have to carry me. I assure you I'll resist." He looks around and shrugs.

A wail of sirens in the distance; police and emergency services rushing to the scene of whatever horror has taken place up ahead. We turn our attention to blue flashes on the carriageway. They're a distraction to both of us, for different reasons.

23

He leaps towards me, covering the ten-foot gap in three strides. A hand grabs my throat, pushes me back, crushes me between body and car. He stabs the gun in my ear, his face, an inch from mine.

"Do it!" he hisses. His breath smells of coffee and weirdly, I recognise cheap aftershave; *'Force'*, the one my ex used to wear. He's gripping my windpipe, I can't speak, I manage a shake of head. He lets go of my throat and slaps me hard; so hard the back of my head smashes into the car. The hand is back around my throat and I can feel blood dripping from my mouth. He slams my head against the car for a second time, blurring vision, shock and pain making me dizzy. "Let's go," he snarls, taking a handful of hair and jerking my head sideways and down. I resist, but the blow behind the ear from a gun handle is beyond vicious, potentially fatal. A word springs to a stunned mind from the edge of consciousness. *Necrophilia.*

Hit the ground like a dead weight, muscular hand on collar, dragged backwards, heels scraping through puddles. Amidst the brain haze, find strength to flail arms and twist body and break hold, but within a second he's on top, brutal punch to the head, hand pressed down, crushing throat, deadly intent. Through the visual fog, glimpse of gun, raised for ultimate blow. Fumble in pockets, weapon descends, raise hands…deep breath…close eyes… pull triggers…

It's good stuff, pepper spray. He freezes in shock, drops the gun and then topples off me, screaming, desperate hands tearing at a contorted face, a vain attempt to wipe away the blinding pain, rolling on the ground shouting obscenities. I get to my knees and stagger unsteadily to my feet, retching, head swimming with nauseating pain. I see him come up for air, lurching towards me with outstretched arms like a zombie. I give him another blast with each hand and step aside like a matador as he collides headfirst with the Mini and collapses to the ground, writhing in agony.

Blue flashes illuminate the car park, the light sparkling in the standing water as three police cars skid to a halt. Doors are thrown open, running men appear in the yard.

"What kept you?" I mumble to one in plainclothes. I'm still concussed and bleeding, but think he looks vaguely familiar.

"Are you alright Miss?" he says, holding my upper arm. Two of his uniformed colleagues pounce on the twitching, whimpering assailant while one stands guard, machine pistol at the ready. One kneels on his neck while another tries to cuff him, his nice white shirt and pale blue jeans, stained front and back by the wet filthy ground. I ignore the question and detach the brooch from my jacket handing it to plainclothes along with the transponder.

"It's all on the bodycam. Ignore the big ugly guy with tattoos unless you want to arrest him for offences under the personal hygiene Act."

"Come with me," he says.

"No."

"You need medical attention."

"No."

He doesn't understand. I won't agree to be examined and I know I'll be fine soon, cracked skull or not.

"I need you to make a statement," he says, getting increasingly anxious.

"That's not the deal."

"I must insist."

"Am I under arrest?"

"No."

"Then I'm going home." I nod at the Sprinter. "That'll keep forensics busy."

He holds up a hand. "Wait! I need a name and contact details."

I walk slowly around to the driver's side, vision clearing, pain subsiding. "Ask Dave Parker."

He looks at me dumbly as I climb in. The Mini dashboard pings, protesting a malfunction, the yellow tyre graphic still aglow. I can go fifty miles.

# CHAPTER 2

Hawsby. A typical Lincolnshire village in the heart of the Wolds boasting wide open spaces and big skies. The landscape is flat to the south and east, and to the north, undulating hills form a gateway to the Yorkshire Dales.

The village has maybe a hundred properties; a mixture of ancient stone cottages interspersed with modern bungalows and four-bed detached houses mostly built over the last fifty years. There's also a new, private development of executive, faux mansions guarded by electronic gates and ten-foot-high brick walls. Hawsby has neither post-office, shop nor pub, the last one closing two years ago, currently shuttered up and forlorn. But it suits me, and for the foreseeable future, it's home.

I rent a barn conversion dating from the seventeen hundreds in half an acre of garden, typical in this part of the country. It's far too big for one, but will do for the time being, until something compels me to move on. I have no plans. No plans, no family, no friends and just a few acquaintances whom I have no reason to contact, but with whom I'm content to engage if, like Sue Jenkins, they choose to contact me. I don't expect to hear from Sue again, unless she needs me. I don't know where this life will take me today, next week or next year.

I got home eventually, via the tyre fitters, at around ten in the morning. I stayed in bed until three, trying unsuccessfully to catch up on lost sleep, giving my wounds time to heal. But the sun is shining enticingly through my bedroom window, so I shower and dress, slide on the aviators and take a stroll down the long garden. It's laid mainly to lawn and hosts a pair of silver birch trees in the middle, a rose hedge down one side and yew on the other. Beyond the fence there's open meadow festooned with wildflowers and long grass, and cattle graze contentedly in the distance.

I've been away for most of the last three months, popping back once a fortnight to make sure everything was in order and for a change of clothes, before resuming my motorised vigil. I hadn't realised how much I'd missed the solitude and tranquillity. It's not that I don't like other people, it's just other people have busy lives and things on their mind: family, jobs, mortgages, health, wealth. Other people tolerate daily existence, struggle through the tedium of the present assuming the best is yet to come, the future, theirs in perpetuity. Unlike them, I have no future, just an infinite present.

A noise shatters the peace. A shriek of laughter and the slamming of car doors heralds another new family arriving at the cottage next door. When I first got here, I tried to make myself known to the neighbours before realising it was a holiday let, so different people come and go all the time. My other neighbour is a hundred yards away. Nate and Jas are young farmers with two kids, three dogs and a cat. They have five hundred acres of arable land and also run a farm shop from an open shed off the main road. They're my landlords and also own the cottage next door. They're a nice family. Something I once had.

*\*\**

My day at the hospital last week was poignant. In the weeks and months after the accident, I'd been able to monitor Clare's progress by phone, but after a while, ran out of fake names and white lies and the hospital began to get suspicious. I had already stopped ringing Mum, deciding it was unfair to continue her torment, and in her increasingly fragile state, thought it unlikely I'd get a coherent answer. She has more than enough to deal with. I did garner enough information to be optimistic my sister might at least make a partial recovery and disciplined myself to leave it alone for a while. There was, after all, nothing I could do for her. A year later, I called again. My timing was impeccable; Clare was being discharged in three days. I felt a massive weight lifted and a reckless urge to see them all again.

I abandon the motorway vigil, drive overnight and sleep in the car until it's light and sit in a small waiting area with a good view down the hospital corridor, watching people come and go. It's four hours before I see a vaguely familiar group shuffling towards me at snail's pace. Mum, a grey, withered old lady pushing a wheelchair containing Dad, a semi-comatose old man. Her hands grip the bars for support, his hang limp in his lap, both stare aimlessly into space. Alongside, hobbling on crutches, my beloved and interminably infuriating younger sister. No wheelchair for Clare, the contrarian. I can hear her. *'Bollocks to that, I'm not a bloody invalid, give me a couple of those sticks',* the crutches, a rare concession to compromise.

Her hair is cut severely short, fine and wispy, her lush blonde tresses the enduring casualty. I can see she's in pain, every tiny step challenging her will, dogged determination etched deep in her face. She's thin and frail, years of battling misconceived obesophobia swept away in an instant by a new, enforced diet; *the near-fatal car crash, twelve months in a coma and another six in rehab, diet.* It's worked a treat. My family, or what's left of it.

The urge to throw myself at them, hug them and make everything alright again, is overwhelming. But even if I could, it wouldn't be fair. It would only make things worse. I thought of disguise; dark glasses, hat pulled down over my ears, watching from a distance, but it's not necessary. I step forward and watch the pathetic sight, shifting my gaze from one sorry soul to the other, tears streaming down my face. They pass by within three feet, oblivious to my presence and then fade slowly into the distance. I'm invisible, to them.

Their neighbour Douglas is waiting up ahead, car keys in one hand, Clare's bag in the other. They'll get home, and then what? Dad is not long for this world; one more seizure will take him. Mum might improve a little when he's gone; she's not even seventy. Clare is a survivor and she'll take charge when she's fully recovered. They got over me once, and I wouldn't make them go through that again, even if I could.

I follow them out of the hospital. Douglas is driving Dad's special mobility vehicle; a van with windows and a ramp at the back for the wheelchair. It takes an age to get them all aboard and strapped in. Clare can't swing her legs in and Douglas looks embarrassed helping her, but she tells him not to be an arse, grimaces in pain and says thank you. As well as her disabilities, Clare has to cope with the guilt. I hope she can come to terms with what happened. She was lucky and has much of her life left to live. She mustn't spend it blaming herself. If I can do anything to help I will, but I risk making things worse. She'll never forget, I know that much, but she must learn to forgive herself. It's the hardest thing anyone can do.

Douglas turns and casts me a glance with a weak smile, not sure whether he recognises me or not, deciding not. My family see nothing; I am nothing and I'm unlikely to see them again.

\*\*\*

A second, high-pitched squeal jerks me back to the present. Next door, there's frenetic activity; two kids and two adults scurrying between car and house, moving their things in. I wander over and a harassed looking woman comes out of the house. Late thirties, slim, long dark hair tied with a band, in her holiday best: designer shorts, linen shirt and boat shoes. She's swiftly followed by two small girls in matching floral dresses.

"Mummy, can we have a Fruit Shoot?" pleads one, aged four at the most.

"Yes, in a minute darling, as soon as we get everything in."

"But I want one now!" she whines, the precursor to tantrum. Her twin sister stands behind impassively, her eyes fixed on me.

"I don't know where they are," says Mummy, leaning into the open hatch of a Volvo, foraging amongst the clutter of bags and boxes. My presence catches her eye and she looks up, scowling, but I can see she's just flustered.

"Hello," I say. "Need a hand?"

She breaks into an embarrassed smile. "No, that's okay. But thanks for the offer."

"Mummy!"

"Emma, that's enough. Go and ask Daddy."

"He said to ask you," says Emma, the whining ramped up a notch.

"I'm talking to this lady."

Emma stamps a foot and goes back indoors. Her sister stays where she is, staring at me intensely. "Sorry about that," she says, sweeping back her hair.

"Nothing for you to be sorry about. I'm the one intruding."

"Not at all. She's been like that since we left home." I cast a glance at the sister who's still staring at me and Mummy turns to her. "Josie, come and meet our neighbour," she says, but Josie turns on the spot and runs inside.

"Kate," I say, proffering a hand over the wire fence.

"Annabel," she replies, shaking it firmly.

"Welcome to Hawsby. How long are you here for?"

"Just a week."

"Nice to get away."

"My idea of getting away is a fortnight for two in the Maldives," says Annabel with heavy irony, hands on hips. "This was all Adam's idea. A short break, he said. Do us good, he said, and he meant it. But all we've done is pack up the

31

madness from home and moved it to an unfamiliar house in a strange place. He'll be on his laptop working most of the time and I'll be trying to make the cooker and the dishwasher work while my darling little monsters run around screaming, causing general chaos." She stops herself, embarrassed again. "Sorry. Didn't mean to rant on."

"Gin and tonic," I say, but it doesn't seem to help as she shakes her head.

"Left the booze behind. I assume there's a pub or shop here?"

"Afraid not."

"Damn. Tap water it is."

"Can't be having that. Not on your first night. Why don't you come over for a drink, once you've unpacked?"

"Oh no, we couldn't," she says, looking surprised but at the same time, tempted.

"Why not? No pressure, I can see you've got your hands full."

She thinks about it for one second. "Can we bring the monsters?"

"Of course! You're all welcome."

\*\*\*

The incident at motorway services is still fresh and raw. The breaking news I heard on the radio while I was driving back this morning, was that police had arrested a forty-six-year-old male on suspicion of murder, following an elaborate operation conducted by the National Crime Service. I'm surprised Dave Parker hasn't called, but suspect he's too busy dealing with the media. I don't need his thanks nor want any credit but I expected contact of some kind, if only to enquire as to my wellbeing. Plainclothes noticed my injuries, even if there's no evidence of them now. I haven't heard from Sue Jenkins either, in fact not since the wedding, but he may have kept her in the dark. I tell myself the police move at their own pace and given the serious nature of the crime could hold the guy for four days before charging him, but they have overwhelming evidence, and that makes it more frustrating.

The call comes around five o'clock. Dave Parker hasn't been doing a round of interviews, basking in the glow of success, proud his officers were able to rescue victim number seven. He was on honeymoon when it all happened. He's nice as pie to me.

"I just wanted to check you were okay and suffered no ill effects from your ordeal last night."

"I'm fine thanks."

"My colleague said you were injured."

"Just a scratch."

"He said it was worse than that."

"I'm fine."

"I did warn you not to get involved."

"But presumably you're happy I did."

"We would have caught him eventually but your intervention was very timely." It was too much to hope he'd admit to being wrong. *Poor Sue.*

"Who is he?"

"Don't know yet. Refuses to talk to anyone except me. I'm going to interview him tomorrow. That's why Sue and I cut short our trip." *Poor Sue.* "Where did you get your information?"

"No comment."

"Why not?"

"You wouldn't believe me."

"But it turned out to be accurate."

"There was never any doubt."

"Perhaps your source can assist us with some of our other ongoing cases?"

"Doubt it. I don't ask her for help, she'll tell me if there's something I need to know."

33

"Ah, it's a 'she'?" he says smugly, as if having elicited some gem of information.

"It was only ever fifty-fifty."

"Of course," he purrs, in his uniquely supercilious way. "You would make a great policewoman, you know. You have a sharp mind; you're willing to graft and you're not easily intimidated." He said *'policewoman'* rather than *'officer'* inferring such qualities in a female deserve special commendation. *We should all know our place.* "You would need proper training of course, but we're always on the lookout for new recruits."

"Are you offering me a job?"

"Might be. What do you say?"

"No thanks."

"Think about it."

"I have. No thanks."

"Well, you know how to contact me if you change your mind. By the way, someone from the West Midlands police will be in touch. They need a witness statement."

"No comment."

"Excuse me?"

"You heard. No names. Remember?"

"I assure you…" he starts to say, but I cut him off before he starts quoting from the NCS manual.

"You have more than enough evidence to put this guy away. I will not be making any further comment about it to anyone, ever, so tell plod not to waste their time."

"But you can't just…"

"I can and have. I have the right to remain silent, remember?"

"You know, names have a tendency to leak?"

From the moment we met, Dave Parker has neither said nor done anything to go up in my estimation. My initial impression and assessment was, and remains, valid. He and I both know I'm not necessary to the case for the prosecution.

He just wants to be in control and have others do his bidding. *Poor Sue.*

"Is that a threat?"

"Just a friendly warning. The press won't give up on a great story. Heroine special agent puts her life on the line to catch notorious killer," he says, quoting from an imaginary paper.

"How about; amateur PI achieves in a few weeks what the combined resources of police and NCS can't do in two years and makes them look like idiots?"

\*\*\*

I open the door to be almost bowled over by two kids, one screaming, one silent, who race past me and run down the full length of the barn.

"Emma, Josie! Come back at once!" shouts Annabel to no avail. "I'm so sorry." They go straight to the kitchen, come back out again and then fly up the open-tread staircase to the mezzanine where I can hear them jumping on my bed.

"Come in."

Annabel and Adam step tentatively over the threshold. He's tall and has to duck to avoid hitting his head on the oak lintel, but before we can be introduced, the girls are sprinting along the mezzanine corridor and down the stairs at the other side, Emma still shrieking and squealing with delight.

"Oi! That's enough you two!" says Adam.

"I'm Kate," I say by way of distraction.

"Adam. So sorry, inflicting the spawn of the devil on you," he says taking my outstretched hand.

"Not at all. I guess they're excited about being somewhere new."

"Daddy, can we play in the garden?" says Emma, the natural spokesperson.

"I wish you would, but don't climb the fence or the meadow monster will get you and eat you for dinner."

Emma hesitates for a second, processing the thought, then gives out a shrill squeak of delight. "C'mon Josie!" she says, and runs back outside. Josie trots dutifully after her.

"Peace at last," says Annabel. She's showered and changed and brushed her hair, as has Adam. A handsome couple with two beautiful children. The perfect family.

"I would have brought a bottle…but," says Adam, scratching his chin. He's six feet, masculine, charming, easy manner. Stone washed jeans, blue shirt, rolled up sleeves, hirsute arms, gold Breitling, enough hair product to achieve that rakish, windswept look and enough facial fuzz to impart ruggedness. He's also ten years older than his wife.

"Which is why you're here. I hope you weren't counting on gin. All I can offer you is champagne, I'm afraid."

"I guess that will have to do," he says, laying on the charm.

"Never say no to fizz," says Annabel awkwardly, looking less at ease. "I'll just check on the children," she says, going to the door.

"Lovely home," says Adam, looking around. "Can I help?"

"No thank you. Take a seat. I'll be right back."

The tray is ready in the kitchen. Flutes, nibbles, paper napkins. All I have to do is get the Veuve from the fridge. I can hear forced whispering in the sitting room but can't make out what they're saying. Random words permeate the air, carrying an intonation that signals tension. I make a suitable noise to warn of my impending return and place the tray on the coffee table.

"Adam, perhaps you can do the honours?"

"Of course."

"How long have you lived here Kate?" asks Annabel while Adam wrestles with the bottle.

"Nine months, but to be honest I'm away a lot."

"Really? What do you do?"

"Writer."

"Really?" she says again, with genuine surprise.

"Boring stuff mostly; articles, features, brochures."

"Novels?"

"One. Published in America."

"Goodness me! What's it called? I'll have to get it."

"It's not available here."

"Why?"

"Because I couldn't find an agent to take it. And I use a pen name. I prefer to publish anonymously."

"How exciting. What's your pen name?" she says, undeterred.

I search in vain for an explanation that will avoid repeating myself and embarrassing her. "Erm…"

"Kate wishes to remain anonymous, darling," says Adam, coming to the rescue. "That's the whole point."

"Oh," she says, disappointed.

"It's no work of literary genius," I tell her. "It's just a routine mystery about a hereditary peer and a family feud that goes back a hundred years. The U.S. market loves that sort of stuff."

"You mean a trashy English crime novel?"

"Something like that."

"So what keeps you away from your beautiful home? I thought writers spent most of their time hunched over a keyboard."

"Research mainly. Finding things out. Investigating, if you like. If you're writing about something you're not familiar with, it's good to delve into the subject, ask questions, get first-hand knowledge."

Adam passes me a glass and gives one to Annabel.

"Cheers."

"What about you?"

"Me? Just a humble housewife. Childminder, cleaner, cook, laundry maid," she says with a rueful grin.

"And a wonderful mother," says Adam. She flashes him a patronising smile, devoid of humour.

"Adam's in investments," she says, emphasising the word in a way that suggests a degree of contempt. I get the impression whatever Adam did for a living would get similar treatment.

"My firm advises international investors, sovereign wealth funds investing in large-scale infrastructure projects."

"He spends a lot of time abroad," she says, the clarification necessary only to make a point.

"Middle East, Singapore, Malaysia," he adds.

"Is that why you've come to deepest, darkest, Lincolnshire?"

"Partly. Air travel can be so tedious."

"Not for those who never get a chance to do it," she says.

He lets it pass. "I'm working on a massive, long term project and only had a week's leave, so we thought we'd stay close to home."

Annabel lets out a faint snort and swigs from her glass. He continues to ignore her and smile at me. I trust they'll keep their row for later.

"Where's home?" I ask, to change the subject.

"South London. Wimbledon. Do you know that part of the world?"

*Do I know it?* I was born and brought up there, lived there most of my life and Clare has a flat there. "No. Only for the tennis."

"It's nice to be somewhere peaceful and remote for a change."

Annabel drains her glass and holds it out for a refill which he does without hesitation or comment. I've hardly touched mine as I want to keep a clear head. The calm is shattered by a scream.

"Mummy! We saw the meadow monster!"

Emma has appeared in the open doorway, followed by Josie three steps behind. Emma is jumping up and down on the spot clapping her hands together with glee.

"Probably just a cow, darling."

"No! It wasn't a cow. I know what a cow looks like and this was a monster with a long neck and fluffy hair. A fluffy giraffe."

"Alpaca," I say. "The farmer next door has about a dozen. One of them must have got out."

"Go and play," says Annabel irritably, waving a hand as if swatting away an annoying insect.

"Don't go near the monster," shouts Adam as Emma runs back outside. Josie waits, staring at me until, like someone flicked a switch, she turns and follows.

"They're lovely."

"Alpacas?"

"No, your girls."

Annabel raises her eyebrows.

"Yes they are," says Adam. "Especially when they're asleep."

"Have you got children?" she says, the alcohol beginning to take hold and having the predictable effect.

"No. I'm not married."

"What's that got to do with it?" She sounds brusque and impertinent, but I cut her some slack. She's obviously not in the holiday spirit, the girls are a handful and she'd rather be in the Maldives. A week in Hawsby doing pretty much what she does at home, but with a greater degree of difficulty, is not Annabel's idea of a break. Adam places a hand on her knee and squeezes gently. It's intended to show affection and lighten the mood, but it's a warning, the rictus grin of embarrassment giving him away.

"Nothing, I suppose. Don't know how I'd find the time."

There's an awkward silence while Annabel contemplates her next sentence. She's either going to row back or press on regardless. It depends on how pissed off she is, and how pissed.

"Are you a lesbian?"

"Whoa!" says Adam, looking at his wife in shock.

"What?" she says, feigning innocence. "It's a reasonable question, isn't it?" she says, turning her attention back to me, clearly satisfied she's provoked a reaction in him. She'll get none from me.

Adam places his glass back on the table. "I really think we should be going."

"Right!" she says, suddenly angered.

"No need," I say, but Annabel knocks back her drink and marches towards the door. She turns before leaving.

"Sorry Kate. I meant no offence." It's a perfunctory statement, not a real apology. "Adam? Are you coming?"

"Thanks for the drink Kate. We've had a long day." As explanations go, it's poor, but we both know what he means.

"I said I'm sorry!" comes the cry from the open door.

"I hope you have a great week."

The door closes behind them but I can hear Emma squealing, the clipped tones of two adults measuring up for major row and I'm left wondering why I didn't mind my own business. *You wanted to engage with people, Kate.* There was no reason to suppose I wouldn't have an enjoyable and civilised exchange with a young family. Pity I picked one in such a fragile state.

# CHAPTER 3

I'm sipping morning coffee, reflecting on the unusual behaviour of my new, temporary neighbours. It's mildly amusing now. I took no offence at Annabel's impertinence and hope she will be more relaxed today so we can try again. Her ill-tempered demeanour last night was in marked contrast to the agreeable if harassed woman I met unpacking her car. I suspect she and Adam may have had words before they came over, and in some perverse way, was using me to get back at him. It's of little consequence; they'll be gone in a few days and I'll never see them again. I simply regret not being able to have some fun with friends, however transient. My thoughts evaporate with the rap on the front door.

"Annabel!" I'd seen the Volvo leave and assumed they'd all gone out for the day, so I'm surprised to see her. She looks uncomfortable. Contrition written all over her.

"Morning Kate."

I open the door wide and she steps in hesitantly. "Everything okay?"

"I wanted to say sorry for last night. Sorry I was so rude."

"Don't worry."

"Especially when you were so kind. I'm not always like that."

"I wasn't offended. I could see you were under pressure. Would you like a coffee?"

"Thanks. Adam and I had a terrible row after we put the kids to bed."

"I didn't hear anything."

She shrugs. "We've learnt to do it quietly, so as not wake the kids." I busy myself with the coffee pot while she perches on a stool at the breakfast bar. "We've been having one or two problems lately."

"I'm sorry."

I can see what's going on here and it fills me with dread. Adam's gone out in the car with the girls, and in their absence, Annabel takes the opportunity to come and give her side of the story, safely unburden herself on someone to whom she has no connection, lives far away, is in no position to judge and won't gossip behind her back. It's all I need at the moment; an emotionally unstable woman ready to pour her heart out.

"It all changed when the twins arrived. I found it difficult to cope and Adam was always so busy at work. He never took paternity leave, you know? Said he couldn't spare the time; too many important clients, which meant lots of foreign trips. Said he'd make it up to me. This is the first time in four years we've been away and he brings me to some rented rabbit hutch in the middle of nowhere!"

The coffee pot gurgles and I fill two cups.

"He doesn't understand how hard it's been for me these last few years. I get so frustrated."

"I wish I could help you but I can only imagine what it's like. I have no experience of marriage or kids."

"Take my advice," she says, "don't give up your independence."

If only she knew. Independence for me is a fact, not an option. There will be no man, woman or kids in my life, or whatever it is I'm living. I'm destined to move on, relationships of any kind, even lasting friendship, inconceivable. "Are you saying you regret getting married and having children?"

"I suppose I am," she says, looking forlorn, the agitation displaced by subdued realisation. "Gosh, that's a terrible thing to say."

I'm tempted to agree. She's probably wanted to say it for a while but doesn't have the courage to say it to those who really matter and who's lives and futures are also at stake. It's been eating away at her and she's grateful for the opportunity

42

to get it off her chest, confessing to a complete stranger; someone who has no knowledge of her history or circumstance, has no axe to grind and won't challenge her thinking. Well, she's wrong about that.

"You said you and Adam had problems." She nods without comment. "Doesn't everyone?" She casts me a glance, somewhere between surprise and dismay. She wants me to put an arm around her, sympathise, take her side, nod passively and make soothing noises, but it's not going to happen.

"It's not that simple," she says, scornfully. She may be right, but I don't want all the gory details; I'm not interested in the self-indulgent behaviour of two consenting adults. All I can think about are the kids. Whatever the rights and wrongs in their relationship, they should focus on what's right for the children, and that means keeping a lid on their problems for at least another ten years. "I should never have had children."

"Then why did you?"

"Adam wanted them."

"You had them just to please him?"

"No! We never discussed it before we were married and then he started talking about it more and more and I thought…"

"Thought what?"

"I thought maybe I wasn't enough for him. I thought he was unhappy and he needed it to keep us together. He talked me into it. Everyone does it."

"Does what?"

"Has kids."

"I don't."

"Yes, but you will. If you're not careful, you'll fall into the same trap I did."

The woman is so self-obsessed she hasn't stopped to think about the sensitivities of others. Notwithstanding I don't have sensitivities, the impertinence is breath-taking. I could tell her

43

the precise reason I'll never have kids but she wouldn't believe me.

"I assumed if we just had one, it would be okay. But then when we knew it was twins, everything changed."

"What changed?"

"It became such a big deal. The pregnancy was awful, I ballooned in size, I got skin rashes, I felt sick all the time, I couldn't have a drink even if I wanted one, which I didn't, and the back pain…oh my God! Then they cut me open and sent me home with these two wrinkly, squealing…things, leaking at both ends. Yuck! Twice the screaming, twice the feeding, twice the effort, no, three times the effort, and he was away most of the time, swanning around the world; '*how are my babies?*', he'd say from fucking Timbuktu or wherever. What about me for God's sake? '*I've got a job to do*' he'd say. So have I, but mine's 24/7!"

"You're blaming them?"

"No! Of course not. I just wish…"

The words tail off and Annabel goes quiet. She may have her regrets, but so do I. I regret being neighbourly and saying hello across the fence. I regret trying to make friends however temporary, and I regret having this self-centred neurotic bemoaning the loss of her independence when she probably has everything she ever wanted, if only she could see it. I think of Emma and Josie and their wildly contrasting characters. Emma, hyper-active, demanding, full of energy, full of life, and Josie, always at the back, quiet, reserved, following her sister, and wonder how much of their own behaviour is reaction to their dysfunctional mother rowing with their frequently absent father. What chance do they have of growing up to be rational, caring, well-rounded human beings?

"Where have they gone today?"

"Adam took them to the coast. I can't bear all that tacky seaside nonsense with bingo and amusements and grotty pubs

44

and fish and chips and ghastly stupid people in shorts and flip-flops."

"The girls will probably love it."

"I do hope not!"

Putting aside her unbridled snobbery, Annabel doesn't even want her kids to enjoy life, not while she's not enjoying hers, or if they must, it has to be on her terms. The woman needs help for sure or the family vehicle is careering towards a precipice with her and Adam fighting at the wheel. I'm no psychologist or marriage guidance counsellor, but it's plain as day to me. The parents both need a good slap.

"What do you actually want?"

She lets out a moan and leans forward, resting her head on a forearm.

"I don't know," she says pathetically, staring into space.

"Do you want to walk away and regain your independence?"

"I can't."

"No, you can't. You're responsible for your two beautiful daughters, you and Adam. You made a decision which you may now regret, but that's tough. You have a duty to do everything, to the best of your ability, to bring them up as well-adjusted young adults and only then, can you think about yourself. That's the way it works."

She lifts her head, the creases of a frown on her brow. "How would you know?" The penny's finally dropped. She now knows I'm not going to mollycoddle her, let her go on whingeing about her self-inflicted problems, and she's about to go on the offensive just like last night, but without the encouragement of alcohol.

"It's common sense."

She nods slowly, a sardonic grin washing over her face. I imagine she's considering her next rebuke or insult, but instead it's a further plea for solace.

"He had an affair, you know."

"How would I know that?"

She ignores the retort and carries on.

"After the girls were born, I couldn't bear him touching me. I couldn't bear to go through that again. Not so soon. I was terrified I'd get pregnant and have another two monsters, wrecking my life. It would have finished me off."

It's understandable she may have been traumatised by the whole childbirth experience, but it's hardly an excuse for celibacy. "Precautions?"

She shakes her head vigorously. "He wouldn't, because he wanted more, and I didn't want to have sex because I saw it as the root of all my problems, not something pleasurable, just something insidious and dangerous."

"But you didn't always think that?"

"God no! We were good, me and Adam. We had a great life. We partied and we socialised and we went on exotic holidays and we did it four of five times a week, wherever we could. Not just at home, but in the car, on a bus once…" I hold up a hand to stop her. I don't want to hear the vulgar minutiae of their sex life. "Sorry," she says, in a rare moment of consideration.

"You refused him his conjugal rights?"

"Rights?"

"It's just a cliché."

"What about my rights?" she says, stabbing her chest with one finger. "The right not to have my body violated by childbirth, the right to peace and quiet, the right to live a normal life, have some fun and not be a slave to parenthood."

"So he went elsewhere."

"Screwed a girl in his office," she says without pause. "Nineteen for Christ's sake!"

"How did you find out?"

"Digital trail. Messages, emails. Usual shit. *'Didn't mean anything'*, he says, *'error of judgment, pressure of work'*, he says, *'you didn't want it'*, he says. My fault? Jesus!"

46

I can't condone it, but from what she's already said and how she's described their relationship, it was inevitable, her own actions a contributing factor, though I don't expect her to admit it.

"When was that?"

"Two years ago."

"Have there been others?"

"Don't know," she says, sadness descending on her. *Or is it self-pity?* "Probably." She wishes there were. It would make things easier for her.

"What about you?"

"What about me?" She knows exactly what I mean and does her best to look affronted. She may have already said she had no interest in sex to avoid reliving the nightmare of pregnancy, but it doesn't rule out retaliation of some sort.

"Have you been unfaithful to him?"

"Of course not!" she says with force, ignoring my second marriage cliché of the day. There's no *'of course'* about it and I don't believe her for a second. Even if she had, she'd never admit it, desperate to keep the moral high ground, unaware that, in my book, she's as much to blame as he is and worse, taking it out on her innocent children. "He's a bloke," she says, as if his gender proves his guilt and affirms her own fidelity.

"Women have affairs. Single women like that nineteen-year-old with married men like Adam, married women with single or married men. Other women even. There's no law against it."

"I'm not having an affair with anyone!" she shouts, angrily slapping the surface of the breakfast bar.

"Okay," I say, and hold up a hand to calm her. "I just meant that you can't blame Adam's behaviour solely on his being a man." She frowns again, wrestling with some thought, and then regards me warily.

"How did you know that young tart of his was single?"

47

I shrug. "I didn't. I just assumed a nineteen-year-old is more likely to be single than not."

Her jaw drops open and she climbs slowly off her stool. "My God!"

"What is it?"

"Who are you?" she says, backing way.

It's not the first time I've been asked that but never in the context of a potential marriage break-up. I stand up and take a step towards her, taken aback by her latest change of mood.

"What do you mean?"

"You say you're a writer. You find out things."

"And?"

"You probe and you question and you gather information."

"And?"

"Asking me about having an affair."

"You started it!"

"Of course. It's all becoming clear now," she says, anger growing, eyes searching, mouth slowly forming a manic grin.

"What is?"

"We need to get away, he says. Get away to the country, have some space and some time to think, he says. He brings me to the arse-end of England where the woman next door introduces herself to me and invites us in for a drink, and thank you very much I say, that's very kind I say, and then, while she's getting the drinks, he says how attractive and nice and friendly she is and I should get to know her, and I say what's the point because we'll be gone in a few days, but he presses me and I tell him to shut up and he winds me up so much I lash out. Then we have this big row where he says I'm losing it and then asks me if I'm seeing someone else, and I remind him he's the one who screwed around and he says we can't go on like this and I agree with him."

She's deranged, off on a rant, words coming thick and fast articulating every random thought that enters her head. If I had a glass of water I'd throw it at her.

"Then this morning he brings me a cup of tea in bed and he's all sweetness and light and says he's taking the girls to the seaside and he knows I won't go so he suggests I have a lie in and he'll get the girls breakfast and maybe I should pop over here and see that nice Kate and make it up to her. She's lovely, he says for the third time. He thinks I'm likely to share personal issues with another woman, especially a stranger, but the thing is, it's all a set-up, isn't it? You do know us because he's already been in contact."

"What?" I wasn't sure where her latest rant was going but I do now.

"I know what you're up to."

"I'm not *'up to'* anything."

"He brought me here on the pretext of a holiday when really, the objective was to find out if I'm messing around. How convenient you live next door to a rental cottage. How did he find you?"

"He didn't. I've never met him, or you."

"Internet, I suppose. Where you find everything."

"I asked you round for a drink just to be friendly, and you behave badly. You then come back, uninvited, tell me all about your husband's extramarital affair and how you wish you'd never got married and had kids. I didn't ask."

"But you would have, wouldn't you? That's what you're trained to do. You get people on-side, get them to open up and when they do, when you've got your foot in the door, you push at it bit by bit until they're telling you their most intimate secrets."

"Don't be silly."

"You asked if I was having an affair!"

"I didn't mean anything by it. It wasn't an accusation. You were intent on blaming Adam for everything and he's not here to defend himself. I don't just accept people who claim all their problems are the fault of someone else, any more than I would believe Adam if he were standing here instead of you. There's two sides to every story."

"And you're on his side."

"I'm not on anyone's side."

"You're working for him. Admit it."

"I'm… not… working for him."

"Has he screwed you too?"

"Enough!"

Mercifully, she stops ranting. In the relative silence, I can hear a blackbird singing in the garden and the rumble of Nate's tractor going by.

Annabel's lips tremble, her face creases up, the shoulders sag and then begin to twitch. She's about to burst into tears. I wanted to slap her a second ago, but, human nature being what it is, we help others in distress, regardless of the circumstances. I put a hand on her arm. She tenses and makes a sudden movement and I brace for the blow but then her arms are around me and she's squeezing me tightly, face pressed hard against my neck, a cool, trickle of tears on my skin. I can feel her body quivering and I pat her back gently, an instinctive reaction to someone else's grief. After a moment that seems to last forever, she relaxes and disengages, wiping the corners of her eyes with a thumb.

"Sorry," she says, gathering her composure. I'm about to tell her it's fine, not to worry, no harm done when, without warning, she lunges forward and presses her mouth clumsily against mine. I push her away roughly and see the look of horror on her face.

"What are you doing?" I say, equally horrified at the assault.

"Oh God, I'm sorry! I must go," she says, hand over mouth, flustered beyond measure. "Sorry." She turns and rushes out of the door slamming it shut behind her.

# CHAPTER 4

I'm having a glass of wine when there's a quiet knock on the door. I saw the Volvo was back but mercifully, there's been no sound of adults arguing or kids screaming.

"Hi Kate. Have you seen Annabel?"

"No Adam, not since this morning. Come in."

I pour him a glass of wine and he sits on the sofa opposite me. He asks if we can leave the door open so he can hear any commotion from the cottage.

"I can't be long. I've stuck them in front of the TV but they'll lose interest eventually."

"Annabel was here this morning, around ten. She came to apologise for last night. I told her there was no need."

"Yes there was. Her behaviour was unforgivable. It's not the first time she's behaved badly in company. As soon as she's had a drink..." He leaves the rest unsaid, clearly worried.

"Have you spoken to her?"

He shakes his head. "I called her around lunchtime and again as we were leaving but she didn't answer. She left her phone behind. I have no idea where she is."

"I expect she's just gone for a walk." I could tell him how emotional she was and why, but he knows her much better than I do, so it would come as no surprise. "Perhaps we should go and look for her?"

"That's what I thought. Could you look after the girls?"

"Honestly, I think it would be better if you stayed here and I went. I'm not experienced with children. And I know the footpaths."

"I can't ask you to do that."

"You're not asking, I'm offering." He's right, in a way. The last thing I want to do is get embroiled in a family dispute, but it's too late to withdraw the suggestion. "Anyway, I'm sure she hasn't gone far."

"What did she say?" He's got a good idea what his wife said because they probably argued about it and he wants to find out how much I know. If I'm not careful, I'll soon be up to my neck in their domestic problems.

"She said you were going through a difficult patch…"

"Is that all?"

"… it's really none of my business."

"Did she tell you I had an affair?" My lack of reaction gives me away. "Thought so."

I'm not going to ask him about it. I'm sure his version of the story will be different, but I didn't take Annabel's side and I won't take his either. I do, however, want to put the record straight on something which is my business. "She suggested I was working for you as a private investigator."

"What? But that's insane! What on earth…?" He and I both know it's not true, and taken out of context, the accusation is risible. But it signifies her state of mind and her confusion. She doesn't trust anyone, including herself. "Why would she say that?"

"I don't know. Her imagination ran away, but it shows she needs help, maybe counselling, somebody to talk her problems through with."

"Would you be willing…?"

"Me? I'm no psychotherapist or marriage guidance counsellor. I'm not qualified on any level to do that."

"I just mean… talk to her."

"Talk to me about what?" Annabel is standing in the open doorway, looking a little weary and dishevelled. "Is this a private party or can anyone join in?"

"Where have you been?" he says, jumping to his feet. "I've been worried sick."

"Have you? That's nice. You two having a debrief?"

52

"For God's sake grow up!" If Adam was minded to mend bridges he'd be well advised to throw away the petrol and matches. I'm not going to jump in and try to explain; whatever I say will look like taking sides to at least one of them, if not both, and I don't want to get caught in the crossfire. Someone needs to stay calm and the best way to do that is to keep quiet and let them give vent to their feelings. "Kate is not working for me. There's no conspiracy here other than the one in your head."

"I honestly don't care," she says casually. He's riled and she's enjoying it. She's also had a glass or two. "I've had a wonderful afternoon in this glorious countryside, taking in the fresh air, listening to the birds and the wind rustling through the trees. Not a single demand, scream or tantrum from anyone. And do you know what I liked most of all? I was by myself."

"Good for you! Well now you've had fun by yourself, it's time we attended to our children."

"I've had plenty of time to think and I've finally decided what I want out of life. It's been staring me in the face."

"Really? You don't know what you want Annabel, you never did."

"I want a divorce."

My heart sinks. I'm witnessing the break-up of a marriage in real time. Daggers are drawn and someone is about to get injured. For a horrible moment I feel a sense of guilt I may have contributed to it, or at least, done nothing to intervene, but they were already on a path of self-destruction and it's probably too late to stop it. I think I know where Annabel is going with this. This morning when she kissed me, it was a seminal moment, and while she's been out thinking and communing with nature, she's experienced the full damascene conversion.

"Have you met someone?" he says, the gauntlet laid down. She breaks into a wide grin and my discomfort deepens. I pray she's not going to make this any more complicated than it already is, but she's on a roll. She's in charge of this conversation and by the look of her, cares not a jot about the consequences. "Who is he?"

"It's not a *'he'* Adam," she scoffs, casting me a glance. "I've been living a lie; I'm sure you know how that feels," she says, taking the opportunity to twist the knife. "I refused to accept it, buried it all these years and finally, can no longer deny it." She pauses for effect, heightening his frustration and making me squirm.

"Deny what?"

"I'm gay!" she says with a flourish, swinging her arm in a wide arc like a Shakespearean actor. "A lesbian!" she adds for effect.

Adam's mouth drops open and he looks at me, blinking.

"Did you know this?"

I don't have time to answer. "Of course she does! She's a woman!"

"Mummy!" Emma is at the door, Josie right behind. "I want trifle, now!"

# CHAPTER 5

The impossibly high-pitched squeal that's the preserve of little girl vocal chords, pierces the calm and awakens me from a short but deep sleep. I cast a bleary eye at the bedside clock; ten-fifteen. My body clock is still maladjusted; another late night begets another late morning, my routine still disrupted.

I go to the window and watch Emma and Josie running around in circles chasing butterflies and small birds. They're identical yet easily distinguishable; Emma is making all the noise and issuing all the instructions, and Josie is three steps behind, doing as she's told. The twins seem to have appropriated my garden as their favoured playground. It makes me smile.

I plod barefoot downstairs, electing for coffee before shower, but as soon as I reach the sink there's a knock on the door. I'm wearing only a long tee-shirt and my dressing gown is upstairs, but I'm not minded to get it. I half-open the door and poke my head around it, careful to keep my scantily clad body hidden from view.

"Adam!"

"Hi. Hope I'm not disturbing you."

"I'm not dressed yet."

"Aren't you?"

"Late night."

"I can come back in ten minutes." *Ten?*

"Thirty would be better."

He glances at his watch, pondering my answer. I wait patiently for his decision. *Take it or leave it Adam.*

"Eleven o'clock?"

"Fine. Will Annabel be with you?"

"No. She's gone off on one of her walks."

I force down some breakfast, then jump in the shower. Lying awake last night, and again standing under the torrent

55

of hot water, I'm thinking about the family next door and how they are going to deal with their problems. Adam's unexpected appearance this morning signals another episode of emotional outpouring. I'm having coffee when he returns. It's eleven sharp.

"Hi."

"Thanks for seeing me."

"I hope you haven't come to apologise again."

"Well…"

"It's really not necessary."

"I think it is. But also, we didn't really finish our conversation yesterday."

"You'll be going home in a few days. Best you just try to enjoy what's left of your holiday. The girls seem to be having a good time."

"Some holiday," he says ruefully. "I don't know what set Annabel off. I've never seen her like that before." I try to stay calm, not assume he's alluding to my conversation with her nor that I might bear some responsibility. He's not making it easy. "I mean, what did she say to you?"

"I really don't want to get dragged into this."

"No one's dragging you into it. I just want to know what she said so I know how to deal with it."

"And I told you I'm not into marriage guidance. I'm not having any more unsolicited, one-sided conversations with either of you just so you can use it against each other."

"But she said she was…gay," he says, struggling with the word as well as the concept. "Is it true or is she just trying to punish me?"

"How should I know? She's the only one who can answer that and I'm not even sure she's sure."

He scratches his chin aimlessly, making a show of incomprehension. "I'm sorry to ask this but, did you two…?" I should have seen it coming.

56

"Out!" He's overstepped the mark by a mile, lucky there's no heavy object nearby to throw at him.

"No! Wait, please, I'm sorry. I didn't mean…"

"What did you mean, Adam? Are you asking me if I snogged your wife or maybe gave her the full-on girl-shag?

"No!"

"Are you asking if I put her up to it, turned her head, seduced her?"

"No!"

"Because I'm not to blame for your personal problems, or hers, so get out of my house!" I say, pointing at the door, weirdly disturbed by my own outburst. It's rare.

"I need your help." He sounds broken and pathetic and only those with a heart of stone would fail to be moved by a grown-up man who's clearly on the verge of a breakdown. I'm naturally dispassionate, more so given my situation, and ordinarily, it would cut no ice. If it were not for the two girls outside, he'd be sent packing. I'm not sure what I can do, but I have to try, if only for their sakes.

"Would you like a coffee?"

He nods dumbly, apparently unable to answer the simplest of questions. "I'm sorry."

"Stop it. Please. I've had enough apologies."

"Sorry."

I roll my eyes and refill the coffee pot. He's hunched forward on the sofa, hands clasped, deep in thought.

"Tell me about the twins."

He brightens a little, with none of the angst or frustration exuded by his wife, but then mother is on the childcare front line; father can take a back seat and do all the nice easy jobs.

"They mean everything to me. It's what I always wanted."

"Twin girls?"

"Not necessarily, just, you know, kids. Makes it simpler, having two at the same time."

"Simpler for who?" He doesn't answer. He's not ready to admit failure on his part. I try another tack, keen to sound less combative. "They're very different."

"Yeah. Emma got all the feisty genes from her Mum, whereas Josie is more like me. She nearly died you know?"

"Josie?"

"Everything was going smoothly and they told us we could expect a natural birth, but around thirty-five weeks they did an ultrasound and it looked like Josie was tangled up in the cord so they had to do an emergency C-section. Emma was fine but Josie was unresponsive. She was blue and floppy and not breathing and they said her heart stopped for a minute."

"She died?"

"Technically, but they brought her back. She didn't cry like Emma and she never has. It's as if she had a glimpse of eternity, knows she was lucky and should be grateful for being here. She's utterly fearless, is our Josie."

I feel a chill. I caught Josie staring at me, more than once. I took it as suspicion or wariness but it could have been fascination. Or understanding.

"But she's okay now?"

"Apart from being perpetually quiet. Hardly says a word except when necessary. But for a four-year-old, she's brilliant academically. Her reading and writing is way ahead of Emma's. Emma's more creative and flamboyant, more of an artiste."

"Drama queen?"

"Yeah," he says with a laugh.

Now there's more reason than ever to help, if I can. I'd like to have a chat with Josie sometime, if she's willing, but can't see how that will come about. She's never parted from Emma and until now I thought it was because Emma was in charge. I'm beginning to think Josie is watching out for her sister, keeping her safe. I pour the coffee and sit down opposite.

"You said you need help." I try hard to keep weary resignation out of my voice.

"Annabel said you were an investigator."

I resist the urge to scream. I said nothing to either of them to indicate that, other than to mention I sometimes carried out research to support my writing. Annabel jumped to a hasty conclusion based on a fantasy of her own making; I had been retained by her husband to spy on her. *You tracked down and caught a serial killer, Kate. What do you call someone who does that?*

"Go on."

"She told you I had an affair."

"She said it and you haven't denied it. That's all I know."

"It's not what it seems."

"Is that a denial?"

"Damn right it is! I would never do that to her, to our kids. I'm not like that!"

He's denying he had an affair but admits there was something that's *'not what it seems'* which means he acknowledges it could be construed as an affair. If I don't call a halt to this madness, I'm going to be sucked in. The shriek of joy from the garden reminds me why I'm even listening to him.

"But she doesn't believe you."

"She didn't initially, but then when I explained it was all a misunderstanding, she eventually relented and said we should forget about it and get on with our lives. It's been hanging over us like a cloud these past two years, but now she's using it to get what she wants."

None of this is fact; just emotionally charged accusations and opinions, arguments and counterarguments going back at least two years and probably ever since Annabel got pregnant. On top of that, his wife is seriously questioning her own sexuality and has alluded to but as yet, not admitted to any relationship. Her coming out, if that's what it is, may be a

59

contributory factor in the breakdown or simply a reaction to it. I can't do or say anything that will put their relationship back together unless both parents want it, and if Annabel really is gay, that's never going to happen. Divorce lawyers would be the only ones to benefit and the twins, the only ones to suffer. The best I can do is persuade them to come to a mutually acceptable arrangement until the girls are old enough to look after themselves. Common sense says I keep my distance, but there's something about Josie that compels me to keep talking.

"I told you both, I'm not qualified or prepared to advise you on how you save your marriage, and I'm definitely not taking sides."

"You've already made that perfectly clear. I'm not asking for that."

"Then what exactly are you asking?"

"I want you to help a friend of mine."

He's thrown me completely. I had assumed he wanted me to get involved in his personal life, talk to Annabel and maybe try to calm her, or else give him advice on what he should do. He obviously thought there was a chance I was gay and might be able to confirm his wife's predilection for women. She teased him with it to make a point, and who knows what she said to him in private? She probably invented some story about our being intimate to wind him up even further, which might explain why he blundered in with his crass question.

"So it's not about you and Annabel?"

"God no. We have to sort out our own problems. We have the girls to think about." He seems to have his priorities straight at least, but something tells me not to breathe a sigh of relief just yet. "No, it's about a young lady who used to work for me."

"Would this be the young lady you didn't have an affair with?"

# CHAPTER 6

My phone rings, and this time, it's less of a surprise. I have a good idea who it will be. My last conversation with Dave Parker convinced me it was time to change my number so I went online to order a new one. I have no need to speak to him again, nor Sue Jenkins for that matter; it's in all our interests that such relationships, however short lived, are not maintained beyond their immediate need. Until the new sim arrives, I'm stuck with the old one and two new people who know my number. I pluck it from my back pocket and glance at the display. Inevitably, I don't recognise the number, so I let it go to voicemail and after a minute the message comes through. There's some hesitancy, someone unsure of whether to speak or what to say, plus background noise. She's hands-free in a car.

"Hello, this is Becca Harding." She accentless, and sounds young, but her words are clipped and she seems on edge. "Adam Cross gave me your number." She's working hard to control her emotions. "Please call back. Thanks." I knew what to expect and in a couple of short sentences, Becca Harding has confirmed the impression of someone distressed. My natural instinct would be to reply immediately, find out what's wrong and try to help, but caution prevails and I resist the temptation. She's probably upset Adam palmed her off, and she didn't say it was urgent, suggesting she feels there's little to gain by talking to a strange woman. I'm also still tired, readjusting from the excesses of the last few weeks and I'm not sure I want to take on another assignment so soon. I said all this to Adam but eventually caved in. Initially, he didn't want to talk about his non-affair two years ago with nineteen-year-old Becca, but I insisted.

\*\*\*

He never expected to hear from her again, but a couple of weeks ago, she contacted him out of the blue. She needed help and she had nowhere else to go. Since then she's called every day, pestering him until he had to act. The price for my agreeing to give her my number was information.

"What did she want?"

"I think it's best she explains that herself."

"Not good enough."

"Kate, please. It's complicated."

"I bet it is, but you must have some idea."

"I really think you should talk to her first. Then you can come to me."

I seem to be pushing water uphill. "Why can't you help her?"

He lets out a deep sigh and shakes his head. "I can't risk getting involved with her again, especially with Annabel the way she is. You can see how it would look."

"She'd think you'd rekindled your non-existent affair."

"Give me a break Kate, for God's sake!"

"Why? Three days ago I didn't know you existed. You and Annabel were complete strangers, but now you both expect me to just accept whatever you tell me without question?"

"As I say, it's complicated."

"I heard you. Tell me about you and Becca."

Reluctantly, he told me she was an economics undergraduate on a gap year, but instead of flying off to Cambodia or working in a kibbutz, she elected for work experience and got a junior admin role in his financial advisory firm. She was diligent, personable, and attractive and soon, they became friends and had lunch together.

"Once?"

"Once or twice." *Regularly then.*

He soon realised she had a crush on him and wanted to take it further, but the CEO picked up on office gossip and told Adam to deal with it. So he made clear to her he was married with two young children, they could not continue working together and she should find another position.

"You fired her."

"I had to!"

"And you didn't take it further?"

The pause says he did, he's just not sure how to present the case for the defence.

"I was stupid."

"How stupid?"

"A couple of weeks after she left, she called me and said there were no hard feelings and she understood why the boss wanted her out, but everything was fine because she had another job and there was no reason we couldn't be friends and maybe have a coffee sometime? I said fine, never expecting her to follow it up, but a few days later I get a text asking me to meet her for a drink. I know I shouldn't have gone, but I did," he says ruefully.

He was the wrong side of forty-five, his wife showed no interest sexually and he was intoxicated by the attentions of an adoring teenager, deluding himself he could remain in control of the situation. He tries to call a halt by sacking the girl but the girl can't resist, according to him. *What's a guy supposed to do?*

"But the drink turns into dinner and we're outside, saying goodnight, when she says her flat is across the road and her flatmate is away and would I like to have a nightcap…?" He tails off, leaving me to fill in the blanks. I'm not going to oblige.

"Go on."

"Alright! I admit I was tempted. She's giving me that doe-eyed look and saying *'please'* and *'no one would ever know'* but I tell her I can't and I have to go home. She starts to cry and says, *'why don't I like her?'* and I tell her I do like her and I put my arms around her to give her a hug and the next thing she's kissing me on the mouth, telling me she loves me and I

63

have to untangle myself and push her away." *Been there Adam, if only you knew it.* He pauses again but there's more to it than that. If he thinks he's finished, he's wrong.

"Then what?"

"Then nothing." He shrugs. "I wish her well and tell her we can't do this again. We say goodnight and I go home."

I'm struggling to believe him. Having gone that far, having taken food and drink, flirted shamelessly all night with an attractive and vivacious young woman who's now offering herself to him and a post-natal wife at home who's lost interest, it would take nerves of steel and an iron will for any man to resist. But now is not the time for full-blown interrogation. He's trying to give me the impression he feels some responsibility for her and it's only fear for his marriage that stops him helping her himself. More likely, he's tried to give her the brush-off and she's not having it. Even more likely, their relationship went much further and for much longer than he's willing to admit to me, or himself. The question is, why would he lie when I'm bound to ask her about it? I'm likely to get a very different version of events, or at least, another perspective.

"How did Annabel find out?"

"Someone saw us together."

"And this someone saw you walk away?"

"Presumably." He's hedging, and it's unconvincing. "But Annabel was still suspicious."

"Maybe Becca told her out of spite?"

"No, she's not like that."

"Have you seen her since that night?"

"No," he says, but his eyes are elsewhere.

"So, two years go by and she calls you out of the blue?" I find it hard to keep the scepticism out of my voice.

"Yes."

\*\*\*

I leave it an hour before making the call. She's still in the car.

"Thanks for calling." Peremptory, unimpressed.

"Sounds like you're driving?"

"Yeah, but it's okay, I'm hands free." It's not okay. Becca Harding sounded upset earlier and unless I've misjudged the tone of her voice, still does. If she's about to get weepy the last place she should be is behind the wheel. "I don't know where to start."

"Becca, before you go on, I suggest you find a place to pull over. Then we can have a good chat."

"I can't. I'm on the motorway."

"How far are the next services?"

"South Alston, about ten miles."

*South Alston?* I know it like I know all the others, just better.

"Call me when you get there."

"Okay."

"What kind of car are you driving?" It may sound an odd question to her but somehow, it matters to me.

"Mini. Why?" *I just knew it.*

"Don't get out of the car. Speak later."

There's someone at the door. At this time of day it can only be one of two people.

"Annabel!" I do my best to sound cheery and casual. I've just been speaking to the young woman who did or did not have an affair with her husband two years ago and I wonder whether she's been listening at the door. She looks nervous and twitchy, which is a good thing, because if she knew who'd been on the phone, she'd be angry and ready for a fight.

"Hi Kate, can I come in?" For someone who's taken years to finally discover the reason for her unhappiness, she shows none of the breezy confidence she displayed yesterday. "I promise I won't attack you." It's meant to be light-hearted.

"Of course. Would you like a drink?" The words are out before I can stop myself and I curse inwardly. I already know

65

how volatile she can be and if she's teetering on the edge, alcohol could tip her over.

"That would be nice, thanks." I get an open bottle of white from the fridge and two glasses. "I'm really sorry about yesterday."

There are only so many apologies I can take from the Cross family, but I've learned it's pointless to bat them away.

"Adam says you've been going out for walks by yourself."

"Adam was here?" It sounds like an accusation.

"This morning. He came over to apologise."

She bristles. "For me?" Her body language is stiff and guarded, and I sense a new storm gathering but I'm not going to smile sweetly or mop any fevered brows.

"For you both. And I'll tell you what I told him. I'm sorry you're having problems but they're not my concern and there's really nothing I can do for you other than wish you well. You're both grown-ups and you have to work it out between you."

"I know. I'm sorry."

"Sorry for being sorry?" I watch her posture ease and she sips her wine. "Does Adam know you're here?"

"Yes. I told him I needed to come over and apologise and he agreed."

"Did you tell him exactly why?" I hope she knows what I'm alluding to. I'm not comfortable being explicit about another woman ramming her tongue down my throat, especially when she's sitting opposite.

"No. That's just between us."

"There's nothing between us, Annabel."

"What I mean is, I'm not ready to confess to him what I did. I was confused; overcome with an irresistible urge. It won't happen again." She flashes me a look that's earnest but also ambiguous. *Unless I want it to?*

"Good."

66

"And I totally agree with you, Kate. Adam and I need to sort this out ourselves. I'm not asking you to get involved. *We* are not asking you to get involved." I sense there's a 'but' on the way and I hope I'm wrong. I'm not. "But…remember I told you he had an affair?"

"You did."

"He's been in contact with her again." I think I know why but to open my mouth here would be like stepping into a minefield. "I heard him on the phone. Nothing specific, just clipped words and when he saw me, he looked guilty as hell and hung up. Business, he said, but I know when he's lying. Female intuition."

"How do you know it's the same woman?" She's probably right and I feel bad stringing her along, but I want to know why she's so sure. If I'm going to help Becca it could make sense to come clean and explain why Adam has been talking to her, which should, in turn, reassure Annabel there's nothing untoward going on. Unless, of course, there is.

"I heard him mention her name. There can't be two of them called Becca."

Annabel knew the nineteen-year-old's name and has never forgotten it. I can clear this up right now, at least in part, and send Annabel away secure in the knowledge the most likely reason Adam is talking to Becca is because I've agreed to help her. But that would mean admitting that I am, after all, working for him, just not in the way Annabel imagined. My previous denial, fulsome and accurate at the time of delivery would be fatally undermined. *It's not your problem Kate!*

"Have you confronted him about it? Have you asked him directly if he's still seeing her?"

"No. He's impossible to talk to," she says, with some diffidence. I'm not fooled for a second. She believes it's an argument she'll never win unless she catches him in the act. I'm also struck by her change of heart. The strident, confident

67

woman I saw yesterday, finally comfortable in her own skin, once more on the back foot, retreating into her shell.

"Why should you care anyway?"

"Why should I care?" Her voice rises, the alcohol kicking in. "My husband's having an affair!"

"But you told him you were gay and you wanted a divorce. That's pretty unequivocal. What's he supposed to do?"

"I certainly don't expect him to go straight back to his teenage mistress!"

"But you're free to snog another woman?" She provoked me and I bit on it. *Not clever Kate, stay calm.* "I shouldn't have said that."

"I knew you'd take his side."

"I'm not taking anyone's side. It's none of my business."

"Precisely."

"Then why bring it up?" *The woman's impossible.* She takes a breath, preparing for her next rant, then thinks twice. "What do you want Annabel?"

"I want you to help me." She takes another sip and I notice her hand is shaking. "I'm sorry I accused you of spying. I wasn't thinking straight, I was just lashing out. I'm so confused about the way I feel. One moment I think how lucky I am to have a family and the next, I wish I was somewhere else, with someone else."

"A woman?"

"Maybe. I don't know is the honest truth. But I'm not ready to give up on us just yet." Adam was right. Annabel doesn't know what she wants, if she ever did. "Which is why I need to know if he's still having an affair."

"Then ask him."

"You don't know him like I do. Adam is clever and manipulative. He'll deny it, spin it around and blame me. I didn't realise it at first but I've learnt he's capable of deceit like no one else I've met."

"You've been brutally honest with him. You're entitled to expect the same in return."

"But what if I'm wrong? What if I challenge him and he denies it or I can't prove it and it turns out I'm plain wrong? Then what? Then we're totally screwed," she says, answering her own question. I struggle to think of a rational response for a woman who's irrational to the core. "There'll be no going back. I need to know for sure."

"I don't know what you want me to say." It sounds defeatist, but it's not my battle and isn't one I choose to join.

"You could find out," she says, brightening, as if the thought just occurred to her.

"Me?"

"Yes. You're an investigator." *I'm not!* "Do some digging, find out what's going on between them and then I'll know how to handle it. I can't do anything without proof."

"So having accused me of spying on you, you want me to spy on Adam instead?"

"You'd be helping us all in the long run."

***

I pour what's left of my wine down the sink. The last thing I need now is a fuzzy brain. I've agreed with Adam I'd help his 'non-mistress' with whatever is troubling her, and at the same time, find out if he's having an affair with her so I can tell his wife.

I can still taste her. It wasn't unpleasant or repulsive, just unexpected. But it was outrageously self-indulgent, something anyone might find offensive. Had it been Adam, it would have taken on a whole new dimension. It's unlikely a man would have cringed with embarrassment as she had, and run off in a state of confusion. Had it been Adam, it would have been sexual assault. That it was Annabel, a woman,

69

should make no difference. But somehow it does. *What does that say about you, Kate?*

It wasn't about me, it was about her. Annabel is still wrestling with her sexuality and given her own reaction at the time, the genuine shock at her own impulsiveness, I'm guessing I'm the first woman she's kissed. It would answer a lot, particularly her frustration, bitterness and utter dissatisfaction with her life. She's been fighting against it and taking it out on her family, but coming out the way she did, blaming Adam for past transgressions, real or imagined and then claiming she's only trying to keep her marriage together, is a strange way of clearing the path to a better life. Unwittingly, and in different ways, they've each asked me to delve into Becca's past. It evens up the score, leaves me feeling a little less duplicitous, and actually makes the job easier.

It's been over an hour since I spoke to Becca Harding. I was relieved she didn't ring while Annabel was here, but now I'm concerned for her. She may have had second thoughts and if I were being selfish, I would regard that as a good thing for everyone. The tangled lives of the Cross family are becoming more entangled by the minute and I risk getting drawn in myself. I call her, but it goes to voicemail. I have no idea what her problem is, but it makes no sense she should call me in a state of some anxiety and then, once she made contact, fail to ring back. She may already be back on the phone to Adam pestering him, asking him why she should put up with some strange woman called Kate, while Annabel earwigs from the next room. I have absolutely nothing to go on, but my instinct still says there's something wrong. Young, troubled woman in a Mini at South Alston; it makes me shiver, even with the killer locked up. My phone pings with a text from her; *"Can't talk now."*

South Alston is three hours from here; my phone tells me it's seven p.m. It may be a complete waste of time, but time is

70

not in short supply, not for me at any rate. If I don't go, I'll simply lie awake speculating. I throw a few things in a bag, lock the barn and fire up the Mini.

# CHAPTER 7

Déjà vu. Three lanes of traffic pound the motorway in both directions, and I'm in the middle of it all, just like before, although this time, I know who I'm trying to find. I think back to the weeks I spent doing this, looking at every white Sprinter that raced by, and wonder where my assailant is now. A handsome, fragrant, serial killer, contemplating the start of a long incarceration, cursing the bitch who got the better of him, imagining what he would do to her if had a second chance. It's another reason I need to remain anonymous. I'll change my car and my phone and soon, leave Hawsby for good.

Along the way, I can't help thinking about my neighbours and their increasingly bizarre behaviour. A neurotic, harassed mother of twins whose initial impertinence set off a chain reaction that has resulted in my chasing down someone who is or is not her husband's mistress, whom he has asked me to help. The Cross's personal problems are of little consequence to me; they'll be gone in a few days and I'll never see them again. Instinct tells me Becca Harding needs me more than they do.

The car park at South Alston is half-full and I cruise the aisles at walking pace looking for a Mini. Not surprisingly I count eight, three of which contain people; two elderly couples and a single man. *Dammit! I should have asked the colour.* I find a spot where I can monitor three at once and then go inside to use the ladies, peeking furtively under the gap between cubicles in the unlikely event I can correctly identify the shoes of a twenty-one-year old. In the main hall, I keep eyes open for someone I've never met, but who might look distressed and could conceivably be her.

I buy a sandwich and a bottle of water and return to find one of the other Minis has gone. It reminds me what I'm doing is probably futile; I can't be sure she even stopped here or if she did, isn't now a hundred miles further north. Along the way, I called her three times to no avail, and I consider for a moment ringing her again but decide it's pointless. She's either changed her mind, in which case she won't answer, or something has happened to her and she can't. Her phone could have malfunctioned, but it's unlikely, and if even if it had, she would have found another way to get in touch if she really wanted to. I work out the timescales again and assuming she did stop here, I estimate she would have arrived at five-thirty at the latest, four and a half hours ago. It gives me an idea.

I leave the car and walk around each of the remaining four Minis. A hand on the bonnet gauging the temperature of the metal gives me a sense of how long they've been here. Three are warm, one is stone cold. It's white, ten years old, a small teddy bear hangs motionless from the rear-view mirror and a *Hermes* scarf is draped over the back seat. It looks like it belongs to a woman; probable, but hardly conclusive. I take a picture of it with my phone.

If I stay here longer than two hours I'll have to pay. I wander over to the ticket machine, dial the number and go through the preamble, registering the white Mini and the location code. The automated message warns me excess parking charges have been running for this vehicle since nineteen-thirty, which means it arrived at five-thirty, about the right time. She didn't register because she expected to be long gone. I cancel and move my car closer to it so I can keep watch. I have until midnight to register and pay for my own, conscious that if it is her car, it could be a long night.

Sitting here in the dark at ten-thirty at a motorway service station three hours from home, staring at a strange car which may or may not belong to a strange woman who may or not be in trouble, I have little to do but speculate on Becca Harding's whereabouts, chilled with the notion that, were the perpetrator of the Triple-M crimes not in custody, she could be his latest victim. I send her a text.

73

*"Hi Becca. Are you at South Alston? [Smiling face]."*

I don't expect a reply.

An involuntary shiver. It's a reaction to the falling temperature, and the realisation I'm back at the scene of a violent assault.

***

A noise startles me. I shake myself awake and look at my phone; *23:19*. The same noise again; a tap on the side window and then torchlight in my eyes, dazzling, the holder invisible in the darkness. A face appears; white cap with chequered band, yellow high-vis jacket with strapped-on gadgets. I press the window button but nothing happens and have to fumble with the ignition before it slides down with a swoosh.

"Evening, Miss. Everything all right?"

"Yes. Sorry. Must have dropped off."

"May I ask where you're going?"

"Er, home." It's a plausible, though disingenuous response. There's nothing to be gained by launching into a detailed explanation.

"Where's home?"

"Hawsby."

He doesn't ask where that is. He's not interested in me.

"You shouldn't sleep in the car. It's not safe."

"No. Thank you. I was just tired. Thought it better not to drive."

I can see another officer through the windscreen. He's walking around the white Mini, peering inside, talking into a gadget clipped to his vest. Their patrol car is parked alongside.

"How long have you been here?"

This is dangerous. If they want to confirm, the CCTV will show my time of entry. They may already have checked.

"Don't know. Since about ten." I prepare myself for the 'Why?' or 'Where have you been?' but it doesn't come.

"Did you see the driver of that white Mini?"

"No."

"Or anyone getting in or out?"

"Don't think so."

"It's been here since you arrived."

I shrug. "Has it? I hadn't noticed. There were lots of cars when I got here. I wasn't paying attention." They know when it arrived and like me, probably know the parking hasn't been paid for, but I don't for one minute think they're on parking duty.

"Did you see anyone taking an interest in it?"

"No."

"Sorry to have troubled you. Keep your doors locked at all times. In future, stay in the hotel. For your own safety."

"Yes. Thanks."

He hands me a card. "Call this number if you see anyone near that car."

He starts to leave and I take a chance. "Officer? Is someone missing?" He regards me without expression and for a moment I fear I've overdone it, but he says nothing and rejoins his partner. They have a brief discussion about me, judging by the glances, before getting back into their car and driving slowly away.

I cling to a thread of hope. If this were about Triple-M, they would have said so to put the fear of God into me and told me to get going, but it's not, because he's in custody. They're looking for the driver, but unlike me, they can't just wait and watch. I'm anonymous, but their patrol car sticks out a mile; anyone returning to the Mini would see it and might keep away if they know the police are looking for them. There's also a chance the police may simply be here to make contact; impart some bad news. Who knows? My gut says it's connected.

I need the loo, but hesitate to abandon watch; sod's law says she'll come back the moment I leave. I have no choice.

*It'll take only five minutes, Kate.* I clamber out into the cool night air, feeling a stiffness in the legs and an ache in the back. I blip the locks and head for the entrance as quickly as tired legs will take me. I'm back in four, and something's changed.

A black Mercedes SUV parked a dozen spaces away catches my attention. I saw it four hours ago when I arrived but didn't give it a second thought. What's different is the engine's running, a wisp of exhaust condensing in the cold, two faces dimly illuminated by the dashboard light. Two men. The driver is talking, demonstrative head movements asserting authority, giving instruction, expressing frustration. They're waiting and they're bored. I duck behind a van to avoid being seen, and to think.

The SUV has been here as long as I have and probably longer, which means they must have noticed my cruising around examining a number of cars before keeping watch on this one. They're waiting for the same thing as I am, as are the police; they're looking for the driver of the white Mini. I peek around the side of the van and take another look. I hear a rustle behind me.

"Jesus!"

A guy is watching me from six feet away. He's scruffy: ripped jeans, stained anorak, beaten up trainers, beanie and a bulging carrier bag in each hand. He lowers them to the ground and I take an involuntary step back. I can see someone in the distance across the car park but I'm not ready to scream. He surprised me and I'm shocked by his appearance but he doesn't look menacing.

"I seen you here before. When that geezer molested you." He doesn't look in the best of health: unshaven, emaciated, staring eyes.

"How did you…?"

"I was there, wasn't I?"

"Where?"

76

"Round back, by the bins." He nods towards the service area. "I seen you with Trevor. He was tryin' it on."

"Big man?"

"Yeah. He's no trouble is Trevor, just a bit lonely." I'll take his word for it. "You gave that other guy an eyeful, didn't you? I was going to take him out but you were brilliant."

"Thanks." I'm not interested in having a conversation with a homeless guy who has delusions of machismo. I just want to extricate myself without causing offence.

"They bang him up then?" I nod my head and take another peek at the SUV. "You're still drivin' a Mini." A statement, rather than a question.

"You're very observant."

"So's that other girl."

"What girl?"

"The one you're looking for." He reaches into one of the bags and pulls out a can, popping the ring and extending it towards me.

"No. Thank you."

He takes a long swig. "You a copper?"

"No."

"Are you with them?" he says waving the can in the general direction of the Merc.

"No."

"What are you then?"

"Friend. She called me and asked for help, but I can't find her. She's not answering."

"I know where she is," he says casually and takes another drink. I take my cue and make a worried face.

"I'm worried about her."

"You a hooker?"

"No."

"Didn't think so. She a hooker?"

"No." I have no idea. I haven't given it any thought.

"Them blokes in the Merc are after her."

"Are they?"

"Must be my lucky day," he says breaking into a smile. I feel a chill, unsure of what he might want, and hope it's only money. "She gave me twenty to tell her when they'd gone. Didn't say anything about you."

"She didn't know I'd be here."

He takes another swig and crushes the can with one hand, tossing it into a nearby waste bin. It holds his attention. "Chuck you out when they're done with you," he says, staring at the bin. "Put your life on the line and then they cut you loose. You're already fucked in the head and they crush you like a tin can. Guys like me all over the place. Can't settle, useless, spent. Still got two arms and two legs though, unlike some."

"Army?"

He doesn't answer. He doesn't need to. I feel for him and all the others like him, but I don't have time to engage in psychoanalysis or the effects of PTSD on good, honest men, if indeed, that's what he was.

"How are you going to tell her they've gone?" He snaps out of his stupor and looks at me like I'm simple. He dips into his anorak and holds up an antique Nokia. I don't know why I'm surprised. "Looks like you could do with an upgrade."

He considers his options, but only for a second. "A ton." I'm not up on monetary slang and it must show in my face, because he feels the need to explain. "Hundred quid."

I'm not interested in bargaining. The money means nothing to me. "Cash?"

"Yeah. Card machine's broke."

"Sorry." *Stupid question.* "I'll have to go inside."

"Go on then. I'll see you back of the yard, behind the bins."

I go inside to raid the ATM and pick up some supplies from the coffee shop, then make my way to the service area. It's just as quiet as it was the other night. He's sitting on a groundsheet behind the bins, carrier bags by his side.

78

"I got you some food and a coffee."

"You're a diamond," he says, stuffing the sandwich into a bag and taking a sip. "Some folks do that, out of sympathy, others look at me in disgust or call security. Most just ignore me, look the other way and pretend I don't exist."

"I'm not into sympathy. I want to ask you something."

"Go ahead."

"What's your name?"

"Is that what you wanted to ask?"

"No. I'm Kate."

"Eddie."

"Eddie, the guys in the Merc. Do you know who they are?"

"They ain't regular cops, that's for sure. I know all the cops around here and those guys aren't regulars. Regular cops tell me to move on, I'm upsetting the public, even though they know I'll take no notice. I mean, where am I gonna go? Anyway, I tip 'em off if there's kids messing around with drugs or whatever or someone's nicking a motor, and the management know that. I'm an unpaid observer and they leave me alone provided I stay out of sight. Yeah, not regular cops. Could be specials, could be villains. And they're armed."

I agree with him. If they were law enforcement officers looking for a twenty-one-year-old, they wouldn't be skulking in the shadows, waiting for her to show herself. They'd just call up the regulars, seal off the place, search the shops and the toilets and flush her out. If these guys are armed, it's not for their own safety. They're above the law and they're dangerous.

"Here's the hundred."

"Ta," he says, tucking it into an inside pocket.

"Call her and tell her Kate's outside."

"I only do text."

"Whatever. Where will she come out?"

"Catering exit, up the end there."

79

"Show me."

He leaves his bags and walks with me along the service area, past some empty metal cages and a stack of wooden pallets, to the far end of building. Up ahead, there's a solid double door with a light above and bins outside.

"Text her. I'll get the car."

I can't avoid them seeing me getting into the Mini, but I ignore them; a woman minding her own business. I drive past them in the opposite direction to the service yard and take a circuitous route around the car park entering the yard from the other side where Eddie's waiting. I turn the car round and get out. He shows me the phone; it has a tiny monochrome screen that displays her reply.

*"WTF?"*

I call her but still get voicemail. "Becca, it's Kate. I'm outside the catering exit with Eddie. Get out of there now. My car's here." I await two agonising, frustrating minutes, certain the guys in the SUV will appear any second.

"I hope you know what you're doing," says Eddie.

I hand him a second wad of cash. "Here's another hundred." I may not do sympathy but this guy needs it more than I do. He stares at it then looks at me suspiciously.

"What for?"

"Donation. Don't you want it?"

"I'll just drink it."

"Do what you like, Eddie."

"Cheers…Kate."

I sense movement to my left, fifty feet away. A door has opened and a head appears, scanning the yard left and right.

"Becca!"

Becca Harding steps outside, clutch bag pressed to her chest. Even at this distance I can see the look of fear and panic on her face. I run towards her and she backs away.

"Who…?"

"Come on," I say, tugging her arm.

80

"What?"

Becca Harding looks like a zombie. It's midnight and a woman she's never met but who knows her name has accosted her in a motorway car park. She's already traumatised. This just makes it worse.

"Who are you?"

"Kate. You called me."

"Kate?"

"Hurry!" Her mascara is all over her face, her lipstick smudged and her hair dishevelled, leather miniskirt topped by a black matador jacket, its sequins sparkling under the streetlight, four-inch heels impeding her progress. She looks older than twenty-one.

"What's happening?"

I open the driver's door and pull the seat forward. Eddie looks on, detached and expressionless. "Get in the back and lie down."

"No! I need to go home."

"Do it now, or spend the rest of the night with a pair of bad guys. Your choice."

"Where are we going?"

"Never mind. Get in now before they come back." She thinks about it for a few seconds, then clambers inelegantly into the back, folding her long, bare legs up to her chest.

I hear a squeal of tires and the roar of an engine but pay no heed; another moron showing off in the car park. But headlights swing around the far end of the building and settle on us, dazzling me for a moment and I have to shield my eyes. Tires screech and doors fly open, two burly men in suits approaching.

"Police!" shouts one. "You're under arrest." I can hear whimpering through the open door.

"You ain't police," shouts Eddie, fortified with half a litre of nine percent.

"Shut it, dosser," says the spokesman. "Becca, sweetheart," he shouts. "Come on now. Uncle Jimmy wants to see you."

"No!" Comes the shriek from within.

"I don't want any trouble," I say, adding a faint tremor to my voice for effect.

One nods to the other and they each step towards me. There's no need for guns, not when faced with two feeble girlies and an inebriated tramp. They're a foot away when I give them both barrels. They stagger backwards and double up, clawing at their eyes, bellowing in rage. I give them each another blast for good measure and stuff the pepper-spray back in my pockets.

"Bitch!" screams one.

Eddie is clapping his hands with glee. "Awesome! Take that, punks," he hollers, acting like a cowboy shooting two pistols. I waste no time, run around the car and dive into the driver's seat. The Mini bursts into life and I floor the pedal, tyres screeching, round the building, heading towards the exit. I break sharply.

The police car is parked, backed into a space next to a portakabin, two coppers with blue-lit faces, watching who leaves. I consider acknowledging them with a courteous wave but decide against it, staring straight ahead; an innocent woman, a member of the public going home. We cross over the motorway to the southbound side and get onto the slip road.

"Wait!" comes a shriek from behind. "My stuff's in the car!"

"Too late." I join the southbound carriageway and put my foot down, heading for Hawsby.

***

It's 3.15 and there's a full moon as I park the car on the hard standing alongside the barn. Not long after we'd escaped, and once I was sure we weren't being followed, I pulled into the next services so she could climb into the front. She was in no fit state to talk, sobbed quietly for several miles and slept the rest of the way. I switch off the engine and she comes awake naturally in the stillness.

"Where are we?"

"My place. Come on, you need food and rest." I go inside, allowing her to follow me at her own pace.

"How did you know?" she says, standing in the open doorway.

"Know what?"

"Where I was."

"You told me you were going to South Alston services in a Mini."

"Yes, but…"

"Not now. There's plenty of time for you to tell me everything, if you still want to. Are you hungry?" She shakes her head. "Drink?"

"Water's fine. Is there somewhere I could I lie down for a while?" I take her upstairs to the spare room and she flings her handbag on the bed.

"Make yourself at home, ensuite's over there." I pull the door closed, fill her a glass of water and take her some towels, a pair of jeans and a couple of tee-shirts, together with an unopened packet of underwear. She's already under the duvet, out for the count, clothes on the floor. I leave the glass by her bed and the clothes on a chair. Sleep beckons.

# CHAPTER 8

But I can't. I lie awake reliving the extraordinary events of the previous night, trying to work out how a simple request from a strange man I've only just met, to help a strange young woman with a problem, turned again into violent confrontation. The parallels with last week are chilling, but this time the threat is harder to gauge. Police, two heavies and someone called Uncle Jimmy all expressing an interest in this young woman; relatively benign compared to the monstrous acts of the guy who killed six women. I stay in bed until six-thirty but have to get up. I'm dozing at the breakfast bar, radio on, nursing a coffee, drifting in and out of consciousness, when the seven o'clock news wakes me like a screeching alarm. It's the Triple-M case. The man helping police with their enquiries has been released without charge. The search continues.

I feel the heat rising up my neck, a surge in heartbeat swiftly followed by a wave of nausea. I can feel his hand on my throat, cold gun metal on my skin. I can smell his cheap scent and see his dark manic eyes inches from mine. *What the hell are they playing at?* The gun clattered to the ground, they couldn't have missed it. And what about the camera? Did I switch it on? Did it malfunction? What about the van? I need answers. Even if fragrant guy is not the Triple-M murderer he's a violent sexual predator and a threat to women. Even if he's a copycat, he's no less dangerous. It's early but this can't wait.

I call Dave Parker and get his supercilious voicemail. I swear under my breath. I'm guessing he's seen it's me and ignored it. Either way, I don't feel the need to introduce myself.

"What's going on? You've let a very dangerous man loose and I want to know why. Call me back." No pleasantries, I'm not in the mood. It takes him thirty minutes.

"What happened?" I say.

"What do you mean?" *You know fine well what I mean. Were you born irritating or do they teach you that in plod school?*

"You let a killer loose."

"There's no evidence. Leave it."

"No evidence? What are you saying?" I promised myself I'd stay calm but he's winding me up.

"You're lucky I don't charge you with common assault and wasting police time."

*"What?"*

"You pepper-sprayed a passer-by who was trying to protect you from being molested."

"He had a gun!"

"What gun?"

"He had a gun. He had one hand round my throat and a gun in my ear. He tried to force me into his van."

"There was no gun. The duty officers searched the scene and found nothing."

"You think I made it up? What about the van?"

"What about it? It's a van. It was empty. It's not even his." I can feel the pulse in my temple. This is not possible. *How can they be so wrong?* "Apparently, there was another guy. Big and bald, tattoos."

"So what?"

"He's the prime suspect."

"No! He was just a chancer."

"Face it. You got the wrong guy."

"What about the footage? It's all there on camera."

"Blank."

"You're joking."

"No I'm not. There was nothing on the chip."

"I don't believe you."

"Go back to your day job, Kate."

I strain every sinew not to shout and scream. I know exactly what happened that night and I know these incompetents have released a very dangerous man, but if Parker is telling the truth, then I'm just as incompetent. I didn't make sure the camera was working and I didn't hang around and make sure they found the gun. I didn't go with them to make a statement or let them treat my injuries. He's speaking again.

"I knew your source was questionable. I was always sceptical about you and your crazy plan from the very beginning and to be frank, if it weren't for Sue, I'd be tempted to throw the book at you. You've wasted police time, assaulted an innocent man and severely embarrassed me. I'll say this again. Leave it to the professionals. You're way out of your depth and if you interfere in police investigations again, I'll come down on you like a ton of bricks."

I open my mouth to speak, but he's already hung up. I'm certain his own embarrassment is the most important thing on his mind, but I'm angry and frustrated and there's no way I'm giving this up. I know what happened and so does the guy who attacked me. I can't prove he's the same guy who murdered six but he's dangerous none the less, and knowing what I know, I have to do everything I can to stop him before he tries again and someone dies. In short, I'm committed, and now, because of my mistakes and the plod's stupidity, I can't rely on any help from them. I'll do it on my own, whatever Parker says.

My source is unassailable. Edith was clear, although I have to consider her tip-off could have been a figment of my imagination. I can't ask her to repeat it and there's nothing written down, but she was accurate in describing the van and right about a smell; all I have to do is find him again. I realise I'm more of a target now. He might just keep his head down for a while, but he might want revenge, considering it a challenge to finish what he started, and if so, he'll be looking for me and my job will be that much easier. I thought the problem was solved and I'm dismayed I have to start again, but I won't make the same mistake twice.

I retrieve the dashcam from the car and download the footage onto my laptop. I find the sequence where I was following the Sprinter, take a still of the number plate and share it with my phone. I look the registration number up on line but it belongs to a VW Golf. The van had fake plates.

My head's still in a spin when I hear someone knock. I'm still wound up. I reach for a kitchen knife, expecting the front door to burst open and a murderer to charge his way in and overpower me. Another knock, gentle but persistent, suggests otherwise, and I go the window, knife raised, and peek outside. I breathe out long and slow and lower the knife. It's time for the daily confessional.

"I know it's early, but I saw the light was on." Annabel's gaze drops to the hand clutching a large blade. "Goodness."

I can't tell whether she's shocked by the knife or my open dressing gown and the flimsy nightdress underneath. I wrap it around me and retie the cord. "Morning Annabel. Would you like some coffee?"

"No thanks. I just came to bring you this." She hands me a fragment of paper with two mobile numbers written in pencil. I recognise the first one because I've dialled it many times already. "Top one's hers. I got it from Adam's phone when he was asleep. That's mine underneath." I told her if I was going to track down Adam's alleged mistress I'd need something more than a first name to go on. Clearly, she was undeterred and well up to the task. "I felt terrible," she goes on, "snooping around like that, but just as well I did because he rushed back to London this morning. Emergency meeting so he said, but I wouldn't be surprised if he's gone to meet her."

I know this isn't true, and not just because the girl in question is asleep in my spare room. Not for the first time, Annabel isn't thinking straight. Whatever the relationship between Adam and Becca, any clandestine reunion could surely wait a couple more days.

"Why don't you ring...her?" In my state of fatigue, I almost blurt out her name, painfully aware Becca is upstairs. I worry momentarily she'll do exactly that, but tell myself I needn't bother. If Annabel was minded to confront the issue herself she would have done it already.

"Who?"

"The girl you want me to find."

"What would I say?" she says, as if I've gone mad.

"You could ask her. Come straight out with it. You'll probably know if she's lying." I'm still angry and frustrated and it shows in the way I speak. Adam and Annabel's problems are not worth a dime compared to the news a killer has been let loose.

"What if I'm wrong? I need to know the truth first." She's oblivious, her mind a prisoner in a world of her own.

"Alright, but think how she'll react to getting a call out of the blue from me, a complete stranger asking about an alleged affair with a married man."

"You'll think of something Kate, I'm sure of it. It's your job and I expect you're brilliant at it." Her praise is generous and sounds nice, but has no basis in fact. If she's trying to sweet talk a reticent amateur sleuth, she's wasting her time; the effusive compliment probably signals another motive. "There's something else I wanted to say," she says, clearing her throat. "While I'm here." She pauses for breath and stuffs her hands in her jeans, as if composing herself for a big announcement, something she's been putting off, but can't wait any longer.

"Go ahead," I suggest with some trepidation. I've heard it all so far. It surely can't get any worse.

"I said yesterday I was sorry. Sorry for kissing you… without permission."

"And I told you it wasn't necessary." I'm dismayed we're about to go round the same loop. I'm too tired for this.

"Well the truth is, I'm not sorry. Not sorry at all. I was driven by lust and desire. Driven by the overwhelming urge to hold you. It was an instinctive reaction to being with you, close to you."

"Annabel…"

"I can't sleep Kate. Every waking moment is spent thinking of you, thinking how I can be with you, how much better life would be if I were with you. I'm in love with you Kate and I'll do anything to make you love me back."

It was the last thing I expected her to say and I'm filled with despair. I judged her reckless outburst of emotion to be just that, something done in the heat of the moment, an irrational act of an irrational woman, desperately confused about who she is and who she wants to be. She's had time to think about it and she's made up her mind. She's deadly serious. But she doesn't know who she's dealing with. How could she?

Even if I were to consider a relationship with her or anyone else, it would be doomed from the start. I shall not grow old. Unless my body is hung, drawn and quartered, burned to ash or weighted down and thrown in the sea, I will never change. If I cut my hair, it grows back to the same length, and no longer. If I break a nail it repairs itself, but I never need to cut them. I waxed the day before the crash, since when my legs have remained smooth and will be for all eternity. I can't be scarred for life; it will heal. I am today, and will be for an indeterminate period of time, what I was the second before I died, frozen in time. It's never easy to be on the wrong end of unrequited love, but for more reasons than she can ever comprehend, it has to be done. She's anxiously waiting for my response, her eyes pleading, knuckles white. She's thrown herself on my mercy, but it's something I don't have.

"I'm flattered Annabel, I really am. Maybe in another time or another place... but, it's not possible. You'll have to find someone else to love."

She begins to shake, the same way she did just before she launched herself at me and I fear this time, I may have great difficulty restraining her. The sobbing starts and then, abruptly stops. Her eyes are like saucers, unblinking, staring over my shoulder. I turn to follow her gaze. Becca is standing halfway down the stairs dressed in one of my tee-shirts. It's long, but not long enough to hide the fact she's got nothing on underneath.

"Hi!' she says, and I turn to Annabel, who has already spun around, heading for the door.

*** 

A faint slap of footsteps on the open stair shakes me out of my stupor. Becca is wearing the same tee-shirt but this time over jeans, she's barefoot and her short, red hair is still wet. She'd been full of questions as soon as Annabel had left, but after Parker's call and Annabel's latest outburst, I couldn't cope. I told her to shower and get dressed. That was an hour ago.

"Is the coast clear?" I ignore the question partly because I know it's rhetorical but mainly because it's irritating and I'm not ready for explanations. "Who was that?" she says with annoying persistence.

"Annabel. She has issues."

"Really? Are you two…?"

"No!" My riposte is unduly aggressive, but I'm still bristling from Adam's similar enquiry and I'm mad as hell at Parker. *She can't know that.* I rein myself in. "I'll tell you later. Do you want some breakfast?"

"Coffee would be good."

She perches on the bar stool and while I make a fresh pot, prepare myself mentally for another round of personal relationship problems. I slide over a plate of pastries and she grabs one without hesitation.

"Thanks," she says, eagerly stuffing her mouth. In the cold light of day, without make-up, she looks her age, and she looks vulnerable. She's also strikingly attractive. "Thanks for looking out for me," she says.

"You're welcome."

"I can't believe you drove all that way on a hunch."

"Me neither. Why didn't you call?"

"I'm sorry Kate, but I didn't know who you were," she says. "And what was I going to say? I'm being followed by two ugly bruisers?" She's right. I would still have rushed up there but she wasn't to know. "You could have been with them, or else told me to call the police, and I can't do that."

"Why not?"

"It's complicated."

I want to know why, but now's not the time to put her under any more pressure. She's had a traumatic few hours and needs to time to recover.

"By the way, if we bump into Annabel again, your name's Maddy."

"Maddy? Why?"

"Trust me. I'll tell you later."

"Cool. How come you know Adam?" It's no casual enquiry. She wants to know if I'm involved with him, and I'm now relieved he went back to London as it gives me time to think. Annabel and Becca clearly haven't met before, so that's a relief too, but it would be highly dangerous to use her real name. I didn't plan this and I can't imagine what would happen if either of them realise they're only a few metres apart, but we are where we are. It's a bridge I'll have to cross.

"I don't know him very well. Met him by chance. What about you?"

"Used to work together. Had a bit of a thing going," she says, flicking her eyebrows. "You know, naive young office girl and the fit older boss. It was fine until his wife found out." She gives me a knowing look, enjoying the recollection without shame or regret. I know if I probe deeper I'll get a different version of events from Adam's, but now is not the time.

"But you stayed in touch?"

"Not really. It was over a long time ago. I haven't spoken to him for...ages." It sounds forced, as if she's delivering a pre-rehearsed line; as if he told her what to say.

"You said you needed help."

"Defo."

"Then why Adam?"

She looks confused. "Didn't he tell you?"

"Tell me what?"

"Why I called him?"

I'm fumbling in the dark. All I know about Adam Cross is what he's told me; he's an international investment advisor who admits to having a non-sexual fling with nineteen-year-old Becca two years ago, has two kids and a neurotic, sexually confused wife. I expect I'm about to find out a lot more and I'm not sure I'm going to like it.

"He thought it was better coming from you."

Her eyes drop, her bubbly enthusiasm gone. "I really thought he'd want to help given what went on."

"Becca, you're going to have to tell me what this is all about."

"He said you were a private investigator."

"Well I am, sort of."

"Sort of? What does that mean?" She's instantly excitable again, but not in a good way. "You know how I got the job, right?"

"What job?"

"Jesus! I need someone to investigate a murder!"

92

I feel a shiver of apprehension, that this is something more than coincidence. Parker's warning about interfering amateurs, is ringing in my ears. "That's a matter for the police."

"Been there, done that. Useless. They said there was no evidence, but I know she was murdered."

"Who?"

"My aunt."

"Stop!" Her mouth's full of croissant and she freezes, looking at me with a dead stare like a waxwork. I realise I've raised my voice. I need to calm down. "Sorry. Just go back and tell me from the beginning. Assume I know nothing. Zero. How do you do, Becca, my name's Kate. What brings you to my barn in Hawsby."

She carries on chewing and takes a swig of coffee, but now seems subdued. "My aunt died recently and I know she was murdered."

"Okay, how do you know?"

"I just do."

She's going too fast. She needs to substantiate her wild assertion, one that seems to be based solely on intuition, but I need to know more about her. I didn't know she existed twenty four hours ago, but since then I've learnt she has history with Adam, she's distressed, she's being chased by two men who work for Uncle Jimmy and the police are looking for her. Now she's alleging murder.

"What made you think Adam could help?"

"I thought he was a friend. And he knows people," she says excitedly. "He's important and he has contacts and he knew my aunt!" she says, on the verge of tears. "I thought he'd want to help or he might know someone who could help, but he said not." Her misery and desolation are heart-breaking. "I don't know anyone else. I don't have anyone else."

It sounds complicated and I can understand why Adam didn't want to elaborate. "When you first called me. Where were you going?"

"Home to York."

"Where had you been?"

"Funeral. I wanted to stay down there and find out who killed her, but I can't do it by myself. I haven't got time, I haven't got the knowledge and I can't afford it."

"Why are the police looking for you?"

"Police?"

"Two uniformed police were sniffing around your car."

"They weren't looking for me! I haven't done anything. They were probably looking for the car."

"What about the car?"

"They think it's stolen."

"You stole a car?"

"Borrowed. Without the owner's permission."

"Who's the owner?"

"Boyfriend. He's such an arse!" she says, agitated again. "I asked two weeks ago if I could borrow it and he says, '*sure babe*', and then when I remind him the other day, he says he now needs it to go on a jolly with his mates and tells me to get the train. Arse! So I get up early before he's awake, drive off and when he realises the car's gone he calls me and messages me, telling me to bring it back, so I tell him it's my aunt's funeral for God's sake and maybe he should get the train. He calls me a selfish bitch and if I don't bring it back he'll report it stolen to the police. Arse!"

I watch her closely. She's clearly passionate, but teetering on the edge. The death of her aunt is obsessing her, causing her to overreact. Police haven't got time to look for stolen cars, unless they have some relevance to a bigger crime. In the unlikely event they were, all she'd have to do was explain the situation and call her boyfriend. They'd realise it was just a domestic, she was on her way home, and they'd let her go.

She could have worked that out for herself, but I cut her some slack; it was midnight, she was traumatised hiding from two men and she'd just come from a funeral. She's wrong about one thing; the police weren't looking for the car because they'd already found it. They were looking for her.

# CHAPTER 9

The lady in *Next* is very helpful: jeans, skirt, tops, underwear, shoes, it's all there. Becca fumbles around in her purse and pulls out a few notes, but it's not even close to being enough, so I tell her to put it away and I pay by card. She changes into some of the new stuff and the lady carefully folds mine like the professional she is, placing it in the outsize carrier along with the rest of the new items. We then raid *Boots* for some toiletries.

We'd driven to Lincoln in virtual silence, other than an occasional comment on the simple beauty of the rolling countryside and the clear, open space; something I appreciate given my origins in densely populated London. Becca came down from her state of heightened anxiety and was receptive to my suggestion we do some light shopping. It was either that or drive back to South Alston and retrieve her bag. When we left, there was no sign of Annabel and the kids, so I assumed she'd taken them for a walk; someone else who needed fresh air and time to clear her head.

The coffee shop is well patronised, over-priced drinks and over-priced snacks no deterrent to the self-indulgence these places offer; the casual decadence of modern living. We find a vacant table outside in the sunshine.

"Thanks for the clothes and stuff. Credit cards are maxed out," she says.

"Forget it. Tell me about your aunt. What was her name?"

"Grace. She brought me up. My mother disappeared after I was born and we never saw her again. Grace had no children. She and her husband tried but…"

"Is that Uncle Jimmy?"

"God no! He's not a real uncle." Jimmy and his heavies obviously play different roles in the life of Becca Harding, and will have to wait until later.

"Grace and her husband adopted you?"

"Yes, but I don't remember him, only a vague recollection. She once said they weren't suited and split up when I was two. I asked her if that was because of me, but she would never admit it."

"Were you happy?"

"God yes! She told me about my mother running off as soon as I was old enough to understand, but no matter, she said, she was my aunt and she could do a better job and we'd have loads of fun; and we did. She was thirty-five when I was born, but she acted like a teenager all her life. Bit of a hippy was Grace. She was a throwback, an eco-warrior with weird clothes and bangles and beads. I remember when she collected me from school, other mums would huddle together, cast a glance, whisper behind their hands. *'Come away Becca,'* she'd say with a flourish and loud enough so they'd all hear, *'leave the philistine proletariat to their gossip mongering, they have nothing better to do'.*" Becca Harding is vibrant, enthused by the memory. "She read a lot," she adds with obvious pride, "and she'd quote from Shakespeare and her favourite, Oscar Wilde. *'True friends stab you in the front,'* she'd say. That's so cool."

"When did she die?"

"Four weeks ago. She was fifty-five."

"Cause of death?"

"Officially? Skull fracture and exsanguination."

"Blood loss?"

"Doctor said she fainted and cracked her head open on the hearth."

"How would he know she fainted?"

"Exactly!" She slaps the table with one hand. "Purely circumstantial. He said she may have had a hypoglycaemic attack."

"A hypo? That's low blood sugar, isn't it?"

"She had type 1 diabetes all her life. She knew what she was doing and how to deal with it. There's no way she overdosed on insulin."

"That's your evidence?"

"I spoke to her the day before!" she says, stabbing the table with her index finger. "She was fine, in perfect health. She was excited because her new guy was staying over and she was looking forward to another night of unbridled passion."

"Who was the new guy?"

"She never said, but she had quite a few in her time."

Becca describes her aunt's attitude to boyfriends as if it's like routine shopping, but the enigmatic, departed Grace is already firing my imagination and it's all I can do to brush the thoughts aside.

"But these things come out the blue, don't they? Isn't that a risk all diabetics have to live with?"

"She was looking forward to end of term when I could go visit. She said so." There's no relevance to either statement; neither support her case. *She's hurting. Back off Kate.*

"You're at Uni?"

She nods. "York."

"What are you studying?"

"Philosophy and economics."

"Grace must have been proud." It's a gratuitous comment, but Becca is already getting emotional again and needs calming, even if it tugs at her heartstrings. She blinks moist eyes. "Where was the funeral?"

"Southwold, but she lived in a village called Holburgh."

"Is that where you lived?"

"Yeah. All my life, until I got a place at York and moved up there. I wish I'd never gone."

Her head droops and she fingers her coffee cup aimlessly, the body language of fatigue and regret; a regret borne of misplaced guilt. She needs something to assuage the guilt, but claiming Grace was murdered is going a bit too far.

"Becca, I'm sorry for your loss, but you need to give me something tangible, something credible, something other than a hunch that makes you believe Grace didn't die of natural causes."

She shakes her head in despair. "I don't have anything, except something Grace said to me."

"Go on."

"She said she'd found out something terrible that was a national scandal and she was going to the papers with it."

"What was it?"

"I don't know! She said the less I knew the better, so I didn't ask. I just thought she'd had a spliff and was being weird as usual."

"Weird?"

"She wasn't your average, fifty-five-year-old. She was a real character. But after she died, it made me think. Maybe she was on to something." There's precious little to go on and now she's told me what's on her mind, she realises it too. "I guess I'm wasting my time, and yours."

"I have plenty of that."

"I can't even pay you. Another reason I asked Adam."

I don't need money, but she doesn't know that and never will. "Forget it. C'mon. Let's go home."

\*\*\*

It's just gone five and there's plenty of daylight left for a glass of wine and a cobbled-together supper on the patio. Next door, the Volvo is still absent but the lights in the cottage are on. At least they won't be bickering or putting on a brave face for the kids before packing them off to bed.

"Who's Uncle Jimmy?"

"Oh, him? Nobody," she says.

It won't wash. Becca Harding is an intelligent, educated young woman but if she thinks she can get away with that, she's wrong.

"You're a bright girl Becca, so don't insult me by trying to fob me off."

Her breathing deepens and she rubs her forehead; a vain attempt to steady her brain. "I can't."

"Can't what?"

"I can't say anything," she says, shaking her head from side to side, as if reliving a nightmare.

"Yes you can. You're perfectly safe here, but if you think otherwise, then I'll happily drive you back to South Alston and you can get in your stolen car and go on your way."

"Please!" It's no longer a request for help, it's a cry. I'm moved to help her out, for both our sakes.

"He sent two of his goons to get you."

Her eyes open wide, remembering the incident. "Yeah! My God, what did you do to them?"

"Pepper-spray. Used it last week for the first time and had some left over. Works a treat."

"Wowzer! Defo going to get some of that," she says, clearly trying to steer the conversation away from my question.

"So who's Uncle Jimmy?" I ask again. She has no answer and tears are beginning to form. "Look, you didn't go to Grace's funeral dressed like that." The leather and the sequins and the heels remain vivid first impressions. *'She a hooker?'* Eddie had asked, and with good reason. The shake of the head is virtually imperceptible, but it's there, and the wine is helping. She exhales deeply, her eyes scanning the meadow as if looking for someone, until they return to mine and find them staring straight at her.

"Spit it out Becca." I sound weary because that's what I am. She had two hours sleep in the car and another six when we got back to the barn. Thanks to her, Adam and Annabel combined, I got zero. It's catching up with me now.

"I'm worried you won't help me if I tell you the truth."

"I won't help you unless you do."

I wait patiently as she bites her bottom lip. "I work as an escort," she says finally, leaning back in her seat. Job done, line drawn.

"I already guessed that. What else?"

"What else is there? You want details?" she says with a flash of anger, folding her arms. "Do you know how much a student loan is?"

She takes my silence as ignorance, which is fairly close to the truth. I graduated ten years ago just before the fees ballooned and I've since read many students, especially women, find it so daunting they resort to desperate measures. "We all do it."

"All?"

"Well, some of us. Women mostly. It's common."

"I'm sorry."

She shrugs. "Pays the bills."

"So who's Uncle Jimmy…?"

She holds up a hand in frustration, mimicking my own gesture to Annabel. "It's a long story."

"It always is."

*** 

While I was knocking up some pasta, she sat at the breakfast bar, talking. The wine unlocked memories and lubricated the tongue, and in the telling, it got easier.

Grace's husband left when Becca was two, but there was always a man in the house. Her aunt's bohemian lifestyle meant Becca grew up in an environment where men came and went on a regular basis. Some lasted a few months, some a few weeks and eventually the turnover was so rapid, she lost track and took it for granted there'd be a new one every time she came home from school. One of those was Uncle Jimmy.

Jimmy Munro used to work in security. He started as a bouncer in the nightclubs of Ipswich, and worked his way up through the ranks to establish a reputation for ruthless efficiency, such that he was both feared and admired by the punters as well as members of his own door team. When one night the boss of the company for whom he'd worked loyally for many years had the misfortune to be stabbed to death outside the *Palais de Danse,* a twelve-hundred capacity cauldron of electro-house, sex and drugs, everyone, including the police, looked to Jimmy Munro for continuity, stability and order, something he delivered in uncompromising fashion.

The boss's widow Charmaine, not wholly distraught at the demise of her habitually violent, womanising, septuagenarian husband, implored young Jimmy to take the reins of the business, organise her financial affairs and, in his spare time, see to her personal needs. Jimmy, not burdened by any lack of ambition, recognised the opportunity of a lifetime, martialled the troops and stepped into the old boy's shoes. The business grew and expanded its operations both geographically and laterally, diversifying its activities into other forms of leisure, entertainment and security.

A working-class lad from Cambuslang, Jimmy craved respect. Despite his bruiser-like facial features, his overtly pugnacious character and lack of formal education, he professed a love of fine art and culture that belied his humble background. He did his duty by Charmaine, but grew tired of her once she'd passed sixty, her skin began to sag, and she spent most of her time drinking gin and watching daytime TV. And although the increasingly powerful Jimmy had access to an unlimited supply of ambitious young women willing and able to sate his natural desires, he preferred and sought the stimulation of a partner with more esoteric tastes. He happened across forty-five-year-old Grace when she attended Tuesday night's *'Mature Singletons'* session at the *5th Avenue* nightclub in Ipswich. She was loud, feisty, uninhibited, and on a mission to seduce any handsome man who came her way, whatever his age. She was also intelligent, independent and loved the arts. She struck a chord and so did he.

Jimmy moved into the cottage in Holburgh and after an uninterrupted, month-long period of fornication, they emerged to establish a new, elite escort business, funded by Jimmy, operated by Grace, a role for which her aunt was eminently qualified. To her credit, Grace continued to ensure Becca, by then fifteen, was protected from the seedy world to which she'd been exposed for several years. Becca was no fool, and even as a teenager, had no doubt what Grace did for a living, but Grace was her de-facto mother and unassailable. Becca would do anything for her and by her sixteenth birthday, her unbridled devotion was put to the test.

"Grace pimped you?" I say, open-jawed, noticing the spoon I'm holding aloft is dripping tomato sauce on the kitchen floor.

"It wasn't like that!" says Becca angrily. She wipes her red fringe out of her eyes and grabs her wine glass. "We had a long talk about it. She said all experience was useful and would stand me in good stead. It was my decision, there was no pressure, but if I wanted to give it a try she'd get someone clean and reliable to make sure I was safe. He'd be handsome, thirtyish, charming and gentle, and it would happen at home so she'd be on hand in case of difficulty. She knew one or two candidates and she could show me some photos. But only if I wanted to."

She makes it sound utterly natural, but Becca Harding is suggesting her Aunt Grace made her a prostitute the day after her sixteenth birthday and, in between other commitments such as school and higher education, has probably been one ever since.

"Did Uncle Jimmy ever take advantage?"

"No! Grace would never have allowed it and anyway, he was very protective towards me, the closest thing I ever had to a father."

I serve up the pasta and open another bottle. Over the next hour, and fortified with food and drink, she tells me how Jimmy's business developed. The nightclub sector had contracted, a long-term consequence of the smoking ban enacted ten years earlier. He'd been forced to diversify into other areas such as retail cash collection, security for sporting and entertainment events, and construction sites. Meanwhile, Grace's escort business was growing and she was able to widen her geographic coverage such that when Becca left Holburgh to go to York, she was able to pursue a part-time career as an escort, managed by her aunt. Over time, Grace and Jimmy's relationship waned, but they remained friends and in regular contact due to their mutual business interests. Then, and thanks to the wine, she begins to go off script. Adam was one of Grace's clients.

"And one of yours?"

"Not at the time. I was studying in York but when I decided to take a year out to work, Grace did some asking around and I ended up getting a job at Adam's company."

It's not the way Adam told it. He implied Becca had turned up out of the blue, conveniently skipping over the fact he'd been a client of an escort business and its proprietor had pulled a few strings. I can see how Grace might have used her influence. The success of her business would be predicated on strict confidentiality and professionalism, but there would be no harm asking a simple favour from one of its esteemed clients. Such casual enquiry would always carry with it the unspoken threat of blackmail.

"Did he know what you did in your spare time?"

"Not at first. I think he assumed I was either unaware of what Grace did, or didn't care. He never mentioned it, I guess

104

he was just trying to keep his distance, you know, maintain the charade because, like most men, he had something to hide."

"And you?"

"Excuse me?"

"Did you exploit his vulnerability?"

She'd clearly never thought about it before, and takes a moment to consider whether I'm being critical or just curious.

"No, he asked me out to lunch and I agreed. I thought it was because he liked me, but maybe he was just being nice to me to please Grace."

"And were you nice to him?"

"Like, did I give him a free shag?" What few inhibitions Becca Harding has, have been swept away by the booze. "Yeah!"

I rather expected Adam was lying about it. It's understandable, but stupid. He couldn't rely on Becca to keep his secret for long and if he thinks it's her word against his, he's wrong. Unlike him, she has no reason to lie. "Whoops! Shouldn't have said that," she says, putting a hand over her mouth and giggling.

"Don't worry, I guessed as much. But I understand word got out and you had to leave."

"Yeah," she lets out a sigh. "Pity, I liked that job."

"But you got another quickly."

"That was Adam. I guess he felt guilty. He got me a place at a firm of lawyers he knew."

He could claim to have done his bit, granted the favour but, unfortunately it didn't work out due to no fault of his own. I think it's more likely Grace put him under pressure. He caused the problem and he had to find a solution.

"And you finished with him?"

"No! The good thing about working somewhere else was we didn't have to play-act in the office. We had lunch and sometimes saw each other in the evening. Whenever he went on his foreign trips he would come home a day early and we'd meet up."

"But you knew he was married with kids?"

"Yeah, but we never talked about it. For me it was just a bit of fun and anyway, it wasn't my problem."

"Did you ever meet his wife?"

"No way! Don't even know her name. Angela or something."

Adam carried on an affair with Becca while she was working for him, and continued afterwards in her new job. How could he think I wouldn't find out? He spun me a yarn about some girl who had an infatuation with him, whom he gallantly resisted out of loyalty to his wife and kids, and who's now resurfaced after two years asking for help. He puts her in touch with me, because he can't be seen to be in contact with her at this critical stage in his marriage. I struggle to rationalise the ineptitude of a guy who purports to be a big noise in international finance.

"I'm puzzled about one thing. How does a high-flying financial services executive from the city come into contact with an escort agency in Suffolk?"

"Nuclear power."

"Explain?"

"They're building a nuclear power plant on the Suffolk coast, have been for years. Won't be finished for another ten by all accounts. Millions of gigawatts, zillions of pounds and Adam's company is involved in the money side. He visited the site many times bringing potential investors from all over the world, selling the project, in effect."

"So how does he meet Grace?"

"Uncle Jimmy. One of his companies provides security for the site. Adam got to know him and Jimmy took him to one of his clubs. They got talking, got drinking, Adam expressed a desire for stimulation, female company, and Jimmy put him in touch with Grace."

"And you hadn't met him at that stage."

She shakes her head. "I was in York." Her phone buzzes for the umpteenth time and she glances at the screen as if to dismiss it like all the others, but this one's different. She carries on reading, her eyes darting across the screen. "Arse!" she shouts, and it's loud enough to make me jump. She's had a lot to drink.

"Who is it?"

"Miles. Boyfriend, ex-boyfriend. I messaged him his car was at South Alston services and if he wanted it back he should go and get it. He just messaged me back. The police have been round his flat and turned it upside down. They found a load of drugs in the car and he told them it was me."

# CHAPTER 10

I can see Emma and Josie, as usual, playing at the top of the garden by the meadow. Emma is feeding grass to the stray alpaca from my side of the fence while Josie looks on. The Volvo is still not back and there's no sign of Annabel. I'm worried she's gone off for a walk and left the girls alone. I wander outside to see them.

"I see you've made friends with the meadow monster."

"He's not a monster," says Emma disapprovingly. "His name is Al and he's a packer," she says, diligently thrusting long green grass into Al's face.

"Just be careful he doesn't bite you with those big teeth."

"He won't bite me. I'm his friend!"

Josie is staring at me dispassionately, unimpressed by her sister's reckless enthusiasm. I look back and for the first time, she doesn't run away. I sense the wheels turning in her mind, assessing and examining the being in front of her, initial apprehension turning to curiosity. She's enchanting.

An ear-piercing scream from the undefiled vocal chords of a little girl breaks the spell. Al the packer rears up on his hind legs and tosses his long neck up and down, while Emma lets rip with another blast that could summon dogs from miles around.

"He bit me!" she screams, holding up her right hand and wailing hysterically. I drop to my haunches and take her arm. She turns up the volume.

"Ssh! Let me see." I examine her hand and all I can see is some half-chewed, pulverised grass and lots of foamy camelid saliva. No blood or missing digits.

"It's okay. He just gave you a nibble."

"Emma! Josie!" A shout from behind. Annabel is sprinting up the garden towards us. "What's happened?" she says, shock written all over her face. Emma turns the wailing up another notch especially for her mother.

"She was feeding the alpaca and her fingers got in the way," I offer helpfully.

"What are you doing, allowing them to do that?" she says with fury, picking Emma up and hugging her.

The heat rises. I'm not having Annabel take her frustration out on me. "I wasn't doing anything! I saw them up here by themselves and came to check they were okay, warn them to be careful. Where were you anyway? They're your kids. You should be looking after them, not me!"

Annabel turns on the spot and strides off towards the cottage with Emma around her neck, little girl cries ringing loud. "Josie!" she calls without looking back, but Josie doesn't move and we both watch them disappear indoors. I put a hand on her head, her fine, golden hair, soft as silk. She presses her head against the top of my leg and wraps her arms around my thigh, squeezing with unexpected force. I feel the warmth of her tiny body and at the same time, a chill up my spine.

Josie isn't like me. Technically, she was stillborn, but was revived and saved, has since grown to four years old and will probably go on to live a normal, happy life. She may have experienced a life changing event, been psychologically damaged by a shortage of oxygen or even by getting a glimpse of what's beyond. As an infant, she would never have been able to comprehend it, but the fact is she has rare characteristics, qualities even.

"I want to stay with you."

It's the first time I've heard her speak. It's no childlike demand; the type kids make when they see an ice-cream or a puppy. It's considered, mature and deadly serious. A statement, not a request.

"I think you should go and look after your sister. And your mum."

She squeezes my leg again then skips back up the garden and disappears into the cottage.

***

Becca's standing by the coffee pot, munching on a slice of toast.

"How's Annabel today?"

"Same as usual."

"Cute kids."

"Beautiful."

"No man about the house?"

"He was called back to his office unexpectedly." I'm reminded Adam could be back at any time and I haven't worked out how I'm going to keep them apart. It sounds like Becca won't be going back to her boyfriend in York for the time being, but she can't stay here indefinitely. "How's your head?" I had to help her up the stairs and into bed last night.

"Fine!" I believe her. Despite two bottles of wine, she's as vibrant as ever. I pour myself a coffee hoping it will wake me up. Her vitality makes me feel lethargic.

"We didn't finish our conversation."

"What about?"

I sigh inwardly. There are now several interlocking strands to this saga and I'm not clear how they fit together.

"Tell me about drugs."

She looks genuinely shocked. "I don't know! Nothing to do with me."

"Miles said police found them in your car."

"His car!"

"Alright, his car. But you were driving it which is why he's blaming you."

"He's an arse!"

"You've said that, but it doesn't explain how they got there."

110

"Well I don't know!" she says, raising her voice.

"Then you'd better start thinking Becca. The police are probably still looking for you and it's only a matter of time before they turn up here." She folds her arms, her face betraying a mixture of defiance and fear. "Does Miles deal in drugs?"

"No. I don't think so. He's smoked a bit of weed now and again like most of them, but I'd know if he was heavily into it."

"Do you?"

"No way!"

"Just asking."

"Miles knows I'm not into that. He just said it to get back at me."

It makes sense. If she took his car without asking, even with good reason, then I can see why he'd be upset and threaten to call the police, but even if he did, he'd just be given a case number and that would be the end of it. It turns out the police were interested both in the car and who was driving it, which means they knew it contained drugs. But it would take more than a few spliffs to make them kick his door down. She has no reason to defend him and it sounds as if he's just as innocent as she is.

"Does Miles know what you do in your spare time?"

"God no! He'd go ape. What guy wouldn't?"

"But Uncle Jimmy does."

"Yeah," she says guardedly. "So what?"

"Why were you dressed like that?"

"Like what?" She knows full well what I mean. She didn't go to Grace's funeral in her working gear. She puts on a confused face but soon buckles under my piercing stare. "Okay, okay. Jimmy said I could do a job on my way home if I wanted. It was very respectable and the client was loaded so it would be good money. I really didn't want to because I was still upset, but he can be very persuasive, can Jimmy."

111

"Jimmy's running Grace's business?"

"No," she says, as if I'm a dimwit. "He wouldn't have a clue. This wasn't one of Grace's usual clients. It wouldn't take long, he said and it was on my way, so I gave in."

I'm about to ask her where it was when she slaps a hand over her mouth and looks at me in horror.

"Oh shit!" Her eyes circumnavigate the room, looking for inspiration.

"What is it?"

"I was supposed to deliver a box. Shit, shit, shit!"

"Did you?"

"I didn't go. I changed my mind, decided I couldn't do it, not straight after the funeral. All I was thinking of was Grace and how I was going to find who did it, and why Adam was avoiding me, so I kept going. And then I'm getting calls from Jimmy so I ignore him and Miles, so I ignore him too, and then Adam calls me and says he knows someone who can help and gives me your number and I forget about the client guy and the box in the back. Shit!"

It's clear as day. Uncle Jimmy used Becca as a mule, dressing it up as a lucrative assignment. The 'client' may or may not have wanted sex, but he certainly wanted the box, Class As probably, given the reaction of the police who found it. The client messages Jimmy and tells him the girl and the package haven't arrived and regardless of whether Jimmy believes him or not, sends the wolves out to find Becca, and they do, but not before she's seen them and they've seen the police. The bit I can't explain is, how did the cops know?

I think back to that night. The police had no reason to believe I was connected and didn't appear suspicious of my being there, but they may have routinely taken down my registration, in which case, they'll be following up enquiries with me. I can't believe Jimmy's flunkeys would be so thorough as to clock my number plate before they made their move, and after I'd sprayed them they'd struggle to do it with both eyes streaming. It's a risk, but one I can mitigate easily.

"I'm going back to Lincoln. Stay here, turn out the lights and lock the doors."

"Where are you going?" She says, suddenly anxious.

"I'll be back in a couple of hours, three at the most. And then we can plan what to do next. Do not answer the door to anyone, okay?"

I grab my bag and keys and leave her looking confused and lonely. It's not ideal, but if anyone is going to track me down in the car, it's best she's not with me. I had already decided to change it. Now's the time.

*\*\**

The Mini dealer obviously doesn't get this very often.

"What, now? Right this minute?"

"Is there a problem?"

"Well, first we have to find the specification you want, then assuming there are no modifications, we put them through a multi-point check, which takes an hour or two, then we valet it which takes another hour or two and then there's the paperwork, both for the new one and the trade-in. Then there's the credit checks, the warranties. We need two or three days minimum."

I should have known, but I'm not deterred.

"I'll take a used one," I say, pointing at the floor-to-ceiling glass through which I can see a neat array of cars proudly displaying their *'Pre-Owned'* signage. "That'll be quicker, I assume."

"Not much. We have quality standards to maintain. It's not in our interests to shortcut the process."

He's clearly not impressed with a cash buyer wanting a quick swap; it's making him suspicious and I'm sure I'd get the same reaction from any dealer other than a dodgy backstreet trader. I'm pushing water uphill.

"Okay. Here's what we'll do. I'll leave my car here with a view to trading it in and I'll put a deposit on that grey one over there. You do whatever it is you have to do and tick all the boxes you have to tick. While you're doing that, you can lend me a demonstrator so I can be sure I like the new model."

He consults with his manager, I give him the details he needs and within an hour, I'm heading back to Hawsby. Changing cars won't make me invisible, but it will slow down their progress until I can work out what's going on.

\*\*\*

It's after four when I hit the drive. There are no lights on, just as I'd hoped. Next door, there's light in the kitchen but still no Volvo. I turn my key in the lock but it's not necessary; the door pushes open.

"Becca?" I call from the open door, but there's no reply. The place is eerily quiet. I call again and go upstairs to the spare room. Her clothes are here, but she isn't. I call her number but it goes straight to voicemail. I rush downstairs, neck tingling, and I feel a cool dampness on my forehead. I run next door. Annabel answers, wine glass in hand, wearing a satisfied grin.

"Kate! How lovely to see you," she gushes. "Do come in."

"Have you seen Maddy?"

Annabel feigns ignorance, pretending she doesn't know who I mean.

"Oh, you mean your attractive young friend? I'm afraid she's left," she says with obvious relish.

"Left? When?"

"I should say around two, two-thirty."

"What happened?"

114

"Two men arrived and knocked on the door. I thought you were both out as it took some time to get an answer but eventually Maddy appeared and she left with them."

My heart starts to beat in my ears. I daren't ask, but I already know the answer. "Were they in a black SUV?"

"Oh, you know them? Well that's a relief because I thought it was a bit odd. Would you like a glass of wine?"

# CHAPTER 11

I declined her kind offer, trying instead to elicit the facts; did Maddy looked distressed or resist in any way, did they carry her or did she walk, was she smiling and chatty or screaming and argumentative? Annabel couldn't add anything useful. "Why would she resist?" she'd said with an unconvincing air of innocent curiosity. She felt spurned, passed over for a younger woman. I led her to believe there was no one in my life and she catches me out with someone ten years younger. I had no choice but to let her have her fun.

I called Becca repeatedly, but after the third attempt realised it was useless, her phone having reverted to a generic voicemail greeting. I searched her room and found her original clothing, the things I'd lent her and one or two unused items we'd bought. She'd left wearing the clothes she was in this morning, so didn't have time to change. Her clutch bag was gone, suggesting she went quietly but her jacket was still hanging up in the wardrobe. I felt around in the pockets and found her car key.

Student services at York University refused to confirm or deny the existence of Becca Harding, *'are you family?'* and searches for her on social media revealed several with the same name, but none that fitted her profile. With nothing else to go on, the only option was to go to York and look for her. I don't believe for a minute she was chauffeured there by Uncle Jimmy's goons, but I figured I might find someone there who knows her.

It's a minimum three hour drive but it was already late afternoon and I wanted first to take a detour. I needed to know what happened after we'd left that night. I tried to get some sleep, but it was fitful, my mind replaying everything she'd said, trying to piece together what little I knew, but primarily, worrying about what happened to her.

I take a familiar route, and find South Alston still exudes an aura of menace, even in broad daylight. Not surprisingly, her car has gone; either towed away or collected by her boyfriend. I check behind the bins but Eddie is nowhere to be seen, so I settle down to wait. It's gone six when I spot a familiar figure. He's lugging two bulging carrier bags as he shuffles past the main entrance, continuing around the side of the building to the rear and out of sight. I find him setting out his mattress and sleeping bag in a recessed area beneath a pair of horizontal grills.

"Well I never," he says. "If I knew you was comin' I'd a got in the wine and canapés."

"How are you doing Eddie?"

"Me? I'm tickety-boo. Just gettin' me bed ready. I like it here because I get a warm blast from the air-conditioning. Nights are drawin' in, soon be winter."

"You sleep outside in winter?"

"No. I go my villa in Majorca."

*Ouch!* I was so concerned for him I wasn't thinking. "Sorry."

"No worries. How's your friend?"

"Missing. Those two guys tracked her down to my place and took her away."

"Didn't you spray them?"

"I was out."

"Bummer. Do you think she's dead?" It sounds grimly matter of fact but in Eddie's world, past and present, fatalism is routine. It's a thought I've already had and tried to dispel.

"I need to find her."

"Are you and her…?"

"No, we're not. It's just when people ask me for help I generally try to oblige."

Eddie nods sagely. "I didn't thank you for the extra."

"You're welcome."

"I didn't drink it…well, not all of it. Got some new socks."

117

He lowers himself to the ground with a grunt and sits on his sleeping bag. "So why come back?"

"That night. What happened after we left?"

"Them two geezers got some water out the truck and doused their eyes. Took 'em a while to recover but then they crawled back inside and drove off. You was well gone by then."

"They didn't break into her car?"

"The white Mini? Nope."

"What about the police?"

"What about them?"

"Did they show any interest in it?"

"Nope."

It's not what I expected him to say. That night, the police told me they were looking for the driver and Becca suggested it was because her boyfriend had reported it stolen. I thought it unlikely at the time, but when she said he'd been busted and then remembered a package, we'd both assumed she'd been carrying drugs and the police had found them. Or at least that's what she wanted me to think.

"But the car's gone."

"Recovery truck hauled it away. Probably sitting in a pound somewhere."

It's possible the car was searched after it was taken away and only then were drugs found, meaning police weren't acting on a tip-off, they just got lucky. But it doesn't explain their initial interest, nor does it explain why Uncle Jimmy's men didn't try to recover the package, if indeed there was one at all. Eddie's observational skills prompt me to ask another question.

"That night I was attacked."

"Yeah?"

"What did the cops do after I left?"

He shrugs. "Usual. Bundled the perp into the car then did a sweep around for clues."

118

"Did they find the gun?"

"Sure. It was under your car, plain as day. Saw it myself. Glock 43 if I'm not mistaken."

"You could tell the make and model?"

"Yeah," he says as if I'm a halfwit. "Nine millimetre, easy to conceal 'cos it's small." *So much for my thinking it was fake.* "I used a seventeen. Bigger, seventeen rounds. The 43 only has five, okay for casual use."

"What do you mean casual?"

"Personal protection. Killing or threatening people close up. Not for goin' into battle with." I ought to be thrilled getting a masterclass in handguns, but instead, I'm even more confused. Parker told me they'd searched the scene and found no gun, even though I knew there was, and now I have a witness.

"They told me there was no gun."

"Oh dear," says Eddie, scratching his chin. "You and me know better don't we? What do you think they're up to?"

"Don't know. Did they take the white van away?"

"Somebody did, 'cos next day it was gone."

"No tape around it, no forensics?"

"Nope. Motorway plod stood guard for twenty four hours but that was it."

It's all wrong, but not something I can think about at the moment. I return to the matter at hand. "Do you know where the pound is?"

"No," says Eddie, lifting a finger. "But I know a man who does."

\*\*\*

I'm sipping a soda and lime in a student bar waiting for it to fill up. I spent the whole day wandering around the campus, asking anyone and everyone if they knew of Becca Harding. It elicited blank looks, as well as one or two suspicious ones,

119

but I judged no one was wilfully concealing information. I'd hoped Becca's outgoing personality may have stood out and I even entertained the fantasy I might bump into her in person, but as time went on, I became more and more pessimistic I was even in the right place. Two male students suggested I try the bar, on the grounds there would be many more people to ask, especially late in the evening.

I had assumed it would be easy to find a student simply by asking around, but when I looked up the university online and discovered it comprised eight separate colleges spread over a wide area of countryside to the south-east of the city, I had second thoughts. I did find the offices of student administration, *'Are you family?'*, but the most they would do was accept a handwritten message asking Becca Harding to get in touch, without any confirmation, one way or another, she actually studied there. I pondered citing a family emergency, but considered it too dangerous. It could prompt official questions or even the attention of the police, and I couldn't in all conscience fabricate a story and hope to get away with it. My suspicion Becca may be in danger is no more reliable than hers that her Aunt Grace was murdered. Then I remembered she said she'd been studying Philosophy and Economics, which pointed squarely to Keynes College. If nothing else, it might narrow down the search.

A group of four girls arrive, buzzing with animated conversation and I wait while they get their drinks and settle at a table before approaching. "Sorry to bother you but I'm looking for a friend of mine. Her name's Becca Harding." The exchanged looks, quizzical expressions and shaken heads say it all. I try a couple of guys at the bar who use it as an opportunity to flirt, trying to prolong the conversation with clever quips. I cut it short and move on. I've heard it all before; nothing's changed since I was a student. The boys and girls serving behind the bar are equally unhelpful but I give it another hour until I'm sick of asking and decide to call it a day.

"Excuse me?" says a voice behind me as I reach the door. A twenty-ish man with floppy centre parting and three-day wispy stubble is posing, hand on hips, gleaming white teeth on show. "Are you looking for Becca?" I glance over his shoulder and see a table with five or six guys looking in our direction, grinning inanely.

"Yes. Do you know her?"

"I do," he says. "In fact, she has a room just down the corridor from me." He's good-looking and knows it, but utterly transparent.

"Is that right?"

"Would you like me to take you?"

"To your room, or Becca's?"

He grins broadly and can't resist casting a glance back at his mates. Their facial expressions urge him on. He thinks he's in with a shout.

"Both," he says, clearly pleased with himself. Another predatory male showing off to mates who probably encouraged him in the first place. There may even be money riding on it. I don't have a problem with boys chatting up girls but being underhand and deceitful makes it unsettling and implies sinister intent. He's a low-level pervert and probably harmless, but this is where they start. I'm also tired and frustrated, and ready for a fight.

"What's your name?"

"Jake."

"Well Jake, you're a liar and a danger to women."

"What?"

"You don't know Becca and she doesn't live next door."

"Yes she does."

"I know what's happening here. I go with you and you knock on a door and shout for Becca but there's no answer; reason being the room really belongs to one of your mates

121

who's down here getting pissed. *'Damn! I forgot she's got a late tutorial',* you'll say. *'Okay thanks, I'll wait for her',* I'll say. *'You can wait in my room if you like?',* you'll say, *'better than standing in the corridor. Come and have a drink'.* And I say, *'Thanks Jake'* and you pour the wine while I go to the loo. So while I'm gone you spike the wine and in no time, I pass out." I watch as he swallows involuntarily.

"When I come to, you're on top of me sweating and grunting and I'm wondering why my pants are over there on the floor and I realise I'm being raped but I'm too weak to do anything except moan and mumble the word *'No'.* Then your flatmate comes in and he's laughing and filming it on his phone, making sure your face isn't in the picture, of course, and when you're spent, it's his turn and you do the filming and say, *'This is going viral, man',* and I'm weeping, asking him to stop but he can't stop because his dick is in control and well past the point of no return." Jake goes white, the arrogant grin dissolved. People nearby are taking an interest.

"So you guys have a drink and a laugh while I try to get dressed, and like the gentlemen you are, you help me on with my clothes, pat me on the head and tell me I'm okay and how great I was and how we should do it again soon, and you call an Uber and shovel me in and send me back to my hotel where I sit on the floor in the shower for thirty minutes trying to wash away your filth, and then crawl into bed and stay there for forty eight hours, curled up in a ball crying my eyes out."

"Now, hold on a minute…"

"Eventually I pluck up the courage to go to the police where I'm kept waiting for an hour before I'm taken to a room with a WPC who's sympathetic and a PC who isn't, who slouches in his chair and sighs heavily while I tell them what happened and eventually, they put me in a car and bring me back to your digs where you admit we had sex but I was well up for it, and the WPC takes me to one side and tells me it's *'He said, she said, love',* and if only I'd come sooner they might have got some DNA but without that, there's no chance of conviction, so I'd better just put it down to experience."

"Crazy bitch!" he says, agitated, pointing a finger at my forehead, hopping from one foot to the other. The sound of student revelry has ceased, all eyes turned to the scene being played out by the door. Jake waves a hand dismissively and swaggers back to re-join mates who are no longer amused. I follow him as he sits down at the table and takes an angry gulp of lager, spilling some down his chin, while the rest of them lean back in their seats as if to keep a distance. I lean over the table and lay both hands on the sticky surface, my face twelve inches from his.

"I spend the rest of my life wallowing in self-pity, cursing myself for being stupid and gullible, consumed with self-doubt, racked with guilt, unable to form relationships or function in any rational way, and all because of something you've done that can't be undone. You on the other hand, go on to spike a few more girls' drinks and enjoy student life to the full before you eventually graduate and make your mum and dad proud. You get a fancy, well-paid job at a hedge fund in the City where you party hard and spike a few more drinks before you meet and marry Samantha and have three beautiful kids. It's then only a short step into politics, where you swiftly rise up the parliamentary ranks, abusing your power as you go, manipulating vulnerable, career-conscious women and touching up any bit of skirt that comes within shagging distance. By the time you've got eight grandkids, a mansion in Surrey and a flat in Mayfair, you're in the House of Lords. An elder bloody statesman with a fucking unassailable reputation!"

"Sod off!" he shouts, banging the table with a clenched fist so hard the glasses jump in the air.

"And not once in those fifty years, did you give any thought to the women who've had to live with the trauma of abuse all their lives, other than to despise them for being so easy and giving you what you rightly deserve!"

Jake drains his pint and in a fit of anger, smashes it on the table, scattering shards of glass and causing his mates to lurch backwards in shock. "Shut up, bitch!" he screams, threatening the jagged rim in front of my face, shattering the silence in the room that starts to fill with shouts and shrieks of fear.

"You don't know Becca Harding and she doesn't live next door, does she?"

"So what?"

"So, that's why you're a liar and a danger to women."

I swiftly run an index finger down the razor edge of the glass and my blood runs freely down onto my hand.

"Oh my God!" screams some woman and "Jesus Christ!" says some man above the heightening murmur.

"You're one sick bitch," gasps Jake, looking aghast as I use my heavily bleeding finger to slowly draw a large heart on the table in my own blood, except there isn't enough to complete the shape. I examine the finger, the flesh clean and unscarred and hold it in front of his face so closely, his eyes cross.

"Sick doesn't cover it."

***

Some would say I overreacted, but the signs were there and I related the scenario line by line with absolute clarity of thought as if it had already happened. *Maybe it had?* The crowds parted as I made for the door, leaving them with something extraordinary and juicy to gossip about, and me no further forward. I'm annoyed with myself. I've recklessly burnt bridges with the student fraternity and that's not going to help. Outside in the cool night air, I look to the southern sky where Orion's Belt is clear, the view unsullied by the city lights, and allow my eyes to trace the path of its constituent stars. They offer little inspiration, so after a moment, I head for the car park.

"Excuse me?"

I reach into my pocket for the pepper-spray. I'm tired and all out of patience.

"Are you looking for Becca?"

I turn to look at him. He's my age, nervous, unthreatening.

"My name's Miles."

***

I park outside the Premier Inn and go back to my room to freshen up. He suggested we meet in the pub next door in thirty minutes, the time it would take him to cycle from the university. The pub is busy and boisterous, but I find him alone in a booth with a pint. I decline his offer of a drink and sit opposite.

"Kate Duvall," I say, proffering a hand. He's guarded, smiling, but only in a polite way. He's not sure of me, which isn't surprising after the show in the bar.

"That Jake has a reputation."

"Does he?"

"There was a complaint, but it came to nothing."

"What sort of complaint?" I ask, but all he does is move his head so we both know.

"He won't like being humiliated in front of all those people. I'd stay away from him if I were you."

"I'm going home tomorrow."

"Where to?"

"What about Becca?" I ask, dodging the question.

"I was hoping you could tell me. How come you know her? You're not police are you?"

*Why is it always the same; copper or hooker?*

"No."

"Because I've had enough of that already."

125

"Becca called me out of the blue and asked me to help her."

"When?"

"Three days ago. I spoke to her, met up with her and then the next day, she disappeared. Radio silence." I'm not going into detail until I get some answers. He looks subdued.

"Why call you?"

"She got my number from a mutual acquaintance."

"Who?"

"You wouldn't know him."

"What sort of help?"

"Hold on Miles. Don't be offended, but I don't know you. Becca's in trouble and my only concern is to find her and make sure she's safe."

"Me too, but it works both ways."

"What does?"

"Trust. I don't know you either. Who exactly are you, Kate Duvall?"

# CHAPTER 12

I left York as soon as possible after breakfast, anxious to get on my way but keen to eat something given I'd skipped dinner. Miles and I talked until closing time and at the end of it, there were as many questions as answers; most of them for the only person not there to respond. Becca Harding.

He'd had a few traumatic days. Yes, Becca went off in his car without telling him and yes, they had a row about it. No, he hadn't called the police, it was just a threat. Yes the drug squad knocked on his door but no, they hadn't *'turned his flat upside down'* looking for drugs, they just wanted to know where the driver of the car was. Yes, he told them Becca had taken it but didn't mean to incriminate her and denied she could be involved. They had a look round the flat, found nothing, so gave him a caution and left. He'd asked about his car; held pending further investigations.

"Were they in uniform?" I'd asked.

"No."

"Did they show you ID?"

"Yeah!" he says irritably, as if offended by the inference he'd been scammed. "National Crime Service."

"Names?"

He'd shaken his head. "They just held them up for a few seconds. I was too frightened to look closely."

"Did you see the car they were in?"

"No," he'd said in frustration, not appreciating the importance of the question. He really regretted sending her that last message. It was meant to be a wind-up but he was so mad at her.

"You sent that after they'd gone?"

"Yeah. I thought for a minute they were going to keep my phone."

"They looked at your phone?"

"It was on the table and one of them picked it up and I said, *'Hey man'*, and he told me to shut up and show him Becca's messages or they'd arrest me."

"Can I see?"

I flick through the thread. I knew he and Becca had exchanged increasingly angry messages; she'd told me. But I can see from the timing they continued after I had left her alone in the barn. They included one from her, saying she was holed up in some barn in the middle of nowhere with a 'friend' that ended with a stuck-out tongue emoji.

*"What friend? [Worried face]."*

*"A friend. [Winking face]."*

*"Where? [Pleading face]."*

*"Dunno. Back of beyond. Hawsby? [Thinking face]."*

*"WTF? [Man shrugging]. Where's my car? [Face with raised eyebrow]."*

The texts that followed were peppered with angry red faces from him and middle fingers from her.

I needn't have worried about them tracing my car. I'd failed to impress on her not to divulge her location to anyone, and consequently, she gave it away. She screwed up, but so did I.

He'd sent the message about the police raiding his flat the night before I left her alone to swap the car. Plenty of time to get from York to Hawsby, cruise around until they find the right barn, or spot the right car, maybe even wait until I've left before knocking on the door at around two-thirty, as Annabel suggested.

"You must be the friend, then?" he'd said, somehow relieved.

Miles is not a student, he's in admin, and although Becca was a student once, she crashed out after her first year and got a job in a supermarket close to the campus. She'd told him her aunt had died but he only knew about the funeral when he got home and found a note she'd left. The supermarket has had no contact either. Becca went AWOL and they haven't heard from her since. He's worried and feels responsible, regretting they argued, but it's not the first time and it's not out of character.

"She's always been scatty and highly strung, at least, for as long as I've known her. It's part of her charm. If I've been dumped, I've been dumped, but I'd like to hear it from her. I want to know she's okay…and I want my car back."

"What about her things?"

"She doesn't have much. Most of the stuff in the flat is mine."

It's consistent and by the end, I'd formed the view Miles was telling the truth. He didn't quiz me about what else I knew or where I thought Becca might be, had never heard of Uncle Jimmy and never met Aunt Grace. I asked him tentatively if Becca had any other work but he said not, just that she sometimes worked the nightshift for extra money. He was clearly unaware of her escort work, just as she'd said, and I saw no merit in bringing it up. He had only known her for a year and had never heard of Adam Cross. He did ask again why she'd contacted me; was it something to do with him? Has he done something to upset her? Was it about the car? All I told him was she was upset about Aunt Grace, particularly the way in which she died. He doesn't need to know about the altercation and flight from South Alston or the arrival in Hawsby of two men who took her away. It will just make him worry all the more. We exchanged numbers and promised to keep in touch if we heard anything.

I hear my phone bleep and I pull into a layby. It's a text from Eddie. *"Pound at Favenham, north of Stoke."* I had planned to head straight for Lincoln and pick up my new car but instead, search online, find the post code and set the satnav, diverting west to go back the way I came.

\*\*\*

It takes an hour before I'm in visitor parking outside a portakabin office in front of a fenced-in compound. Beyond the razor wire lie hundreds of cars, vans and trucks of all sizes, abandoned and forlorn. There are cameras, floodlights and various signs giving instructions or issuing warnings, the largest designating the site a division of a multi-national plc. The portakabin is occupied by two men and a woman behind computer screens, all in matching uniform; black trousers and zip-up fleeces with corporate motifs. She taps away on her keyboard, ignoring me for a minute or two, then looks up. Her name badge reads *'Michelle'*.

"Can I help?"

"I'm looking for this car." I show her the picture on my phone and she taps in the registration number.

"You the registered keeper?" she says without looking up.

"No. It belongs to a friend."

She looks at me, unmoved. "You have to be the registered keeper," she says in a monotone. It's something she's said a hundred times before and it bores her.

"I just want to know if it's here." One of her colleagues has overheard and wheeled himself over to look at her screen.

"You got any ID?" says *'Darren'*.

"I already told you it's not mine."

"But have you got any ID?"

"Why does it matter?"

"You want to know if we are storing the vehicle in question," he says, as if that explains everything.

I show him my driver's license. He looks at it carefully, then at the screen and repeats the exercise before handing it back. The girl rapidly types some more characters, clicks her mouse and they both stare at the screen, making we wait. I guess they're looking me up as well. *Good luck with that.*

"You're not the registered keeper," she says finally.

"We've already done that."

"What's your interest in this vehicle?" he says.

I have no choice but to give them the bare bones. I don't know where it will get me but it's worth a try. "A friend abandoned it at South Alston services. I picked her up but she left her bag inside and wants it back."

"Why doesn't she come herself?"

"She's in hiding." It's stretching the truth, but the reality is I simply don't know.

"From who?"

"Domestic issues. I'm just trying to help her out." They look at each other and I can see I've struck a chord with Michelle. Darren is scratching his chin, formulating his next response. "Look. I don't know who the car's registered to but it's certainly not me and I'm pretty certain it's not my friend Rebecca. Am I right?"

"Correct," he says grudgingly.

"I'm guessing the owner is called Miles." No answer. "Okay, the registered keeper." No answer.

I reach into my pocket and pull out the key, dangling it in the air. "I don't want the car. I just want what's inside."

"The contents belong to the registered keeper. He'll get a letter telling him to come and collect it."

"When?"

"Sent yesterday." Miles would get it tomorrow or the day after. "And there are charges of three hundred and twenty pounds to pay before it can be released."

"What?"

"Parking fees and penalties, towing away, storing per diem," she says officiously "which…"

"…will continue to clock up." I finish the sentence for her as she nods in satisfaction.

"So the police didn't tell you to bring it in?"

"No. The car overstayed it's welcome that's all. Happens all the time."

"I'll pay it."

"We can't release the vehicle without the registered keeper's permission."

I call Miles and explain the position. *What? Jesus man!* He can't afford the fees, he'll just have to leave it there. I tell him I'll settle it and park it close by. *You're an angel!* I'll leave the key behind the visor. *It's okay, I have a spare.* Okay, I'll lock up and send it on. He has to give written authorisation. *Thanks man!*

It takes another hour, and while I sit in my car waiting and thinking, something drops into place. The regular police were never looking for Becca at South Alston. That night, all forces were told the Triple-M suspect had been released, told to warn women drivers, especially in Minis, and look out for a tattooed tub of lard in a green Transit, especially at the services where he'd been seen last. The guys in the SUV said they were police but then mentioned Uncle Jimmy and were more interested in Becca than what was in the car. If they were Jimmy's men who just wanted his drugs back, they wouldn't have waited for her to appear, they'd just smash the windows and take off. They must have been drugs squad and found the package after we'd gone, despite what Eddie said.

Miles's ID, the car's V5 and the dealer receipt eventually come through. I pay the fees and drive his Mini out of the pound, parking it next to mine. I unhook teddy from the mirror and slip the Hermes scarf into my pocket, then pop the hatch. Inside, there's a compact umbrella, battered pair of men's trainers, a plastic bag containing an empty can and fast food container and a large soft holdall.

There's also a parcel, a heavy package wrapped in brown paper. I stare at it dumbly for a moment or two and instinctively glance left and right to see if I'm being watched before transferring it and the holdall to my car.

I drive Miles's Mini to a city centre car park and buy parking for twenty four hours, text him the location and call him.

"I owe you one Kate."

"Forget it. Don't be late or else they'll tow it away again and you'll be back to square one."

"Gotcha."

"Let me know if Becca gets in touch."

I hang up and turn on the satnav. The most recent destination is York, with Holburgh further down the list but the one I'm most interested is second from top. *Chevenham Hall, Norfolk,* complete with post code.

*** 

The taxi drops me back at the pound ten minutes later. Curiosity gets the better of me and I open the hatch to stare at the contents. I unzip the holdall. There are two pairs of jeans, several tee-shirts and blouses, two sweaters, a few pairs of knickers and some flat shoes. There's also a small bag containing toiletries and a hairbrush plus three packets of assorted condoms and a portable hairdryer. She was planning to be away more than a day or two.

I think of opening the heavy package, but something stops me. I close the boot and slump into the driver's seat, taking a deep breath, suddenly overcome with fatigue. It's not physical exertion, it's mental overload, continuously juggling contradictory facts and assumptions, knowing the answers are in plain view, just not being able to see.

Row upon row of abandoned vehicles stare at me pathetically through the vertical bars of the razor-wire-topped fence, waiting for their oppressed, punishable owners to cough up for their release. I want to go home and sleep for a month but there's work to be done.

It's lunchtime, and she's on her own. No greeting this time, not even of the perfunctory type I received earlier.

"Is there a problem?" says Michelle, looking up from her screen. I take a pen and yellow sticky note from her desk, write down a registration number and hold it up. She gives me an almost respectful smirk and taps away. "VW Golf," she says. "But…", she hesitates, a frown forming.

"…on a white Sprinter." I hold up my phone to show her the still taken from my dashcam.

"You're very knowledgeable."

"It's here isn't it?"

"I'm afraid…"

"Listen Michelle, I really need some help here. I mentioned a friend who's in hiding. She's been hiding from some bad guys who want to do her harm. Now, that van with the fake plates belongs to a really bad guy; a guy who does really bad things to women and gets away with it. The cops arrested him then let him go so he can do it again. It's up to us to do something about it."

"Your friend. Is this Rebecca?" she says, remembering the name I gave her.

"Yes."

She bites her bottom lip, continuing to stare at the screen.

"What can I do?"

"Tell me who it's registered to."

"I'm not allowed…data protection and all that," she says awkwardly. I can tell she's wavering. She fiddles with her pen and stares back at the screen. "What did he do? This guy."

"He abducts women, forces them into that van at gunpoint and they're never seen again." Michelle goes white and puts a hand to her neck. "Do I need to go on?"

She's thinking. Thinking about consequences. "You can't see it. It's gone."

"Gone where?"

"He collected it two days ago."

"Forty-something, good looking, strong aftershave?" She looks like she's about to throw up. "Seemed like a nice guy?"

134

She nods then shivers noticeably. "I knew there was something about him." She scribbles on the back of the yellow sticky note and hands it back. "This didn't come from me."

*** 

It's gold. Jason Palmer, address in Solihull, mobile number. *What are you going to do about it Kate?* Arrested then released due to lack of evidence, Palmer's got his van back and is free to continue where he left off. I hope and expect he'll lay low for a while, let the dust settle. Meanwhile plod, under the spotlight of media attention, frantically resume their search just as they did the other night. He'll trade in the van or at least get some new plates, but inevitably, the perverted addiction that drives him will prevail and someone else will die. *What are you going to do about it Kate?*

Somehow I have to get new evidence. There's not much I can do except set him up, catch him in the act, this time with several witnesses, and hope plod don't screw up again. I think back to the night he attacked me and the evidence that was in plain sight, disregarded or dismissed, and it comes back to me. Though concussed and bleeding, I thought I recognised plainclothes. He was Parker's best man.

135

# CHAPTER 13

The journey eastwards was arduous, taking over three hours, the only consolation being I've been able to mull over the facts, and rationalise the connections. It's not easy to do alone.

It was Parker's best man who arrested Jason Palmer. After I'd gone, he picked up the gun and ignored the van. Parker denied this and told me the bodycam had failed, so either his best man lied to him or Parker is lying to me. He also told me the suspect demanded he talk directly to him. I took this to be another example of Parker's tendency to self-aggrandise, but in no time, Palmer was released due to lack of evidence, or so he said. More likely, he was released because they knew each other and Palmer needed a favour.

Adam Cross knew Uncle Jimmy who knew Grace, who provided him with escorts and put him on to Becca, with whom he probably had an affair. I rescued Becca from South Alston, the same place Palmer attacked me and both his van and Becca's car were hauled away and ended up in the same pound. *Coincidence or connection?* Two men in a black SUV claiming to be police and then citing Uncle Jimmy tried to abduct Becca from South Alston. Two men purporting to be police harassed Miles in his flat, on the pretext they were looking for drugs. Two men in a black SUV took Becca from my house. *Coincidence or connection?*

The best way to solve an intractable puzzle is to talk it through with someone totally unconnected. Someone with no preconceptions is more likely to spot the blindingly obvious, the one fact that was staring you in the face all along but your mind kept dismissing as irrelevant because you'd already reached a conclusion and you wanted to make the facts fit. Translating jumbled thoughts into the spoken word slows down the process and compels you to present the facts in a systematic and coherent way. For a while, I pretended there was someone in the passenger seat, listening, as I related out loud everything I know and everything I think I know. But talking to yourself is a sign of madness and your brain knows it, which is why it won't let you continue for more than a few minutes. Eddie would be a good sounding board, but he's not here, and as each minute passes I'm heading further and further away.

It's late afternoon when I reach the chequered flag, but there are no villages, houses or obvious signs of life. I'm on a 'B' road in an area of dense woodland, with an ancient red brick wall running down one side. I carry on until I reach the junction with the main road, turn round and go back the way I came. In half a mile I pass heavy wooden gates set into the wall, accessed by a short turn off the road. I'd noticed it the first time but quickly dismissed it, because I was looking for signage and a large house. I turn around again and take another look. The gates have the appearance of a mediaeval drawbridge, strong and impregnable and there are no push buttons or panels to communicate with whoever is on the other side. There are however, two cameras mounted on poles pointing down at the short drive.

I'm thirsty and haven't eaten anything since this morning. The car needs fuel too, so I return to the main road and after three miles find a service station.

"I'm looking for Chevenham Hall," I say to the young Asian woman behind the counter, who's flicking through a celebrity gossip magazine.

"Sanjeev?" she shouts without looking up, then rattles out an elongated sentence in Hindi that ends with *'Chevenham'*. Sanjeev appears from the storeroom, replying in equally incomprehensible terms. They continue their dialogue for a few moments as if I weren't there, and I begin to wonder whether he's just telling her they've run out of toilet rolls.

"You are looking for Chevenham Hall?" he says in a thick Indian accent.

"That's right," I say, smiling politely despite my weariness and growing impatience.

"It is three miles up this road and turn to the right. It's half mile along."

"Wooden gates set into a tall brick wall?"

"Yes, this is the place."

"I've passed it already but wasn't sure. Thanks."

"But you can't go there."

"Why not?"

"It is private place. You have to make appointment."

"Really?"

"There is private hotel and conference centre, spa and wellness for rich people," he says, looking me up and down as if a casually dressed woman in a Mini doesn't meet the required standard. "They will not let you in."

"I don't want to stay there."

"Are you having interview?"

"No," I say, mildly perplexed.

"You cannot see from the main road because of big gates and big walls. But you can go across field." Sanjeev points out of the window. There is footpath across field. I take Durga sometimes."

"Durga?"

"My dog. You drive for two miles in your car to the next roundabout and turn to the right. Then after a while you will see dirt road on the left."

"Thank you."

"Good luck to you," says Sanjeev without a trace of humour.

*** 

The single track is unmarked, with no signage from the main road to indicate it leads anywhere other than a dead-end in the Norfolk countryside. The Mini bobs and sways along a

138

potholed dirt road more suited to tractors and Range Rovers. After five minutes I'm beginning to wonder if Sanjeev made a mistake or is playing a prank, as the track narrows and tall grass on each side slaps the Mini's flanks, obscuring my view across the fields. Eventually the road widens where there are metal gates on each side and deep ruts full of water indicating a tractor has turned off into a field. I pull into the side, switch off and climb out.

The silence is almost complete, broken only by the rustle of long grass, sporadic birdsong and the pinging of hot metal. I step around the ruts and climb onto the gate to see if I can get a better view up ahead. The field drops away to the left but I catch a glimpse of chimney a mile distant. I climb as high as I dare on the gate, gripping the top bar between my knees and stretching to full height. Several chimney stacks and castellated towers come into view. It's a stately home, set in a small valley.

A distant, rhythmic thump invades the silence, making me look up. A helicopter appears from the south, floats above a wooded area ahead of me and drops out of sight, the sound diminishing as it goes. I'm no aviation expert but this isn't a plaything. It had twin rotors and several oval windows along a bulbous fuselage, with obvious capacity for many passengers and cargo. I guess it's the preferred mode of transportation into and out of Chevenham Hall.

I drive on into the wooded area where the track widens and the light reduces dramatically under the tree canopy, judging I'm within half a mile of my destination. I leave the Mini and proceed on foot through the trees, bemoaning my inadequate footwear, picking my way carefully amongst the ferns and fallen branches, brushing nettles that sting the backs of my hands and puncture my jeans. The trees part and the ground drops away steeply so I sidestep down a bank to an eight-foot-high razor-wire fence. Chevenham looms into view, two hundred yards distant.

It's a vast, gothic pile; a monument to Victorian vanity with fountains and landscaped gardens worthy of Capability Brown. The helicopter sits on a concrete pad in a field to one side, it's drooping blades rotating lazily to rest. An extensive gravel driveway hosts a number of luxury cars and a tarmac road snakes away uphill and out of sight in the direction of the main road.

Several black Mercedes SUVs are amongst the vehicles on display, but my eye is drawn to the helicopter, where the door swings open and people emerge to descend a flight of steps. Two pilots in short sleeves stand on the pad greeting passengers as they alight: three middle-aged men in suits, two bearded Arabs in white thobes and red and white keffiyeh. Five smartly dressed young women follow, some in flowing dresses, some in short skirts, holding hands and giggling as they help each other totter down perilous steps in heels. I try to focus on the faces but they're too far away. There's one with short, reddish hair, the length of her slender legs accentuated by the shortness of her skirt. Like the others, she's relaxed, happy and engaged in lively conversation. I watch the party climb aboard golf buggies that take them the short distance to the main entrance where they disappear inside.

I sit on a tree stump, contemplating the image, relieved, yet deflated. Captains of industry, junior government officials, members of the international business elite meeting at a luxury hotel and health sanctuary with escorts in tow. *'Are you having interview?'*. I'm flattered Sanjeev thought even I might qualify. It's all very calm and civilised; no distress, no coercion, no drama. The place may be exclusive and secretive, but it's not a prison. A girl who looks like Becca Harding is there and it doesn't look like it's against her will.

I return my gaze to the building and scan the lush grounds then dial her number for the first time in two days. The phone still has a generic voicemail greeting. Before I can consider leaving a message my eyes come to rest on a tall pole fifty

140

yards away, one of several dotted around the grounds. On top of the pole is a camera and it's pointing at me.

# PART 2

# CHAPTER 14

Smokey is waiting. He's stretched out on the path, basking in the sunshine, and when he sees me, rolls around on his back as if to banish an itch, but more likely, showing off to earn a treat. I crouch down to rub his white belly and in an instant, all four paws grab my hand. Smokey likes to be in control, and if showing who's boss means puncturing my skin simultaneously with four, needle-sharp claws, then so be it. I wait a moment and he releases his grip. I examine the pin-prick spots of blood and offer him a look of admonishment. His eyes and whiskery snout suggest contrition, but only in my imagination. Cats have no such emotion. He jumps to his feet, confident he hasn't forfeited the right to a tasty snack.

He's not my cat. I'm not sure he's anyone's cat, and if he is, he's not called Smokey, but that's the name I gave him. He's a creature of habit, visiting twice daily, and I always have a tub of crunchy titbits to offer him. He never says, *'Thank you Kate'*, he simply takes what he can and moves on. He lives in the moment. No past, no future, only the here and the now. It's something he and I have in common; something I can empathise with.

He holds his tail aloft and rubs his fur against my legs while I unlock the door of the cottage. He strides purposefully ahead of me into the kitchen, waiting by the cupboard he knows is the store of hidden delights; cat cocaine, I once heard someone say. For my own juvenile amusement, I place the open tub on the floor, but he looks at it dispassionately, and then at me, refusing to dive in or tip it over and gorge on the spillage. It's a power struggle. He wants it served properly, six pieces, placed just so, and what Smokey wants, Smokey gets. I know my place, and acquiesce. He appears to inhale the pungent pellets as in seconds, they're gone. Without further reference to me or anything else, trots back outside to continue his mission, whatever it is.

When I collected my new car, I signed the papers with grim irony. I'd worried the men in the black SUV might find my address through the car registration but it turned out, Becca made it much simpler for them. I considered cancelling the deal, but was still motivated to preserve what's left of my anonymity and start a clean sheet, so when I moved, I left the registered address at Hawsby. My new sim arrived so I bought a new phone, deciding to keep the old one alive for a few weeks in the event she deigned to make contact, but deleting my voicemail greeting to add an extra layer of privacy.

When I got home from Norfolk, the cottage was empty, meaning Adam had returned from London but only in time to pack up the family belongings and head back south. I don't have his number nor any motivation for re-establishing contact. Neither he nor Annabel waited to say goodbye, nor called me about my respective assignments. They either found a way to iron out their differences or both concluded a woman living in a barn in the Lincolnshire Wolds was unsuited to the task, especially now they were going back to Wimbledon. I have a vision of Josie staring mournfully through the rear window as they pull away. Somehow I'm confident that young lady will survive the choppy waters ahead.

I opened the package I found in Becca's car with some trepidation, unsure of what I would do with two kilos of Class A drugs, whilst not at all convinced that was what it might contain. Under the brown paper was a gift-wrapped parcel and a *'Congratulations Jules – Love Jimmy'* label, and under the silvery paper, a wooden presentation case stamped *'Moet'*. A sliding panel revealed a bottle of vintage champagne lying in a bed of straw on one side, with two crystal flutes and a small carton of Belgian chocolates on the other. I was tempted to pop the cork, but it would have given me no pleasure, so I closed the box and brought it with me as a reminder of recent events.

It's not just about Becca and her wild assertion about the demise of her aunt. It's also about repulsive men in suits driving sinister cars, arrogant and incompetent police and a violent predatory male still on the loose. Whatever happened, happened for a reason, and those who ignore the consequences do so at their peril. I don't have it in me to walk away and leave the guilty to prey on the innocent, without at least understanding why. I was subjected to misinformation, supposition and subterfuge, some of it the product of insecurity and fear, much of it, I have no doubt rooted in good, old-fashioned duplicity and malfeasance. I have all the time in the world to uncover the facts, and I will.

I told Nate and Jas I had to leave for a while and wasn't sure when I'd be back, but they said they'd look after things. They said they'd miss me, they couldn't have wished for a better tenant, especially one who'd had paid a year up front at twenty percent over the asking price. I have no regrets about that arrangement, happy to support a resourceful, hard-working young family. I packed a suitcase, put my laptop and personal items in a flight case and, together with the champagne and chocolates, loaded up the car.

My destination was never in doubt. A quick search had revealed the semi-detached seventeenth century pile of stone, wattle, daub and thatch, for rent.

"It's charming," says Dean the agent. "The last occupant lived there over thirty years until she passed away. When would you like to view?"

"I've seen the pictures, I don't need to view," I tell him. "Who owns it?"

"Recently sold to a private landlord."

"Who?"

"Professional based in London. Buy-to-let. Part of his retirement fund."

"Name?"

I can sense Dean's discomfort at my persistence.

"Operates under a limited company."

It's no matter. The name will be on the lease. "Send me the bank details and I'll transfer a year's rent in advance, plus ten percent, plus security deposit." I spell it out, so there's no misunderstanding.

Dean stutters, clearly thrown. "That's very generous Miss Duvall…"

"Kate."

"…Kate. But I'm obliged to do background checks, references, you understand?"

"Go ahead Dean, but I'm paying you a hefty premium, in advance. Do your checks later and if there's anything you don't like about me, you can terminate the lease and keep three months' rent plus the deposit."

"I'll have to speak with the owner." It takes five minutes. "By the way, despite the photos, the cottage is unfurnished. The previous owner had no family and the only contact I had couldn't be reached. No one has come forward to claim any of her belongings, so we had the place cleared and put into temporary storage." *No family?* I'm surprised Becca didn't make herself known if only to retrieve items of sentimental value.

Smokey greeted me on day one, showing me around the place and demanding payment for services, although I was woefully unprepared for him and he went off in a huff. I wondered if he belonged to my neighbour in the adjoining cottage, but there was no sign of life so I bought some cat snacks the next day and he forgave me. I took myself for a walk around the village to see what was what. Slightly bigger and with more houses than Hawsby, which barely warrants a place on the map, Holburgh has a working pub, a corner shop and a church. That it saw the genesis of a successful escort business, seems incongruous.

I throw my bag on the counter, pour myself a glass of wine and sink into my brand new sofa. I survey the meagre surroundings; a far cry from the luxurious and spacious barn in Hawsby.

The sitting room is open plan into the kitchen and between the two there's space for a small dining table. The kitchen cupboards date back to the eighties and the electric cooker has seen better days, but there are no other large appliances, just gaps where they might have been.

Upstairs, there are just two bedrooms and a bathroom. The smaller bedroom I assume was Becca's. The only storage is a cupboard built into an alcove and the woodchip on the walls has been repainted to cover up blemishes. I smile when I imagine a teenager sticking pop posters on the walls with BluTack, just as I did.

The larger bedroom has a built in wardrobe, so I've been able to unpack some of my clothes, but my suitcases remain open on the floor, their contents gradually spilling out onto the cheap beige carpet. I'm destined to sleep on the sofa until my new bed arrives.

I got the keys a week ago and presented with a blank canvas, had to go on a furniture shopping spree, most of which is being delivered next week. Inevitably, the online photos exaggerated the size and condition of the place, but it was no less than I expected. I've had the windows open permanently since I arrived but the carpets and curtains still exude the sickly, sweet smell of weed combined with the aromatic odour of joss stick and cheap perfume. Dean told me he'd had a commercial cleaner come in to freshen the place up and he'd recommended to the landlord the sitting room carpet be replaced. I suspect this was due to an indelible blood stain in front of the fire. The open fireplace has a simple red-brick surround, the hearth covered in polished tiles that extend a few centimetres over the front edge, one of which has a chunk missing. I'm guessing this is where Grace fell and cracked her head open, and on close examination, I can see discolouration on the exposed edge of the broken tile; blood that seeped into the porcelain, Grace's DNA on permanent display.

This is where Grace lived, in this village, in this very cottage. Despite the absence of any personal items or loose furniture, I can feel her presence, as if she's popped out to the shops and will be back at any minute.

"Coo-eee!" The shriek is so loud and unexpected, my body tenses and I sit up abruptly, spilling wine down my shirt. I jerk my head towards the door, realising someone has let themselves in. "Aah, there you are!" says a buxom woman with a beaming smile. She's sixty-plus, wearing a voluminous white blouse stretched tight over her extra-large bosom, red Bermuda shorts, sandals and sunglasses that perch on top of her head astride a rigid mass of silvery hair streaked with pink and purple. "I hope you don't mind me letting myself in," she says. "Force of habit. Miriam. We're neighbours," she says, pointing at the adjoining wall. "I have a key," she adds, dangling it from her other hand. "Goodness me, where's all your stuff?" she exclaims, looking around at the virtually empty room. I jump to my feet and hold out a hand, still shaken by her unannounced arrival.

"Kate. Pleased to meet you."

She offers me the tips of her fingers like royalty, wrists and hands adorned with a plethora of assorted jewellery.

"When I left, all her things were still here."

"The place was cleared before I arrived. New furniture is on its way," I assure her without further explanation. I'm not minded to get into a conversation about me at the moment, but I needn't worry as Miriam's more interested in herself.

"Just back from a fortnight in Tenerife," she says, "topping up my tan for the winter. Go every year, same place, same hotel. They know me well and see to my every need. I have the same room every time with a gorgeous sea view."

"Really?"

148

"Food is superb, cocktails to die for," she gushes, lost in her holiday reminiscences, "wonderful infinity pool and jacuzzi, there's a sauna, hot tub, they have their very own spa with a gorgeous masseur called Carlos," she says, with a twinkle in her eye, "and where would Senora Miriam like her massage today?" she continues in a cod-Spanish accent. "Ooh la-la," she says, switching nationalities and winking.

"That's nice."

"I've booked same time next year, although I'm tempted to go back in the Spring. I just love it."

"Have you ever thought of moving out there permanently?" I know it's mischievous and based entirely on first impressions, but I couldn't resist it.

"Oh yes. Every time I step off the plane into that sunshine, I say to myself, 'Miriam, you're not getting any younger, do it while you still can', but I worry it might lose its attraction. Spending most of one's time here in England shivering in the wind and rain, makes going there feel all the more special."

"Does the grey cat belong to you?" I ask, to change the subject.

"What? That verminous little tyke? Certainly not!"

"I thought he was rather sweet," I say, moved to defend Smokey's honour.

"Ugh! Grace used to say that!"

"Grace?"

"The lady who lived here. Oh, it's so sad," she says, her ebullience deflated. She takes her sunglasses from her head and folds in the legs. "I knew her for ten years, she was a good friend of mine."

"What happened?"

"She had a terrible accident. Fell and hit her head. It's just too awful for words." I fear Miriam is about to burst into tears, but she manages to control her emotions. "We were supposed to go for coffee in Southwold, we go every Monday and do a little shopping, and I'm getting ready when the phone rings

149

and it's Dr Webb. He's been trying to call Grace but there's no answer so he asks if I mind going next door. So, I knock but there's still no answer. But I have a key, you see? I've always had a key, and she has a key to mine and I let myself in and call *'Coo-eee Grace'* and…" she pauses for a sharp intake of breath "…that's when I find her, dead on the floor!" She puts a hand over her mouth, reliving the shock. "Right there by the fireplace, in a pool of blood. Her eyes were wide open. I'll never forget it."

"That must have been terrible for you."

"I called Dr Webb and he came immediately, a lot quicker than an ambulance, I can tell you, but it was too late. Poor Grace was…gone." She dabs at her eyes with a tiny lace hankie.

"I'm very sorry."

"Comes to us all. But she was only young. She had so much life in her. It wasn't her time."

"What about her family?"

"That's the saddest thing. She didn't have any. She died alone and there was no one to grieve for her."

It's not what I expected to hear. "No one?"

"Well, hardly any. People turned out for the funeral, you know, people from the village who knew her, plus an old boyfriend of hers who looks like a bouncer. The only blood relative was her niece, who's at university up north somewhere. She only came back if she wanted something, money usually. She turned up, but spent most of her time with the bouncer. She came back here to see what she could salvage. You should have seen what she was wearing, and for a funeral?" she says, shuddering at the thought. "Looked like a tart, that's all I'm saying."

Miriam's disparaging comments are surprising, given Becca's professed love for Grace and her allegations of foul play. But something doesn't ring true. Becca claimed she changed into her working clothes implying she was more

150

soberly dressed at the funeral. Also, Miriam describes Becca as if she's just an acquaintance when, if she'd lived next door to Grace for ten years, she would have seen her grow up and presumably known her well.

"Is Dr Webb close by?"

"Yes. The practice is on the edge of the village. Manages it himself with a receptionist and a part time nurse."

"Thought I should register."

"Good luck! I think he's full, if you know what I mean. He is rather dishy." Miriam's eyes twinkle again, grief at losing her friend temporarily set aside by new, lustful thoughts. "Must get back, I have to unpack and do the washing. Welcome to Holburgh!" she says, striding out of the front door.

# CHAPTER 15

It prompts me to dial Becca's number again, this time using my old phone, the one she might recognise, but I still get the same generic greeting. If she has access to it, she'll know she's missed my call but I have no reason to suspect she's in danger and no expectation she'll get back in touch. I check with Miles, but he hasn't heard from her either, not since he gave up trying. I do my best to assure him she's okay without actually providing any evidence.

I go online to Companies House. There are five Grace Hardings listed as directors and a further eight who have Grace as a middle name. I work through them, eliminating several on grounds of age and location, settling on one, born fifty five years ago, director and secretary of Nubilis Limited with a registered office in Ipswich. The giveaway is her co-director, one James Munro, who has fifteen other directorships. She and Uncle Jimmy may have ended their personal relationship, but remained business partners until the end.

Nubilis was classified as a micro-entity, operating in the entertainment sector, which meant it had annual turnover of less than six hundred thousand, although the exact figure is not shown. The last unaudited accounts comprised merely a simplified balance sheet showing net liabilities of over three hundred thousand pounds meaning it was technically insolvent and only able to trade because it's creditors allowed it to. The first annual return, filed twelve years ago, shows James Munro as a 99% shareholder and Grace with 1%. Ultimately, their escort business was a commercial failure and her modest home bears that out. I say was, because six months ago, it was placed into administration.

A check on Jimmy's other directorships reveals companies of varying sizes in security, entertainment and consultancy. I flick through the companies, looking at the names of other directors all of whom mean nothing to me. Out of interest I look up Adam Cross. There are several but the company that sticks out is ISW Associates, classified as international investment advisors, the company he presumably works for now and where he met Becca. Another former directorship of a company recently dissolved, lists James Munro as a fellow director.

It's interesting, but not very informative. Adam's relationship with Uncle Jimmy, starting with a drink in a nightclub two years ago continued for a short while in a professional capacity. There is a generic website for ISW with bland pronouncements of its expertise in international finance and consultancy, illustrated by stock photos. Nothing obviously untoward and pretty much how Becca described it, yet I know in my heart something's wrong. Without thinking, I call ISW and ask for Adam Cross. I'm surprised to be connected quite quickly. He skips the pleasantries, sounding a little flustered.

"Kate, can I call you back?"

It's no surprise. He's a busy man in with an important job. I'm amazed he's even in the country. It's thirty minutes before my phone rings, caller ID withheld.

"Adam?"

"Hi Kate!" He sounds more relaxed and I can hear background noise. Ever cautious, he's stepped out to a coffee shop. "How nice to hear from you."

"Have you spoken to Becca Harding recently?"

"No. Not since we were at the cottage."

"Do you know why she was asking for help?"

"Sort of. She said her aunt had died in suspicious circumstances."

"Why come to you?"

"I told you. She sounded desperate, thought we still had some sort of friendship and didn't know where else to go."

"Rubbish."

"Excuse me?"

"Come off it Adam. I know you were a lot closer to Becca than you're prepared to admit, I know you were one of Grace's clients and I know you're an acquaintance of Jimmy Munro." All I can hear is the hubbub of background chatter and the clatter and hiss of coffee machines. "What did you expect? Becca would give up once you'd palmed her off onto an amateur like me? Or did you think I'd panic when I found out what the problem was? She's alleging murder, for God's sake!" No response. "And now she's gone missing. Speak to me Adam!"

"She can get hysterical, be a bit irrational."

"So you're not denying it."

"We need to talk."

"When?"

"Not now. I'll have to call you back."

***

It's listed in the *'Useful numbers'* section of *Holburgh News*, a free quarterly publication featuring articles and people of local interest, funded largely from advertising by local tradesmen and subsidised by the parish council. It arrived through my letterbox this morning. I know it's closed on a Sunday and I won't be able to register as a patient, but take a walk in the summer sunshine and familiarise myself with the village.

I find the surgery without difficulty. It's a relatively unattractive seventies-style residential property with an even less attractive, flat-roofed extension, which suggests the good doctor both lives and works here. It's the last house on Southwold Road, separated from its closest neighbour by a footpath that snakes off into a field. I take it, gauging it will bring me out at the other side of the village.

154

The air carries the aroma of Sunday roast and there's only birdsong and the occasional barking dog to disturb the peace. One canine miscreant sounds close by and particularly agitated, and I turn to see a head poking between the bars of the wrought iron gate to the surgery. I'm no expert on dogs but can identify one or two, including the Staffordshire Terrier that's barking vociferously in my direction. I take no heed; it's just a dog flaunting its courage from the safety of its own domain.

I realise I'm wrong when it takes a step back and vaults the top bar, racing towards me like a demonic express train, barking angrily. Before I have time to react, it takes a flying leap and sinks it's teeth into my left ankle, emanating a deep, guttural sound. The animal has formidable strength given its diminutive size and I'm grateful it isn't a German Shepherd or a Rottweiler, either of which would have had me on the ground. The pain however, is exquisite and I'm looking down at the beast, twisting and tugging at my leg, when its bulging eyes look up and catch mine. It lets go immediately and staggers backwards like a drunk, barking wildly, long trails of blood-stained drool stretching to the dusty ground.

"Samsung!" comes a cry from behind the surgery gate. "Samsung!"

The dog that's named after a phone continues to bark hysterically, desperate to resume its attack, but equally, unsure whether it should. I take a step towards it and it whimpers pathetically, turns on the spot and races back down the path, passing a flustered individual who has appeared from nowhere waving his arms in the air.

"Samsung! Oh my God!" he says, rushing towards me. Blood is already trickling onto my nice white trainers and I briefly challenge the wisdom of wearing a skirt in preference to jeans that might have afforded better protection. "Are you okay?" he says, already out of breath, having run a mere thirty

155

yards. He's in his forties, wearing a checked shirt, chinos and brown brogues. "I can't believe he did that."

"It's fine. Just a scratch."

"Come with me," he says holding out a hand.

"I said it's fine."

"It most certainly is not!" he says with an air of authority. "I know what I'm talking about." *No you don't.* "I'm a doctor. Come inside and I'll see to that wound, it looks really nasty. I insist!"

I ignore the outstretched hand and follow him back down the path to the house. There's no sign of Samsung. The dog was clearly spooked when I first went by, but in attacking me, bit off more than he could chew. Animals have no concept of mortality other than a deep rooted instinct to survive. He tasted my blood and made the mistake of looking into my eyes, caught a glimpse of the dark side and something flipped in his minuscule brain.

The man I assume to be Dr Webb leads me into a kitchen that's perfectly tidy and bears no sign of culinary activity. I expect another human being to show themselves but he appears to be alone.

"Come through into the surgery," he says opening a frosted glass door and striding purposefully down a short corridor before turning into a small consulting room. "Sit on that bed, please," he says with the air of someone used to giving orders to a dog. I clamber onto the edge of a narrow surgical bed covered in a sheet of blue plastic and dangle my legs over the side. He brings two stools and sits in front of me. "Pop your leg on that one, so I can see what the damage is. I can't believe he did that!"

"So you said."

"Take off your shoe."

Hastily, he fills a stainless steel basin of warm water and swabs down my wounds with cotton wool, then dabs the skin with something that stings.

156

"Bleeding has stopped already. Remarkable given the state of your shoe. No shortage of thrombin there!" he quips. I assume it's a medical term but I have no idea what he's talking about, nor, in my case, does he. "Only superficial I think," he says, holding my calf with one hand and gently moving my foot in a circular motion with the other. "Does that hurt?"

"No."

"He's never like that. I don't know what got into him. What on earth did you do?"

His nose is inches from my foot and I could easily kick him in the face. It's a triumph of will I stay calm.

"I think I was taking a walk along a public footpath, minding my own business. Remiss of me not to anticipate an unprovoked attack from a vicious dog with a name like a smartphone."

"Samson's not vicious."

"Not usually."

"Not ever!"

"First time for everything."

"He's not a bad dog," he says with some irritation. *There are no bad dogs Doc, just bad owners.*

"I'll take your word for it."

"Look. I'm really sorry."

"I said it was fine. I won't report it, if that's what you're thinking." He looks at me as if contemplating an expression of gratitude. "Just as well the first time was with an adult rather than a three-year-old." It's not fair of me. I know what freaked the dog. It was me, and the mutt won't come across people like me very often, if ever. But now he's got the taste of blood, who knows?

"That's very generous of you."

"Not at all."

He carefully winds a bandage around my ankle. "Sorry about your trainers."

"No worries."

"I'll give you a tetanus jab."

"No thanks."

"When did you last have one?"

"Can't remember, but it's not necessary, I assure you."

"I'm the doctor! I'll decide when you need a tetanus jab."
He is, of course, wrong about that; not about being a doctor,
but that I need any protection from *clostridium tetani* or any
other neurotropic virus such as rabies. They can't survive in
my body, but he's not to know that.

"If you insist. Samsung was certainly agitated. Does he
have rabies?" I ask, just to be mischievous. I'm rather
enjoying Dr Webb's discomfort.

"It's Samson, and no, of course he doesn't."

"Just asking."

He leaves the room and is back within a minute carrying a
tin tray, a phial of serum and a needle. I let out a sigh as he
goes through the motions and jabs me in the arm.

"There. That'll head it off at the pass."

"Are we done?"

"You're welcome to stay as long as you like. I'd prefer it
if you waited twenty minutes or so, in case you have any
reaction."

"I'll be fine."

"Let me make you a cup of tea."

***

"Nigel Webb", he says, pushing a steaming mug of tea
towards me and holding out his hand. I shake it firmly.
"Holburgh village doctor."

"Kate Duvall, Holburgh village resident and prospective
patient."

"You must be new around here. I know most people but I
haven't seen you before."

"Moved in last week. I'd like to register, if that's okay?"

"Always room for one more!" he says without conviction. "Anyway, I think you've earned your place after today."

"No sign of Samsung."

"It's Samson," he says with a hint of reproach, knowing fine well I'm teasing. "Where do you live?"

"Rose Cottages, the one on the right."

"Grace Harding's place," he says lowering his eyes. I want him to tell me what he knows about Grace without having to prompt him, but the chatty doctor has gone quiet. He's a good looking guy who's thinning on top and developing a paunch. He reminds me of Adam Cross with his easy, open manner.

"I understand she died."

"Yes. Very sad. Very sad indeed."

"You probably see a lot of that."

"A lot of what?"

"Death. Being a doctor."

"Oh, yes. I suppose I do. There's a steady turnover amongst the older members of the community, but not many like Grace."

"What happened?"

"She had a bad fall and sadly, she didn't recover."

"Was she elderly?" I'm treading dangerously here, feigning ignorance when I know she was fifty-five.

"Mid-fifties, but she wasn't well."

I'm surprised he describes her in those terms. Type 1 diabetes is a serious condition but perfectly manageable, especially by those like Grace who had it all her life. I want to know more, but if he's a proper doctor, he won't tell me anything that compromises his professional ethics. On the other hand, he should realise by now I'm fairly direct, so I have no compunction about asking the question.

"What was wrong with her?"

He gives me an awkward look. *It was worth a try.*

"I can't tell you that I'm afraid. Medical ethics," he says in such a way that suggests he'd like to tell me, but is burdened by professional obligation.

"Sure. Sorry, didn't mean to pry. It's not every day I move into a place to find the previous tenant died in tragic circumstances. Rather puts a dampener on it."

"I'm sure you're not a believer in ghosts."

*If only he knew.* Edith hasn't given me the benefit of her wisdom recently but it's only a matter of time. "Not at all." I get up and make a show of testing my injured leg. If Dr Webb were to remove his extremely neat bandage, he'd probably find the wounds were already well on their way to healing. "Must get back. Do I have to run the gauntlet with Samson again?"

"Look. I feel really bad about this."

"Don't."

"Let me make it up to you? Let me buy you dinner?" He looks nervous in the asking. He's stuffed both hands in his pockets and shifted his weight twice in three seconds. I cast a glance around the kitchen and down the hall.

"Is there a …Mrs Webb?"

"No!" he says, rather too quickly. "What I mean is, we split about a year ago."

"Sorry."

"Her choice."

If Dr Webb is looking for love, he's come to the wrong place but he still might be the source of valuable background information. I should take him up on his offer without appearing too enthusiastic. But first, I have a question.

"Is it okay?"

"Okay for what?"

"Okay for a doctor to go on a date with a patient?"

He grins sheepishly, embarrassed at the inference. "It's not a date, as such. I'm just buying you dinner. I mean, we can't take it any further than that. I'd have to refer you to another

160

surgery," he gabbles, his ears going red. I watch him blink erratically. "What I mean is …"

"I know what you mean."

"And you're not a patient yet, at least not officially."

"I get it. Okay. When?"

He relaxes visibly. "How about tonight? Village pub, if you're up to it. It's just pub grub but perfectly adequate and Sunday nights are usually quiet."

"Alright."

"And I can make sure you're still okay. See you there about seven?"

He shows me out and we look up and down the path for an angry attack dog.

"Samson!" he shouts but there's no reply. "I'll have to go find him." We go in separate directions and I resume my walk across the field. I hear Dr Webb calling as he goes off in the distance and then find Samson lying under a hedge fifty yards away. He stares at me and growls but is afraid to make a move.

"You and I are going to be best buddies. I can tell."

# CHAPTER 16

The Fox and Anchor is busy, despite what Dr Webb said, and I have to scan the occupied tables until I see a figure standing in the corner waving at me. I sense the eyes of fellow diners as I pass by and when I look at them, they glance away, restraining their curiosity. Dr Webb is well known, separated from his wife and understandably, dining alone. Or, on this occasion, not.

"Kate!" he says, grinning nervously and holding out a hand. "Nice to see you again. How's the ankle?" He's wearing a crisp, checked shirt under his tweed jacket and I get a waft of fabric conditioner and gentleman's fragrance.

"It's fine."

"No aftereffects?"

"No."

"Shall I take a look?"

"Now?" I say, looking around the busy pub.

"Why not?"

The bandage is redundant, but I left it on in case he enquired or happened to notice it under my trousers. Anyway, it's a curious suggestion, that I might stick a bare ankle on the table or have him look closely between my legs.

"No, it's fine."

"Okay, you're probably right. Any pain?"

"Leave it!"

"Sorry."

"Did you find Samson?"

"Skulked home shortly after you left. I gave him a good talking to and he spent the rest of the afternoon asleep in his basket. He's certainly not himself."

"Maybe he caught something from me?"

Dr Webb manages a weak grin, not sure whether I'm joking, but a waitress arrives with menus and I order a gin and

162

tonic. He's already two thirds through his pint and orders another.

"You're sure you're not taking a risk, compromising your ethics being seen socialising with a patient?"

"No! Anyway as I said, you're not a patient yet."

"What about gossip?"

"I'm not going to worry about that, fact of life around here. Even quacks are allowed out sometimes and you're here because I owe you a personal apology and this is my treat."

"It's forgotten already."

"What brings you to Holburgh."

*I'm investigating the suspicious death of Grace Harding.*

"Change of scenery. I move around from time to time, can't seem to settle. I'm a writer, so I can do what I do from anywhere."

"What do you write?"

"All sorts. How long have you been in Holburgh?" I say, switching the conversation around. I don't want to discuss me or my past, it will do neither of us any good.

"Three years. Moved from East London, decided a sleepy country practice was more appealing than dealing with drug addicts, domestic abuse injuries and knife wounds."

"And is it?"

"Of course!"

"But your wife didn't?"

"It's complicated."

"I'm sorry, none of my business." He'd be well within his rights to concur, but if he wants what I think he wants, he'll tread carefully, at least until he realises the way is barred. All I want from him is information and I haven't yet decided how far I'm prepared to go to get it. "Let's agree on something. Stay away from personal history for now. Pretend we have no back story, no past; just talk about the present and find out what we have in common."

163

"Interesting," he says, encouraged, yet unconvinced. "Who we are is largely a product of who we were and what we've done, don't you think?"

"Yes I do, of course. But what I mean is… why don't you tell me your taste in say, music and literature, food and drink, recreational drugs…?"

"What?"

I've succeeded in throwing him off balance and I chuckle. "Just joking. I'm not into that."

"I might have had the odd bit of weed at Uni," he says, pleased to share a wicked secret. I act suitably shocked but at the same time, amused.

"Really? The good doctor was a student dopehead?"

"Ssh! You'll get me struck off!" he says, joining in the joke, and then has to keep a straight face as the waitress takes our order, a task he finds difficult because I'm grinning at him provocatively.

"I think the late Grace Harding must have been partial to some of that stuff," I say when she's gone, continuing the theme. "The place reeks of it. She sounds like a very interesting character."

"What makes you say that?"

"Miriam next door. She said they'd been friends for years. She said she was the one who found her and you came rushing over to help."

"Yes, Miriam was in quite a state. You can imagine how terrible that would have been for her. Nothing I could do, I'm afraid, she'd already gone."

"Maybe she overdosed?" He looks at me and shakes his head. "Sorry, done it again. You're not supposed to say." I run thumb and finger across my lips, as if zipping my mouth shut.

"Cause of death isn't confidential. I have to put it on the death certificate, so it's public knowledge. I knew she had a history of taking weed. She told me, but you can't overdose on it and it certainly isn't going to kill you. It was something

164

far more prosaic. She cracked her head open on the hearth, died from a skull fracture and blood loss. If someone had been there at the time; if I'd been there for example, I probably could have saved her. Assuming of course she didn't have catastrophic brain damage."

"There's a big chunk out of one of the hearth tiles."

He shrugs. "Accidents happen all the time in the home. People assume they're safe at home, but they can fall downstairs, electrocute themselves, gas themselves, cut themselves with a knife or on broken glass, all manner of hazards. And it's those who live alone who are most at risk."

"Miriam said she had no family."

"One daughter, as far as I know. Rebecca," he says as if thinking fondly of her. "But she went off to university and was away when it happened. Just bad luck I'm afraid."

I'm struck by his use of the term 'daughter' instead of 'niece'. It may not be significant. He's been here three years, so he'd have barely got to know her before she left home, and knowing of her doesn't mean she or Grace ever explained their relationship. They shared a surname and acted like mother and daughter; what was there to explain?

"It would be nice to meet her. Just to say hello and offer my condolences."

"I'm seeing her next week; I'll tell her."

I try not to look surprised. His statement is innocuous and it doesn't warrant a reaction. He might be mistaken. It may be a long standing appointment which she can't now keep because I know she's otherwise engaged. I do my best to sound normal and not overly inquisitive.

"Please do. What day is it, so I make sure I'm around?"

"Wednesday. We're having lunch. Here, in fact!"

The food arrives just at the right time and allows me to vent feelings, a heady cocktail of confusion, suspicion and excitement. I tracked down her location but she was

165

inaccessible, and now I find she's strolling back into view as if nothing happened.

"Wow! This looks good."

I tuck into the sea bass, questions whirring in my head. There's nothing to dislike about Nigel Webb. He's affable, considerate, earnest and straightforward. It could be the forty-something doctor is on the prowl; he's separated and already got a twenty-one-year old meeting him for lunch, so until then, may as well fit in a thirty-one-year old for dinner, and who would blame him for that? Fortunately for me, he's on his third pint, and it's fuelling his loquacity.

"Why don't you join us?" he says with more enthusiasm than warranted; as if he's just had some splendid idea that involves three in a bed. I try not to laugh, but the gin is doing me no favours.

"I'm not sure about that. I don't want to intrude."

"You won't," he says through a mouthful of steak and ale pie. "Her mother's stuff is in my garage and she wants to take a look and buy me lunch as a thank you."

I realise I'm gobbling my food, but it's the only way of stopping my mouth running away. I make an effort to compose myself and slow down, wondering whether the 'stuff' he's referring to is a stash of cannabis.

"What stuff?"

"Her stuff. Furniture and well...stuff."

"You've been storing Grace's belongings?"

"Rebecca had to clear out the house for the new tenant, that's you," he says, pointing his fork at me and winking, "and had nowhere to put it, so I offered the use of my garage."

"That was nice."

"Not really," he shrugs. "I met her for the first time at the funeral and she looked so unhappy I said if there was anything I could do... you know how you say these things never expecting people to take you up on it... but then she needed storage space and I was only too happy to oblige."

166

It's one of those reset moments. You collect fragments of information from loosely connected people, most of it incomplete, most of it compromised in the telling, either by virtue of the teller's own preconceptions or by human instinct that drives them to ameliorate their own standing. Much of it is motivated by personal prejudice, but will always contain an element of truth. You try to assess it, process it, filter out the inconsistencies, match up the commonalities and try to arrive at a coherent conclusion without allowing your own assumptions to get in the way.

Becca Harding was taken from my home against her will by two men from whom she'd been hiding. They were intimidating and aggressive and deserving of a good blast of pepper-spray. They claimed to work for Uncle Jimmy, a former bouncer, drug dealing pimp and all-round dubious businessman who was once close to Grace, whom Becca believes was murdered. Becca's phone number may be active, but it may as well be offline, perhaps destroyed, because she can't be contacted, despite my knowing where she last was. She's a missing person according to her boyfriend Miles and even now, may be dead like her Aunt Grace. That's my assessment, my conclusion, my assumption, and it's why I'm here.

But there's no evidence the two men who took her were the two men who stalked her at South Alston, or the two men who terrorised Miles. There's no evidence they actually work for Jimmy Munro and no evidence Jimmy tricked her into taking a consignment of narcotics to a fat-cat client. A reset moment, like throwing the pieces of a jigsaw into the air and trying to reassemble them using the picture from a different puzzle.

"I'd love to, but can I make a suggestion? Don't mention I'm coming."

"Why not?"

167

"I don't want her to feel awkward. I'll just turn up and you can introduce us. We'll know if she's uncomfortable and doesn't want to chat, and if so, I'll just make my excuses."

"That's very considerate, but I'm sure Rebecca will be delighted to meet you."

\*\*\*

He insists on walking me home even though it's in the opposite direction to the surgery. "It's not far. Nothing's far in Holburgh."

We get to Rose Cottages and Smokey appears as if from nowhere.

"Hello cat," says Dr Webb with little affection.

"This is Smokey." Smokey miaows loudly to remind me he's hungry.

"Is that his name? I've seen him about," he says.

"It's the name I gave him. I think I've been adopted."

"Not one for cats," he says with some distaste. "Prefer dogs."

"Thanks for dinner."

"My pleasure. Let's do it again."

"See you on Wednesday."

He's clearly not sure what to do so I help him out with a quick kiss on the cheek. He looks happy enough, but weirdly disturbed by Smokey's presence. I turn and glimpse a vertical sliver of light through a gap in the curtains next door, quickly extinguished.

# CHAPTER 17

I find Southwold crematorium on the outskirts of town. Set in landscaped gardens with far reaching views across the Suffolk countryside, it's a beautiful final resting place but paradoxically, only for the living, as the dead don't have a clue where they are. It sounds unduly cynical, and more than most, I'm aware of the blurred lines between life and death, but for someone in my position I feel uniquely privileged to be able to appreciate the beauty of my surroundings, regardless of its purpose.

Row upon row of headstones, urns and plaques line the myriad paths that snake through the grounds. It would be time consuming, but not impossible to find a particular one if one didn't know where to look. I need someone with the knowledge. The office opening times are posted on the door. I can see a middle aged woman inside sitting behind a desk, and she can see me, but keeps her head down. She won't open up for another twenty minutes according to the notice, so I go for a walk around the grounds, reading each name, imagining who they were, how they lived, how they died and the journey they took to end up in this, their final home.

My half of Rose Cottages now feels like home, but for how long, I can't say. My furniture arrived and I'm looking forward to sleeping in a real bed for the first time in a week. Miriam made a pretence of tending her minuscule front garden so that she could watch the men carry it in, then unable to resist, started directing operations, inviting herself in to make helpful suggestions about where everything should go.

"Grace used to have her dining table over here…" she'd said "…and two armchairs here. Goodness me that's a large bed," were among her less irritating comments. Smokey kept well away, probably due to the unusually feverish activity

169

rather than Miriam's presence; the enmity she feels towards him not reciprocated, much to her annoyance.

I don't know what I expect to find here, but it's part of the picture, a piece of the jigsaw, however tiny and insignificant, and somehow brings me closer to Grace. Despite my state, I'm not a believer in the afterlife and I still refuse to accept we go to another place when we die, yet can't escape the inevitable conclusion there are others like me. All of the people beneath my feet though, are dust, pure and simple; whether their spirits live on, is a matter of faith. Edith would have something to say about it, I'm sure, and I wish I could ask her, but our conversations are one-sided and only happen when she's in the mood.

I don't need the woman behind the desk. I've been directed subliminally to Grace Harding's brass plaque, sandwiched between Samuel Rosen and Molly Weaver, both significantly older than Grace when they died. There's no room on it for a eulogy, and it brings home to me how short was her life and, whether by accident or design, how precipitate her death. I want her to speak to me and tell me what happened, it would be far easier for everyone if she did, especially Becca, who, without some resolution, will remain forever tormented. She's probably wrong about murder; neither Miriam nor Dr Webb suggested Grace's death was anything other than a tragic accident and in her final weeks and months they were arguably closer to her than Becca. I'll be pleased to see her again tomorrow and find out what really happened in Hawsby.

The point is, Grace is dead, a fact borne out by the name on the plaque. *There's one for you in Wimbledon. Explain that!*

***

I look for a white Mini in the car park, knowing it was highly improbable. It's been over a month since I saw her and in the

170

meantime she's refused to engage. When I think through the mess she was in, and the happy and relaxed young woman I saw at Chevenham, it points squarely to this being a false alarm. She won't be here.

But she is.

Nigel Webb is sitting at his favourite table, facing the door. Becca is seated opposite, back towards me. The hair looks longer and has lost some of its colour, the shock of red giving way to a deep auburn, and any expectation of sparkly top and leather miniskirt is quickly dispelled. She's casually dressed in jeans and cashmere sweater. Webb looks up as I approach.

"Kate! Nice to see you," he says, playing the chance meeting to a tee.

"Hello Nigel. Don't let me interrupt you."

"Not at all. Rebecca, this is Kate. She recently moved into your mother's house." Becca Harding pushes her chair back and nervously rubs palms down the leg of her jeans. The features are just as I remembered. Those high cheekbones, good complexion and brown eyes. Strikingly attractive, was my original impression and it hasn't changed.

"Hi Kate," she says politely, forcing a nervous smile and extending a hand. "Nice to meet you." She looks through me without a flicker of recognition, as if I'm a total stranger, and why shouldn't she? We've never met.

\*\*\*

I offered her my sincere condolences, made my excuses and left them to it. I have no reason to believe the lunch arrangement was anything other than that, a gesture of gratitude combined with a practical discussion of what was to happen to Grace's furniture and belongings. I could have made a contribution, but I would have been distracted by the ever growing list of questions forming in my head. Whatever I had to say to Rebecca Harding was not for the doctor's ears.

I left them with a small lie. I had found something personal belonging to Grace, something the house clearance firm had overlooked and I thought she should have it. It's only small, but it may have sentimental value.

"What is it?" she'd said, curious but unconcerned.

Without answering, I'd checked my phone and said I was late for an appointment, but if she had time, perhaps she could drop by the cottage and collect it. I'd be back by three if that wasn't too late?

"Not at all," she'd said, still intrigued, but not enough to pursue her questioning.

In the intervening two or three hours, I repeatedly ran through the sequence of events from the day I arrived home from South Alston. I met the Cross family and their enigmatic children, learned quickly of an unstable marriage ruptured by claims of infidelity, exacerbated by sexual disarray, Adam's connection to Becca, then Grace and ultimately Jimmy. The tortuous nature of their interlocking relationships, in which each player has something to hide, means verifiable facts are few and far between. The scope for dishonesty is absolute, half-truths a given. I've unpicked Becca's story again and again and come up with a different scenario every time. The only thing I know for certain is that Grace Harding is dead, because I've seen her grave with my own eyes.

It's three-thirty before she arrives. I'm struck by the similarity but there's no longer any confusion in my mind. They're twins.

"I wondered what it looked like," she says glancing around the room like an excited child.

"When were you last here?"

"I've never been here."

I wanted it to be another reset moment. Time for a totally new approach predicated on the crucial assumption Rebecca is a complete innocent and knows nothing of what I'm about to tell her. I'm hoping whatever she does know will make

172

sense of all the rest, but she's thrown me immediately by claiming she's never been in her mother's house.

"As you know, all Grace's possessions are with Dr Webb. Everything here is new."

"I need to go through it all, I just don't know when. I couldn't let it be thrown out, not after all this time. What was it you found?"

"Rebecca..."

"Becky."

"Becky, how much time do you have?"

She glances at her watch. "My train from Southwold is at four-twenty."

"There's something I need to talk to you about."

"Okay."

"It may take some time."

"Okay, go ahead."

"Like, a few hours."

\*\*\*

She called home to say she wanted to make a start sorting out Grace's things, so she'd be staying overnight.

"Where's home?" I ask her over a glass of wine.

"Hampshire."

"How long have you lived there?"

"Always."

"I assume you're not a Harding."

"No, I'm a Saunders."

\*\*\*

Rachel and Philip Saunders from Chetworth, Hampshire married in 1985 and within five years, had produced three sons. Teacher Rachel, and fund manager Philip, doted on their boys and at the millennium all three were boarding at public

173

school on the south coast. Rachel, by then in her forties and with a comfortable lifestyle, was nevertheless discontented, spending most of her days alone in a rambling former vicarage. Rather than return to work, she announced her intention to produce a girl, since only then would their family be complete.

Philip was minded to indulge his wife in her every desire but, ever the pragmatist, felt obliged to point out that it had been a full twelve years since her last child and so she'd not only be running a risk to her health, there was no guarantee she could even get pregnant again, never mind produce a child of the specified gender. What if it was another boy? How many more rolls of the dice would it take to produce a girl? Adoption was the only way to guarantee that outcome.

The couple were assessed by a local adoption agency and found to be eminently suitable but it was one of Philip's business connections that led them to their adoption of a one-year-old baby girl from Suffolk.

"When did you find out?"

"I was ten. I had an argument with one of my brothers and he came out with it."

"That must have been a shock."

"You bet it was, but we got over it. It made me special, in a way and I never once regarded my parents as anything other than real. I love them as much as I ever did and I love my brothers too. They're my family."

"But at some stage, you decided you needed to track down your real mother and the trail led you to Holburgh."

"I wanted to know why. I could only imagine this woman and her circumstances. What made her give up her child? Was she single, homeless, poor? The more I thought about it the more I realised I had to find out, otherwise it would fester in my mind for ever. Like one of those songs you can't get out of your head, even if it's one you don't like. They drive you mad. I had to know who she was."

Becky Saunders is far more grounded than her twin, more measured in her approach and less emotionally challenged. I'm reluctant to throw another potentially harmful variable into the mix, but I've discovered I can't do this all by myself and I have limited options. I can drop in some apparently innocent questions and try to steer her towards the answers I want, but it might just further muddy the waters. It's time I trusted someone to tell me the truth which means I have to be truthful myself.

"I have a confession to make. I don't have anything of Grace's here for you. I just said that to get you here."

"Okay," she says, sounding guarded.

"I turned up at the pub today expecting to meet someone else. Someone who asked me for help and then disappeared."

"I'm not with you."

"I thought I was meeting your sister."

"I...don't have a sister," she says slowly, bracing herself for a new revelation.

"Yes you do. You're a twin." She shifts her eyes, processing the statement, not sure if she heard me correctly, formulating a response that doesn't come. "Not only do you have a twin, she has the same name as you, although she's a Harding."

"I really don't understand."

"Today was the first time you met Dr Webb wasn't it?"

"Yes, and he was a bit weird. He referred to our talk at the funeral and I was confused because I wasn't there, but he kept blethering on about being a village doctor and being single and asking me what I was going to do now and I thought he looked a bit lost and lonely. I decided he was the one who was confused."

"At the funeral, he was talking to Becca, your twin sister."

"Becca? Same name?"

"Yeah, I know it's confusing."

"Gosh."

175

"How come you weren't there?"

"I only found out about Grace a month ago, and then that she'd died and her funeral had just taken place. If only I'd started looking for her sooner. Now I'll never know what my real mother was like."

"Becky, there's a good chance Grace wasn't your real mother."

"What are you saying? How would you know that? I've got a birth certificate with her name on it. What have you got? I don't even know who you are." The emotions are catching up with her, delayed reaction to not one but two extraordinary new facts and the wine isn't helping. Her suspicion is understandable. She's never met me and has no reason to trust me. She's disturbed, as disturbed as Becca, but for very different reasons.

"Let's have some dinner. I have a story to tell you."

\*\*\*

We sit on the new sofa sipping tea, watching the flames dancing in the open fire, casting flickering shadows on the walls.

"Right here? In front of the fire?"

"There's no evidence of murder, just Becca's intuition, but we're dealing with a number of dubious characters who, one way or another, are engaged in questionable activities, and I include your Aunt Grace in that; enough to suggest she may have put herself in danger. The fact that Becca disappeared after making the allegation might add some substance to her belief Grace was murdered."

"I'm sorry to ask you this Kate, but what are you getting out of this? Why are you so interested in what happened to a middle-aged ex-hippy protestor who may not have been my mother and my disappeared twin sister, if indeed, that's what they are."

176

It's a good question and a lot of the answer is tied to my own being, my unique circumstance, something I can't begin to explain. The police will investigate a crime if they think one has been committed and they have a reasonable expectation of both solving it and getting a conviction, not because they have a burning desire to deliver justice for the victims. It's their job, but they only ever scratch the surface. Who speaks up for the victims?

"It's about victims; not just Grace, but your mother, you, Becca and to some extent, me too. You were adopted by a caring family after something bad happened to your mother and once you found out, you felt compelled to find her because until you did, the doubt and uncertainty of who you really were and where you really came from and why, would stay with you forever. You had to find out. Well, like you, this story worm got into my head and it won't go away until I find out what really happened, who the real victims are and who was responsible."

"And if you do find out?"

"One step at a time. We need to fill in the blanks."

"We?"

"You set out to find your mother only to discover she's probably your aunt, she may have died in questionable circumstances and that potentially, your real mother may still be alive. Don't you want to find her, and your sister?"

# CHAPTER 18

I turn up as arranged at five-thirty. Nigel told me surgery should be finished by then but he's obviously running late as two people are still in the waiting room flicking through greasy, dog-eared copies of *Country Life*. There's no one behind the reception counter and a sign bearing the handwritten word *'Closed'* makes clear the receptionist has done her work for the day, even if the doctor hasn't. Nevertheless, she suddenly appears from behind a screen pulling on her coat.

"Sorry, we're closed."

"I can see that. I just wanted to know how to register."

"Dr Webb isn't taking any more patients," she says, wrestling with a scarf.

"He's making a special case for me," I say, smiling sweetly.

"Can you come back tomorrow?"

"I'm here now."

The girl tuts and has a brief look under the counter. She hands me two sheets of paper and a glossy pamphlet. "Fill out that questionnaire and give it back when you're ready. Appointments are weekdays nine 'til twelve and two 'til five except Tuesdays and Thursdays when he does telephone appointments until three," she says briskly. "It's on the info sheet. Have to dash," she says, disappearing behind the screen. I hear a door slam shut.

I take a seat in the waiting room. "I've been here over an hour," grumbles an elderly man. "If I were you I'd come back tomorrow."

A middle-aged woman sitting opposite tuts and sighs and tosses her magazine back on the table. She checks her phone and sighs again, sharing her boredom. They both perk up in anticipation as a woman with a walking stick emerges from the frosted glass door and hobbles across the room. I hold the outside door open for her just as Nigel's disembodied voice crackles from the wall speaker.

"Mrs Firth?"

The woman leaps to her feet and strides purposefully through the door watched enviously by the elderly man.

"Tell him to be quick," he says to her back, then looks at his watch. "I got bowls tonight and I ain't had me tea yet."

While I wait, I think fondly of my evening with Becky and how motivated she was to help. I drove her to Southwold station after breakfast and saw her onto the train. We'd stayed up late discussing what we were going to do and by the end, she was more excited than ever to discover the truth. She slept in Becca's room and in the morning, thought she'd had vague recollections of purple walls and a green ceiling, a bed with bars either side, and another baby chatting endlessly. She also remembered the smell of sweet sickly perfume. I only have her sister's account of life in the Harding household and that was long after Becky was adopted. I'll brief her on what little I know of Grace's past when I see some evidence. She has a job offer in London but isn't due to start for another three months, so in that time we resolved to try to finish what she started, together. First she would have to go home, explain to her parents what we were doing and pack a suitcase.

"Just tell them you found out Grace wasn't your real mother after all but you've met someone who can help."

"Okay."

"Don't mention the M-word whatever you do. It's just speculation at the moment."

Becky was fine with that, and at the time I thought it was sound advice but on reflection, telling her to withhold sensitive facts from her parents, mislead them almost, leaves me feeling uncomfortable. They'd be worried if they thought Becky was planning to get involved in a murder investigation, and understandably, want to talk her out of it. Speculation or

179

not, murder is still a possibility and although I have nothing to lose and nothing to fear, I'm putting Becky at risk by having her tag along. But the genie's out of the bottle now. Even if I chose to leave the matter alone and abandon her, she'd carry on by herself and I worry who and what she might come up against. I made the decision to tell her the truth rather than keep her at arm's length, and now she's fired up. She's my responsibility now; my responsibility to make sure she stays safe.

Mrs Firth is out in five minutes, tutting loudly as she heads for the door and the old boy is on his feet before he's even called. "Mr Clarke," squawks Nigel, but he's already halfway there. I know he'll be quick because he has bowls. He's out in five, holding aloft a slip of paper in triumph, trotting towards the door and his dinner.

"Good luck," he says.

I make my way through to the consulting rooms and knock on the first door, figuring there's a possibility, tired and harassed, he may have forgotten me. He has.

"Oh my God! Kate!" Dr Webb looks up from a mound of paperwork, exotic fountain pen in hand, sleeves rolled up, stethoscope around his neck, just like in the films. He snaps the cap back on his pen and clips it to his shirt pocket. "It slipped my mind."

"Busy day?" I say, taking a seat alongside.

"No more than usual. Sorry about the wait."

"You look like you could do with a drink."

"As your doctor, I'm obliged to point out alcohol is a poison, pure and simple. Despite what the Chief Medical Officer recommends, there is no safe level of alcohol consumption."

"I bet he likes a tipple."

"I bet he does. Come on, let's have a glass."

I like Nigel Webb; he's easy and unassuming and I'm left wondering what his wife was like and what she found intolerable about him or life in Holburgh. I would love a glass of wine, but I want to get the job done.

"Can I have a look in your garage first?"

***

It's full. So full you can hardly move around. Two mahogany wardrobes stand guard at the front, chests or drawers, dismantled beds, mattresses, sofas, armchairs, dining table and chairs down each sides piled on top of each other, along with packing cases and plastic storage boxes, the usual paraphernalia of home; an Aladdin's cave of domesticity. Grace's life, squashed into a space one tenth the size of her cottage, condensed, just like her body, to fit into a small container. I don't know what I imagined but had hoped to be able to inspect her belongings to see if there were any clues to her life as well as her demise. That won't be possible in Nigel's garage. His own stuff, piled up at the back and down the sides is inaccessible too. I wonder what he thought he was taking on? I tell him I've seen enough, so we go back indoors and I follow him into the kitchen. He fetches a half-full bottle of white from the fridge and two glasses.

"Do you lecture all your patients on the damage drink is doing to their livers?"

"Sometimes, if it's extreme. Otherwise, I call it explaining."

"But you don't follow your own advice?"

"It's a risk, that's all. People need to know the risk and then it's up to them whether they take it or not." We chink glasses. He's obviously decided it's worth the risk.

"I'll arrange to have Grace's stuff moved, then you can have your garage back."

"You will?"

I'm going to have to trust him and like the wine, it's a risk. Becca was disparaging about the doctor's verdict on cause of

181

death, her implication being he was either negligent or covering up. But if I had to choose whether to trust Becca or Nigel, I'd have to go with the doctor.

"You spoke to Rebecca at the funeral and offered your assistance."

"Yes."

"And later on she contacted you to take you up on the offer?"

"No, she never asked me directly. The agent did, said she needed space."

"The agent? Why would he say that?"

"Dean and I play tennis together. He just mentioned it and I told him I'd already met Rebecca and offered my help." He takes another mouthful and then his face creases up in a frown. "Wait a minute. I'm a bit confused…"

"Are you're wondering what it's got to do with me?"

"I wouldn't have put it like that, but, now you mention it."

"The girl you had lunch with isn't the girl you met at the funeral. They're twins."

His expression says he's not convinced. "But, they're both called Rebecca."

"Yes. The girl at the funeral was Becca, the girl in the pub was Becky."

"Why didn't she say?"

"She didn't know."

"Didn't know what?"

"Didn't know she had a twin sister and didn't know you'd met her."

"I'm bloody astonished. Mind you, it explains why she wasn't that responsive in the pub. Now I think about it, she was very offhand at the funeral, well, the other one was, but I just thought she was upset about her mum."

"Aunt."

"What?"

182

"Grace was their aunt, not their mother." He stiffens noticeably, his expression, a mixture of suspicion and doubt. "What's this got to do with me?" I say, reading his mind. He nods slowly.

I tell him about Becca contacting me, our eventful meeting at South Alston, the drugs she thought were in her car and her abduction. I mention no names and he listens attentively, neither reacting to the more dramatic events, nor interrupting to ask a question. At the end he looks more confused than ever. He empties the last of the wine into my glass and opens another bottle.

"Do you know someone called Jimmy Munro?" He shakes his head. "He was with Becca at the funeral."

"I remember a big Scottish guy with a scowl that more or less told me to back off. Not someone I'd like to bump into in a dark alley."

"Did they leave together?" He makes a show of trying to remember and then sits upright.

"Wait a minute! Kate, I think you're lovely and I'd really like to get to know you better, but you're beginning to worry me."

"Why?"

"Are you police?"

"Would that bother you?"

"Not at all!" he says, getting agitated for the first time. "It's just that you keep firing questions at me. I mean, who are you? What's going on here?" He's right, and telling me I'm lovely earns him a few points. *Maybe in another life.* He's making all the right noises and neither said nor done anything to suggest he isn't a decent, considerate human being, but I don't want to tell him the main reason I'm here. It'll put him on the defensive; it won't help him and it won't help me.

"I met Becca, the girl you saw at the funeral, about a month ago. She was disturbed, she told me about her Aunt Grace and then disappeared without warning. I think I know where she

183

is, but I'm very concerned for her and I want to talk to her and make sure she's okay. So when you told me you were meeting her for lunch..."

"I thought I was!"

"...I had no idea it would be someone else."

"Me neither."

"And now Becky, her twin, knows Grace wasn't her mother but her aunt, so I'm going to help her find her mother and her twin sister and bring them together."

"Good for you. But that doesn't explain who you are or why you're doing it."

I think of Annabel Cross being in denial all those years, the frustration and torment it caused her and how she took it out on her family and realise in effect, I've been doing the same thing. I have no one to live for, nothing to look forward to and no plans for the future other than to expect more of the same. I can only live in the moment because that's all I have, a recurring, interminable moment, a space in time during which people will come and go on a journey to wherever. Everyone else on the conveyor belt of life sees the world through their own personal prism, their actions guided by their own view of the future and what it might hold, their expectations constantly confounded and modified by random events and interactions with others. Some would say I'm lucky, or gifted, or cursed, but I wouldn't wish this on anyone. I'm uniquely placed to help them find their way; altruism in its purest sense. I've been in denial. Time to stop.

"I'm a private investigator. People need help, so I help them."

He looks relieved, but still wary. "Are you telling me you moved into Grace's cottage in the expectation of finding the 'missing' Rebecca and mopping her fevered brow?"

"I know she lived here and grew up here and I know Grace once had a relationship with Jimmy Munro who's a colourful businessmen in this area. I also know the guy who introduced

184

me to Becca and with whom she had an affair, has business ties in Suffolk and is also connected to Grace and Jimmy. It seemed like a good place to start."

"Why did this guy introduce you to Becca?"

"He said she needed help and he was right."

"So why did she need help? She wasn't the one looking for her mother." *He's not stupid is Dr Webb. You either trust him or lie to him, which is it going to be?*

"Becca got herself into trouble. She upset some people; people Grace had been threatening to expose. A national scandal, she called it. Becca went to the police making allegations but they brushed her aside which only made it worse for her and is probably the reason she disappeared."

"What sort of allegations?" says Nigel. It's a reasonable question, motivated by confusion or curiosity, but not when accompanied by a sudden change in mood and demeanour. He's tense, sensing danger, concerned how it might affect him. My main concern now is why he should feel like that.

"Don't take this the wrong way Nigel."

"Take what?"

"No one is questioning your professional judgment."

"But?"

"Becca believes Grace was murdered."

He looks shocked, then indignant. "Nonsense!" he roars.

"She has no evidence, it's just her intuition," I say, trying to placate him. I haven't seen him wound up and angry until now and it's unedifying. *We all do it Kate, even you.*

"It's still nonsense!" He paces up and down, agitated, the body language of exasperation. "I know exactly what happened."

"And as I said, the police aren't interested."

"Of course they're not! It was an accident! Why can't people just accept it? It happens!"

"Believe me Nigel, Becca knows it now. She knows she has nothing to go on."

"Then why raise it now?"

"Because you asked me why she needed my help. That's why." I was afraid something like this would happen. I expected him to challenge Becca's theory, possibly be mildly offended or dismissive, but his reaction has taken me by surprise. "But since Becky has come on the scene, my primary focus is on making sure Becca's not in any danger and bring the family back together. That includes finding her real mother."

\*\*\*

There's a small, dried leaf on the carpet beyond the doormat, one of the sofa cushions is out of position and a drawer in the desk is open a few millimetres. In the kitchen, there's a scuff in the paintwork behind one of the cupboard pulls and upstairs in the bedroom, the deep pile carpet I hoovered this morning shows footprints. In the drawers, clothes have been lifted and replaced, but not in the right position.

Someone has been in the cottage.

# CHAPTER 19

Becky calls to say she's coming back on Saturday. I tell her I've rented part of the village hall for two weeks and organised a man and van to move all Grace's things there in the morning. The space is self-contained, lockable and five times the size of Nigel's garage so will give us room to spread everything out and decide what to do with it. I don't expect the large items of furniture to yield anything useful but there are several boxes which might contain papers and memorabilia that will help paint a picture of her aunt.

"Train's due in at three fifteen but I'll text you when I know for certain," she's saying, when we're interrupted by the doorbell.

Miriam doesn't appear as ebullient as the day she came back from Tenerife. In fact, she has a face that oozes formality, as if she has something unpleasant to say. "May I come in?" I offer her tea but she declines. "I won't be staying," she says, as evidenced by coat and handbag.

"I couldn't help noticing Rebecca stayed here the other night. I see she was actually wearing some clothes this time," she says huffily.

It's no surprise. I already assumed Miriam would be a founder member of neighbourhood watch even before she spied on Nigel and me last Sunday. It's interesting she confused the two girls, but she couldn't have had a good view peeking through the curtains. "Nice to think someone is keeping watch on the place."

"You never can be too careful," she continues, missing the dig. "Especially with those you don't know."

"She seemed quite charming to me."

"Well, looks can be deceiving. I know that young lady rather well and I wanted to warn you."

"Warn me about what? All she wanted was to see what I'd done to her aunt's cottage."

"Is that what she said? I don't believe a word of it," she says with a sniff. "Poor Grace did her best to bring her up in very difficult circumstances and got precious little in return. I always thought she was hyper as a child but as soon as she hit sixteen, she changed dramatically for the worse, hung around with some very dubious friends, dressed provocatively, stayed out all night drinking and taking goodness knows what. You should have seen her at the funeral! She was either drunk or spaced out on something and you wouldn't believe what she was wearing."

"You said."

"You'd think going off to university would straighten her out but it only made her worse, but I suppose that's what you get when you mingle with those student types. The trouble with young people is they think they know everything when what they really need is a few lessons from the university of life. I'd check she hasn't pinched something, if I were you."

"When did you last talk to her?"

"Why?"

"Well, the girl you're describing is not the girl I met." This is of course, factually correct, but Miriam wouldn't know that. I already knew Becca had a big personality and that she may have moved in circles Miriam would find unconventional and disturbing, but the woman's exaggerating to prove a point. I'm receptive to another insight into Becca's character and background, but I could do without the rant and hyperbole.

"She blanked me at the funeral. Stayed close to her sugar daddy. Knows what side her bread is buttered, does that one."

"Sugar daddy?"

"Jimmy the bouncer. He and Grace had a thing going at one time. Rebecca obviously decided to carry on where her aunt left off." She may be right, but my guess is Miriam is making this up, embellishing her story with lurid speculation to make Becca's behaviour appear more outrageous. She's bitter about something; something that happened before Grace died and she has neither forgotten nor forgiven.

"She's coming back on Saturday to stay for the weekend." Miriam looks suddenly aghast, a reaction I find curiously satisfying. "She asked me to help her go through Grace's things."

"What things?"

"All her stuff is crammed into Dr Webb's garage. We're moving it to the village hall on Saturday, pending disposal. Maybe you'd like to help?" Her face goes red and she puffs up her bosom until I think she's about to burst, but manages to calm herself.

"I don't think that would be appropriate. I expect she wants to scavenge whatever she can."

"Is there anything you'd like?"

"Excuse me?"

"Amongst Grace's possessions. Is there anything you'd like to keep to remember her by? I'm sure Rebecca wouldn't mind."

"Oh no, that would hardly be right," she says, shaking her head vigorously in such a way I can tell there's a 'but' coming. "Well actually, now you mention it, there is something I would like that would remind me of Grace and has a special relevance to me."

"What's that?"

"It's a necklace. Nothing fancy, you understand, just thin, braided leather, but with a silver medallion inscribed with the word SANE. She wore it a lot. Got it in the nineties when she was in the protest movement."

"SANE?"

"Southwold Against Nuclear Energy, an offshoot of CND. They all got them, in memory of their great victory."

"What victory?"

189

"They managed to disrupt the development of a new power station on the coast. Long before I moved here," she says, sighing audibly, "otherwise I might have joined them!"

"Grace was an eco-warrior?"

"Oh, that's such a hackneyed phrase," she says, screwing up her face. "She was far more than that. This was in the early days of global warming, as they used to call it. They were pioneers! Took on big industry, big finance, government, the lot of them, and won!" she says with pride. "Or, at least, managed to delay things with a public enquiry. Her sister was involved too." Miriam has caught my attention. At last she's said something interesting.

"Her sister? Becca's mother?"

"Yes, but Rebecca didn't know that, didn't even know her name. Grace never talked about her. Swore me to secrecy. Less said about Fleur the better, she said."

"Her name was Fleur?"

"Yes. Pretty name."

"Do you know what happened to her?"

"All I know is she dumped her child on Grace and disappeared. I gather she was a bit… unstable, mentally. It's no surprise her daughter ended up the same way."

"Grace sounds like a very colourful lady. Was she always involved in climate change protests?"

"She and her husband were student hippy types, both active in SANE, both thought they could change the world. I never knew him of course, but Grace said he lost interest in the protest movement and when they were forced to adopt Rebecca, that was the last straw. He left, she needed money and that's when she started a temp agency. Did very well for herself. She was a survivor."

The irony of her last statement seems to be lost on her, and Miriam is either unaware of the true nature of Grace's business or is trying to protect the reputation of her late friend. But it's her hostility towards Becca that interests me. It goes

190

beyond simple criticism of teenage behaviour and her being inappropriately dressed for a funeral. Time to put Miriam on the spot.

"What did Rebecca do to you?"

"I beg your pardon?"

"You came here to warn me about her but all you've really said is she was a bit wild as a teenager. Weren't we all? And why do you dislike her so much?"

"I'm afraid I can't go into it. It's personal," she says prissily.

"Then I'll ask her when she gets here."

Miriam puffs up her chest, the colour rising in her neck. I recognise she's someone who likes to get their own way. "Do as you wish!" she bellows while heading for the door. "Don't say I didn't warn you!" The door closes with a bang, leaving me as confused about her as I am about Becca. I'll need to keep her away from Becky but given her antipathy towards Becca, that won't be difficult. I'm left thinking that, despite the tirade, she gave me some useful information.

# CHAPTER 20

They're about my age, attractive, have a welcoming smile and professional manner. "Do you have an appointment?" says one of three, attractive, well-dressed women behind the long reception desk.

"No, but I'm sure he'd like to speak to me. It won't take long."

"What is it concerning?"

"The death of Grace Harding and the abduction of her niece Rebecca."

She goes a little pale and her nearest colleague looks up with interest.

"And your name is?"

"Kate Duvall. I'm an investigative journalist."

It has a predictable effect. Her nose twitches like she's noticed a bad smell, but she manages to remain pleasant and civil. "From which publication?"

"Freelance."

She asks me to take a seat while she taps a few buttons and I hear her speaking in hushed tones. I cast an eye around a room that's minimalist in design; plain cream walls adorned with striking works of modern art, rich, deep pile carpet and solid light oak furniture. It oozes wealth and success. There are business newspapers on the coffee table together with a corporate brochure for the Munro Group extolling its expertise in commercial security across a wide range of sectors.

I know it's a risk, but one I had to take sooner or later. If Jimmy Munro recognises my name, it'll prove the men who chased and abducted Becca were working for him, and even if he doesn't, he'll be curious an investigative journalist is making a surprise visit. I'm guessing he'll make me wait. The last thing a powerful businessman will do is to react quickly to a stranger who's turned up out of the blue issuing a thinly veiled threat. That would only fuel suspicion he has something to hide.

While I wait, I call ISW again, irritated Adam hasn't got back to me. The receptionist asks me to hold but is back within twenty seconds.

"I'm sorry Miss Duvall, Mr Cross is about to go into a meeting and asks if he may call you later? May I take a note of your number?"

"He already has it."

"Just in case," she persists. Adam may be playing hard to get, but there's no merit in refusing.

A tall, slender woman in heels and a red business suit appears from one of the mirror-door elevators, her footsteps echoing loudly on the polished granite floor. I get the impression that in order to work for Uncle Jimmy, one has to meet some fairly strict criteria, at least in terms of gender, age and looks.

"Miss Duvall? I'm Karen Small, Mr Munro's personal assistant. Would you like to come this way?" I follow her into the lift which stops on the third floor. "This way please." There's no need for chitchat, the smile, fixed and inscrutable, the swagger and sway, indications of a former career. She shows me into a half-glass meeting room with a projection screen at one end. Mineral water and glasses sit in the centre of a polished mahogany table where two places are set with notepads and pencils. Karen Small takes a seat on one side and directs me to the one opposite. "Please take a seat."

"Is Uncle Jimmy joining us?"

I expect a flicker of disdain, but she's very good, is Karen.

"Mr Munro regrets he's busy at the moment. He asked me to deputise in his absence and make sure you were comfortable."

"Is that a yes or a no?"

"Why did you want to see Mr Munro?"

"Didn't your receptionist tell you?"

"I understand you're a journalist."

"I'm also a friend of Becca Harding."

Karen doesn't react to the name. "Don't journalists have a notebook or some device to record what was said?"

"I've a good memory."

"Miss Duvall, you can understand my caution. We don't know who you are, or why you're here."

"Didn't your receptionist tell you that either?"

"I understand you're investigating someone who's disappeared."

"Abducted. And a suspicious death."

"What has that to do with Mr Munro?"

I lean forward. "I'm not sure whether he'd want you to know this, but I know Uncle Jimmy had a relationship with the deceased and he knows the missing person who is, or rather was, her niece."

Karen Small already knows that, so it's no shock. She leans forward herself to show she's not fazed, gives me a superior look and rests her chin on the back of two hands. "And your point is?" We could do this dance all day but I'm not in the mood. If Karen thinks I'll be intimidated, she's wrong. I'd much rather be dealing with the organ grinder and at this precise moment, I wouldn't be surprised if he's watching.

"My point is, Karen..." I move my head in a wide circle, as if seeking out a monitoring device, "...Becca Harding believed her Aunt Grace was murdered, and she made a lot of noise about it, so much noise in fact, that she was tracked down by two of Uncle Jimmy's goons and then taken against her will. I simply want to know where she is and what he has to say about her aunt's death before I make a great deal of fuss and report the matter to the police."

Karen Small is good, but not that good. It takes her precious seconds to compose herself, her superior grin

194

yielding to an uncomfortable smirk redolent of someone with trapped wind. "Those are serious assertions Miss Duvall. Best our lawyers get together to discuss them."

"And I forgot to mention the Class As he put in her car and told her to deliver to a sex client."

"As I said…"

She stops mid-sentence and glances at the door. I resist turning to see who it is because I already know.

"Thank you Karen. I'll take it frae here."

The deep, smoky Glaswegian burr is unmistakeable, the delivery, slow, clear and unambiguous in its meaning, imbued with a seductive warmth that belies the underlying threat. Karen sashays out of sight, her place taken by a bulky man in a Ralph Lauren suit, Charles Tyrwhitt shirt and red silk tie. The Rolex sparkles under the LEDs as do the copper wristband and multiple rings. He's clean shaven, the back-combed, dark grey hair freshly groomed and the cologne subtle, reminiscent of a serial killer in a car park, only far more expensive. He releases the middle button of his jacket to expose an ample girth and lowers himself into the chair opposite with the air of a man who finds this whole exercise too tiring for words but for whom courtesy and respect, in all matters, is paramount.

I stifle the urge to laugh. Jimmy is a powerful man who holds sway over his domain, and he knows it. With a look, a wink, or a glance to the side, he could, like a mafia don, intimidate and enfeeble mere mortals in fear of their safety if not their lives. I'm not so afflicted, but he's not to know that. We do the boxer stare for a while, waiting for the other to blink, the tiniest deviation from the norm an admission of weakness. The ball's in his court; his turn to serve. The eyes don't stray for an instant; eyes of a bouncer facing down an inebriated punter twice his size who's demanding entry to the club, telling him that, despite appearances, he's doomed to fail, with or without injury. His choice.

195

"I'm worried about Rebecca," he says. "Did you say she was missing?"

Expect the unexpected, someone once said. I expected feigned ignorance, denial, then threat; nothing too explicit or obvious, just enough to put the fear of God into the wee lassie so she'll run away blubbing and not come back. But instead he's gone for the innocent, concerned look. I don't buy it.

"If you were that worried you'd have met me yourself, rather than sending your secretary to threaten me with lawyers."

"Karen's my PA. You arrived unannounced while I was in a meeting and I asked her to greet you. She was being hospitable, and protective."

"You know where Becca is, your men took her."

"What men?"

"The men in the black SUV who stalked her to South Alston and then took her from my house in Lincolnshire."

"I don't know what you mean," he says, deadpan. "Are you saying she was abducted?"

"When did you last see her?"

"Answer the question."

"Yes. When did you last see her?"

"Grace's funeral. She said she was driving straight home."

"And you've not been in touch since?"

"Rebecca doesn't stay in touch."

"She believes Grace was murdered."

"She said the same tae me, but it's nonsense and I told her so. She was distraught, looking for someone to blame when the truth was much simpler. Grace was ill and troubled, and lived by herself once Rebecca had gone to university. Nothing wrong with that; all kids grow up and leave home at some point, but Grace had an accident and Rebecca felt guilty about it; responsible in some way."

"Alleging murder is a little extreme don't you think?"

"Rebecca can be a little extreme, Miss Duvall. What makes you think she's missing?"

It's a good question from an astute businessman. I put together the facts as I know them and drew a conclusion. Becca's insistence Grace was murdered, the men at South Alston who cited 'Uncle Jimmy', the men Annabel saw, her unanswered mobile and her continued radio silence, my sighting of her at a secretive and private stately home with high-powered men, all suggesting something sinister and untoward, all happening against a backdrop of prostitution, drugs and potential criminality. But none of it proven or verified by me or anyone else. At this very moment, Becca Harding could be stacking shelves in a supermarket before going home to her boyfriend's flat, all thoughts of Grace, death, murder and some foolish amateur sleuth banished to history. It's a question I should have asked myself.

"Are you telling me they weren't your goons?"

He stares at me with cold, blue eyes. "I don't employ goons."

"So you don't know where she is?"

"If she gets in touch, I'll tell her you were asking."

"She's not answering her phone or responding to any messages."

"Maybe she's gone off grid." He shrugs. "Maybe she just doesn't want to speak to you."

"I don't believe you. I'm sorry."

"Are you?" he says. I can tell by the curled lip I've insulted him and know immediately it was a mistake. Up against a man like Jimmy in the bravado stakes, I'm always going to come second. "You're not taking notes. What kind of a journalist are you, exactly?"

"One who's concern for the welfare of a young woman transcends any desire to tell a story."

"And what story would that be?"

"There may not even be a story, but Becca asked me for help and hasn't withdrawn the request. She's vulnerable and I'm going to find her, if only so she can tell me to go away."

Jimmy Munro relaxes and sits back in his chair, the buttons on his shirt straining to contain his bulk.

"Takes balls to come in here and throw around accusations. I'm guessing you already decided what sort of man I am. It's the reason you've rushed to judgment without a shred of evidence, but doesn't explain why you'd feel safe doing it. That makes you very interesting tae me."

Jimmy's perspicacity is impressive, proving it takes more than brute force to build and sustain a business empire. He may well find me interesting, but he'll never find out who I am.

"Tell me about Grace."

He regards me intensely, making me wait.

"Karen?" he says, fixing me with a smouldering stare. "Miss Duvall and I will continue our meeting over lunch. Can you organise it please?"

"Yes Mr Munro," comes his PA's voice from some invisible source.

***

The *Ristorante Il Forno* is busy. Lots of tables where men in suits engage in earnest, hushed conversation conducted between mouthfuls of gnocchi and Barolo. A few mixed couples, none under forty, make up the numbers. The clientele and style suggest this isn't for young, fast-food afficionados.

Jimmy Munro leads the way, glad handing here and there, slapping a back or two, playing to the audience like the local celebrity he is. I'm acutely conscious of my plain linen jacket, jeans and trainers, and eyes are on me, my dress sense adding to the intrigue. Jimmy has a reputation after all.

He orders without looking at the menu, the waiter nodding and bowing obsequiously as he backs away towards the kitchen.

*"Signor Munro,"* says an oleaginous, moustachioed manager, identifiable from his jacket and bow tie. *"Come stai?"*

*"Sto molto bene, Franco."*

*"Signorina,"* he says to me with a nod and a knowing smile before moving on to the next table.

I'm beginning to think this was a mistake. I went along with it because I guessed he was unwilling to discuss aspects of his private life in the office. But I'm not hungry, not impressed and not going to play Jimmy's bimbo for much longer.

"Tell me about Grace."

The waiter brings two flutes of champagne and Jimmy lifts a glass, extending it towards me. "You're very persistent."

"I don't drink."

"Pity. *Luca? Acqua minerale per favore,"* he says to a passing waiter in his strong Glaswegian accent.

I confess the man has a certain charm. He's physically unattractive and battle-scarred, and the expensive tailoring doesn't hide the fact he's overweight. He exudes authority and has an air of menace. He could strike fear into most men with the blink of an eye, but adopts a softer approach with women. I have no doubt he's had some success with this technique in the past. Many young woman choose to associate with rich and powerful men, despite how aesthetically unappealing they may be.

"What do you want to know?"

"You were in business together. Nubilis."

"You've done your homework."

"Not difficult."

"That was her thing, I just funded it. I fund loads of businesses for different reasons."

199

"Why this one?"

"Why not? Grace asked me, I said yes."

"Do you always say yes?"

"To people I like and admire. I liked Grace. We had fun together, for a while. I thought she'd be good at it and she was, for a while."

"But you didn't want to keep the business going?"

"Escort agencies don't fit into my portfolio."

"You don't do prostitution?"

"Do you?" I meant to be provocative and throw him off guard, make him angry and tell me to keep my voice down in a public place, but it's backfired and I can feel the heat rising up my neck. "Thought not," he says.

He could leave me to stew, enjoy my embarrassment while he reasserts his authority, but for some reason, lets me off the hook. "Grace wasn't into prostitution. She simply connected rich people, usually men, to beautiful people, usually women, in return for an introduction fee. That's not much different from a dating agency. What those men and women did in private in their own time, was their own business. Nothing illegal, or disreputable about it. By the way, if I thought you were into prostitution, you wouldnae be sitting here."

"Why am I sitting here?"

"I like you. I admire yer... courage. I was actually gonnae offer you a job." He takes a sip of champagne and watches for a reaction.

"What kind of job?"

"So... you'd be interested?"

"No!"

"Then why are you asking?"

He's playing with me. I'm not going to get one over on Jimmy Munro and I was naïve to think I could. The waiter arrives with two bowls of pasta. I stare dumbly at mine.

"Are you gonnae tell me you don't eat as well?" he says, tucking a napkin into his shirt collar. I poke around at the food like a recalcitrant child, but it smells and looks so appealing I take a mouthful, annoyed to find it's very good.

"I don't want a job, but thanks for the offer."

"How much does a freelance journo make anyway? Cannae be much."

"I don't need money."

"Everyone needs money."

He's a messy eater, pasta sauce oozing out of the corners of his mouth. It's vaguely repulsive and I try not to look at him while he's chewing.

"I don't need any *more* money."

"So who's payin' you for this gig?"

"No one."

He laughs and I'm sure I feel a tiny splash of something wet on the back of my hand. "You cannae be doin' business like that."

"It's not business. It's personal."

"Some wee lassie called Rebecca rings you up out the blue and asks for help and all of a sudden, it's personal?"

He's right to question my motives. I'm not related to her, never heard of her before and have nothing to gain. But when a vulnerable and frightened young woman is exploited and hounded by aggressive men, it becomes personal. I'd like to think Jimmy Munro would agree with me but I don't know him well enough.

"Did you ask her to deliver drugs?"

His expression darkens and he puts down his fork, glancing left and right. "Be careful what you say, young lady. I wouldnae want anyone to overhear and misunderstand." It's the first time he's been remotely threatening. I can tell by his eyes and the tone of voice.

"So she lied about it?"

"I've no idea what she said to you, but let me tell you this. Rebecca is a disturbed wee lassie, sometimes, a fantasist. I

201

would strongly recommend you treat everything she says with caution."

"Who's Adam Cross?"

Even Jimmy Munro can be caught out. He makes a face that implies ignorance and casual indifference, but he's too slow. He's taken time to think about it and it's given him away. He can concoct some lie and bat it away or go straight for the threat. He doesn't know how much I know, so silence would be the best option. He gives me an exaggerated shrug to suggest he neither cares nor knows, but is meant for me to elaborate. I touch a napkin to my lips and push my chair back.

"Sorry, I have to go."

"I take it you're declining my job offer?" he says, relaxing again.

"Another time, maybe."

"There won't be another time. You have to take yer opportunities when they arise."

It's clear. He's telling me I'm either with him, or against him. He'd rather have me on the inside where he can find out who I am, placate me, control and neutralise me and eventually, make me dependant on him. One of his acolytes, just like Karen. On the outside, I could be a nuisance, an irritant, a buzzing insect.

"Thanks for lunch."

"My pleasure. Can I give you some advice?"

"Go ahead."

"Rebecca has got you running around chasing shadows for reasons known only to her. I know Rebecca well and I'm sure she's perfectly content, so don't waste your time looking for something that isn't there."

\*\*\*

I'm driving home when my phone rings. It's Miles.

"Hi Kate. Have you heard anything from Becca?"

"Afraid not Miles, but I'm still looking for her and I think I'm getting close. I'm beginning to think she's just keeping her head down, staying out of everyone's way for a while." It's the least I can say after my session with Jimmy.

"It's just that I've collected up the rest of her stuff. I'm not sure what to do with it." He wants closure. He knows her better than I do and is convinced she's not coming back, so he wants to clear out the flat.

"What is there?"

"Usual stuff: clothes, cosmetics, books, an old phone and a laptop. I've thrown out the stash of condoms." *He knows.*

"Can you do me a favour?"

"Sure I can. I got the car back thanks to you. I owe you one."

"Can you box it up and send it by courier? I'll text you the address. And I'll pay."

"Sure I'll send it, but this one's on me."

# CHAPTER 21

Terry and his son Ed managed to load up Grace's belongings in less than hour but due to my directing operations, took twice as long to unload. I wanted to arrange all the furniture so we didn't have to move things around and now it's out of Nigel's garage, there's less than I first thought.

"Not much, is there?" says Becky, surveying the scene, strolling around like she's browsing a second-hand furniture shop. "And everything's such a jumble."

She's right. The stuff in drawers is topsy-turvy and most of what was hanging up in wardrobes is lying in a heap on the floor inside.

"They obviously didn't waste time packing things neatly, just picked up each item and threw it in the van. I'm surprised Becca didn't find time to do a clear-out after Grace's death. Maybe she was too upset, but then she was two hundred miles away.

"There's no computer," I comment.

"Maybe she didn't have one."

"She must have. There's a desk and an office chair and a few loose cables. She ran a business from home."

"Really?" says Becky. "What kind of business?"

I hesitate to come out with it but Becky's a grown-up and never knew her Aunt Grace, so nothing should surprise her. "Escort agency."

"What? You mean…?"

"Well-heeled male clients seeking the company of young women."

"Gosh. Did my sister know?" I don't need to answer. I just give her a look that says it all. "Really?"

"There's nothing illegal about it, provided it's all done in private and the agency doesn't control or profit from the procurement of sexual services," I say, having looked it up, surprised at myself for mimicking Jimmy Munro. Becky Saunders crosses her arms as if feeling a chill. Life would have been much different for her if she and Becca had not been separated so early. "Someone has taken the machine, maybe because it was the only thing of any value..."

"...or because it contained confidential records or incriminating evidence," she says, finishing my sentence.

"Quite."

We start with her clothes on the assumption they are unlikely to reveal anything of interest, sorting the items into black sacks, those for disposal and those destined for the charity shop. The smell of weed combined with perfume pervades the air.

"What are we looking for?"

"No idea, but check the pockets. You never know what you might find."

An hour later, and with all wardrobes and drawers now empty, we're left with a scrunched-up post-it note bearing a phone number and the name 'Des', a three-year-old shopping receipt, a small key that looks like it might open a filing cabinet or desk and a pile of used handkerchiefs."

"I'm surprised there's no jewellery," says Becky.

"Becca probably took it along with anything else of sentimental value. She would have had a key to the cottage. She probably has the necklace Miriam asked for."

"What necklace?"

"A cheap leather thing with a medallion. Something to do with the protest movement Grace belonged to when she was young."

I feel a tingle at the back of my neck, a connection clicking into place. "God, I'm an idiot!"

"What's the matter?"

"How did you find out all this stuff was in Nigel's garage?"

"The agent told me."

"You didn't arrange it?"

205

"No. I turned up at the cottage, saw the 'To-Let' sign and had a peek through the window. The place had already been cleared so I called them and asked what happened."

"Dean?"

"Yeah, that was him. He told me what happened and that all her stuff had been moved out."

"Did you tell him who you were?"

"I told him I was family, just not that close. The news came as a shock and I was upset. I didn't feel like giving him any background. Actually, that explains something."

"He thought you were Becca?"

"Yes. He said he was pleased I got in touch because he'd been trying to contact me and had left several messages. I asked him what number he was using but I didn't recognise it."

"Becca's number. It went quiet as soon as she was taken from my house."

I call his office and he answers personally. I put him on speaker so Becky can listen.

"I need to ask you a question."

"Fire away," says Dean, always keen to please.

"Grace Harding's daughter."

"Rebecca?"

"Where did you get her phone number?"

"Er…" I can almost hear the cogs whirring. He's considering whether there are any data protection or confidentiality issues he needs to be wary of. "…why do you ask?"

"You tried to get in touch with her to arrange house clearance."

"Yes of course." He's on solid ground here, confident he carried out his responsibilities diligently by consulting with the family. "You were moving in and I had to get the place ready."

"But you didn't speak to her."

206

"No. I did leave messages, though."

"But she eventually called you."

"Yes."

"After the house had been cleared."

"Yes, I think that was it," he says, as if not sure. I leave him a few seconds to stew. "I had to do something," he says, suddenly defensive, "otherwise you would have been severely inconvenienced."

"I'm not criticising you Dean."

"We have rights under the lease, anyway," he goes on, sniffily.

"Of course. I just wondered where you got the number from, that's all."

"Why does it matter? What's the problem?"

There was of course, no problem, until I asked the question. Dean has decided he's either going to resist simply because I've rattled his cage or he's unwilling to say because it'll open a can of worms.

"There's no problem, Dean. I'm just trying to clear up some confusion."

"What confusion? I'm not confused."

"Yes you are."

"No, I'm not."

"Rebecca is with me now. She's the one who called you and asked what had happened to Grace. Weren't you surprised she didn't already know?"

"I suppose so, but she said they weren't close. I didn't think any more of it. Just told her to get in touch with Dr Webb."

"The person you were trying to call was someone else called Rebecca."

"Okay, now I am confused. Grace Harding has two daughters called Rebecca?"

"Partly correct. Except they're not daughters, they're nieces."

207

"Right," he says with weary resignation. "What do you want me to say?" He's waving the white flag and for good reason. I'm still struggling with it myself.

"Who gave you the number for the other Rebecca?"

"Next door neighbour. Mrs Lamont."

"Miriam?"

"Yep. Fearsome woman." I can imagine Miriam's disdain; her reluctance to assist a low-life estate agent trying to contact a recalcitrant young woman. "Said it would do no good and she was right."

"You knocked on her door?"

"No. I went to the cottage to see what was there and make sure it was secure. I found Mrs Lamont there."

"She was inside Grace's cottage?"

"I thought it was odd, but she said she'd always had a key. She said she and Mrs Harding had keys to each other's houses in case they got locked out or there was some other emergency."

"Did she say what she was doing there?"

"Same as me. Checking everything was okay. She gave me the key back, said she didn't need it anymore. That's when I asked if she had contact details for any family members."

"And she gave you Rebecca's number?"

"What's this about Miss Duvall?"

"Kate."

"Is there some problem with the cottage?"

"Not at all. As I said, there's been some confusion. Wires have got crossed and I'm trying to uncross them. Thanks for your help."

I cancel the call, hoping he's feeling a little vulnerable, worried he's done something wrong. He might try to rustle up another useful nugget of information just to prove he's on my side.

"Can't wait to meet the fearsome Mrs Lamont!" says Becky.

"We should be careful."

"Why?"

"Miriam was very scathing about your sister. I don't know what went on between them and Becca never mentioned her, but when you came over last week, she was peeking through the curtains. She mistook you for Becca and then went to great lengths to warn me off."

"Really?"

"It would be fascinating to know if she can tell the difference close up, but as soon as you open your mouth, she'll know."

"How?"

"I've met you both, remember?"

"Why don't we just tell her? Maybe she can give us some background on Grace."

"At the moment, you and I are the only ones who knew Fleur had twins."

"Fleur?" It came out without thinking. I completely forgot Miriam had revealed her name and didn't think to mention it before. "Was that my mum?"

Becky Saunders looks haunted, and I can understand why. She arrived in Holburgh believing she'd be reunited with her birth mother only to find the woman she'd been searching for was actually an aunt who'd died recently, and her twin sister, whom she didn't even know she had is alleging foul play. I haven't had time to ask her how she felt about it then or how she feels about it now. The initial, uncontrollable urge, the work that went into the search, the euphoria of finding a person from just a name, the doubts about whether you're doing the right thing, the fear and trepidation that's part and parcel of meeting long lost family and finally, the knowledge it's all been futile, a mistake that can never be rectified. And now I've given her a new name, she has to start the process all over again. I told her Grace wasn't who she thinks she was, but the fact is, I'm not really certain what's true and what isn't.

209

"Yes, I should have said. Sorry."

"How do you know?"

It's a good question. Becca never mentioned her mother by name, just claimed she'd run off and she'd been brought up by Aunt Grace. That was Miriam's understanding too, but that could only have come from Grace, as presumably, did the name Fleur.

"I don't know for certain. Miriam told me when she asked about the necklace, although Grace swore her to secrecy. She could have made it up."

# CHAPTER 22

It's Saturday night and The Fox and Anchor is predictably busy. We have to wait at the bar for half an hour before being seated at a tiny table in the corner. I was in two minds about bringing Becky out for dinner, conscious there may be people in the village who knew Becca and want to say hello, but so far, no one has come forward.

"I'm sorry I forget to mention Fleur."

"It's a lovely name."

"It may not even be true. I only have Miriam's word for it and she got it from Grace."

"Why would she lie about it?" *Why indeed?*

"That conversation I had with Dean. He said he found Miriam in the cottage and she gave him back the spare key."

"Yes."

"Well, she still has one. She surprised me by letting herself in shortly after I arrived and yesterday, I came home to find someone had been in there sniffing around."

"You think it was her?"

"Probably. And I don't believe the story she gave Dean about checking everything was okay in the cottage. She was looking for something."

"The necklace?"

"Maybe, but I can't believe it's that valuable."

We'd spent an hour going through the packing cases and only got halfway before deciding to call it a day. We'd carefully unwrapped and laid out on the floor a mishmash of crockery, cutlery and glassware, all manner of kitchen utensils, porcelain figurines, collectables and trinkets, but as yet, not a single photograph, nor significantly, any files or paperwork.

A large, florid-faced woman brings us our food. "Hello darlin'," she says to Becky with genuine surprise, but it's lacking in warmth and the smile looks forced. Becky casts me a quick glance. "Not seen you here for a bit. Sorry about your Mum."

"Thank you," she replies. "This is Kate. She's moved into the cottage and is helping me sort through her things." I admire Becky's cool but she's on shaky ground pretending to be her sister and I'm beginning to fear the woman will expect an introduction, when she does it herself.

"Hello Kate," she says, folding her arms. "I'm Viv. Didn't I see you in here with the doctor the other day?" The pub is clearly a hotbed of gossip in the village and Viv, one of its main protagonists. I steer her away from it.

"You must be in charge around here?"

"For my sins," she says rolling her eyes in mock frustration before turning back to Becky. "Ah, I miss your Mum, so I do. Always good for a chat she was."

"Yes," says Becky. She's pushing her luck, and casts me another glance. I sense she's made a decision and give her a surreptitious nod. "But I think you might have mistaken me for my twin sister Rebecca." It takes the wind out of the landlady's sails.

"Really? You're not Becca?"

"No I'm Becky."

"Now that is confusing," she says. "You're a dead ringer, and how come you got the same name?"

"Don't know. I never knew Grace. I was adopted as a baby."

"Well I never," says Viv, excited by the potential for a juicy new piece of gossip. "What sort of woman has twins and gives one of them up for adoption?"

"You tell me. You probably knew her better than I did."

"She never once said." Viv's probably a bit miffed there was something she didn't know. "Even when we had too much gin, she never said."

"Did you know Jimmy Munro?" I ask. Viv takes a moment to think.

"Yeah. Scottish fella. She used to hang out with him. I reckoned he was up to no good. I told her, but she wouldn't have it."

"You weren't at the funeral then?"

"No. Me and Gaz were in Lanzarote."

"So when did you last see Becca?"

"A year or so? That was a real to do, that was."

"What happened?"

"Rebecca had a bit of a moment. Caused a scene."

"Really?"

"Grace was in here having dinner with some bloke. Put herself about did Grace," she says, "know what I mean?"

"Not really." I know exactly what she means but I expect Viv will have a unique take on Grace's lifestyle and I want her to expand on it.

"You girls eat your dinner and I'll come back when it's quietened down a bit," she says looking furtively round the pub. "We can have a chat then."

"She's a character," says Becky once Viv is out of earshot. "Becca and I must really look alike."

"Yes you do, but you have totally different personalities."

"Probably the way we were brought up."

"Maybe. But I know another set of twins with wildly different characteristics and they're only four years old. Been like that since birth. One's hyper, scatty and emotional and the other calm, subdued almost, but arguably more intelligent."

"Which one am I?" she says, laughing.

My phone pings as if on cue. It's a text from Adam. He's in Ipswich next week on business and suggests we meet up, offering a time and place.

"Weirdly, that was the father of said twins," I offer by way of explanation.

"Are they relatives of yours?"

213

"No. Adam is the guy who asked me to help Becca."

"Does he not know where she is?"

"He says he doesn't and hasn't had any contact, but I found out he was less than honest with me and I had to put him under pressure. I'm interested to know what he has to say."

It's interesting Adam suggested we meet near Ipswich. I didn't tell him I'd moved to Suffolk so logically, he would have picked somewhere closer to Hawsby. Word has got to him where I live and the most likely culprit is Jimmy Munro who's done his research and knows I'm in Grace's cottage.

***

Becky declines a nightcap and opts for an early night. We have a full day tomorrow unpacking the remaining boxes and as she's planning to return home the day after, wants to get some rest. I'm not ready for bed, kept awake by an overactive mind trying to make sense of an ever-growing body of information in relation to the lives of Grace and Becca Harding. Following our visit to the pub, that's now supplemented by another barrage of fact, or possibly fiction. Viv's story was clearly embellished and over-dramatised, her ebullient nature and the passage of time conspiring to distort events in her mind. But if nothing else, it's further evidence of Becca's highly-strung personality and Grace's bohemian way of life.

About a year ago, Viv said, Grace was having dinner with this handsome hunk, which wasn't unusual as she'd been introduced to at least a dozen others over the years. But this one was different. This one was dishy and cool and repeatedly reached across the table for Grace's hand as they engaged in intimate conversation. Due to their hushed tones and the general hubbub in the pub, Viv was unable to hear what they were saying, but it was 'clear as day' they were 'an item'. Grace would fiddle coquettishly with her hair and at times, laugh out loud, which, according to Viv, she did solely to attract the attention of other diners and pique their prurient curiosity.

They'd finished their meal and were on coffee and brandy when it happened. Becca had come home unexpectedly for the weekend and forgotten her key. She knew Miriam next door had a spare but the *'old bat wouldn't let her have it'*, told her Grace was down the pub with one of her boyfriends and she should go there instead. Viv had been excited in the telling, relishing the memory of the drama that unfolded.

"So in she comes, wheeling her bag behind her, asking where Grace is and then she spots them in the corner having a bit of a snog. Orders a pint of lager, marches up to the table and throws it all over Mr Hunky. Oh my God! Then she launches into a tirade against them both. I mean, I've never heard such language in all my life. Made me blush I'm telling you, and I've been around so I have. But then she storms out again and that's the last I seen of her."

"So you don't know what it was all about?"

"Yeah I do. It were obvious weren't it? Grace was shagging Becca's boyfriend and she caught them at it. Pure and simple."

"But I thought you didn't know him."

"I didn't. Never seen him before. But young Becca knew him alright. Called him by his name and the way she tore into him, you could tell they'd been, you know…intimate. Twice her age he was too! Grace had had a few and laughed it off, but he wasn't amused and left straight away. Never saw him again."

"Did you get his name?"

"I did," she said, preening. "His name was Adam."

Another half-truth to further muddy the waters. Adam Cross having a congenial dinner with Grace Harding, she who procured escorts for his personal entertainment and who, either as a favour or perhaps even a demand, asked him to give

215

her niece a helping hand with some work experience, with or without the knowledge it might evolve into something more serious. If Grace already knew about Becca and Adam then she must have been untroubled by it or else why meet him for dinner and, as Viv alleged, carry on a relationship of her own? And if she didn't know about it and heard it for the first time from the vitriolic mouth of her niece, why able to laugh it off, as Viv suggests? The more I think about it, the more certain I am Becca and Adam were indeed intimate, Grace knew of it and may even have planned it from the beginning.

Becky had looked bemused throughout, not surprising given she's still struggling to rationalise the behaviour of her erstwhile family. When we get home, she throws another spanner in the works.

"How do you know this guy Adam?"

"Pure chance. I met him with his wife and twin girls a couple of months ago. They rented a holiday cottage next door to my house."

"And he asked you to help Becca?"

"Becca asked him, and he referred her to me because he got the impression I was a private investigator. He said he wanted to help but needed to put distance between him and Becca; stay out of it in case his wife found out."

"He has an affair with a nineteen-year-old, then does the same with her mum or aunt or whoever she was, and he already has a wife and two kids? Sounds like a bit of a shit to me."

Adam denied having seen Becca since the night outside her flat when he claims he resisted her advances, but here he was, in Holburgh, with Grace, getting a dousing and a serious tongue-lashing from Becca. For all his passive nature, easy manner and good looks, there is no doubt he's been economical with the truth.

***

We're sitting on the floor in the village hall, surrounded by packing cases, piles of brown wrapping paper, an ever increasing collection of books and memorabilia spreading out around us. We've been here all day and I can imagine Grace Harding watching over us, hand on hip, berating us for intruding on her most personal possessions. But, imagination is all it is. In the middle of the night I half-expect some form of contact either directly or via Edith, but there's been nothing. It would save a lot of time if Grace could just tell me what happened. Becky is cross-legged, hunched over a hardback notebook, flicking pages back and forth.

"What you got?"

"It's a diary, but there's only one."

"What year?"

"2000."

"Maybe she started at the millennium and then gave up?"

"Don't think so. This one's pretty full, with an entry almost every day, some of them quite long. Aunt Grace looks like she was a prolific diarist, at least she was in 2000."

"Becca said she was well-read and into classic literature."

"She wrote pretty well herself," says Becky and then takes a sharp intake of breath. "Oh my God!"

"What is it?"

"Fleur's pregnant! *'My crazy sister is up the duff'* she writes on the tenth of December, *'She's distraught, doesn't even know who the father is, doesn't know how she's going to cope and frankly neither do I. She can barely look after herself never mind a child. I'm going to broach the subject with Des at some point. There must be something we can do although it's going to be an uphill struggle with him'.* Wow!"

"Des. The name on the scrunched up yellow slip. Must be her ex-husband. When were you born?"

"May 2001."

"And that was December 2000. I guess they didn't know twins were on the way. There must be other diaries."

217

Becky jumps to her feet and rips open another box, rummages around in the contents then moves to the next. The first glimpse of her origins recorded for posterity by her Aunt Grace spurring her into action with renewed vigour. I attack some of the others but there is no sign of more diaries.

"I don't believe that's all she wrote," she says scratching her head. I agree with her, but it means someone else has taken her diaries and begs the question, why? My phone rings and I glance at the screen. My heart sinks. I know who it is and I consider ignoring it, but there's no escape. I've had no contact since the day Becca went missing and I had hoped that would be the end of it, but she found my new number and I think I know how.

"Kate, darling. How are you?" I'd forgotten how good she was at condescension.

"Hello Annabel. How's things?"

"How's things? I'll tell you how things are, love of my life, but then I expect you already know."

"Know what?"

"Come on Kate, have a guess."

"Easier if you just get to the point?"

There's a second or two of silence, during which I reflect I may have come across as a little too irritable and dismissive. "You hurt me, you know?" Her mood has changed instantly. She's moved from condescending to needy, and it's two short steps to tears and aggression. I don't want to fight with her but I have enough on my plate at the moment.

"I'm sorry, I didn't mean to, but there's really nothing more I can say." The conversation is uncomfortable. I'm not sure what Becky can hear, but I can see her attention's still focused on the diary and she's unfolding a sheet of paper she's found inside. I turn my back on her and take a few steps to one side.

"Don't worry," says Annabel, "I got over it. I got over you, in fact."

"You didn't call to tell me that."

"No."

"Have you been looking at Adam's phone again?"

"See? I said you'd be good at your job and I was right," she says, bypassing aggression and moving on to smug. "But actually, once we started negotiations, he changed his password so I couldn't spy on him."

"Negotiations?"

"Divorce. I meant what I said."

"I'm sorry."

"Don't be. Gosh, how funny!"

"What is?"

"You were the one who kept telling us not to apologise and you've just done it twice!"

"I mean sorry for you, not me."

"Whatever. Divorce is the right thing to do."

"For whom?" I ask, already worried about Emma and Josie.

"For everyone. The twins can grow up without their parents being at each other's throats all the time. They'll be perfectly happy with Adam and his young girlfriend. I've already done the hard bit and I'll see them from time to time. Emma has already bonded with Ciara."

"Ciara?"

"My partner. We met at Pilates."

"What about Josie?"

"Not so much. Strangely, she keeps asking about you. You made quite an impression, but then, you made quite an impression on both of us. Think where we would have been if…"

"Okay Annabel," I say, jumping in before she becomes too maudlin. "So why the call?"

"I know you and Adam have been in contact, so don't try to deny it. We were going to marriage guidance and I was in his office reception waiting when you called. Goodness! How my ears pricked up when I heard your name and I do confess to having a slight flutter as well."

It's bad luck she overheard. Given her mood swings, I can't tell whether she called me simply to show how clever she is or whether she wants to try again. Being free to explore her sexuality with Ciara has done nothing to mitigate her chronic neurosis. And she hasn't answered the question.

"So, why the call?"

"You lied to me!" It's loud enough for Becky to hear and I glance back at her. She can't help turning to look and I wink at her to indicate it's not serious. "You denied working for Adam!" she goes on at full volume, working herself up to a frenzy, "and I find out it's a lie!" Her voice is cracking and I can visualise the tears, the heaving shoulders, the emotional devastation about to overwhelm her once again. If she were standing in front of me now, I'd have to put my arms around her, regardless of the risks.

"Listen to me."

"I loved you!" she wails between gasps for breath. Becky refolds the paper and regards me intently. I can't tell whether it's friendly concern or suspicion.

It's the betrayal Annabel can't bear and I feel a crushing weight of responsibility towards her; not because I spurned her advances, but because she's a victim too. She's never heard of Grace Harding and can have no idea how her life has been impacted by a deceased stranger. She's not a party to this mess, even though her husband is.

"I said listen!" I pause and give her a second to calm down. For all her faults, I judge Annabel is innocent, worthy of support and therefore, potentially useful. I baulk at the notion I'm exploiting her, but I convince myself it may help her too. "I'm not working for Adam and never have. He never once asked me to dig around in your personal life, insisting it was up to you two to sort yourselves out, which is exactly what you seem to be doing."

220

"Then why are you still speaking to him?"

"I'll tell you when I see you."

"What?" It comes out as a whimper. I've taken the wind out of her sails and I know it's cruel, but playing on her emotions is the only way to get her attention. It's not possible to discuss it on the phone, especially when I haven't had time to think exactly how much I'm going to tell her. I'm meeting Adam in Ipswich next week and I need to see her before then.

"There's a wine bar in Wimbledon called *Picasso*."

"I know it."

"I'll meet you there for lunch tomorrow."

"But I'm not sure if..."

"Tomorrow. Twelve noon." I'm not going to negotiate because I don't need to.

"Okay," she says meekly.

"Adam must not know about this."

"No. Of course not."

I end the call and Becky looks away but remains ominously quiet. She only heard snippets of conversation and is probably trying to fill in the blanks. By necessity, I've become a solitary, private individual and have no reason to offer explanations about my life, past or present. On this occasion, however, I'm driven by something that's out of my control, and I know what it is.

"That was Adam's wife. She can be quite…impassioned."

"I could tell."

"Their marriage is in trouble and I got caught in the crossfire."

"Because of Becca?" It would be easy to say yes but it wouldn't be the whole truth and this is not the time for explanations.

"I need a drink. Let's go home."

# CHAPTER 23

Smokey is squatting on the mat outside the front door but sits up and has a stretch when we arrive.

"Who's this?" says Becky going down on her haunches to greet him. He lifts his tail, arches his back and rubs himself against her knees while she gives his neck a good scratch.

"I have no idea who's he is or where he lives, but I call him Smokey. You're honoured. I don't get affection like that. He just uses me as a slave, demands a few treats and then disappears." I open the door and Smokey trots inside heading straight for the kitchen cupboard. "See what I mean?"

"He must have known Grace."

"I suppose so. I bet he knows what happened to her." I give him a handful of snacks and within seconds they're gone. He licks his lips and heads out the open front door.

"Do you think she was murdered?" says Becky.

"We have nothing to go on but your sister's gut feeling. The police aren't interested, Nigel Webb said it was an accident, and I believe him. Miriam found her and she hadn't been dead long. It's hard to believe someone killed her, here in her own living room on a Monday morning and slipped away without anyone seeing anything. Miriam's a champion curtain twitcher."

"Coo-eee!" comes the predictable cry from the hallway. "I thought you were home," says Miriam with a satisfied smile. She's holding a large cardboard box covered in tape and emblazoned with courier's stickers.

"Hello Rebecca," she says haughtily. I knew this moment would come and hadn't quite worked out what to do; whether to introduce Becky as Becca's twin or keep quiet and see what happens. Nigel Webb knows the truth but I can safely rely on his discretion and that's more than I can say for Miriam. The woman could be a useful source of information but only if she's onside, and her antipathy towards Becca will make that difficult if she thinks we're good friends. Becky casts me an awkward glance, not sure what to do or say. Miriam hands me the box. "This arrived today." On top, there's a carrier bag full unopened mail. "And these are for you," she says to Becky.

"Me?" says Becky, looking inside.

"I've been collecting Grace's mail. I tried to give it to you once before if you remember," she says, puffing out her bosom.

"Thanks Miriam. By the way, this is Becky."

"I know that!"

"No, actually, you don't. You know Becca. This is Becky, Becca's twin sister."

Miriam looks back and forth between us, the colour rising up her neck and cheeks, her facial expression an evolving blend of outrage and suspicion. Her mouth opens and closes like a hungry goldfish while she searches for a response.

"Nonsense!" she declares finally.

"It's true Miriam," says Becky, trying to be helpful. "How do you do?" she says extending a hand. Miriam stares at it with horror then shakes her head.

"Is this some sort of joke?"

"No," I say. "It's not a joke. Fleur had twins, Grace adopted one, that's Becca, and the Saunders family from Hampshire adopted the other, that's Becky here."

"I didn't know I had a sister until I met Kate," adds Becky helpfully, "so it was a surprise for me too." Miriam looks down at her outstretched hand and nervously takes it.

"I can't believe it," says Miriam, blinking repeatedly. "I would never have guessed. You look just the same."

I offer her an obvious explanation for her confusion. "That's because they're identical."

"Yes, now I think about it, you may look the same but you don't sound the same as the Rebecca I know. You don't act the same. You seem, how can I say, more grown up."

223

"Sit down Miriam. I was just about to open a bottle of wine."

***

It had the desired effect. Once the alcohol had started to do its work, and once Miriam had accepted the young lady sitting opposite was not her nemesis nor I, her enemy, the words began to flow.

She told us at length of her life in the eighties as a young woman, protesting at Greenham Common and their campaign against nuclear missiles. I wasn't born then and have only a vague knowledge of the subject, but I was struck by the vibrant and passionate reminiscences of someone who, back then, was my age, sobered by the reminder that old people were once young people. The mental jump from Miriam the young activist to Miriam the caricature of middle-age conceit is difficult to grasp, however hard you try to look under the surface. Those who live together all their lives have a different perspective, the gradual transformation in looks, attitudes and character virtually indiscernible until an old photo or random event triggers a reconnection to the past.

I watched Becky like she was an infant at primary school, clinging to teacher's every word, listening to ancient history taught by the wisest of the wise. Becky will remember Miriam when she herself is old and no doubt reflect fondly on her encounter with the departed soul. Becky and Miriam are mortals. They will evolve, grow old and die, their time is limited. I am immortal, my body frozen, but only for a limited time. It's a salient reminder my association with these disparate characters, will, by necessity, have to end soon whether I like it or not.

Miriam and her late husband had no children and after he died, she moved from Berkshire to Suffolk, where the couple had previously enjoyed many a holiday. She moved into No.2

224

Rose Cottages and bonded immediately with Grace, discovering they had a shared past in the protest movement with the common goal of fighting for something in which they passionately believed. Saving the world from itself.

Rebecca aged ten was a beautiful but boisterous young lady and if Miriam were to criticise her late friend for anything it would be her failure to apply a little more discipline in her upbringing. Obviously, being a single parent is never easy, she conceded, but it seemed to Miriam that like her aunt, Rebecca could do or say anything she liked, however inconvenient or upsetting it might be for others. Education and discipline at an early age pays dividends, she'd told Grace, but her advice had not been heeded by a woman who floated through life on a cloud of entheogenic substances.

She never knew Desmond, who'd left many years earlier and had, presumably, anticipated the difficulties of bringing up someone else's discarded child, but she was introduced to a succession of Grace's male companions, so many that even Miriam could not keep up, each relationship shorter than the last. Then along came the bouncer.

"Grace was besotted," she'd said, in a manner that conveyed both her doubts about Grace's judgment and her dislike of Jimmy Munro. "Vulgar and uncouth in both style and language. The man had no respect for anyone. I really have no idea what she saw in an overweight, uneducated hoodlum from the Gorbals, but somehow they stayed together for several years, before finally drifting apart."

"And what about Becca?" I'd asked. "How did she cope with all the comings and goings and did she get on with Jimmy?"

"Cast from the same mould," she'd said stuffily. "He was definitely a bad influence on her, not that she needed it," she'd added sanctimoniously, "but when I tried to warn Grace she just laughed it off. *'Life's for living'* she said to me, *'Becca's a free spirit'* she said, *'I want her to experience all that life*

225

*has to offer, find her own way, make her own mistakes and have no regrets'.* Pah!" she'd said, with a wave of her hand.

"But it didn't affect your friendship with Grace?"

"The woman could be infuriating at times, but we never fell out. Grace was incapable of getting angry at anything or anyone. Must have been something to do with… her habit."

"Drugs?"

"Weed or pot or something or other," she'd said prissily. "She once tried to give some to me and I told her a dry sherry on a Sunday was perfectly adequate for me," she'd said proudly, then on her second refill of Muscadet.

"Did Becca take drugs?"

"I never saw her smoke anything, but she must have."

"Why?"

"Well, how else would you explain her outrageous behaviour?"

Becky had flashed me a look, thinking what I'm thinking, wanting to know but at the same time, not. Before either of us could decide whether to prompt Miriam to elaborate, she was off. She'd only paused to have another drink.

"Sixteen she was. Sixteen! They had a wild party next door for her birthday… I was invited but I made my excuses… couldn't cope with all that drunken mayhem… and the music…that Jimmy organised it all, sent some of his gang to maintain order and keep out gate crashers…"

Despite the appalling anti-social behaviour next door, Miriam could not call the police. Grace was her friend after all. But others did, and a couple of bobbies came in their car and had a word and the party was broken up and *she* got the blame. Not from Grace, you understand, who thought it was all a hoot, but from that young madam.

"The next morning around eleven, there she was outside in a flimsy robe, hand in hand with a tall, dark, handsome man, who picked her up and slapped her bare bottom and gave her a good old snog in public view of anyone who happened to be

226

passing, before he got into his car and drove off waving and tooting his horn. And do you know what she said to me? She said, all cocky, *'That was Paolo, my birthday present from Grace'* she said, laughing her head off. Well, I was so shocked I didn't know where to put myself. Sixteen! And then you'll never guess. She said, *'I'll give you his number if you fancy some?'"*.

Becca had told this story in her own way and hadn't felt the need to mention Miriam. Why should she? I couldn't bring myself to suggest Becca, given the environment to which she was exposed, probably lost her virginity long before that with or without Grace's knowledge. It would be too much for Miriam to cope with. But Miriam wasn't finished. Over the next year or so, Becca seemed to bring home as many boys and men as Grace, making damn sure Miriam saw them, until Grace told her Becca was leaving to go to university and she could breathe a sigh of relief. Some form of normality might return to Rose Cottages. The sting in the tail, though, the *'coup de grâce'*, as Miriam put it, was the day she left.

"She handed me a present as she was leaving, all nice and humble, saying sorry for all the trouble and that she would come back a grown up and I was very gracious and said, *'thank you Rebecca, I wish you every success at University'* and off she went. But when I opened it…" At this point Miriam had gone pale and put a hand over her mouth and her eyes had filled with tears of shame and torment and it took another refill before she recovered her composure. "It was…one of those disgusting artificial…thingies."

I look at Becky, mouth open, willing her not to react. In another time and another place and in different company, it might have provided for riotous laughter and much merriment, but any thought of humour is buried under the weight of humiliation Miriam must have felt then and probably still feels today. I'm sure Grace would have laughed it off, unwittingly compounding the offence. Miriam and

Becca; two disparate characters, poles apart, in a permanent state of conflict and antagonism, each deluded their way is the right way and the other must change and conform. It would be nice to bring them together and bury their differences.

"So that's why I had no compunction. None whatsoever." I can tell by her frown Becky is as confused as I am.

"About what, Miriam?" I ask tentatively.

"About telling the police!"

I've had a drink too and I'm tired and ready for bed. May as well get to the point. "You reported Becca to the police for giving you a dildo two years ago?"

"Heavens no! Of course not. About the drugs!" A light has come on from an unpredictable, but with hindsight, obvious source. I sit forward in my chair, realise her glass is empty and reach for the bottle. "Oh, no more for me," she says, "well, maybe just a little."

It was a week or so after Grace's death. Miriam saw Becca arriving and enter Grace's cottage and then she heard noises. She'd been there a good hour banging and crashing, before Miriam could stand it no longer and went to investigate. She wanted to know what that little madam was up to. "And I wanted to give her Grace's mail. Someone needed to deal with it. People had to be told or else it would just keep coming." Getting no reply, she let herself in with her key.

"Rebecca was rummaging around, drawers and cupboards open, stuff strewn across the floor, making a terrible mess! I asked her what on earth she was up to and she was very rude."

"And?"

"She positively bellowed at me, telling me to get out. She was very disturbed, but that wasn't the worst of it." Miriam drank some more wine and sat for a moment looking into space. She was either marshalling her thoughts or had lost her place. I had to nudge her.

"And?"

228

"There was a box on the floor full of white bags. Well, I've seen enough of those detective programmes on television and I know what's white and comes in small bags and it's certainly not sugar! I knew straight away and it turns out I was right."

"Knew what?" Best let her spell it out.

"Well, drugs of course! She saw me looking aghast and when I remonstrated with her she told me to get out and mind my own business."

"So you called the police?"

"I wanted to, but I'm sorry to say I was afraid. What with Grace's death, I confess I hesitated. But then I needn't have worried. A couple of days later two nice policeman arrived."

I can see their faces; two burly men in dark suits in a big black car. "Plain clothes?"

"Yes."

"Did they show you any ID?"

"Yes of course! Very courteous they were. They said they needed to search the house, and did I know where the owner was and I said I had a key, so I let them in. Then after a while they left with two black plastic sacks and asked if anyone else had been in there, so I told them."

"About Becca filling a box?"

"Yes and I gave them her number. But that wasn't the end of it." Miriam is building herself up into such a frenzy I fear she'll have a seizure before she gets to the end of the saga.

"Go on."

"It was the day of the funeral. She and that ruffian Jimmy had ignored me completely and I came home quite distressed. Then she's banging on my door and I open it and she's dressed like a tart and she starts shouting at me, wanting to know where Grace's jewellery box is, accusing me of stealing it! I mean, how dare she? I've never stolen anything in my life," she says with outrage. "I gave her a piece of my mind, told her the police must have taken it, and she says, *'What police?'*

229

and I tell her the police who searched the house and know all about the drugs."

She sits back and closes her eyes. She's exhausting herself and Becky looks at me, concerned, but it's all new and important information. She can't stop now. "Miriam, take a deep breath. I know it's been very traumatic, but I need to know what happened next."

"Rebecca swore at me, called me terrible names and then stormed off in her car. And about an hour later, those nice policemen were back asking where the young woman next door was. Well, I told them everything, of course. She'd left in a white Mini heading for York, and they sped off."

\*\*\*

It's past ten when Miriam goes home, merry yet subdued, tomorrow's hangover already looming. Once she'd finished her dramatic story, we'd opened the parcel to reveal a layer of white air-filled bags. She'd gasped in shock until I popped one and proved to her it was just protective packaging. She conceded it looked very similar to the white bags she'd seen before.

I had wanted to scream at her, tell her what a foolish old woman she was, those men weren't police, or if they were, they were up to no good, and because of a petty personal vendetta going back years and her failure to identify innocuous white packaging, she'd put Becca's life at risk. I simply shook my head. Miriam wouldn't understand, and if she did, she'd be mortified and like the rest of us, and unable to do anything.

We removed the air bags to find a laptop, an old phone, Becca's clothing and personal items, several diaries, and a leather necklace with medallion.

"That's the one!" Miriam had exclaimed, but the delight was short lived. "Oh. Is that it?" she said, holding it in her hand, a frown forming.

"What did you expect?"

"Oh, nothing. It's not as I remembered. Maybe Becky here had best keep it. As a memento."

Becky and I open another bottle and nibble on some toast.

"Can you believe it?" she says.

"Sounds like the guys who attacked us in South Alston. I still don't know whether they were police or Jimmy's guys, but they eventually caught up with her. Becca told me Jimmy had given her a package to deliver and she later assumed it was drugs and that's what they'd been after. But it turned out it was just champagne and chocolates for someone called Jules. She'd obviously packed up and taken the laptop and diaries long before the funeral in case anyone else got their hands on them."

"I wonder where she is now?" says Becky. "I hope she's not in trouble." I knew Becca was disturbed from the moment I heard her voice and over the years she's mixed with some dubious characters, including Grace. But it doesn't make her any less worthy of help and support. I feel sorry for her and in a strange way, responsible. When I first met her she was frightened and vulnerable, but if she's now content to pursue her escort career in an exclusive country hotel, then even that might be progress.

"We'll find her," I say, but its wishful thinking and raises another question. "If you never found out what happened to Becca and Fleur, would you be able to go home and put it all behind you?"

Becky shakes her head without hesitation. "No. We're identical, we have the same genes. I've always felt there was something missing, just never knew what. Becca and I were conceived together, shared a womb together and Fleur looked after us and delivered us into the world."

231

"Are you afraid of what you might find out?"

"Yes of course. But not knowing is worse."

She passes me a folded sheet of paper. It's a black and white photocopy of a photo from a newspaper; two young women, arms around each other, happily posing for the camera. There's no doubt who they are; Grace and Fleur over two decades ago, sisters bonded in love, beads and flowers in their hair. In one corner there's accreditation in tiny print: *'Photo: Des Harding'*. I turn it over and find handwriting on the back: *'Southwold Chronicle 1998'*.

"I found it in the back of the diary. When you were talking to Annabel."

"Gosh. Aren't they lovely?" She's sitting on the sofa, Smokey on her lap. She nods but doesn't meet my gaze and doesn't have anything to say. "Are you okay?"

"I don't know what I expected. My mum and my aunt, not much older than I am now. They look so happy." She wipes a thumb across one eye then the other. "It's weird to see them."

Fatigue and alcohol have taken their toll. I move cross to the sofa and sit beside her. She leans over and rests her head on my shoulder and I put an arm around her. "We'll get to the bottom of this," I tell her, unable to resist caressing a few strands of her hair. I examine the faded picture. Behind the two women stands a young man with long hair and a beard. He's side-on and out of focus, talking to someone else, unaware he's in the shot. I strain to see through the blurred image, seeing something vaguely familiar. The hairs stand up on my neck. I think I recognise him. I think his name is Adam.

# CHAPTER 24

I needed an early start if I was to get to Wimbledon by twelve, but Becky was up at dawn preparing breakfast, insisting I needed sustenance for the drive. She said she'd start to go through the mail and the contents of the box. She had been due to go home tomorrow but now, given the emergence of a set of diaries and a laptop, things have changed. She said she'd call home to tell them she'd decided to stay a couple more days. I gave her a hug and she told me to drive carefully. It wasn't the casual remark of a friend looking out for another. It was heartfelt.

I slept badly; the image of Grace and Fleur with a young Adam Cross standing behind kept me awake, and as I drove south, continued to burn in my consciousness. It was the last thing I expected. I had understood it was Jimmy who'd introduced Adam to Grace, but it looks like they knew each other long before that. It puts Adam in a new light and I have to work out how to broach the subject when I see him. But I have other thoughts to contend with and someone else on my mind.

After the Triple-M fiasco, Parker threatened to throw the book at me, alleging it was only my friendship with Sue that stopped him. He made it clear I'm persona non grata, at least when it comes to police matters, but I happen to know he's wrong about the guy they arrested and so quickly released. He's extremely dangerous, he carried a Glock 43 and shoved it behind my ear. He hit me with great force and tried to abduct me, so worth locking up for that alone, even if he isn't the Triple-M guy. I also know his name; Jason Palmer.

Parker is wrong about the gun. I don't need Eddie as witness to know that and I doubt they'd believe him anyway, but he saw the police find it, which means someone is lying. Parker said they found no evidence in the van; it wasn't even his, but I know it is and according to Eddie, they didn't even look. Ineptitude on this scale is not conceivable.

So I texted him my new number asked how they're getting on with Triple-M because I had new information. Even if he thinks I'm a timewaster, he can't afford to ignore it. If he's part of a conspiracy, he'll want to know what I know, so I can be corrected or neutralised, one way or another. I give him an hour and call him. I know he won't answer but it's worth a try. As expected, it goes to voicemail.

"Hi Dave, hope you're well," I begin jauntily. "You've got my new number, but I wanted to let you know that the guy who attacked me was carrying a Glock 43. Hope that helps! Love to Sue."

An hour later I call him again. He's still not picking up. "Hi Dave, forgot to mention, the white Sprinter had fake plates belonging to a VW Golf. I assume your boys noticed that when they examined it. Talk later!"

I get to Wimbledon in plenty of time to give Parker another go, aware the stakes get higher each time. I know it's provocative, but I'm running out of patience.

"Hi Dave. Guess who?" I figure if that doesn't annoy him what I'm about to say will. "You're a busy man I can tell, but this is really quite important. Fact is, the reason I know the make and model of the gun is I have an expert witness who saw one of your men pick it up. Apparently it bounced under my car. The same witness claims your men never examined the van. The local plod watched it overnight and twenty-four hours later, it was gone. Now, as you were quick to point out, I'm no expert in police procedures, but I would have thought it routine to secure the area as quickly as possible in search of evidence, and at the very least carry out an inspection of a van with false plates, especially one found at the location of a serious crime. I fear your best man was either slapdash or else he's not telling you the truth. Just wanted to give you my feedback. Hope this is all helpful, and talk to you later. Byee!"

I mute the phone. I don't want to be interrupted when I'm with Annabel and if my messages do provoke a response then my being unavailable will annoy him even more.

***

Annabel is sitting at a table in *Picasso,* chin on hand, swiping her phone aimlessly, an open bottle of Prosecco in a clay chiller. She's smartly dressed in cashmere and leather, has cropped hair with blonde highlights and she's wearing makeup. She looks up as I approach, but appears unsettled. I give her my warmest smile and don't stint on the greeting, giving her a big hug. Our cheeks touch and linger, and her aromatic fragrance fills my senses.

"Hello Kate," she says breathlessly, taking both hands. She looks at my mouth and I brace for the unauthorised kiss, but mercifully, she controls herself and meets my eyes. "It's lovely to see you." She tries to pour me a glass, but I place my hand over it.

"Not for me, thanks. I'm driving."

"Yes of course," she says, and pours water instead. "How are things in Lincolnshire?"

"Fine. How are the girls?"

"Starting school next week, thank God!"

"Adam?"

"Bahrain. Back next week, but I expect you know that already." She can't help having a poke; it's just the way she is. But it's obvious Adam lied to her because he's meeting me in Ipswich. It reminds me he used to come home early from his overseas trips to spend time with Becca. Or so she said. "Josie keeps asking about you."

"That's nice."

"I miss you too," she says soberly, stretching a hand across the table, her expression earnest, full of longing. I thought this would happen. On the phone, she said she'd got over me, but

235

she was just lashing out. Despite what I said to her then, she's been fantasising about our meeting, keeping alive a glimmer of hope I've come here to be persuaded, driven all this way to see her and tell her I made a terrible mistake. Make everything alright. I was content to give her that impression and although I don't want to mislead her, I do need information. One way or the other, someone is going to get hurt.

"I'm sorry, I meant what I said."

She withdraws her hand abruptly, still able to surprise me with her instant mood swings. "I know. You're with Maddy," she says with finality. "Can't say I blame you."

"No, she's just a friend."

"I saw you together!" she says in frustration.

"We're not together."

She shakes her head, unable to comprehend, still clinging to that ray of hope. "Then why can't you…?"

"I'm celibate."

"What? Why?" she says, incredulous.

"I have a condition." It's as close to the truth as I'm prepared to go, but I realise it won't be enough when she swings from angry to concerned to relief in a trice.

"But my darling, that's okay!" she says, remotivated, enthused. "It's not about sex. It's about love and companionship. It's about being together. We'd be wonderful together." She's leaning across the table, eyes bright, searching my face for acquiescence or any endorsement, however slight.

"I live alone."

I'm strangely moved by my own pronouncement; genuinely regretful to admit it, and also to cause her such disappointment and anguish. It's a simple matter of fact that no one can change. I have no option but solitude unless I happen across someone with the same condition, and that in itself would be contradictory, caring and loving and protecting someone who doesn't actually need it. Sometimes, when I lie awake at night, I imagine Edith will appear and take my hand. She tells me it's time to go and I'm content and we disappear in a puff of smoke, or crumble to the ground like dust to be blown away in the wind. I wonder when and how it will end if I don't end it myself. I told Eddie that when people ask for help, I generally try to oblige, because I have nothing to lose and there has to be some upside to this endless enigma. I can't give Annabel what she wants and I can't explain why, but I can help her and her children to a better future.

She plucks a tissue from a sleeve and dabs her eyes. "Then why did you come?"

"Maddy is the reason I came."

"I don't understand."

"Maddy is not her real name. It's Becca."

She blinks and glassy eyes stray, focus on a random object then move on to the next. It's coincidence, she's thinking. She has no reason to equate the two, but her husband's alleged affair with a girl called Becca has been festering in her mind for over two years, so the name has never been out of her mind. She knows it's the same girl, she just doesn't know why.

"What was she doing in your house?" she says uneasily, fearing the worst.

"I rescued her from two villains, thinking she'd be safe with me, but I made the mistake of leaving her alone for a few hours and they tracked her down."

"You mean...those men? Oh God!" she says, wrapping arms around her chest.

"She admitted having an affair with Adam, but she also claims it was over and they hadn't been in contact for two years."

"But I heard him on the phone to her. I gave you her number."

"She called him because she wanted his help. But Adam refused and he didn't want you to know because you'd think he was seeing her again. So he referred her to me."

"Why you?"

"Because you two got it into your heads I was a private investigator."

"Aren't you?"

"Well I am now!"

"So he's not seeing her?"

"Why would you care anyway?"

"Excuse me?" she says, affronted. "My husband's re-established contact with his pretty young mistress at the same time we're trying to salvage what's left of our marriage. Why shouldn't I care?" This is the other Annabel, the sensitive, emotional alter ego quickly eclipsed by the self-centred, conceited hypocrite devoid of self-awareness.

"You made your decision after the twins were born and you've made your feelings clear now. No wonder he was tempted to look elsewhere when the chance came. You've jumped into bed with Ciara and you'd have me between the sheets given half the chance, despite which, he wants you to stay together. You can't blame Adam for the fact you're gay. No one's to blame for that."

I'm acutely aware I'd raised my voice and she sits in stunned silence. I expect a flood of tears. People around us have lowered their voices to a whisper and some are silent, ears primed for the next instalment.

"I'm very confused," she says sadly. "About everything."

"We all are. But right now, Becca might be in danger and I'm trying to help her. I think I know where she is but I can't be sure she's not being held against her will." Annabel looks me in the eye, sullen, as if weighing up the options. She needs a kick. "She's twenty-one!"

She lowers her eyes and refills her glass. She's torn between the natural desire to rail against her husband's

238

infidelity and the instinctive urge to assist a vulnerable young woman. I check my phone for messages and see one from Becky, along with a missed call.

*"Hi, I know you're busy, but I got onto the Southwold Chronicle online archive and found the original article about Grace and Fleur and the SANE protests back in '98. I downloaded the original photo which is top quality. [Smiley face]."*

I take another look at bearded man, now more certain of his identity.

"How can I help?" she says finally.

"How long have you known Adam?"

"About twelve years."

"What was he doing?" She looks puzzled. "What job?"

"Same as now. Financial services."

"No, before that. What was he doing twenty five years ago?"

Her mind's still on me and her and Maddy and Becca and it takes her a moment to think. "He said he was once with the police."

A feel a prickle in the neck "Police?"

"Domestic Counter Terrorism or something. But I didn't know him then."

"Are you sure?"

"That's what he told me," she says.

It's the last thing I expect her to say and immediately blows a hole in my theory. *The guy in the picture is a lookalike?* I can't accept it.

"Did he ever mention being involved in protests?" She shakes her head but more in confusion than denial. "What's his opinion of protestors?"

"What sort...?"

"You know, environmentalists, Stop Oil, XR."

239

"Oh, them. He hates them. Thinks they should be locked up or shot, or both! He's got a big job on, getting investment for a major energy project on the east coast."

"Nuclear?"

"Yes. And he says those bloody communist hippies are aways there causing trouble, banging on about green energy and the fact funding is coming from the Middle East where they have terrible human rights. He calls them lunatics, half of them the great unwashed, and the other half middle class hypocrites; pinko, liberal lefties who drive home to their barn conversions in Range Rovers."

"What if I said back in the late nineties he was active in an organisation called SANE; a protest movement based in Suffolk. He had long hair and a beard and sandals. One of the great unwashed."

"No way! Adam?" I show her my phone with the photo and she shakes her head, bewildered. "What's this?"

I hand it to her. "Look at the guy standing in the background." She enlarges the picture and lets out a gasp, putting a hand over her mouth. "This isn't possible," she says, whilst at the same time knowing it's true.

"So you didn't know him then and you didn't meet for another ten years. Question is, what did he do in the meantime?"

"He never talks about it and I've never asked."

"Let me throw some names at you. Jimmy Munro?" She shakes her head. "Scotsman, looks like a bouncer."

"Sorry."

"Grace Harding? Dave Parker?"

Her eyes flicker. "Parker's a name I recognise," she says, "but I'm not sure where from." I shouldn't get too excited, it's not an uncommon name, and only a slender thread. Annabel has already given me plenty to work with and I'm still reeling from the knowledge of Adam's past. "Why are you asking me this? Are you saying Adam is mixed up in something?" She

240

sounds like the dutiful wife defending her husband's honour, which would be perfectly reasonable if I wasn't aware of their circumstances.

"Tell me about the men who took Becca away."

"I can't. They looked fairly normal to me."

"Did she fight?"

"No, I told you, she seemed calm."

"Smiling? Did she laugh or share a joke?"

"Not that I saw. One of them held her by the arm. I thought he was just being comforting."

"Comforting? She was being abducted."

She looks embarrassed and defensive. "I didn't know that! You weren't there, I thought maybe she got bored and called for a taxi. I don't know!"

"Admit it. You were jealous, so whatever the reason, you were happy to see the back of her."

"That's not fair!"

She's right. If Becca had put up a fight it would have been obvious. Whatever Annabel thought about her, she wouldn't wish that on another woman. "Sorry. I shouldn't have said that."

"Yes, okay. I wanted to try again, with you, but then you shot off, Adam came back from London and said we were going home."

"Did he ever explain why he had to go back to London?"

"Just that something had come up and he needed to go to a meeting."

"Not one he could do on the phone or online?"

"No. Adam never explains anything about his work, assumes it'll be too complex for my simple brain or I'm not interested. But I *am* interested. Maybe if he'd shared more of himself we wouldn't have drifted apart." Sounds like Annabel is looking for another reason not to blame herself, conveniently forgetting that coming out as a lesbian is pretty much a deal-breaker as far as straight marriages are

241

concerned. But it reinforces the view Adam had something to hide, and now even more so. "You've worried me now Kate. What do you think he's done?"

I'm curious she professes to be worried. They set a course for separation and seemed to be sanguine about it. But I need to calm her, prevent her from speaking out the moment they start to row about something, at least until I've seen him. I try to adopt a measured tone.

"I'm not worried about what Adam may have done in the past nor should you be. You know him better than I do and anyway, you're going your separate ways. He had no idea I'd met Becca or was bringing her back to the barn and never called me again to find out if we'd spoken and if so, how we'd got on. He washed his hands of her so she couldn't get in the way of his trying to repair his marriage. I called him that day in his office simply to ask if Becca had made contact and he said not."

"So you're not doing this for him, or me?"

"You're intelligent grown-ups. You've made your own decisions and I wish you well. I spent two days with Becca and in that short time, learnt a lot about her life, and I've learnt a lot more since. I don't think she's ever been able to make decisions for herself and I'm worried something has happened to her. She's a victim in all of this."

"I'd like to meet her one day," she says pensively. "I hope you find her and she's alright."

"So do I." I glance at my phone. As well as the missed call from Becky there's one from Parker. "Time to get going."

I settle up the bill, and outside, she lingers on the pavement, looking awkward. I open my arms and give her a hug and she holds on tightly for as long as she can before I can ease us apart.

"Not a word of this to Adam."

She dabs her eyes again. "No, of course not. He'd think there's some great conspiracy afoot. It won't help me get what I want."

I ignore the inference. "Give the little monsters a hug from me."

\*\*\*

I leave Parker to sweat and call Becky. She sounds excited.

"Kate! How did you get on?"

"Annabel confirmed it's Adam in the picture but she said something else."

"What?"

"She said twenty five years ago he was in a special branch of the police. Domestic Counter Terrorism, she called it."

"Really? So why is he in the picture?"

"Don't know. I'll have to try and find out when I see him."

"I've got loads to tell you," says Becky. "I think I know where Fleur is. She's in a care home in Brighton. Been there for twenty years."

"So she didn't run off like Grace said."

"You only have Becca's word for that."

"Where's the truth Becky?"

"We'll get there. There's a lot more, but no smoking gun. Not so far."

"Well done. I'll be back around five."

If Becky and Fleur can be reunited then something good might still come out of all this. But Fleur can't be more than fifty, so if she's in a care home, it's not for the elderly. It means she's incapable of looking after herself and Grace wasn't willing or able to do it.

Parker left me a curt voicemail. I call him, expecting no reply, but this time he picks up. He can see who it is but still pretends otherwise.

"Parker."

243

"Hello Dave."

"Kate. Thanks for ringing back." Obsequiousness doesn't suit him. He's laying the ground. "I must say I was disturbed to receive your messages." *I bet you were.* "You wilfully ignored my advice."

"What, to go back to the day job?"

"You've raised serious matters and made very disturbing allegations."

"I've given you key information that I know to be true."

"Then tell us who your witnesses are so we can interview them and get a statement."

"No."

"You're prejudicing police enquiries."

"Then why don't you arrest me?"

"I may have to, if you continue along this path."

"I say again, I have witnesses."

"Then give me names."

"No."

"Then you have nothing."

"Nor do you, not any more. You had him and you let him go."

"We have a suspect. A picture has been circulated."

"Fat bald guy with tattoos? You're wasting your time and you know it. And what about the gun?"

"We're looking into it."

"Ah, I get you. You'll find big guy, the gun will miraculously reappear and you can pin it on him."

"Tread very carefully, young lady. I won't say this again. Leave it alone. You're bang out of order."

"Noted. Who's Adam Cross?"

I wanted to spring it on him. The police service has thousands of people working for them and many thousands more who did and have since left. The chances of him knowing Adam from twenty five years ago are negligible, yet instinct tells me otherwise. *Connections.*

244

"Who?" He's almost convincing, but he took too long to reply and I know he's lying. "No idea. Now stay out of police business. I won't tell you again." He hangs up, confirming my suspicion.

His threats mean nothing and I consider for a moment ramping up the pressure, telling him I know the name of the guy who attacked me and where he lives, but decide for the moment to keep my powder dry. I'm thinking about Becky's latest discovery when Annabel calls.

"I've been trying to get you. It's just come back to me."

"What has?"

"I remember who Dave Parker is. He came to our wedding. I didn't know him then but Adam said he was an old colleague."

I feel my heart begin to race. "Did you speak to him?"

"No, not really."

"Was his wife with him?"

"Yes, I remember talking to her. Her name was Julie."

"Some memory."

"I remember because it was my happiest day, yet she was very unhappy. She tried to hide it but I found her sobbing in the ladies. We had a long chat and I got the distinct impression she was a victim of domestic abuse."

"From her husband?"

"Yes. She didn't come straight out with it, not wanting to spoil things for me, but we women can tell, can't we?"

I don't rise to it. "Do you have a number for her?"

"No, sorry. I never saw her again after that. Kate, who is this Dave?"

"National Crime Service. He's a big noise in the East Midlands."

"Police?"

"Not a word about this to Adam."

"Yes, yes! You already said that," she says irritably, but I know she's wound up and I now fear I've told her too much.

If he provokes her, and she can use it against him, she will. But the time for skulking around is coming to an end. The dots are beginning to join up.

"Sorry. I'm just worried about a young woman."

"You keep saying sorry."

"Must be catching."

"Look, I understand. She's a victim. I'll do all I can."

"Thanks."

"Love you."

She couldn't resist it. She means it and it makes me sad.

*Connections.*

Parker denied knowing Adam, but it's a lie. You may forget an old colleague but not one whose wedding you attended. He's also lying about Palmer and he's trying to silence me with threats; silence the truth. Adam lied about Becca and by omission, lied about Grace. We're each connected in some way with the dead woman at the centre.

But now, there's something else bugging me. I don't believe in coincidence, so why did Adam Cross, a former colleague of Dave Parker, rent a holiday cottage next door to me?

# CHAPTER 25

Becky can't wait to tell me. She's hyper, gabbling incoherently about what she found in Grace's diaries and mail. Her primary aim was to find Fleur and meet Becca and now she thinks she has all the answers she needs. My priorities are different; finding Becca and putting Palmer away, neither of which I expect to achieve hearing Grace's life story. And on the way home, it got worse.

The traffic was bad and the journey took longer than expected. I stopped for fuel and the newspaper rack outside the service station screamed at me, most of the front pages carrying a photo of the suspect and fugitive. A bald, tattooed tub of lard with a personal hygiene problem, already pronounced guilty by the tabloids for no other reason than he looks it. It was inevitable. Palmer blamed Trevor for the attack, claiming Trevor was armed. Palmer bravely came to my assistance and there was a struggle in which Trevor dropped the weapon before he sped off in a green van. The girl didn't mean to pepper-spray him, he just got in the way while being a hero. All of which would be plausible were it not for the fact that Palmer's prints are on the gun, and I have a witness, Eddie, who saw the whole thing. Whether Eddie would vouch for Trevor and, given his social status and propensity for booze, be regarded as credible, must be in doubt. But particularly galling is the fact that the photo of Trevor in tabloids was taken from my bodycam, the one Parker said was blank. I refused to give evidence at the time believing it wasn't necessary, but it would have made no difference. Palmer would have been released anyway.

"Pub!" I said to Becky the moment I walked in and ten minutes later, we've ordered food and are on the gin. I'm reminded of my wrestling with conflicting facts on the drive to Chevenham. Now I have Becky as a sounding board and it has a synergy that makes analysing theories ten times quicker. I briefly wonder whether Becky would join me in my adopted career. We'd make a great team. *What sort of team is that, Kate?*

"Becca was followed to South Alston by two men in a black SUV, who purported to be police but also mentioned Jimmy Munro. Uniformed police had already been sniffing around her car and later on her boyfriend's flat was raided by guys who claimed to be police looking for drugs. Men turned up here claiming to be drugs squad and Miriam thought the white packaging was drugs too. Even Becca thought the parcel Jimmy gave her contained drugs but it turned out just to be just champagne and chocolates and Jimmy got quite shirty when I mentioned the *'D'* word to him. Eventually, someone caught up with Becca and she disappeared. This has nothing to do with drugs and everything to do with Becca and by extension, Grace."

"You said Grace was onto something, some national scandal. Is that what this is all about?" says Becky.

"Anything's possible. Now I find out Adam Cross was known to Grace twenty five years ago and he's connected to Parker, who's connected to Triple-M. They're all linked."

"Whoa," says Becky, who was following the thread diligently but now feels the need to interject, and rightly so. "Who's Parker? And what about Triple-M? Do you mean that serial killer that's been in the news?"

I got carried away, thinking out loud. I thought I was fighting two battles at once, but the possibility it's all one has been gathering pace in my mind. It's just I never mentioned the incident with Palmer to Becky. She's looking at me expectantly but now's not the time. I don't want to appear evasive, but for her own safety I need to think carefully before I tell her everything. My phone pings a welcome distraction.

*"Cops are after Trev. That you? [Grumpy face]."*

Becky's still looking at me, waiting for an answer. "It's a text from Eddie."

"Who's Eddie?"

"He's a dosser at South Alston."

"Excuse me?"

She thinks I've gone mad or had too much gin, or both. There's no going back now, but first, I send him a reply.

*"No. It's a stitch up. I'll speak up for him when the time comes. Will you? [Questioning face]."*

"Becky, trust me. As of today, there's a whole new dimension to this. I promise to explain all when we get home. Here is not the right place."

"Okay," she says guardedly.

"Tell me about the diaries."

"They go back to 1995," she says. "But there's nothing between 2001 and two years ago when she started again and even then, she didn't write every day, just when she felt she wanted to record some event or get something off her chest."

"What does she say about Fleur?"

"About ten years younger as far as I can tell and more committed and passionate about environmental campaigns than Grace. It reads like Grace was only there to keep an eye out for her little sister. Didn't stop Fleur getting arrested which she did on more than one occasion, like in 1998 when there were mass demos against a nuclear power station and there were clashes with police. Sad to think it was all in vain because the plant they were protesting against is now under construction."

"Did Fleur ever live in the cottage?

"No, she and the other diehards lived in a tented village on the outskirts of Southwold, camped out in a farmer's field. That was until she got pregnant. According to Grace, Fleur was pretty loose with her affections, they all were, but there was a guy there called Mal Devlin to whom she was

249

particularly close. He and Fleur got together in the late 90s and Grace is convinced he was the father."

"Only convinced?"

"She was never sure but as soon as Mal found out Fleur was pregnant, he disappeared. Fleur kept talking about him as if he was still there and had just gone for a newspaper. She wouldn't accept he'd left, kept telling Grace he'd come back for his children but after they, er, I mean we, were born and he still hadn't shown, she went off the rails."

"And he was never heard of again?"

"He hasn't cropped up in any other diaries so far, but they fizzle out after we were born. She must have got bored doing it." Becky appears excited and almost detached about the story. I might have expected her to be more emotional, even traumatised by it. It's probably just the thrill of finding out the truth after all these years, if indeed it is the truth. "Fleur gave birth in a tent but afterwards left us alone for hours at a time and went around in a daze looking for Mal. She could barely look after herself never mind screaming twins and Grace had to step in. She took us and registered the births, put herself down as the mother but without naming the father."

"Becca said Grace and her husband wanted children but it didn't happen."

"Grace did, but she doesn't say much about Des. He was certainly nervous about adoption and definitely wasn't happy with twins. He eventually agreed they could have one but she'd have to find a home for the other."

"But it didn't last."

"It caused a rift, but Grace writes she and Des would have split anyway, adopting Becca was just the final straw. Anyway, Fleur was sectioned and spent the next two years in a psychiatric hospital before being transferred to a care home."

"Where she's been ever since?"

"Yes. She was twenty five."

250

"Have you called them?"

Becky's eyes drop and then she shakes her head, appearing moved for the first time. It's all happened so fast she hasn't had time to consider the consequences. She could leave it at that and walk away; if Fleur has a mental disorder, she's unlikely to form any kind of relationship with her now. She risks making everything worse for them both. I can see the dilemma, how far does she take her curiosity and what damage will be done in pursuing it? Viv appears just in time with two plates.

"Caesar salads, ladies? Alright Becky?"

"Thanks," she says with a weak smile.

Viv looks like she wants to linger. It could just be her gregarious nature but given the chance, she'd want to catch up on the latest gossip. "Can we have a bottle of white and two glasses please, Viv?" I say, mainly to move her along.

"Pinot?"

I nod and she trots off, dwelling at another table to engage with an elderly couple and their dog.

"It's not simple," says Becky, poking at her food.

"Go on."

"Grace was bankrupt. The files from Becca's box are full of demands for overdue debts; credit cards, utilities, you name it. She also gave a personal guarantee on a business loan."

"For the company that went bust?"

"Yep, but it gets worse. She was addicted to online gambling. It was a fairly recent development so she must have turned to it thinking it was a magic fix. Her accounts are still live and her inbox is full of reminders to log back in and try her luck."

"I've read about this. They let you win a few times before gradually turning it around, by which time you're hooked, desperate to repeat your earlier success and you just keep going until you whole world implodes. What's the damage?"

251

"I've done a spreadsheet. It comes to over seven hundred grand."

"Oh God."

"She re-mortgaged the cottage twice and the bank took the rest to satisfy the business loan. There are six credit card companies fighting over scraps."

"So who's been funding the care home?"

"NHS mainly. Fleur was originally deemed to have a primary health need, but I've looked up the home she's in now and it isn't National Health, it's far better than that."

"So Grace has been subsidising it?"

"Her company may have, but I've found no records for Nubilis. In any event, it was all about to change. Six months ago Grace got notice that following a routine assessment, they decided Fleur was fit to return to society and they're going to withdraw funding. Grace had to pay all the fees to keep her in there or take care of her herself."

"That sounds like the final straw."

"Yeah. I've seen her bank statements and there's no way she can pay five grand a month in fees. Her income tailed off over the previous twelve months and all she's had is the odd lump sum from a company called Timeos to pay off the overdraft."

"Timeos?" I get my phone out to look it up.

"Already done it. It's a subsidiary of Munro Group."

"Jimmy," I say, thinking out loud. "Is there a will?"

"Yep. Becca is executor and sole beneficiary."

"But there's nothing left apart from a few old bits of furniture, and some pots and pans."

"Doesn't look like it and there's no insurance as far as I can see. Becca obviously informed interested parties that Grace had died and there are a few acknowledgements, but most just state their claim on the estate."

"So Becca must have known all this when she approached Adam asking for help. She didn't say anything to me about it, but then we didn't have much time together."

"Maybe she was happy to disappear and not have to deal with the fallout? There was nothing to inherit so why even bother?" I think back to the happy relaxed young women I saw at Chevenham. If one of them was Becca then she's well out of it. "You said you'd explain." Viv brings the wine and glasses giving me a moment to think.

"I will. I promise. It's pretty harrowing and I hope not connected to you and your search for Fleur, but then the more we find out, the more connected it becomes. When are you planning to go home?"

"I can stay longer if you like?"

"That would be great. I'd like that." I reach over to squeeze her hand and then, I'm jolted. I'm behaving like Annabel. Becky's looking at me, slightly bemused.

"It's okay. This is all very... thrilling."

I'm embarrassed. I wasn't thinking, and now I'm concerned eagle-eyed Viv may have spotted us and will spread gossip. *Let her!* "I have a lot to tell you," I say, clearing my throat, feeling the heat rise up my neck, painfully aware it sounds ambiguous. "What can we do with the laptop?"

"What do you mean?" she says, stuffing chicken and lettuce in her mouth, unperturbed by my intimate gesture.

"There must be a password."

Becky waves her fork in the air. "Easy-peasy. I have a degree in IT and Computer Science. One of the first things they teach you is how to hack into a PC."

"Really?"

"The only way to beat hackers is to learn how to be one."

I want to hug her. "What about that old phone? It must have been Grace's or an old one of Becca's because I saw her with a smartphone."

253

"Battery's dead but even if we had a charger, it's so old it wouldn't tell us much." *What a great team.*

***

Becky is stretched out on the sofa, eyes closed, Smokey snuggled up beside her. They look like they're sleeping but I guess she's just resting as she's gripping a glass of wine. Smokey has never shown me affection like that but I'm not offended. I suspect instinct kicked in and he's not sure what to make of me, preferring to keep his distance from the strange one.

Fleur's developing situation posed a terrible dilemma for Grace and now threatens to do the same to Becky. She'll feel torn, wishing to meet her mother at last, but anxious about her mental state and now, worried she'll have to assume responsibility for her care. Regardless of her adopted family's resources, it's an emotional and financial burden she can do without. And where does responsibility lie? According to Grace, Fleur failed to care for her babies and whether she gave them up willingly or not, was judged by the authorities incapable of even looking after herself. Grace stepped in to help, but probably only to satisfy her desire for a child, not to do Fleur any special favours. Grace talked disparagingly about Fleur in her diaries and kept her confinement a secret from Becca for twenty years, either through shame or guilt or perhaps even expedience. That was all about to end with news the Fleur was ready to be released from care.

That news, together with Becca leaving home and her own bankruptcy, must have left Grace desolate. Jimmy Munro tried to help with sporadic lumps of cash, for old times' sake, but even for him, there's a limit as to how far he would go to bail her out, especially if he knew she was gambling it away.

It's all very sad. I can understand Becky's reticence about going to Brighton and wouldn't blame her if she now bitterly regrets embarking on the search for her mother. *Careful what you wish for.* I have no reason to go there myself and, assuming Becca ever resurfaces, I would think twice about telling her as it would put her in an equally difficult position. But the facts point to suicide rather than murder as a more plausible explanation for Grace's demise and if Becca knew that, it may help her move on. As regards Fleur, conscience dictates the least I can do is find out her condition for myself, before rushing to judgment. Whether Becky chooses to accompany me, I'll leave to her.

Becky's eyes open and Smokey yawns before jumping off the sofa and having a long stretch. He trots off towards the door for his evening hunt and waits for me to let him out.

"You were going to tell me about Eddie the dosser," says Becky, stifling a yawn.

"Tomorrow."

# CHAPTER 26

I tried three times before he finally called back. I can't blame him because I don't answer unsolicited calls either, but at the third attempt I left a voicemail. I'd thought long and hard about what I was going to say, nervous that if I didn't strike the right tone, he'd never reply and I'd have to track him down the hard way. In the end I felt I had no choice but to resort to subterfuge, and good old fashioned greed was the carrot.

He told me he lived in Norwich and that he was 'usually very busy' but he could juggle his diary to fit me in. We agreed to meet at eleven at a coffee shop in the city centre. By eleven-fifteen I begin to think I've been stood up. I call Becky.

"Did you manage to hack into Becca's laptop?"

"Yes. But's it's not Becca's, it's Grace's."

"Of course! Becca took it from the cottage."

"That's the good news. The bad news is there's very little on it."

"What do you mean?"

"There's nothing on it apart from the operating system and the default applications. Nothing about Nubilis, no software, no client/customer database of the type you'd expect. There's a small accounting package for billing and accounting, but no accounting data, because the system is looking for it on an external drive. No emails, nothing. It's as if it's been initialised. I even used data recovery software to see if stuff had been deleted and potentially restorable but it's been cleaned professionally, all available disk space overwritten multiple times by specialist software."

"No photos or documents?"

"Nope."

"Do you think she wiped it herself?"

"Maybe. The system file dates show it was done before she died, but I never imagined her as a techie."

256

I spot a middle aged man by the door in a vintage tweed three-piece.

"He's here. I'll call you later."

He walks in tentatively, wearing a nervous expression and clutching a flat cap. He fidgets with it and scans the room until his eyes land on me and my deliberately warm, inviting smile.

"Mr Harding?"

"Miss Duvall?" he asks, hesitantly.

"Would you like a coffee?"

He frowns, considering the question as if it's a starter for ten on astrophysics, or questioning whether, being old-school, the male is obliged to pay for everything and he's not comfortable with women taking the lead.

"Er…"

"Americano, skinny latte, cappuccino…?"

"Yes!" he says, relieved to hear one that's recognisable. I'm back with the coffee in a few moments to find him perched on the edge of a chair, deigning to make himself comfortable. He's already decided it won't take long. "Sorry I was late," he says. "You can't rely on public transport these days."

"I'm sorry to be the bearer of bad news."

I told him on the phone that I was acting for her family and had taken charge of all her personal possessions. It was true, in a way, if disingenuous. I didn't actually say I was executing her will, but there's no doubt he got that impression. Unfortunately, if Des Harding thinks anything of value is coming his way, he'll be disappointed.

I'd no idea what to expect. Before we'd made contact, I'd formed a picture of a self-centred guy who knew what he wanted out of life and chose to leave his wife rather than agree to adopt his niece. But the impression I got on the phone was quite the reverse. He's reserved, timid almost, an idealist who perhaps married for love and forever, only to find circumstances forcing them apart, his other half increasingly

257

erratic and ultimately, intolerable, such that with regret, they agreed to part ways. He may have suffered abuse, physical or verbal, or unlike his wife, may just have grown up and grown tired of protesting against the system and being a hippy. It's not fair of me to judge him or Grace but given what I've learned about her colourful life, I can't see the mutual attraction.

"It's been eighteen years," he says wistfully.

"You've had no contact in that time?"

"Oh yes. Quite recently as it happens. How did you find my number?"

"On a sticky note in one of her pockets."

"She called me about six months ago, said she wanted bygones to be bygones and it would be wonderful for me to meet Rebecca. She'd grown up to be a beautiful young woman."

"She has indeed. Is that all?"

"She wanted to know how I was doing, asked where I lived and what sort of house I had and what my job was and wanted to know all about my family. Typical Grace," he laughs mirthlessly. "Wanting to know the ins and outs of everything." More likely she was fishing around for someone, anyone, who could help her out financially having exhausted all other avenues. But I don't have the heart to tell him that.

"You have a family?"

"Yes," he says brightening. "Two boys, eight and twelve. My wife's a nurse."

"Good for you. Rebecca had the impression she might have been the cause of your break-up with Grace, that she wanted children but you didn't."

"Indirectly, yes."

"How do you mean?"

"I was happy to have children but not happy for Grace to be a mother. She wasn't suited. Neither was her sister."

"Fleur?"

258

"Yes. Self-obsessed, rebellious, free spirits the two of them. Thought they were changing the world but were just society drop-outs."

"But weren't you were involved in climate change protests too?"

"Yes. That's how we met, but I was fresh out of university and had a scientific view of the problem for mankind, whereas Grace and Fleur were, to my mind, more stimulated by the ideology and romance of it all, the anarchy of protest. Fleur was certainly. She'd be regarded an extremist nowadays whereas Grace simply got tired of it all, could talk the talk but never really put herself out. You'd never find Grace camping out in a field. We were already drifting apart when Fleur got herself pregnant …"

"Got herself pregnant?" I say, bristling at the pejorative remark.

"Well, they were all into free love, just like their hippy parents. It was bound to happen," he says without apology.

"Was Grace like that?"

"Probably. I didn't want to know."

Des Harding cuts a sad figure; dreams he had as a student and an earnest young man, roundly trashed by bohemian excess. He doesn't even look happy now, despite having a new family.

"Are you still active in climate change?"

He shakes his head, looking morose. "Waste of time. No one will do anything unless it's staring them in the face. No one is going to sacrifice their cosy little existence unless waves are lapping at their door or their neighbour's house spontaneously combusts. Millions have to die before the rest finally wake up."

I didn't come for a debate on the rights and wrongs of climate change or the imminent annihilation of the human race. Most people Des's age won't be around to see it. If it ever happens, I'll be uniquely placed to judge who was right.

259

"Grace was bankrupt when she died."

"Figures," he says, nodding sagely.

"All that's left are some personal possessions and bits of old furniture."

"Then I'm not sure why you wanted to see me."

"I need your help Des. Rebecca believes Grace was murdered."

"Murdered?" he says, scanning the room in case anyone has overheard. It's genuine shock. Like most of us, Des is the type for whom murder is played out on the TV screen, in fantasy drama or film, or if it is real, is detached and remote from our own lives.

"I must say, I have my doubts. The more I look into it the less certain I become of anything. After you separated, Grace was involved with a variety of colourful characters. She set up an escort business with a former nightclub bouncer and, it seems, had many relationships over many years. She lived life on the edge. Maybe she got too close."

"That's Grace. But surely this is a police matter."

"They concluded it was an accident and aren't investigating further."

"Are you a reporter?"

"I'm part writer and part investigator. I'm working for Rebecca, except that she went missing soon after telling me of her concerns. I think she made some people uncomfortable and they're trying to make sure she doesn't cause any trouble."

"Good grief!" he says, looking suddenly agitated, wringing his hands. "That poor child." He's thinking had he not abandoned them, none of this might have happened.

"Now, by chance, her twin sister has turned up."

"My goodness yes! There were two of them. Grace called them both Rebecca. She thought it was a hoot."

"Is it true you agreed to adopt one but not two?"

"Not at all! I had my doubts about Grace but I couldn't stop her so had to give it a go. It was Grace who said she couldn't handle more than one so we had the quiet one adopted."

"The quiet one?"

"Yes. One of them hardly made a squeak while the other one wouldn't stop bawling. Typical Grace to pick the one she thought had a feisty character."

"Did you know the adopting family?"

"No," he says shaking his head. "It was all done through an agent, anonymously. Grace wanted there to be no trace back to her, or Fleur."

"But Becky, the quiet one, managed to do it."

"Good for her. I hope she finds what she's looking for," he says without any sense of optimism.

"Did Grace ask you for money?"

Des plays with his cap. He looks haunted, thinking back to that unexpected, unsolicited call from his irresponsible, free-spirited ex-wife, the first for eighteen years, in which she tries to rebuild bridges and roll back the past and getting little in the way of reciprocity, cuts to the chase. "Yes," he says eventually, another reason to feel guilt. "She said she needed it to pay for Fleur's care. I said I couldn't help her, I'm not a rich man and I have my own family to think about."

"So you said no."

Des is animated again; on the defensive. "I didn't believe her. She never talked about Fleur once she'd been put away. It was if she'd never existed. She never went to visit and had virtually no communication from the home. I couldn't imagine where this sudden burst of family responsibility came from. I thought she was just making it up."

"But you and Grace split up a couple of years after Fleur was sectioned. Maybe Grace re-established contact?"

261

"Doesn't sound like the Grace I knew. I suspect she wanted something for herself. I'm sorry," he says, "speaking ill of the dead."

"It's not your fault, Des," I tell him, but he doesn't look convinced. My phone buzzes in my pocket and I glance at the screen. "It's Becky, the quiet one. Do you mind?"

"Kate! I know you're in a meeting but I found another diary from 1999. Grace had a thing going with Mal Devlin before he got Fleur pregnant and it caused an almighty bust up. I wondered if Des knew about it?" I glance at Des but he's head down, lost in thought.

"Thanks. I'll ask him."

"When will you be back?"

"Can't say, early evening."

Yet more drama emanating from Grace's diaries. I don't want to cause Des any more distress than necessary, but he's already alluded to the promiscuity of his wife and her sister, so it should come as no surprise.

"Des?" He looks up, his face a portrait of misery. "Can I show you a picture?" I hold up the screen so we can both see the shot. "This is the only photo we have and it looks like you took it. We found it amongst Grace's things. I assume it's Grace and Fleur?"

He perks up, looking surprised and alert for the first time. "Yes it is. But I can do much better than that." He pulls a phone from his coat pocket. It's top of the range, with a big screen and three camera lenses, incongruously high-tech for a timid, middle-aged bloke in a cloth cap. "There's loads more." He taps and swipes at the screen using two thumbs with the dexterity of a teenager. "Grace had all these. After I refused her money she asked if I had any old photos because she was writing a book about SANE. They'll be on her computer."

"It's blank."

"Well I can't explain that. These are all scans of slides and prints. I didn't move to digital until after the millennium and I had thousands of these taking up room in the house."

"You're a photographer?"

"Was," he says with an enthusiasm I haven't seen until now. "Just a hobby now. But I digitised everything and got rid of them."

"They're all on your phone?" I say, wondering how much storage he can possibly have.

"No. There's a lot in the cloud. Here we go."

He starts swiping. The first is of two young women, one noticeably younger, arms around each other, happy and gay, smiling broadly. They're wearing garish batik tops and flowery harem pants, the younger one with a headband made of marigolds atop her long red tresses. I already know who they are and I don't know why I'm so surprised to see them. Until recently, they were ghosts, but now they have an identity. It makes all the difference.

"That's them. Grace and Fleur in happier times," he says. "Before Fleur got pregnant." He swipes again and again and I want to slow him down but he's in full flow. "Don't worry. I'll send you a link and you can download the lot."

He stops at one and scoffs. "That's him. That's the one I was looking for. His name's Mal Devlin. There was always something about him I didn't like. He was too charming for his own good and I warned Grace and Fleur but they wouldn't listen," he says getting worked up and I feel my own pulse quicken. In the photo, Mal has his arm around Grace and Fleur is looking on, caught off guard, the camera capturing her displeasure.

I decide there's no time for sensitivities. "Did Grace have an affair with Mal?"

"Yes, he bloody did!" he says, voice quivering with anger.

"And then got Fleur pregnant?" He nods.

263

My brain has gone into overdrive, thoughts careering around like a pinball in a machine, bouncing from pillar to post then slamming down between the paddles. Des and Grace knew him as Mal Devlin; I know him as Adam Cross. I compose myself and he swipes on to the next and the next and the next. Group shots mainly, fuzzy, low definition images of banners, campfires and tents. Lots of shots of Fleur but very few of Grace. He stops at one.

"That's me with Devlin, before I found out" A young moustachioed Des, swigging beer from a bottle with a young Adam Cross, his wife's toyboy.

"How can you be sure he was the father?"

"She and Mal were together, married, good as. Fleur forgave him his dalliance with Grace; which is more than she did for Grace. But as soon as she announced she was pregnant, he disappeared without warning. Her affair with Mal caused a serious rift between her and Fleur, and Grace eventually got tired of the whole protest thing. We both did."

"Why?"

He sighs deeply, reminiscing, reliving the times and his own thoughts, never sure he'd done the right thing. "As a movement, we were in disarray. There were lots of arguments about strategy, where and when and how we'd organise the next protest, what form it would take, who would lead. And invariably we found the police were there waiting for us, putting up roadblocks, bringing out the heavy mob in riot gear. I mean, we were peaceful until they started beating us with sticks and we'd fight back with our bare hands. They'd haul off one or two at random and bang them up for a few days and then charge them with public order offences or release them on bail, but it was sapping our resources and our sponsors started to get concerned. Some of the women who were arrested and then released said they'd been assaulted while in custody, strip-searched and humiliated. The police knew who the main players were and picked them off, made life a misery for them, delved into their past and threatened them, and some walked away. It was all very disheartening. And on top of that was the endemic promiscuity, we were becoming a degenerate rabble, we'd lost focus on the core objective which was to stop big money destroying the planet."

"And you took all these pictures?"

"Yeah. Video too, from tapes. It's a bit grainy."

He swipes a few more, too quick for me to see and screws up his face as if he's smelt something bad. Whatever it is, it's painful for him. "There was another guy; Ged Connor." He leaves the name hanging in the air but it means nothing to me.

"What about him?"

"He joined the movement before Devlin. He was a photographer as well and his job was to get pictures of police brutality and give them to this journalist contact he knew, but it never amounted to anything. He spent more time snapping us. He originally hooked up with Fleur, but then Devlin came along," he says with a curled lip. He swipes past a few more and stops.

I feel as if the air has been sucked out of the room. Four young men, long hair, unshaven, camaraderie on show, arms round each other's shoulders like members of a rock band.

"That's me and Devlin plus Ged Connor on the left and a guy called John Franklin. Slimeball if ever there was one."

Des is still muttering but I can't hear what he's saying, the thumping in my ears drowning out his words. I can't tear my eyes away from the photo. Des Harding, arm and arm with Adam Cross, Dave Parker and a true slimeball, Jason Palmer.

\*\*\*

The lunchtime news reports the arrest of a forty-two year old man on suspicion of murder. Trevor was hardly inconspicuous and probably gave himself up rather than go on the run. I think back to that night. My hunt for Palmer was where this all

265

started. Then, seemingly from nowhere, came the call from Becca Harding; someone else with a problem, yet unconnected. I resolved neither and struggled to prioritise the two; the risk to an unknown number of women now that Palmer was loose again, versus the safety of a vulnerable young woman, pursued by villains and the police. Ultimately, they're linked, I just don't know why. I didn't tell Des I knew all three men, but I did ask if he'd ever served with the police in any capacity. He laughed at the notion. They were the enemy, as corrupt as the criminals they claimed to pursue.

"Franklin was kicked out of the group," he said. "Some of the women complained about him. One accused him of rape and I could well believe it. We all did."

"You didn't report it to the police?"

He looked at me as if I hadn't been listening. "The enemy? What were they going to do? We were vermin as far as they were concerned. Lived like animals, behaved like animals."

"Have you seen any of them since?"

"No," he said. "I have no idea where they are now."

"And what about Fleur?"

"Twenty years ago she was in a mental hospital and she was still there when I divorced Grace."

I thanked him and wished him well, asking if I could call him again if I needed to. I felt sorry for him. Alone amongst all these men, Des was a victim too, but there's nothing I can do for him.

There's now a whole new dimension to this and it gives me a profound sense of foreboding. I can't be certain Adam knew who Becca was when Grace asked him to give her a job, nor can I be certain Becca knew who Adam was when she took it. But Des believed Mal Devlin was the father and so did Grace because it's in her diary, and only a year or so ago, Grace renewed her affair with Devlin, now known as Adam Cross, because Becca found them together in the pub at Holburgh. *What on earth was Grace thinking?* Becca claims she slept with Adam; Adam denies it. Whatever the truth, it makes sick to think about it.

# CHAPTER 27

The number is answered almost immediately.

"Munro Group, Sandy speaking, how may I help you?"

"Jimmy Munro please."

"May I ask who's calling?"

"Kate Duvall."

"From?"

"Just Kate Duvall."

"One moment please."

I'm treated to Vivaldi's Four Seasons while I wait. *What did you expect? Hip hop, house, dub?* Within two minutes, it's beginning to wear me down.

"Good morning Miss Duvall, it's Karen Small. Mr Munro is unavailable at the moment."

"I just need to make an appointment."

"He's asked me to make a dinner engagement for you tomorrow night."

"I don't want dinner."

"That's all I can offer you I'm afraid," she purrs. I can imagine the smug expression that shows she's in control, not me.

"I only want five minutes. Surely it's simpler if I just pop by?" I say, knowing it's futile and I have to play the game according to Jimmy's rules.

"*Le Coq Qui Chante* in Welstead, 7 p.m.?" *The Crowing Cock, how apt!* "Shall I send a driver to pick you up?"

"You don't know where I live."

There's a pause, but it's a half-second longer than it needs to be. "Why don't you give me your address?" *She already knows.*

"That won't be necessary. I'll find it."

"Is there anything else I can help you with?" she adds, for no other reason than to be irritating.

***

I'm getting in deeper and immediately, I think of Becky, because while she's with me it could get dangerous for her too. At breakfast, I dodged telling her about Eddie the dosser, my escape with Becca from two thugs, and the incident with Palmer. It could wait. But at breakfast, there was only a tenuous link. Now, after my meeting with Des, it's cast iron. It brings her in closer and that worries me. I can't possibly explain to her on the phone that I've seen a picture of her father, arm in arm with a corrupt cop and a serial killer; it will have to wait until I get home, if at all. But I need to check she's okay.

"How's your day going? Any more diary revelations?"

"No, I had an idea about the laptop. There's no web site for Nubilis but there is a domain name registered to Grace paid up for another two months. I got into the online control panel and downloaded her emails."

"You got in?" I ask with some trepidation.

"Don't ask."

"The inbox is intact. I've been wading through them and there's an interesting exchange between her and Jimmy Munro about three years ago." Becky sounds fired up.

"What is it?"

"Jimmy asks if she can provide company for one of his London based associates whenever he's out here on business. Once a month at least. Jimmy vouches he's kosher and has funds, but she won't do anything without a name and a photo. Then a week later he sends her a pic of a guy called Adam Cross and she tells Jimmy he's the spitting image of a guy she used to know called Mal Devlin. Jimmy says she must be mistaken but she tells him not to mention her name to Cross until she's sure who he is. What the hell's going on Kate?"

I take a deep breath. I wanted to download Des's photos and go through them with her in person, but she's catching up fast and likely to find a lot more damning evidence amongst the emails.

"Des has hundreds of photos and videos which have obviously been erased from the laptop. He showed me some of them and pointed out Mal Devlin straight away. He says Mal had an affair with Grace while he was still with Fleur, then got Fleur pregnant and disappeared."

"Okay, so Devlin is a creep. We already know that."

"I know him as Adam Cross."

"What? The guy with the young twins?"

"Yep."

"Married to Annabel?"

"Yep."

"Our father?"

"Yep."

"The guy who Becca...?" I remain silent. It's too uncomfortable. "Jesus! Do you think Becca knew?"

"I have no idea, but Grace did."

"The bitch!"

"You can't be certain Grace knew about their affair until Becca caught them together that night in the pub."

"Really? Come off it Kate. Grace had been *in the business* for many years and sucked Becca into it too. She must have known what would happen when she put Becca and Adam together."

Becky is a clever girl. I didn't want to think the worst of Grace without proof but the evidence is pretty overwhelming. I just hope Becca wasn't a willing party to it. Nonetheless, I need to bring Becky up to date with everything I know, notwithstanding the danger. She's already got the bit between her teeth and there'll be no stopping her.

"You're right."

"What a scumbag."

270

"Who?"

"Mal, Adam, whoever he is my. My bloody father! Grace too!"

"He's not your father Becky. Not really." She goes quiet and I imagine her holding back tears, struggling to understand the implications, confused beyond measure, wanting to know the whole story yet at the same time, afraid of what she'll find. "There's more you don't know. Des showed me another photo of four guys together: one's Des and one's Adam, but I also know the other two."

"And?"

"And I need you to listen carefully and do something for me. Lock the doors, lock the windows, do not go out and do not answer the door to anyone."

"Why?"

"Do you understand?"

"Yes, but…"

"I'll be back in an hour or so. Then we can talk."

I end the call and let out a deep breath, tempted to rush back there immediately. It may just be overreaction, yet it gives me a chill, repeating to Becky the warning I gave Becca when I left her alone in the barn. Becky is more grounded than her sister and more capable. Becky is the quiet one and she's diligent, compared to Becca who's reckless and unstable. Becca took no notice, goaded her boyfriend and gave her location away in the process and then probably left of her own accord. Becky is anonymous and not a threat to anyone. Unlike me. *No one knows where you live Kate! Really? No one apart from those who live in the village, plus Jimmy Munro, Adam Cross…and whoever they've told.*

## CHAPTER 28

Smokey's waiting and he's not happy. He sits up and miaows loudly and repeatedly as I approach a door that now sports parallel, vertical claw marks. I phoned Becky when I was a half-hour away and said I'd call again when I was outside. The curtains are closed and the place appears uninhabited.

"Smokey and I would like to come in."

There's a rattle of keys and chains and the door opens a few inches, closes again and then opens wide. Smokey slips through the gap instantly and disappears inside. Becky is standing nervously in the corridor, hands in pockets.

"Thank God you're back," she says. I put my arms around her and she clings on tightly. It feels so good I don't want to let go. "You frightened me to death. I wouldn't even open the door for the cat."

"I'm sorry. I was hit by a wave of paranoia, that's all. When your sister stayed with me in Hawsby, I left her alone with the same instructions, but when I got back, she was gone."

We're interrupted by an impatient miaow from the kitchen and Becky relaxes her grip. I kiss her on the forehead. She doesn't flinch, and I don't apologise. I'm responsible for her.

She gives Smokey his snacks and he trots straight back to the front door, demanding to be let out. I lock and bolt it behind him. The risk is still negligible, but now I'm back, probably greater than before. It would be sensible for Becky to go home sooner rather than later.

I notice the enticing aroma from the kitchen. "You've been cooking."

"Wasn't sure if you wanted to go to the pub."

"Not tonight. We have lots to talk about and I don't want to be overheard."

"That bad?"

"Depends what you call bad. I'm going to take a shower. Get the wine open."

*** 

I stay in there longer than usual, head bowed, allowing the water to sting my shoulders and chest until they form red patches on the skin. I'm thinking about Becca and Grace and Fleur and all the men in their lives, how they all fitted together then and how they fit together now. Poor Becky was only looking for her mum and she's been dragged into this mess. There's no way back for her now. She's doomed to discover the truth, however hideous and awful it might be.

"So my dad slept with my mum, my aunt and my sister. My Mum's a basket case, my aunt's dead, my sister's a tart and gone missing. Apart from that, we're a normal happy family," she says, handing me a glass of wine.

"Don't think badly of Becca."

"I don't know what to think. I don't know her and at this rate I may never get to know her."

"Do you want to? Do you want to meet Fleur and Adam for that matter?"

"Maybe it would be better if I just went home and forgot all about it."

"Can you do that? What would you tell your folks?" She looks glum so I put my arm around her. "You can't bury the truth for ever. You're not responsible for the past and there's nothing you can do to change things. Confront it, deal with it and move on. The worm in your head won't give up. It'll eat you away from the inside."

Over dinner, I tell her about the search for a serial killer, the violent attack on me, the arrest and subsequent release. I tell her Eddie the dosser witnessed it and the entire incident was recorded on a bodycam but the NCS let him go despite knowing he was guilty. I tell her how I found out where he

273

lives and that I have to do something to stop him, but I was distracted by Becca's cry for help in the wake of Grace's death.

"But what's the connection?"

I find the photo I downloaded using the link from Des and hold up my phone. "These four guys, left to right: Des Harding, former husband of Grace; Mal Devlin, aka Adam Cross, once a copper in Domestic Counter Terrorism, and allegedly, father to you and Becca; Ged Connor, aka Dave Parker, currently head of the East Midlands NCS, most recently responsible for the release of this guy, slimeball John Franklin, aka Jason Palmer, the guy who attacked me and is most likely, a serial killer and perpetrator of the Triple-M."

"Jesus!"

"Des is the only one who appears to be innocent. Parker has warned me twice about interfering again and they're planning to stitch up some hapless fool to take the rap, but I'm not letting it go. My main worry is he tips off Palmer and Palmer comes after me, which is why I panicked and told you to lock all the doors."

"Are you seriously suggesting a senior policeman is protecting a murderer and covering up terrible crimes just because they were once mates?"

"I don't know why he would do that unless Palmer has something damning on him."

"And you can't go to the police…"

"Because I already have and I wouldn't know who to trust. But what's clear is that you need to go home as soon as possible, like tomorrow. If Palmer wants to silence me, I don't want you in the firing line."

"I'm not going."

"You must."

"I'm not going to disappear and leave you alone. Anyway, he doesn't know who I am."

"You're not listening Becky. He's a monster and a danger to all woman. I was human bait once before and I'm prepared to do it again, but not while you're in close proximity. You need to keep a safe distance. He may not know who you are, but that won't matter if you get in the way."

Becky pours more wine and lets out a sigh. Her face creases up in a frown.

"It was Adam who put Becca onto you wasn't it?"

"Yes, and I know what you're going to ask."

"Which is?"

"How come Adam and his family just happened to rent a holiday cottage next door to me when he's connected to Palmer, the guy I got arrested a couple of days earlier?"

"Yeah."

"No idea. It's a hell of a coincidence."

"Do you believe that's all it is?"

"No."

"Do you think Adam is dangerous?"

"I don't think so. Annabel didn't once suggest or even allude to any sinister behaviour by Adam in the time they were married, other than his so-called affair with Becca."

"Do you really think he and Becca..?"

"Adam vehemently denies it, Becca emphatically confirms it. Neither are very credible."

"And neither know who the other is?"

"No. Not yet anyway."

"How did you track down Palmer?"

"Tip-off."

"Who from?"

I can't tell her for reasons she'll never understand. "A distant relative."

"You never talk about your family." I knew this was bound to come up despite which, I'm ill prepared and somehow lost for words. I don't even trust myself to speak, so profound is

275

the sadness threatening to engulf me. It must show in my face as she lays a hand on mine. "Sorry. Another time."

She takes our empty plates and stacks the dishwasher.

"While I've been locked inside your cottage I've been hard at work poring over Grace's diaries and foraging around in her emails."

It's enough to bring me back to reality. "I thought there were no more diaries."

"There weren't until around 2020 when she started writing them online."

I wonder at her technical skills and how many others out there can do the same thing. "Is any of this…legal?"

"It's right and proper though, isn't it?"

\*\*\*

Grace Harding got a kick out of it; she said so in her handwritten diaries. She'd revelled in her illicit relationship with Devlin, writing explicitly about their sexual exploits conducted behind the backs of both her sister and her husband with no semblance of regret or guilt. Fleur subsequently made peace with Devlin, but not with Grace. What Devlin did to Fleur was bad, Grace wrote, but then Fleur had always been naïve and gullible and at the end of it Grace got what she wanted, which was a child. She didn't plan it that way, it was just circumstance. Once Mal and Fleur had made up, Grace Harding referred little to him, other than to assert he was the one who got Fleur pregnant before running off.

Years later, when Becca told Grace she was taking a gap year, Grace canvassed some of her more professional clients asking if they had any space for an intern; you scratch my back, so to speak. Few were willing to take her up on it, understandably nervous to keep any connection to Grace at arm's length. But it all changed when Jimmy put a new client her way. *'He calls himself Adam Cross'* she wrote in her

276

private online blog, but when she saw his picture there was no doubt in her mind, despite not having seen him for twenty years. She asked to meet him, on the pretext she wanted to better understand her client's needs and improve the service her company could offer, so Jimmy arranged an introduction at a restaurant in Ipswich, without divulging her name.

'*Still a hunk, despite carrying a little more weight and with flecks of grey around the temples. I swear his eyes lit up when he saw me and the penny dropped, but he was nervous, suspicious he was being set up. I was able to put his mind at ease.*' Following that reunion, Grace and Adam rekindled their relationship. '*I told him Fleur had miscarried, subsequently left the SANE movement and emigrated to New Zealand, figuring if you are going to tell a lie you may as well go big. I also told him she and I were estranged, which was largely true, but, I needn't have worried; it was exactly what Mal/Adam wanted to hear; that this particular skeleton would never come out of the closet. I asked him why the change of name? He said he didn't want anyone to know of his participation in the protest movement. It was entirely contrary to what he was involved in now and would damage his credibility.*'

Grace didn't need to provide Adam with the services of her escort agency; she was able to satisfy him single-handedly. It suited Adam too. Being unfaithful to his wife may have weighed on his conscience, but far less so with a former lover, than if he were paying for sex with a professional escort.

'*Well, well,*' she wrote after a weekend of unbridled passion. '*Mal Devlin, poacher turned gamekeeper. From reactionary eco-warrior to professional mover and shaker in international investment specialising in the not-so-green energy sector. Who would have thought it? And the delicious irony, it turns out he's the proud father of three-year-old twins, blissfully unaware he has another set approaching twenty-one!*'

277

She maintained the deceit for a while, but inevitably, it began to unravel. Adam was more than happy to help her undergraduate daughter Rebecca with work experience, that is until Becca told Grace how dishy Adam was and it started alarm bells ringing. At the time, Grace wasn't aware Becca had actually flunked university and was looking for any opportunity to buy herself a comfortable future with a well-off, mature professional, married or not. *'I put Becca and Adam together. It seemed to me appropriate a father should help his daughter in her career, even if neither of them knew who the other really was. There was nothing to be gained from telling them and I feared Adam would disappear again if he knew, especially as he now had a family of his own. I trusted he wouldn't prejudice our relationship by consorting with my daughter and for a while, I enjoyed the subterfuge. But it was naive of me to assume Becca wouldn't apply the skills I had taught her, nor that Adam wouldn't eventually succumb. I had to warn him.'*

As luck would have it, pressure from Adam's CEO caused Becca to be moved out of harm's way, but soon after, she told Grace excitedly she remained in contact with Adam and they had a date to meet for dinner.

*'He came to the cottage and I warned him off Becca. He insisted he hadn't encouraged her, she was all over him and he found it flattering, but also vaguely embarrassing. I told him I had lied to him. I told him Becca was Fleur's daughter, not mine and he went momentarily white before getting angry and then defensive. He said Fleur had put herself about, been with other men besides him and as soon as he found out she was pregnant, he left because he didn't care to take responsibility for someone else's child. He demanded proof, which of course I couldn't provide, and we agreed to keep it to ourselves, recognising that, whilst there remained some doubt, he had better keep Becca at arm's length.'*

"Why on earth did Grace not simply tell Becca that she was flirting with her dad? That would have been the obvious thing to do," I say, interrupting Becky in full flow.

"Grace thought about that and wasn't ready. She thought it would re-open old wounds and damage her relationship with Adam. She thought Becca would want to know more about Fleur and whether Adam knew what had happened to her. Grace had kept Fleur's incarceration a secret from Becca all her life and told Adam she'd emigrated. The lies were catching up on her."

# CHAPTER 29

I make him wait. I know it's petulant, but it's the least I can do to assert some degree of independence, exercise a modicum of control. But the fact remains, I'm the one who asked for the meeting. He has something I need and he knows it. Dictating terms is a demonstration of primacy, and, given the venue and occasion, an indication he wants something in return.

I looked it up. It's flash and boasts a Michelin star; no slumming it for Jimmy. I dispensed with the jeans and scrubbed up a little, without wishing to give him the wrong impression. I told Becky I didn't intend the evening to drag on, but the orders remained the same; lock and bolt the door and wait for my call, or else go next door and stay with Miriam. She said she'd lock and bolt the door.

I pull into the restaurant car park at ten past seven. It's almost full but one in a private space stands out from the others; an 'S' Class Mercedes with driver and personalised plate 'JM1'. I'm met at the door by a young woman who knows my name without asking. "Miss Duvall, please come this way." The restaurant is half-full, classy and exotic. It's subtly lit, with classical music playing in the background. Jimmy is sitting alone in a semi-circular booth, checking his phone, a bottle of mineral water on the table. Just like last time, I feel out of place and uncomfortable, as if all eyes are on me, Jimmy Munro's paid-for date.

"Sorry I'm late."

"Nae problem. Glad you could come," he says, half-standing, making no attempt at physical contact.

"I did feel like I was being summoned."

"Not at all. You asked to see me."

"True, but I didn't expect dinner in a fancy restaurant."

280

"It's more conducive to having a civilised conversation. I thought you'd prefer it."

"Of course."

"I've taken the liberty of ordering. I hope you don't mind," he says, pouring me a glass of Evian.

"Aren't you drinking this evening?"

"I don't like to drink alone. Have you had any luck tracking down the elusive Rebecca?" he says conversationally, as if only mildly concerned about Becca's whereabouts or welfare. Either he trusts in her independence and self-sufficiency or he already knows where she is.

"Yes, actually. I believe she's staying at a place called Chevenham Hall." I watch for a reaction but there is none. "It's a stately home about an hour from here that's been turned into an exclusive and secretive hotel and conference centre."

"I know it," he says. "And what makes you think that?"

"I found her car in a pound. It was on the satnav."

"Well done you," he says as if praising a child for passing a simple test. "But does that prove anything? I mean, have you been there?"

"As I said, it's secretive. You have to be invited."

"Is that a no?"

"No, I haven't been there." It's true, if you define 'there' as being inside. Jimmy turns his phone around so I can see the screen. There's a grainy shot, taken at distance of a figure on the wrong side of a perimeter fence looking at the camera. "We're responsible for security there."

Round one to Jimmy. I'm sure he has one or two other tricks up his sleeve, but I'm not fazed by it. I had already concluded only fools underestimate Jimmy Munro.

"Then you knew she was there the last time we met."

"Aye, I did."

"Then why didn't you say something and save me a lot of time."

A waiter arrives and lays down two large plates with three rocket leaves, two eyeball-shaped morsels of paté framed by eyebrow-shaped smears of unidentifiable purée. *"Bon appetit."*

"I'm impressed how resourceful you are," he says, as the waiter backs away. "But not surprised. When I saw the picture I assumed Rebecca had told you where she was going."

"She said you'd asked her to go and meet a private client and deliver a parcel. At the time, she led me to believe the parcel contained drugs."

Jimmy spreads half an eyeball of paté on some toast and bites into it, crumbs clinging to both sides of his mouth. "Just goes to show how things get twisted when you make assumptions instead of finding out the facts."

"The champagne and chocolates are in my car, if you want them back?"

"Not at all. Consider them a gift from me, but then I forget, you don't drink do you?"

"I lied about that, I'm sorry. I was just being stroppy."

"Would you care for a drink now?"

"No thanks, I'm driving," I say, poking around in a blob of foie gras. "Who's Jules?"

Jimmy watches me eat with an attention that makes me unusually self-conscious. "I had no reason to tell you where Rebecca was," he says, brushing aside the question. "Some young woman walks in off the street unannounced and starts firing questions and making accusations. I want to know what she wants, what her motives are and whether she's entitled to know the answers. Most of all, I want to know who she is."

"You were going to offer me a job having only just met me."

"I was impressed by your attitude, but confidence and directness are not the only qualities I demand of my employees. It disnae matter because I'm afraid that ship has

282

sailed. But had you accepted, then I would have had to do my research."

"Understandable."

"The thing is, even though you declined my offer, I decided to do it anyway." I feel a frisson of nerves and try to cover it by wiping goose fat from my lips with a napkin. I'm not sure how far Jimmy and his researchers got. Not very far, is my guess. "The first thing that's striking is you have zero social media presence. I mean, there's quite a few Catherine Duvalls out there, but none of them are you. I would have thought for a freelancer like yourself, it was important to be out there, connecting to other professionals, commenting on this and that, picking up on issues of the day, firing your imagination."

"I used to be. I closed all my social media accounts because I couldn't bear the trolls and the morons and the vulgar narcissism the online world represents."

"Fair enough. I just said it seemed strange that's all." He pauses, waiting for me to add further justification, go too far in explaining or excusing my behaviour and opinions.

"I'm not the only one to go off-grid. Becca did it too." It's meant to steer the conversation in another direction, but he's not deflected.

"I've also had people trawl through the International Publication Database for articles you may have written. The last one with your byline was published three years ago. Are you going through a lean patch?" He's probing, trying to put me on the back foot and I don't want to push back too much. I'm sure he's saving the best to last.

"Not everything I do turns into print. In the last couple of years I've done more private investigative work than anything else. If anything of public interest comes from that, I will always consider publishing it."

"So what is the nature of your... investigative work?"

"It varies."

283

"From what to what?"

"Family breakdown, lost relatives, inheritance, fraud, hypocrisy, dishonesty, duplicity. Men in power preying on the innocent."

"Very comprehensive, and very worthy I'm sure, but how do you get your work? I'm genuinely interested."

"Word of mouth, just like Becca. Adam Cross referred her to me," I say, returning to the issues I want to discuss, my personal history not being one of them. For the second time, I sense a reaction to the name. He blinks, but presses on with his own agenda.

"So we went back to basics and looked at birth certificates between 1985 and 1995. Please forgive the presumption I know your age," he says, feigning humility with a disingenuous grin. "I wouldnae want to offend a lady. It turns out there are only two Catherine Duvalls and sadly, both died; one at birth and the other about two years ago."

"How interesting. I obviously picked a rare name."

"Picked?"

"Lots of people change their name for all sorts of reasons."

"So it's not your real name?"

"Yes it is. Why does it matter to you?"

He leans forward and places his hands on the table. "It matters, Kate, because like you, I am disturbed by dishonesty and duplicity. If you changed your name, you did so for a reason. Are you one of those who assumes the identity of a dead person in order to pursue…nefarious activities?"

"Why don't you be the judge of that? Let me tell you what I want to know. You don't have to answer and there's nothing I can do to make you. But maybe you'll be persuaded my motives are honourable?"

He finishes off his starter. "What do you think of the foie gras?"

"Delicious. Pity the poor goose."

"Aye. There is that. But then, humans are a predatory species. It's in their nature to exploit animals, resources, other people, for gain and sometimes pleasure."

"Is that what you do?"

The waiter clears our plates and Jimmy refills the glasses.

"If you want my help, and you want to get to the truth, I'd suggest you remain a little more open-minded. Perhaps consider alternatives before jumping to conclusions."

"Why send Becca to Chevenham?"

"I didn't send Rebecca anywhere. I advised her that it was in her best interests; a safe place where she could take a deep breath, consider her future and earn good money at the same time."

"As an escort?"

"That's what she does. That's what she wants to do."

"She thinks Grace was murdered."

"I know she does. What do you think?"

"I think Grace put herself in danger. I think she'd lived all her life on the edge. She was free-spirited and sexually promiscuous, anti-establishment, rebellious, flirtatious, smoked weed, associated herself with dubious characters who behaved in dubious ways and eventually, it caught up with her. That doesn't mean she was murdered, it just means Becca, who knew her best, has suspicions that are worthy of investigation. On the day of her aunt's funeral, Becca was tracked to a motorway service station by two heavies who put the fear of god into her and told her Uncle Jimmy wanted to see her. I fended them off, but they found her hiding at my place and took her away. It sounds and looks very much like you wanted to keep control over her, stop her repeating her suspicions about Grace, keep a lid on it by making her a prisoner until she finally realises what's good for her."

I'm surprised Jimmy hasn't interrupted. I was blunt and critical, accusing him, by inference, of exploiting Becca and maybe Grace too, if not for gain, for his own preservation and

285

perhaps, amusement. I don't expect a man like Jimmy Munro to tolerate such a scurrilous attack on his integrity, so I anticipate an angry reaction and the inevitable threat to my safety. I watch him and my surprise turns to astonishment. His eyes are moist. The waiter sidles over as if to ask a question, and Jimmy waves him away without looking. I think the night is about to end prematurely when he leans forward and clasps his hands.

"I know what you think of me, what you think I am and what you think I do. You're like all the others who judge me based on personal prejudice and without resort to fact." I haven't heard Jimmy Munro speak so slowly and quietly and with such restrained passion. It's as if the gentler he sounds, the more frightening he is.

"I was born in a slum. My family was poorer than poor, barely existing in abject poverty and deprivation, where out in the street they'd knife you for a bite of yer jeely piece, that is, if yer maw could afford the jeely in the first place. In a life-threatening situation, you learn to talk tough and act tough, and you learn to fight. I don't mean fight as in doin' what others do, takin' what they want and preyin' on the weak, kill to stay ahead. I mean fight for yer self-respect, fight to protect yoursel', fight for survival. Well I fought and I survived. And all along the way, because of where I'm from and how I sound and how I look, people have judged me badly, underestimated me badly.

"I'm not proud of everything I've done. I've had serious challenges to deal with and gone head to head with those who seek to destroy what I've built because they want a piece of it for themselves. I've cut corners here or there, broken the odd rule, but I've never once preyed upon the vulnerable or the disadvantaged, or exploited anyone just because I could. And you know, there are plenty out there who tried to exploit me, pretend to care for me, pretend to love me, not for who or what I am, but for what I have."

He leans closer and I fear he'll either explode with rage or burst into tears. "Whatever you may think of me, young lady, let me tell you this. I am not a bad person," he says, the intensity of the moment heightened by his gently tapping the tablecloth with an index finger.

Against all odds, I'm chastened and deeply touched, the atmosphere across our small table, electric. I glance around the room, relieved to see no one is paying attention, *Le Coq Qui Chante* frequented by a discerning clientele who have respect for discretion and privacy. I need to stay calm. He hasn't stood up, smashed anything or sworn once and he's not likely to now. Instead, he raises one finger and the waiter scurries over. I fear he's about to ask for the bill.

"We'll have the main course now Antoine."

"*Oui, Monsieur Munro.*"

I take my cue to continue. "Did your men try to abduct Becca from South Alston?"

"No."

"Did your men abduct her from my place in Hawsby?"

"No. Would you care to rephrase that last question?"

"Did your men...take her from my house?"

"Yes."

"Why?"

"Rebecca eventually returned my many calls and told me where she was. She said you'd risked your life rescuing her from two scumbags, armed with nothing more than pepper-spray. I asked her who you were, and she said she knew nothing about you, but that Adam Cross had recommended you. I asked how it was you drove three hours to South Alston to help a stranger and she couldn't answer. I suggested I sent a car to take her to Chevenham Hall until we found out what was going on. She agreed."

"Why didn't you just tell me this last time?"

"Because I had no reason to trust you. I didn't know who you were and I still don't."

"So do you trust me now?"

"No, but I might be willing to give you a chance."

I need to give him something. He's making that clear. There is no point my trying to explain. No one in their right mind would accept the truth as it is, but I have to tell him anyway.

"I'm the one who died two years ago."

Jimmy Munro nods slowly, taking in my response, neither laughing nor shouting nor dismissing it with a wave of the hand, nor, mercifully, getting angry. I leave the phrase hanging, waiting for the reaction. "I knew there was something about you."

I don't want to dwell on it and he doesn't seem motivated to press me, so I take it as consent to proceed. I pull out my phone and flick through the photos until I find the one of four men, arm in arm. "Do you recognise any of them?"

He retrieves a pair of glasses from his jacket pocket and studies the picture long and hard. "I know three."

"The one on the left is Des Harding, Grace's ex-husband."

"I never met him."

"And you recognise Adam Cross, second from the right?"

"Aye."

"I already know who the other two are."

"Then why are you asking me?" he says, handing back the phone and removing his glasses. We're briefly interrupted by Antoine serving the main course. "Are you happy with Dover sole?" says Jimmy. "Because I can get you something else."

I'd like to think trust is growing but it's still early days. "It's fine, but thank you for asking."

*"Bon appetit,"* says Antoine.

"Could I trouble you for a bottle of your best white Burgundy and two glasses?"

"Not for me thanks."

"I know, but you might change yer mind. Ryan can take you home if you do." Antoine bows and walks off. "You

288

haven't answered my question," he says, tucking the linen napkin into his shirt collar. "Why are you asking me?"

"Did you know Adam used to be in the police?"

"Aye."

"And the guy second from left, Dave Parker, is still in the police?"

"I hear he's a big noise in the National Crime Service." I'm not surprised Jimmy knows that. "Saw him on TV recently."

"And the one on the far right, Jason Palmer?"

"Palmer? Is that his name these days? He was a copper too but I hope he isn't now."

"Why do you say that?"

"No, no," he says through a mouthful of fish. "Your turn."

I begin to tell him the story. He knows about Triple-M, everybody does, and like everyone who watches the news or reads the headlines he knows they arrested someone but are now looking for someone else. I tell him what really happened and how Palmer is still free and dangerous. He finishes his main course almost before I've started.

"I have to add courage to yer list of attributes," he says, sipping his wine in such a way I'm tempted to join him. "Along with breath-taking stupidity. What in God's name did you think you were doing?"

"Someone had to stop him."

I tuck into the Dover sole and he looks at me, shaking his head in disbelief at my recklessness. "I'm gonnae tell you something, but first, you have to tell me what this has to do with your concern for Rebecca and her claim Grace was murdered?"

"Grace Harding knew all these guys, they all have something to hide, and now she's dead."

***

289

Sometime in late nineties, Jimmy found himself running a late night entertainment empire after the sudden death of his boss. He spent a lot of his time at the flagship venue, *Le Palais de Danse,* the most successful and consequently, the most valuable nightclub in the East of England. Like all night-time venues, it appealed mainly to young girls and boys out having a good time hoping to meet someone of the opposite sex on the dance floor. But it attracted a small number of low-life scum, peddling drugs, carrying knives and out to cause trouble. Jimmy's security team were tasked with filtering out the bad boys before they got inside and being constantly alert for trouble if for some reason any managed to slip through.

Both club management and door security strove to co-operate and maintain cordial relations with the local police, since the presence of drugs in a nightclub could be severely detrimental to its chances of retaining its license. Losing a late night license would be commercial disaster for the club's owners and was to be avoided at all costs. But it was also in the interests of police that *Le Palais* kept its doors open, otherwise fifteen-hundred horny, hormone-rich teenagers would be out on the street causing no end of mayhem, making policing an endless round of street battles, riot gear and flashing lights. The nightclub performed a valuable role in corralling and keeping thousands of youngsters happy and safe in one place. Sheep in a pen instead of dogs running loose.

Whenever drugs or weapons were found inside, the miscreants were taken out the side door and taught a few harsh lessons by the bouncers. They would then be handed over to the police to issue on-the-spot fines, administer summary justice in a manner of their own choosing, or, in the case of knife carriers, hauled away and charged with being in possession of an illegal weapon. No further questions asked. Naturally, this all came at a cost.

"You bribed the police?"

"That's a wee bit harsh. We did our civic duty to keep young people safe inside our venue and off the streets where otherwise they'd be prey to drug pushers, pimps and slave traders. We made a lot of money and deserved to. The coppers played a vital role in that arrangement and considered a reward or commission scheme appropriate, as did I."

"So you bribed the police?"

"Semantics, young lady. Everybody was happy, even though one or two rules were applied with discretion."

"So how do you know these three guys?"

"Can't you guess?"

"Were they the friendly, malleable police officers who helped you control the streets of Ipswich?"

"As I said, it was an arrangement that suited everyone. Parker was the senior man, Cross his eager puppy sidekick and the other guy, was just a fuckin' lunatic. Excuse my Glaswegian."

"But this photo was taken before the millennium?" Antoine collects the plates and I stare at a two hundred quid bottle of Burgundy, allowing the thought to process, pondering the notion half a glass might help. Then it comes to me and it's blindingly obvious. "They went undercover."

"Well done," says Jimmy. Approbation, not sarcasm. "Parker told me he and the boys were going on a special operation that might last a year or two, and were handing over their routine responsibilities to another bunch of enthusiastic, open-minded colleagues."

It's coming at me in waves. I can see them all. The tents the beards, the protests, the banners and the confrontations with police. "They infiltrated SANE, gathered evidence and photographs and reported back to their masters. They formed relationships with some of the women, exploiting them for pleasure, as well as gain. One of the perks of the job. Then, before anyone got suspicious, or when they got someone pregnant, they promptly disappeared, leaving shattered lives and emotions in tatters."

Fleur Harding, knocked up by Dave Parker and Adam Cross and subsequently banged up in a mental hospital for over twenty years. Jason Palmer too may have feasted on the pleasures Fleur, her sister and others had to offer, free to indulge his perverted sexual appetite with impunity. All of them, soldiers on the battlefield, anonymous and unassailable, enjoying the spoils of war. Jimmy Munro has nothing to add or correct. I take it my summation is accurate.

"Did you know?"

"Not at the time. I forgot all about them until Parker resurfaced a few years later and married one of my managers."

It comes to me in a flash. "Julia? Jules? The one the champagne was for?"

Jimmy Munro eyes me carefully, suddenly suspicious. "Tell me that was a lucky guess?"

"Adam Cross's wife remembers Dave Parker coming to their wedding with his wife Julia."

"You have been a busy girl. Jules was his second wife."

"Second?"

"He saw her at one of my clubs around ninety-nine. Told me he was going to have her and divorce his wife. She was young and impressionable and her head was turned by a big swinging dick in a uniform. They went on to have two kids but as his career progressed, he became violent towards her. I think the modern term is, controlling and coercive."

"I went to his third wedding. I knew his fiancée. He admitted he'd been married before."

"Aye. Well I helped Jules put her life back together and got her the job at Chevenham. She manages the entertainment division," he says without a hint of irony. "Her teenage daughters live with their father now, and their new step-mum."

"It was at the wedding reception that news came through about another Triple-M attack. I later got a tip-off and told Parker I'd track him down."

"Tip off from who?"

"A dead person."

"One like you?"

"Similar." I'm thrilled Jimmy is prepared to make light of it and doesn't feel the need to probe. I'm sure he will at some point but in the meantime, I feel like it brings us closer together.

"So you found this Triple-M guy, they arrested him and then let him go?"

"Yep. It was Jason Palmer, their former colleague and undercover cop."

"Doesn't surprise me. He was bad news. By the way, forgot to mention," he says pouring some wine into his glass. "I said I knew that bastard but not the name. Back then he was Jason Parker."

"Parker?"

"Dave's wee brother."

I feel a surge of heightened anxiety, a blend of euphoria finally seeing a key piece of the jigsaw click into place, along with the dreadful, life-threatening certainty I'm confronting and exposing high level corruption rather than simple incompetence. "May I have some of your wine?"

# CHAPTER 30

It's after midnight when the 'S' Class pulls up outside the cottage. Becky and I had twice exchanged texts during the evening to check each was okay. I said it was going to be a long night and I may be back late, but I'd be back. When we left the restaurant, I told Ryan my address to which he'd casually replied, "Thank you Ma'am," before I noticed it was already plumbed into the satnav.

"You know where I live," I'd said to Jimmy sitting next to me.

"I own the cottage," he'd replied and I'd cursed myself for not checking out the company whose name was on the lease. Mercifully, it doesn't matter, but it shows I need to sharpen up. "I bought it from the bank. Thought maybe Rebecca would like to go back there one day and if not, well, you cannae go wrong with property can ye?"

"I have Grace's laptop."

"You'll find nothing there. When Nubilis went bust I had IT transfer everything to our systems and then erase the laptop. Some of the material was highly confidential and as a director, I wanted to ensure it remained so. Grace was already being harassed and I didn't want it falling into the wrong hands."

"What about her personal stuff?" Jimmy had said nothing at first. It's a characteristic I've come to recognise; no need to answer the question immediately, because, given time, the one asking it can usually work it out for themselves. "It's somewhere else."

"Aye. The boys gave her an external drive. I'm afraid I don't understand the technicalities."

"So where is it?"

"I have no idea. I thought you might have come across it by now. Apparently all the stuff relating to Grace's past life is on there. She was writing a book about it."

"And you were content for me to find what Grace was doing before she died and maybe, just carry on where she left off? Someone you don't actually trust?"

"Trust is something that takes time. But I formed an impression of you when we first met and you've done nothing to disabuse me of it. Quite the opposite in fact."

"What impression?"

"That your motives were honourable. That you were genuinely concerned for Rebecca. She told me what you did beating off those two chanty rasslers, and how you were kind to her. And since then, you've satisfied me you're not trying to stop her. You're trying to help. So maybe with the information to hand, you can finish the job."

"And what job's that Jimmy?"

A flash of light catches my attention. Miriam's curtains open a fraction then close again when I move my head. *Neighbourhood watch is up late tonight.*

"I loved Grace," he continues after a moment. "I tried to support her. I felt responsible because it was me who told her Adam Cross had once been a cop and it set her off. But she was out of control, what with her gambling, and she wasn't interested in making the world a better place. She suddenly knew stuff about people and tried to put pressure on them to bail her out."

"Blackmail?"

"It's a crude term but that's what it amounted to. I couldn't get involved in that and told her not to pursue it, but well, Grace was Grace. Free spirited, you called it, and you never even knew her."

"And if you hadn't introduced Adam to her, she would have been none the wiser."

295

"I had no idea their paths had crossed twenty years ago. I was just trying to help an old acquaintance and get Grace some high-quality business."

"Then I'll ask you again. Do you think she was murdered?"

"No. Whatever the cops did to her and her sister, they've done to hundreds of others in hundreds of different ways. It's disgusting what they did, but Parker was never going to be troubled by any of that. Adam maybe, but that's because he's actually a decent enough chap."

"And Palmer?"

"She didn't really know him. She was after Adam, looking for compensation for what he did to her sister and for his daughter Rebecca. And if he didn't play ball, she would go up the food chain with Parker."

It sounds straightforward and plausible and I don't believe Jimmy is lying; he's far too clever for that. I'm rather beginning to like him. "So that job you were going to offer me? Looks like I'm already doing it."

Jimmy Munro turns his head and gives me a nonchalant look. "Karen Small and my lawyers have done most of the admin and frankly, there's nothing much left of Grace's to worry about. But I'm sure between us we can settle Rebecca down, manage the situation with her mother coming out of care, and help them both move on. With or without Adam's input."

"I'm not finished with Parker, or Palmer."

"And I'm sure nothing I say will stop you. I just wonder how many lives you have left." It's a friendly warning, telling me to be cautious, but also telling me I'm on my own. "Pity you can't speak to Jules. She knew Grace and now she's looking after Becca."

"Jules and Grace knew each other?"

"You forget Grace and I had a relationship for several years, so they met once or twice at the club. And when I recommended Jules for the job at Chevenham, it was Grace who taught her about the escort business. They spent time together, got talking about the past, realised they both had history with Parker. Then when Adam reappeared by chance it all fell into place and set her off. Given the trouble she was in financially, she thought there was an opportunity."

"To put right the wrongs of the past, or to squeeze Adam and Parker for money?"

Jimmy doesn't answer. "By the way. Where did you get those photos if you don't have the drive."

"A source."

"And a journalist never reveals her sources." Jimmy checks his Rolex. "It's late. I think you should be going to yer bed." Ryan takes his cue and jumps out to open the doors. "I'll walk you to the door," says Jimmy.

I feel a growing apprehension. I desperately hope he's not expecting to come in or worse, stay. It would shatter the positive impression I've formed tonight. Jimmy Munro has a charm and an enigmatic, smouldering personality that's brought him business success, wealth and power. Some women would go weak at the knees, look past his unprepossessing physical appearance, his bare-knuckle, streetfighter persona, maybe even lust over it. But I'm not one of them. Rejection would ruin a perfectly pleasant evening and be extremely awkward, as would his discovering Becky, who's still up and waiting for a text to say I've arrived. I deliberately haven't mentioned her and he's given no indication he knows she exists. I need to send him away.

"Thanks for dinner Jimmy. And for the conversation. If I need help, can I call you?"

"If it's in my power."

"Could you arrange for me to see Becca?"

"It would be easier to get you into the nuclear facility," he says. He's not joking. "Rebecca's there until she decides to leave. She can't have any contact and anyway, she's in safe hands. Yer car will be back soon," he says, deftly changing the subject. "Ryan will put the key through the letterbox."

We stand there awkwardly for a moment.

"Aren't you goin' in?" he says. I open my mouth, not sure what to say, when I see him glance over my shoulder. Something's caught his attention and they're not Miriam's curtains twitching for once, they're mine. "Someone's waited up for ye."

I give him a swift hug and a peck on each cheek. "Goodnight Jimmy. Thanks again."

\*\*\*

I feel emotionally drained, mind still reeling from the last few hours, yet mellow from the effects of the fine food and wine and the enigmatic company. I'm relieved to be home and find Becky safe and all I want is a hug. Unfortunately, she's clearly got something on her mind.

"Did you not want to invite him in?" The words suggest consideration and generosity, even at this hour, but her chin is up and her arms folded, the body language of fatigue, suspicion and jealousy. Her expression is severe and her tone says she wants an answer.

"That was inspired."

"What was?"

"Peeking through the curtains."

"I was worried!"

"What I mean is, I had no idea how I was going to get rid of him without causing offence and having to introduce Becca's twin sister and all the complications that would entail. You got me off the hook."

"Is that what I am? A complication?" There's fire in her eyes, ready to be doused by tears.

"What's the matter?"

"Nothing!" she says and heads for the kitchen.

"Becky?" I throw my jacket and scarf on the sofa and follow her. "Tell me."

"Tell you what?"

"What's wrong?"

"It's time I went home." It's abrupt, revealing not a considered judgment but a reaction. She's upset.

"Okay," I say calmly. "When?"

"Tomorrow." Her back's turned, arms still folded. I place a hand on her shoulder and feel her tense. "It's all getting too much. Crazy families, drugs and prostitutes, police and villains, death and serial killers. Me cowering under the table all night, frightened half to death about who's going to come knocking on the door while you're out schmoozing with Mr McMafia. I don't need this anymore!"

She's right, of course. An innocent call for help a few weeks ago had turned into something sinister and potentially dangerous, especially for me, and I knew it was happening. It's why I wanted her to take precautions. But now, I've drawn her into this mess. All she was trying to do was find out the circumstances of her abandonment as a baby, fully aware there might be an emotional price to pay. But instead, she's discovered she's the by-product of dysfunctional individuals who lived in a world far removed from her own, who were subjected to exploitation and abuse that persists to this day and which is now dragging her down too. It's no wonder she's beginning to react. The wonder is she hasn't reacted before now. I wrap an arm around her chest and pull her back against me.

"You're right. I'll take you to the station in the morning." There's only ten years between us, but I'm overcome with a sense of maternity I've never experienced before, a sense of responsibility and devotion combined. It's precious and wonderful and fills me with love and trepidation in equal measure. But that's not all it is. Her hair tickles my nose and lips and I gently inhale the aroma of fresh shampoo and it makes me tingle. I can't help what I feel, but I have to keep it at bay.

"I was jealous," she says, almost in a whisper, laying one hand on my arm. She's had wine and time to think and knows exactly what she's saying. I've had wine too and my emotions are in freefall.

*Back off Kate!*

    *...take yer opportunities when they arise.*

*You know this will end badly.*

    *...do I deny myself, just because of what I am?*

*You're selling her a lie.*

    *...a truth like mine, with no believers, has no value.*

*You have the power. Use it, don't abuse it.*

    *...how can love be abuse?*

*She's mortal, Kate. You'll watch her wither and die.*

    *...it's a price I'm willing to pay.*

*She'll hate you for it. Are you willing to pay that?*

I spin her around and wrap both arms around her, pressing her head into my shoulder, every single cell in my body telling me to resist, stop the unstoppable force.

"You've had too much wine," I whisper in her ear.

"Or not enough."

It lightens the moment and I feel the mists clear. "This is not going to happen Becky."

"I know. I understand."

"Doesn't mean I don't love you."

She squeezes me harder and it's my cue to release. She wipes a hand across her eyes.

"Sorry. I'll stay if you want me to."

"I have loads to tell you. Maybe we can discuss it in the morning?"

# CHAPTER 31

It takes ninety minutes to get to the main entrance. There is no signage, nothing to indicate there's a stately home and landscaped gardens behind the eight foot stone wall and heavy wooden gates. I drive slowly past twice but there is no sign of activity, the doors remaining steadfastly shut. There's no phone number and no panel of buttons that I can use to even try to talk my way in there and if I approached the gates, the CCTV would pick me up and two heavies would arrive to see me off. I drive on for a quarter of a mile and park in a layby.

I found the key on the mat and the Mini parked outside, just as Jimmy had promised. By seven, I'd already been up for two hours reading Grace's paperwork and emails and looking at Des's photos when Becky joined me for breakfast in bare feet and tee-shirt, just like her sister had on the first day. Her hair was tangled and she yawned as she filled the kettle.

"I'm sorry about last night," she said sitting opposite me at the table. "Call it tired and emotional."

"I need to apologise, not you. I didn't appreciate what you were going through. Too wrapped up in my own thoughts."

"Don't you ever sleep?"

"I will when this is all over."

"When what's all over?"

I told her everything about my evening with Jimmy, explained the connections between the players and the increasing likelihood that Grace's death was not sinister, just an unfortunate accident.

"Do you trust him?"

"Yes, I do. He has nothing to gain. He wants to make sure Becca is looked after, just like I do."

"So why didn't Becca go to him for help? Why come to you?"

301

"She did. But he didn't agree Grace was murdered, and given the knowledge he had, felt he couldn't explain why. They weren't that close anyway. They lost touch when she was sixteen and he and Grace split up."

"I'd like to stay and see it through," she says, staring into her mug. "I want to meet Fleur and be sure she's okay and I want to meet my crazy sister and check she's okay too," she said with an ironic laugh, before turning anxious. "Are you still going after Palmer?"

"The first thing I'm going to do is visit Chevenham."

I lock the Mini and return on foot, following the line of a wall that seems to go on forever. There is no breach, no sightline to what's beyond and no possibility of climbing over. Deflated, and unsure what to do next, I return to the car and dial Becca's number. I get the generic voicemail as expected.

"Becca, it's Kate. I've met Jimmy, and Miles has sent me Grace's laptop and files. I know where you are and why, and I know it's very difficult for you, but I'd love to see you. I have a lot to tell you." I don't know if she'll see it, whether her phone is being monitored or has been confiscated, but it might just provoke a reaction. It's dangerous, but I suspect more dangerous for her career than for me.

A white delivery truck trundles by and catches my attention, a welcome distraction from frustration and creeping paranoia. It looks incongruous on a 'B' road in the middle of nowhere. I follow at a distance. *'Elite Catering Supplies – Servicing Prestige Hospitality'* reads the lettering on the back. It slows down as it reaches the entrance to Chevenham and indicates to turn in towards the gates. I speed up and turn with it, slipping in close behind, hidden from the truck's mirrors. There's no overt communication but within moments, the heavy wooden gates swing open and I follow the truck along a winding tarmac road, staying as close as I dare.

After half a mile, the house looms into view and the truck turns onto a side road leading to the rear of the property. I stay behind until we reach a gravel car park lined with shrubs. No luxury vehicles here, most of the cars are modest and of varying ages. *Staff car park.* The truck trundles on ahead and I slip into a space between two cars. I've set off no alarms, and no armed guards in SWAT gear have appeared, screaming at me to get out.

I leave jacket and phone in the car and stride purposefully towards an entrance but the wired-glass door is locked, controlled by an electronic panel on the wall. I proceed around the building, following the route of the truck and find the driver unloading by the open service doors, lowering wheeled cages on a hydraulic tailgate. Once they're on the ground he rolls them through the doors one at a time before coming back for the next. I wait until he disappears inside the truck before walking briskly through the opening. Four cages stand in a passageway, some full of boxes and shrink-wrapped packaged foodstuff, one devoted to cleaning supplies, another stacked with baskets of fruit and vegetables. The whoosh of extractor fans fills the air and up ahead, lights and sounds suggest the frenetic activity of a busy kitchen.

I walk towards it and come across an open cupboard, shelves stacked with kitchen uniforms: tunics, aprons, bibs and bandannas. I grab one of each and hastily slip them on as I hear the clatter behind me.

"Can I have a signature please?" says a voice from behind. The driver is in a brown two-piece uniform. He hands me a pen and a four-page multi-coloured delivery note and I stare at it, not sure what to do other than glance up and down at the cages before appending a squiggle. "Cheers sweetheart," he says, taking back the sheaf of papers before separating the copies and handing me the blue set.

I step tentatively towards the kitchen and take a look through half-glass doors. I count twelve people in various grades of uniform, heads down preparing food, or moving purposefully from one place to another, dodging each other with practised skill. I take a deep breath and push at the doors. The heat hits me in the face, the volume, magnified by a factor of ten. A young black man in similar garb to me is working at a bench by the door, hunched over a chopping board, slicing vegetables at high speed.

"I'm coming," he says without looking up.

I waive the papers in the air. "I got it."

He looks up and frowns "Who are you?"

"Temp. What do I do with these?"

"Office," he says, jerking his head towards another set of doors before resuming his work without further comment. So consumed are they by their tasks, no one pays any attention to me as I walk confidently through the doors into a corridor that has walk-in fridges on each side and doors, marked *'Dry Goods', 'Consumables'* and *'Cellar'*. I reach the end where it crosses another, looking left and right, unsure what to do, when a guy in shirtsleeves and jeans suddenly appears.

"Lost?"

"Office?" I say, holding aloft the blue papers.

"Down there," he says, pointing over his shoulder before continuing on his way.

The door has a glass panel and I can see activity inside. I grasp the handle and push the door open a few inches. Six women are seated at desks, tapping away on keyboards, plus a man on the phone at the far end behind a glass partition.

"Excuse me? Where do I leave these?"

"In that tray darlin'," says a middle aged woman, who removes her glasses and looks me up and down. "Who are you then?"

"Kate. I'm temping in the kitchen." She nods in acknowledgement and goes back to her work. It feels like the inner sanctum, the administrative engine room for the entire operation. Despite the apparent security, it was easy to get in, but I can't keep up the charade for long. Jimmy Munro's voice rings in my ears. *You have to take yer opportunities when they arise!* I take a deep breath. "Becca recommended me," I continue. "Becca Harding. She's a good friend of mine." They ignore me. "Don't suppose you can tell her I'm here? I'm on a break." Still no reaction. "I'd tell her myself but I'm not allowed a phone for some reason."

A young woman opposite exchanges a glance with middle-aged, then taps on her computer and speaks through her headset. "Shar? Is Becca busy at the moment? Girl in the kitchen wants to see her."

"Kate," I offer helpfully.

"Kate. Yeah, okay. Here in the office."

"No! I'll see her outside, behind the kitchen."

"Service yard," she says into the mouthpiece and then looks at me. "Five minutes."

"Thanks."

"How long you here for Kate?" says middle-aged.

"Last day."

"Enjoyed it?"

"Yeah. Hard work though."

"Mind how you go."

I retrace my steps past the storerooms and fridges and back through the kitchen, increasingly nervous of being challenged, but thankfully, everyone's too busy, apart from black guy.

"Get the dairy and perishables in the fridge," he says without looking up.

"Yes chef!"

I leave the way I came in and stand outside. The truck has gone and there's no one about. I can only risk five minutes before someone comes by or comes looking. I wait and wait, increasingly anxious. I'm looking left and right when I hear the click of footsteps behind me.

"Kate?" She looks stunning, her dress casual yet sophisticated, with trademark heels, professional make-up and exquisitely cut hair with subtle highlights. "What the fuck?"

"I hope you moderate your language for clients."

Becca Harding gives me a big smile and runs forward, throwing her arms around me. Her scent is Chanel or Dior; whatever it is, it's expensive. "How did you find me?"

"No time for that Becca. Are you okay?"

"Yeah! I'm great."

"You're not a prisoner here?"

"God no! What makes you think…?"

"No matter. I needed to know you were safe, that's all."

"Aw, that's sweet. Yeah. I'm good. Loving it."

"So why the radio silence?"

"Have you been messaging me?"

"Of course I have! I thought you'd been kidnapped, for goodness sake."

"No, it wasn't like that," she laughs. "I so wanted to let you know but they wouldn't allow it."

"Who?"

"Jules. The management. I had to give up my phone and contacts, stay off grid while I was here or else leave. It's the rules; all about client confidentiality, you know, no bragging on Instagram about which president you shagged."

"I need to talk to you."

"Go ahead."

"Not here, not now. Can you get time off?"

She laughs again, radiant and intoxicating. just like her twin but in a far more expressive way. "Are you kidding? It's a one-way ticket. Once you leave you leave and you don't come back. Those are the rules."

"Then leave."

"I can't. I'm earning mega good money here. What am I going to do out there?" she says, waving an arm at nowhere in particular.

"It's got to end someday."

"Kate. I'm sorry I wasted your time. I'm over all that now. Jimmy convinced me, and it was never my fight anyway. But at least now I can pay you for your trouble. And the clothes! How much do I owe you?"

"Nothing! You don't owe me anything. But I have unfinished business and this time I'm asking you for help."

"I don't know what I can do."

"There must be special dispensation? Time off for family bereavement or something?"

She shakes her head in frustration. "What's so important anyway?"

I fear we'll run out of time. If we carry on arguing like this someone will come by, I'll be uncovered as an imposter, an investigative journalist disguised as a kitchen porter, talking to one of the escorts. I'll be kicked out, or worse, and she'll be fired instantly. Getting her dismissed might be a good thing in the long run but she'd never forgive me. It has to be her choice, but I don't have time to explain.

"Everything I have is in there," she says pointing at the gothic pile behind her. "My work, my friends, my life is in there, doing what I do best and I'm paid well and treated well. There's nothing out there for me. I don't have anyone anymore."

I understand her and I'm torn. She looks happy and content and if she's going to stay in the trade, better she does it in opulent surroundings at premium rates with all the safety and security a place like Chevenham can provide, rather than go on the street and be at the mercy of some low life. *Take your opportunities*. Grace made her what she is and it gave her a living, but Grace is gone. We both know what she has here is unsustainable, that she'll be cast out in a year or so. But the

307

truth is the truth and however painful and inconvenient, it will be told, even if hearts are broken.

"What about your mother?"

"Grace is dead."

"I mean your real mother."

"What about her?"

"I know where she is and I know who your father is."

She shakes her head, wrapping her arms around her chest. "They're nobody to me."

"And your twin sister."

Becca backs away a step, shaking her head in denial. "No, I don't believe you."

"She's staying with me at No.1 Rose Cottages. Holburgh. Her name's Becky."

***

I drive home, relieved to see Becca in such good spirits, despondent she chose to go back, but in the round, respectful of her decision. It's not for me to dictate to adults their choice of lifestyle, but I wanted her to do it in full possession of the facts and we simply had no time. It's a dilemma for her and one I wouldn't wish to have. But maybe it's for the best.

I gave her another hug then stripped off my kitchen uniform and handed it to her. She made no promises. She didn't think it was possible but she'd think about it and one way or another, get a message to me. She had to prepare for a client. He'd asked for the pretty redhead again; a Middle Eastern deputy minister of finance with a hundred billion dollars invested in Europe, a tiny fraction of it on the Suffolk coast. He's courteous and polite and generous with his tips. She's one of a complement of twenty that includes women to suit all tastes, two gay boys, and one of each who are trans. The common factor is they are all unattached, have no close family and no responsibilities.

"So my sister really is a prostitute," said Becky, handing me a chilled glass of white wine. "Albeit a high class one."

"Were you in any doubt?"

"Suppose not. I just hoped..."

"Do you think any less of her because of it?"

***

We've had dinner and Smokey has come to visit. Becky's stretched out on the sofa, and he's lying on her belly, eyes closed, but constantly alert. The dead one needs to be watched.

"How did she react when you told her about me?"

"Same as you did. Shock, disbelief, suspicion."

"Was she not even a little bit curious about her father?"

"She didn't have time to think about it. I didn't give her a name; there was no way I could tell her about Adam. It was all too much to dump on her in the time available. I just wanted to get her attention."

We're interrupted by a loud knock on the front door. Smokey's immediately awake, ears twitching. He jumps down and heads for the kitchen. We look at each other and she checks her watch.

"It's eleven-thirty."

"Get the rolling pin," I say, struck by the absurdity of using it as a weapon, but it's all I can think of in the moment; we have nothing else. Becky leaps to her feet while I tentatively approach the door. The knock comes again, louder this time. "Who is it?" The letterbox flap pulls open and I jump out of the way, just as Becky returns wielding a smooth cylinder of hardwood.

"Kate?" says the voice through the letterbox. "Is that you?"

I look at Becky and Becky looks at me, slack jawed. I release the chain and unlock the door and throw it open.

"Hi," says Becca. "Can I come in?"

# PART 3

# CHAPTER 32

They didn't know what to do, nor what to say. Apart from the hairstyle and colouring, it was as if each were looking in a mirror, staring at an image of someone familiar looking back at them, each unable to tear their eyes away. It was Becca who finally broke the silence.

"Wow. You weren't kidding. Hi sis," she said, noticing the rolling pin for the first time and looking a little bewildered. Becky handed it to me and Becca dropped her bag on the floor. They threw their arms around each other, gripping tightly.

"She certainly wasn't," said Becky, but her voice cracked and she began to shake. "Welcome home."

I offered her wine but she wanted water and I offered her food but she wasn't hungry. She said she was tired and I told her to sleep in my room but she insisted on the couch. Smokey wandered back to see what the commotion was and I introduced him. Becca had never met him before, but he made a thorough assessment of the visitor and chose the couch too.

We had so much to say, it was impossible to say anything, so we agreed to keep our thoughts to ourselves and start with a clear head the next day. I lay awake, relieved to see her, but not at all certain what this reunion was going to achieve and where it would all go from here. I could see the light in Becky's room and it stayed on until well after midnight. I checked downstairs at around 3 a.m. and Becca was fast asleep. Smokey had gone out hunting.

I watched the clock until five, talking to Edith from time to time but she was obviously too busy to reply and the next thing I knew it was after six, so I must have finally dropped off. An hour should be enough. Radio news reports the man arrested for Triple-M has been released on bail pending further enquiries. They've ruled Trevor out as a prime suspect but figure they can still get him on minor charges like sexual harassment, just to show a positive outcome. Despite the accusations I levelled at Parker, they would never get his prints on Palmer's gun.

\*\*\*

We're at the breakfast table, waiting for Becca to finish her shower, when Becky says, "I heard you talking in your sleep. Who's Edith?"

"Edith is my great, great, Grandmother. What makes you think I was asleep?"

"You were talking to a dead person wide awake?" she says, more in pity then genuine curiosity.

"How do you know she's dead?"

"She'd be a hundred and fifty by now."

"Who would?" says Becca rubbing her shock of red hair with a towel and pulling up a chair next to Becky.

"My great, great, Grandmother Edith Hawley. She worked in Soho at the beginning of the 20th century."

"Soho?" they say together like a double act, then laugh out loud.

"Yes, she was a prostitute."

"Oh wow," says Becca, then almost as an afterthought, "I hate that word."

"She was mistreated and abused and took the only way open to her," I say quickly, not wishing to dwell on semantics.

"But...she's not still alive?" says Becky, hesitantly.

"She was hanged in 1912."

"Oh God!" says Becca, one hand over her mouth. She has something in common with Edith so it's especially disturbing for her to hear.

"She stabbed Lord Julian Fitzgerald to death in a house of ill repute, and they hanged her for it."

"Jesus!" says Becky, joining in.

312

"He deserved it, she didn't. But ever since I found out about her, I've been asking her for advice, which she never gives. She does, however, sometimes give me advice I don't think I need, until I do. She can be quite infuriating." The twins give me that look, unsure whether I'm pulling legs or not but it would be pointless to explain. Instead, I make scrambled eggs with smoked salmon while I listen to Becky telling her sister about her family in West Sussex.

"Three brothers?"

"Yep?"

"Any of them rich, famous and hot?" says Becca with a glint in her eye. "I'll take any one from three."

"They're brothers!"

"So? They're not mine."

"Good as. Anyway, two are married with kids and Ben the youngest is gay."

"Too bad!"

We're having fun, and it's a joy to have two vivacious young woman around my table, but I have to be realistic. We have emotional hurdles to jump and they're coming up fast.

\*\*\*

She's unnecessarily contrite. "I had no idea who you were," she says, once we've cleared away the breakfast things and are on a fresh pot of coffee. "Adam made me so mad and Jimmy's hassling me on the phone and then I almost get run off the road by a big black Merc. I'm beginning to think everyone's after me, so when you turn up, I don't know whether you're friend or foe. I mean, no one drives two or three hours at night on a hunch and claims to be acting in the best interests of someone they've never met. Do they?"

"Not usually. It was instinct. Just like yours about Grace."

"I felt it was more than instinct, but I couldn't say so at the time…"

313

"Because you didn't trust me?"

"I didn't know you!"

"You still don't know me."

"I know you better now, and anyway, my twin sister vouches for you," she says brightening and winking at Becky. It's pure Becca. She wants to make light of everything, despite how serious it might be. I would like to join in the bonhomie, but we have to face the truth whatever that might be. "I want to explain." She notices my sober expression. "Why the serious face?"

"So, explain."

Grace was anxious. Anxious in a way Becca had never known before. She'd blown everything through her own stupidity and now she was alone and penniless and there was nothing anyone could do. Becca said she'd give up university and they'd work on the escort business together but Grace wouldn't have it, insisted she kept up her studies, unaware she'd already left. Grace told her she had her own life to live and she needed to keep away for her own safety. Grace had one last throw of the dice, a lifeline, which, if it worked would allow her to get back on an even keel.

Jimmy Munro introduced Grace to a man she'd known twenty years ago. She didn't tell Becca his name, who he was, or why she knew him, but Grace had learned something about his past to be able to put pressure on him to help ease her financial burden. She also knew he had acquaintances in high places who had something to hide. Not just infidelity; she'd never betray the confidence of her clients, even those she knew were complete scumbags and deserved it. This was corruption pure and simple, the sort that ruined people's lives and needed to be made public, unless of course, the men concerned were prepared to be accommodating. Principles are all very well but first we need to eat.

"That's all she told me. She said best I didn't know any more for my own safety, and it frightened me. She sounded so

314

confident I believed she'd be okay and because she wouldn't give me any details I couldn't help her even if I wanted to."

"You didn't tell her you flunked university after year one?"

"How could I? She would have been so disappointed. I wasn't doing very well there, I didn't want any more student debt and she didn't have any money, so I had to earn it for myself, day and night."

"Adam Cross was the guy she knew from twenty years ago."

"Adam?" she says, genuinely shocked. "I knew what they were up to, I caught them at it in the pub one night, all schmoozy and lovey, dovey."

"And you threw a pint of lager over him."

"Yeah," she says, laughing at the memory. "Okay. I was jealous. I admit it."

"They had a relationship before you two were born."

"Oh wow."

"I have to ask you something Becca and I want you to tell me the truth."

"Course!" She glances at Becky who looks away nervously. She wishes she were somewhere else.

"You told me you and Adam had an affair."

"Yeah. So what?"

"Did you sleep with him?"

Becca looks back and forth between me and Becky. Unlike me, Becky can't look at her.

"Nah. I tried, but he kept making excuses."

"You told me you did."

"I just said that. Sometimes I just say things," she says, as if it's something outside her control. "I wanted to, and I thought maybe he and I had a future. He was fit and well off and he wasn't happy at home because his wife refused to have sex with him, so I thought there was an opportunity for me. But he kept resisting until I gave up and then found out he and Grace had a thing going. That's why I got so mad."

315

"Grace didn't explain who he was?"

"Only to say she knew him from way back."

"Tell her," says Becky, joining the conversation.

"Tell me what?" says Becca, unsettled by her sister's intervention. There's no reason not to. I don't know what I would say if she insisted she'd been intimate with Adam, but it's beginning to look like he was telling the truth. He resisted Becca's advances, firstly because he was already having a relationship with Grace and secondly, because he feared she might be his daughter. He may have denied it to Grace, but he couldn't be certain, and he wasn't prepared to take a chance. Instinct may have played a part too, Becca's appearance and mannerisms leading him to believe Grace's assertion of his paternity was more than just bluster and blackmail. He just might have gone up in my estimation.

"There's a good chance Adam is your father."

Becca takes a sharp intake of breath, her mouth and eyes wide open in shock.

"Mine too," says Becky, so as not to be left out.

"Jesus! I almost…"

"But you didn't."

"So he knew?"

"He only knew what Grace told him, but he said it could just as easily have been someone else. There's no proof, unless we get a DNA test."

"Who's someone else?"

"Any one of several," says Becky. "Apparently Fleur was quite promiscuous."

"Fleur?"

"Our Mum. She's in a psychiatric home in Brighton."

"That's not right! She abandoned me and ran off." Becca's shock, now compounded, is making her argumentative.

"She flipped and was sectioned. She's been there for over twenty years."

"How do you know?"

316

"It's all in Grace's files. I'm amazed you didn't find out when you were packing up that box."

Becca shakes her head, still reeling from twin revelations about her parents. "I didn't even look at the paperwork. I didn't have time. I got into her laptop but there was nothing there. She had nothing, she'd lost the cottage and Jimmy said he'd deal with it all and I was in a rush and I was being threatened and then that nosy old cow next door is hassling me..." She buries her face in her hands.

"Easy Becca," I say. "It's a lot to take in."

Becky pulls her sister towards her and they hold on tight. Mutual support. It's a moment before Becca comes up for air and I hand her a tissue. "Have you seen her?" she asks.

Becky shakes her head. "To tell you the truth, I was a bit afraid what I might find, but...we could go together if you like?"

"Don't know if I could handle it. Did she really go mental?"

"She had a breakdown of some sort," I say. "But Becky's found correspondence that suggests she's better now. They've judged her fit to leave."

"Wow," says Becca, shaking her head.

\*\*\*

Over the next few hours we chat, drink tea and coffee, laugh a bit, cry a bit, discuss Fleur and Adam and of course, Grace, speculating on how she met her untimely end.

Becca had already formed the view Grace was in danger. Grace told her she'd been to a national newspaper but so far had little success because she didn't have enough evidence. Jimmy knew what she was up to, the information Grace had, came from him in the first place, starting with Adam.

"Jimmy owns the cottage," I say out loud. "He told me he bought it in case you wanted to come back."

317

"Did he really?" says Becca. "That's very sweet of him."

"Can't wait to meet Uncle Jimmy," said Becky.

"Oh, you'd like him," says Becca. "He frightens most people but he's really a pussycat."

I roll my eyes, partly at the image of Jimmy Munro as a pussycat and partly because the saga is getting more complex by the hour. He urged her to take the assignment at Chevenham Hall, for which she'd be well paid. He asked her to deliver a parcel for him. I showed her the champagne and chocolates and the card addressed to Jules that I found in the back of the Mini.

"Wasn't drugs then?" says Becca, mildly relieved.

"Jimmy wasn't happy when I accused him of using you as his mule."

"I can imagine, but what was I supposed to think after that text from Miles? Jesus!" she says, having a sudden thought. "Is his car still at motorway services?"

"It was taken to a pound near Stoke. He's got it back now. I went to York looking for you and I found him."

"How was he?" she said.

"Worried, and a bit shaken at having the cops come round, but then when you cut all communication, he assumed he'd been dumped and you were on the run."

Becca looked contrite. "I had no way of contacting anyone. But, I admit I was going to dump him when I got home, that much is true."

"Call him later."

She had already been to the police insisting Grace's death was suspicious but they weren't interested in pursuing it and in desperation, she got in touch with Adam, but he said he couldn't get involved. Jimmy told her to leave it. He was sure Grace's death was an accident. Then she started getting anonymous emails and texts, telling her not to pursue or repeat her assertions to anyone and threatening her with harm if she did. I told her there were never any drugs. The guys who

318

turned up at the cottage on a 'drugs bust' were probably the same guys who tracked her to South Alston and the same guys who raided Miles's flat on a pretext. Heavy-handed cops trying to intimidate her, sending her a message to shut up.

"I should have trusted you, I'm sorry," she said at one point.

"You had no reason to."

"After you left me in the barn, I kept getting messages from Jimmy to call him, so eventually I did. He asked where I was, because I hadn't turned up at Chevenham and I told him about you and those bad guys. He asked who you were and I said you were a friend of Adam's and he said it would be better if he sent a car to take me to Chevenham. He said Jules would let me stay a while until the dust settled. So I said okay. He asked me if I still had the parcel and I had to tell him I'd lost it. He said not to worry, it wasn't that valuable."

"The police weren't looking for drugs. They were looking for you. But why didn't you go to Chevenham in the first place?"

"I was on my way, but this big SUV came up close behind flashing his lights and what with all the messages and threats, I got panicky and had to swerve off the main road to lose them. I was frightened and still upset about Grace and I wasn't in the mood for shagging some strange guy, but when I got there a couple of days later I was amazed. It turned out to be a big operation, nothing like I expected. If I'd known that at the time, I wouldn't have hesitated."

Jules interviewed Becca at length over the course of the next few days, introduced her to two of the more experienced women and decided she was suitable to work there. Due to the highly sensitive profiles of their clientele, strict secrecy was demanded. Like all the others, she had to agree to give up her phone and for the duration of her stay, have no contact with the outside world apart from limited, carefully controlled and monitored internet access. Anyone found guilty of an indiscretion or breaking the rules would be instantly dismissed and all their earnings forfeited. She didn't have access to money; she didn't need it because everything was provided by Chevenham, but she had online access to her joint bank account so she could see her earnings accumulating. These would be released to her if and when they decided to terminate her contract. She'd already earned over thirty thousand pounds in the short time she'd been there.

"You said Chevenham was a one-way ticket. Have you burned bridges coming here?"

"I honestly don't know. I told Jules at the outset I had no family ties because it was true, and then you come along and tell me otherwise. She said I could have a week to find out the truth and then if I wanted to go back, she'd think about it. She said she'd miss me, but realistically, a lot of escorts don't last more than six months before they're moved on."

"Did you tell her about me?"

"Er, yeah. Is that okay?"

"Jules is an old friend of Jimmy's. Grace taught her about the escort business."

"Wow," says Becca for umpteenth time. "She never said."

It's no surprise. Admitting she knew Grace might have inferred special status on Becca and Jules would want to keep her at arm's length like all the others. But it may have been a factor in agreeing to give Becca leave of absence; if she really did have a family out there, best find out now. I'm certain she would have checked me out with Jimmy, which means he now knows Becca is here.

I checked the time and made us some lunch. Becky told us about her upcoming job in Internet Marketing Strategy for a major multi-national and Becky told us about the Arab deputy finance minister. "This time he just wanted to watch me and Leah act out one of his fantasies and take video of us, you know, getting it on."

"Is that it?"

320

"Yeah. Don't know what he paid Chevenham, but we each got a two grand tip."

"I'm in the wrong job," says Becky.

"No you're not. The boys and girls talk about it a lot, and we all fear the day one of us gets hurt."

I tell her about what happened to me at South Alston and the connection between Adam, Parker and Palmer.

"You actually went looking for the creep?"

"I can't be sure he's the Triple-M guy, but I do know he's a violent sexual predator."

It begs the obvious question and in the spirit of truth and honesty, I tell her about Annabel.

"That woman hitting on you was Adam's wife?" says Becca with amazement. "But how come she was next door?"

"Coincidence," says Becky. "It's just Kate doesn't believe it."

"I have no explanation, but I'll find out eventually."

"So that's why you called me Maddy? Jesus! And she thought you and I were…?" I nod in agreement. "No wonder she was pissed off. And no wonder their marriage is on the rocks. Where was Adam?"

"Went back to London for a meeting. At least that's what he told Annabel. They're getting a divorce."

"Because of me?"

"And because she's decided she's a lesbian."

"Wow!"

"By the way, she doesn't bear a grudge against you."

"She didn't do anything," says Becky, leaping to her sister's defence.

"But Annabel thinks she did."

"Well, he was still unfaithful with Grace."

"Our dad," says Becca wistfully.

"Annabel doesn't know her husband may have been your father."

"That's going to come as a shock," says Becca.

321

I give her my phone and she calls Miles and they have a long chat. He's relieved she's okay, annoyed she's not been in contact and only half believes the story she wasn't allowed to contact anyone, is sad they're splitting up but accepts it's the right thing to do and, he said, at least he got his car back.

"Arse!" says Becca when she's finished.

"Don't be too hard on him. At least he sent back your stuff along with Grace's laptop."

"Yeah," says Becky. "And this necklace." She feels inside her tee-shirt and pulls it out.

"Forgot about that, but you can keep it. I never liked it."

"I need to be getting home," says Becky. "Mum and Dad will be wondering if I'm ever coming back. Maybe I could catch the four-fifteen from Southwold?"

"Okay. Becca can have her old room back until she decides what she wants to do."

"Don't go sis. Stay another night. We've loads to talk about. So much to catch up on."

Becky doesn't take much persuading. She calls her mum and tells her she'll be back tomorrow.

"So, Grace was threatening to expose Adam and Dave Parker for being undercover cops twenty odd years ago. Not just for all the emotional damage they did fathering you two and maybe others but for causing Fleur's mental breakdown. Grace picked up the tab for one of you and the state picked up the tab for Fleur's care but that was about to end. It looks like Grace wanted money to keep quiet; money to settle her own debts and money either to keep Fleur locked up or able to support herself. She obviously rattled cages and by the sound of it, the police were trying to stop her and stop you carrying on where she left off."

"It was Jimmy who told me to clear the place, take her laptop and any paperwork that was lying around."

"He'd already removed all traces of Nubilis and he'd got you settled at Chevenham, but didn't want to take responsibility for dealing with Fleur and any fallout from the cops. But he knew I did."

"What's Jimmy got to gain in all this?" asks Becky.

She's right. I asked him the same question last night and I didn't get a definitive answer other than bland comments about helping to settle Becca down and coping with the aftermath of Grace's death, especially in the context of her mother's imminent release. He appeared to do the decent thing keeping Becca out of harm's way when she was being harassed by two men, denying they were his and implying they were police. After a cautious start with me, he's now conciliatory if not downright flattering, listing my attributes, praising my attitude. To what end? I may simply be a challenge, someone who spurned his offer of a job in his organisation, his 'harem', and needs to be persuaded, for his own gratification. Or is there still work to be done and he wants me to do it?

"I don't think he's on any crusade to expose malpractice in the police. It's not in his interests and I suspect he's seen much worse than that in his time. But that's different from murder. He knew what Palmer was like twenty-five years ago, so he's not surprised at his behaviour now nor the fact he's the prime suspect. He has warned me to stay away for my own safety."

"But you won't," says Becky flashing me an angry look, the sort of look that's reserved for family. Loved ones. "What on earth can you do? What on earth can any of us do if we don't have police on our side?" She slumps back on the sofa and tucks her legs underneath her.

"Do our best."

"And get killed in the process?"

She's right of course. No one in their right mind would even try. But those of sound mind are burdened by their mortality. I need to change the subject.

"Jimmy says there's a separate hard drive with all Grace's personal information on it, and presumably all the evidence

323

she gathered regarding the undercover police operation. We just don't know where it is." I think of Grace and Fleur and undercover cops with their arms around Des and his number written on a yellow post-it note that I found in a jacket along with a mysterious key. It makes me go into the kitchen and retrieve the key from a storage jar where I kept it safe. "Do you know what this is?"

"Yeah. It looks like the key to her jewellery box," says Becca.

"What jewellery box? It wasn't with her other stuff," says Becky.

"She had nothing valuable, mostly costume jewellery and hippy trash. Just like that necklace. She wore it all the time and used to keep that key on it, so she didn't lose it. But the box was definitely here the day I took the laptop. I remember seeing it. But when I came by after the funeral, it was gone."

"Dean the estate agent let himself in before the place was cleared."

"I can't believe Dean took it," says Becky. "Not his style at all!" she continues, laughing and I'm pleased to see her lighten up. Then I look at her and she looks at me.

"Miriam," we say in unison.

"I accused her of nicking it," says Becca, "but she denied it. Said the police took it."

"She still has a key to the cottage."

"Really? I'd get that back if I were you."

"She told me about the dildo."

"Oh God! Is she still bitter?"

"Just a bit. Maybe it's time to kiss and make up?"

Becca grunts and sits back on the sofa, arms folded, not entirely convinced. I go next door and knock. She's wearing yellow latex gloves.

"Hi Miriam. I wondered if you knew what happened to Grace's jewellery box?"

"Why do you ask?"

324

"Because it's not amongst her belongings."

"Yes I do," she says prissily. "I took it for safekeeping. I didn't want those removal men to steal it. Anyway, Grace said she was going to leave it to me because Rebecca didn't want any of her...trinkets."

"Do you mind if I take a look?"

Miriam's face clouds over. "Why?"

"I'm guessing you can't open it. Unless you broke the lock?"

"I did no such thing. I took it to a locksmith in Southwold, but they were sniffy because I couldn't prove it was mine."

"I have the key."

"Oh!" she says brightening. "Well then that's okay." I almost expect her to hold out a hand.

"Rebecca's here. Both of them. Perhaps you'd like to come over for a cup of tea? There's something she wants to say to you."

"Who?"

"Becca. The one you used to know."

"What? Now?"

"Yes, and bring the box with you, if you don't mind."

"Why?"

"I think it would be a nice gesture if you asked Becca's permission to keep Grace's jewellery? Asked both of them, in fact."

Miriam's face says it all. "I have nothing to say to that young...woman," she says, spitting out the word. "Grace said I could have it and that's that!"

"Maybe, but it's not in the will so technically, it belongs to Becca. I'm sure the girls will accept your explanation, and I know Becca has no interest in her 'trinkets', as you say. But Becky has the right to take a look, don't you think?" Miriam puffs out her chest and her face goes red. "And Becca wants to apologise."

"Does she indeed?"

"And so do you."

"What for?"

"For letting yourself into my home last week to look for this key?" I hold it up in front of her nose and she squirms. "I think it's time to let bygones be bygones? I'll go and put the kettle on."

***

It takes her fifteen minutes. She's changed into smarter clothes, doused herself in perfume and done something to her face and hair to soften her appearance. In one hand she's carrying a plate with a cake and under her other arm, a leather-covered box. Both wrists are laden with multi-coloured bangles, trinkets of her own.

"I brought a lemon drizzle. As a peace offering."

The twins get to their feet, all three of them looking awkward. We'd already discussed it and surmised Miriam had no interest in the necklace, all she wanted was the key to the box. It's Becca who takes the lead.

"Hi Miriam," she says sweetly. "Thanks for bringing the jewellery and for the yummy cake!"

"Yes, thanks Miriam," says Becky.

Becca steps forward and gives Miriam a hug which makes her tense up, unsure how or whether to reciprocate.

"I'm sorry I was such a bitch," says Becca. I'm praying she's not about to remind us exactly what she did. I made her promise not to, however tempting.

"Well, we all make mistakes," says Miriam. I brace for a reaction from Becca but it's just Miriam's cackhanded turn of phrase. "I'm sorry I came snooping around looking for the key. I should have asked first. It used to be second nature letting myself into Grace's house. I forget she's gone. I miss her terribly."

"I miss her too," says Becca.

326

I make the tea and we demolish half the cake. Becca and Miriam talk fondly about old times while Becky and I can only listen. They venture close to the edge at times, referring to each other's behaviour under pressure and how the other reacted, but here in this atmosphere, enjoying a shared experienced and out of respect for the dear departed, they're both able to see the funny side.

"She used to keep the key around her neck. I never understood why she bothered to lock her jewellery away when there was nothing of any value."

"Why bother indeed?" I say, tiredness descending. Miriam never wanted a souvenir. She just wanted the key. "I found it in one of her jacket pockets along with her ex-husband's phone number. "Becky and I have been through all Grace's things and the jewellery box is the last piece."

"But what do you expect to find?" asks Miriam, genuinely confused.

"We don't know," says Becky, who's been quiet until now. "We're looking for clues."

"What clues?"

"You were the one who found her," says Becky.

"Yes. I'll never forget it," says Miriam, staring grimly at the fireplace.

"Becca believed she'd been murdered."

"What! Goodness gracious! You don't think I...?" says Miriam, glancing back and forth between us, beginning to panic.

"No, not at all," I say swiftly, to calm her down. "It's just that Grace recently learnt of something that goes back to her time in the protest movement. We believe she was threatening to expose a conspiracy of some sort, something that involved the police and has links to international investment and possibly, prostitution," I add, for good measure. Miriam goes white and does her goldfish impression. It's a world she knows nothing about.

327

"But we haven't found the evidence," adds Becky. "Her files and her laptop have yielded very little. We do know Grace was bankrupt and her house was being repossessed. Her whole life was about to come crashing down and she was desperate."

"I didn't know that. Poor Grace," she says. "But I don't see what that has to do with a box full of cheap jewellery." We all stare at the box sitting ominously on the table, like a time bomb about to explode.

"It's not the Holy Grail," I say. "But let's open it anyway."

I slide the key into the lock and it turns smoothly with a click. Inside there are three separate trays divided into various compartments containing a jumble of bangles, bracelets and necklaces, mainly silver, some garish beads, fake pearls, leather and copper wristbands and crystal earrings. It's in the bottom of the third tray. It's slim and chrome, smaller than a little finger. I hand it to Becky who smiles at me and then Becca, who nods and smiles back.

"What is it?" asks Miriam, feeling left out.

# CHAPTER 33

"Well I never!" Viv's voice booms from behind the bar and she scurries over, wiping her hands on a tea towel. "Hello darlin', how the devil are you?"

Becca gets to her feet and gives Viv's bulky frame an awkward hug. "Hi Viv. Been a while."

"I do have the right one?" she says laughing. "Hello sweetheart," she says to Becky, placing a hand on her head like she's a five year old, making her grimace. "You back for good then?" she asks Becca.

"Not sure. Kate here is helping me sort things out. She's helping us both."

"Aah, ain't it lovely? You two girls together again," gushes Viv.

"We met for the first time last night," says Becky. "Feels like we've never been apart."

"If only poor Grace were alive to see it. Her daughters reunited."

"Actually Viv," says Becky casting a glance at Becca. "Grace wasn't our mother. She was our aunt."

Viv's mouth drops open. "Well I never. Really?"

"Our mother was Grace's sister," says Becca. "She had mental health problems after we were born and went into a psychiatric hospital. Becky here was adopted by a family in Hampshire and I lived with Grace. I knew she wasn't my real mum but it never seemed to matter."

"Grace never mentioned me for some reason," says Becky.

"That's families for you," says Viv, turning philosophical for a moment. "So who was that Mr Hunky you drowned in beer?"

Becca begins to open her mouth but she's interrupted by Becky who's not fooled by Viv's disarmingly innocent question. "Just one of Grace's boyfriends."

"Oh, right," she says, clearly disappointed. "I'll get you some menus."

"What are we going to do?" says Becca when Viv has gone.

After Miriam had left, Grace's jewellery box under her arm, we wasted no time examining the flash drive. It contained all the photos and videos Des had digitised all those years ago. Images of Des, Grace and Fleur and other members of SANE; in the camp, on the march, handcuffed to railings, being carried off by police. Grainy, low definition video of police brutally attacking protestors with truncheons and tear gas, grabbing women by the hair and beating up the men.

She'd written a book entitled *Twice Shy*. The entire story of SANE and police undercover operations as told by the people who were involved and whose lives had been forever damaged, witness statements from present and former members of the movement whom Grace had tracked down in the last couple of years. Her inbox contained emails she had exchanged with national newspaper journalist Charlotte Anders, in which Grace claimed undercover police infiltrated SANE and other protest groups, their objective being to destabilise their organisation and provide intelligence to the regional police to counter what they termed 'domestic terrorism'. Officers had exploited their positions, developed intense personal relationships with some of the women, and even fathered children, before disappearing. Grace herself had evidence of one officer who fathered twins by her sister and another whose wife alleged was guilty of domestic abuse, controlling and coercive behaviour and was currently a senior detective with the NCS. She'd written everything down and was looking for a publisher. Anders was interested in pursuing the story and several times suggested they met to discuss it, but then Grace died. Getting no response, Anders gave up.

"Grace was trying to play both sides, pretending to go through with her threat, and maybe the journalist thought she

330

was just a crank. I'll go through everything at home and try to piece it together," says Becky.

"Call Des. He didn't know what Grace was really up to I'm sure he'd be interested in helping."

A familiar figure walks in led by a Staffordshire terrier straining on the lead. He looks around and spots us at the corner table. I wave at him and he looks awkward, but makes his way over. Samson begins to bark.

"Samson!" says Nigel Webb angrily, tugging on the lead, but Samson doesn't need restraining as he's cowering in front of our table, head down, snarling. I stare at him and point a finger at his nose and the bark becomes a whimper. He spins twice around like some demented pooch chasing his own tail and hides under a table opposite, where he can still see what's going on. "Stop it!" says the good doctor, "or I'll take you straight home!" he says, more for our benefit than Samson's.

"Nigel, you've met Becca and Becky," I say, ignoring the grunting, groaning animal.

"Hello doc," they say in unison.

"Hello ladies. You two certainly had me confused for a while."

"Thanks for storing Grace's stuff," says Becca.

"My pleasure. Kate here managed to track you down then?" Affable as usual, but his discomfort is evident.

"What's the matter with your dog?" asks Becky.

"He took a chunk out of my ankle," I answer for him. "He thinks I want revenge."

"He's usually perfectly placid, Kate" says Nigel. "I don't know what got into him, or what's troubling him now."

"Maybe we should take him for a walk together, so I can get to know him."

"I'd like that," says Nigel. Samson whimpers again, as if this time, he actually understood.

"Come and join us."

331

"Are you sure?" he says, quickly pulling up a chair before anyone can think twice. *That a middle-aged man might decline an offer to keep the company of three young women?*

"We wanted to ask you a question."

"I have to tell you, I never dispense medical advice while consuming alcohol," he announces jokingly. *Make them laugh Nigel.*

"About Grace."

The grin dissolves immediately. "Look, I've pretty much said all I can about that."

"Watch out!" says Becky under her breath.

"Hello Nigel," says Viv, who's appeared from nowhere. "What's the matter with Samson?"

"Nothing Viv. He's just having an off day."

Viv takes our order and wanders off, out of earshot.

"We need to be discreet," I say.

"Okay," he says nervously.

"I told you Becca here asked me to help her."

"Yes you did. And you explained why, if I recall?" He turns to Becca. "I understand you didn't accept Grace died of natural causes."

"I was suspicious, Nigel. I knew what Grace was up to and I believed there were some people who wanted to silence her."

"She died from blood loss following a blow to the head. She fell, and hit it on the hearth."

"Becca believed it was murder," says Becky.

"It wasn't. Trust me."

"Why?" says Becca. "You didn't see it happen. You arrived afterwards."

"True, I didn't see it happen, but it could not have happened any other way."

"The point is Nigel, is there any way Grace could have been attacked, hit over the head, or maybe poisoned and made to look like an accident?"

Nigel Webb looks decidedly uncomfortable. His inquisitors are waiting patiently for the answer to a very serious question. "Look, anything's possible, but not in this case."

"Did you do a post mortem?" says Becky. "Test her blood?"

"No."

"Why not?"

"I'm a GP. I don't do post mortems. Anyway, it wasn't necessary because her death wasn't suspicious to me."

"How do you know?" says Becca, getting more anxious by the second.

Nigel Webb has three women staring at him with varying degrees of intensity. I know he's faced with a dilemma, but I also know he won't get out of here without explaining.

"Here you are doc!" says Viv, appearing from nowhere with a pint. "Aren't you the lucky chap this evening?" she says, winking at us.

Nigel grins sheepishly and rolls his eyes. The evening isn't panning out the way he had imagined three minutes ago. He takes a long swig of beer. He leans forward and lowers his voice. We all lean in to hear.

"I have a duty of confidentiality to all my patients, even the deceased. But I accept these are exceptional circumstances and you two are, after all, the only surviving family, so you have a right to know. Grace had type 1 diabetes…"

"I know that!" says Becca, jumping in.

"…but she also had high cholesterol and severe hypertension, that is, very high blood pressure, all of which I was treating her for and all of which contributed to her coronary heart disease."

"What?" says Becca.

"She was booked for a bypass, and she'd already had one heart attack. The second one caused her to fall."

"She didn't tell me she was ill," says Becca.

"Your mother…"

"Aunt!"

"…aunt, was very cavalier about her illness. I doubt she believed it was serious enough to mention or perhaps she simply didn't want to worry you?"

"So the crack on the head and the bleeding?" says Becky.

"Her heart may have been pumping when she hit the floor and the blow to the head itself probably wouldn't have killed her. The heart attack may have proved fatal but loss of blood finished her off."

It's sobering; talking about Grace in her final moments, sitting around a pub table like co-conspirators, quaffing beer and wine. It should remind us all she was a living person.

"I told the police all this when they arrived."

"You called the police?"

"Of course! I had to. It was an accident even though it was an accident waiting to happen. There were no suspicious circumstances as far as they were concerned and I had no hesitation issuing the MCCD."

"What's that?" says Becky.

"Medical Certificate of Cause of Death. There was no reason to involve a coroner."

Becca sits back in her chair and lets out a sigh. "So that's that."

"It doesn't alter the fact that the police behaved appallingly," I say. "Those three guys still need to be brought to justice."

"Which three guys?" says Nigel.

"It's a long story," says Becky. "Not sure you really want to know."

334

# CHAPTER 34

Adam keeps me waiting. He suggested we met at noon at a village pub outside Ipswich as it would be more discreet. He arrived on time, but he's spent the last fifteen minutes sitting outside in the Volvo talking into space; hands free on the phone. He comes in looking flustered.

"Sorry!" he says touching cheeks as if we're old friends. "Had to take a call." I'm tempted to ask if it was Jimmy or Dave or maybe even Jason the slimeball, but decide to go easy for now "How's deepest, darkest, Lincolnshire?" he says.

I shake my head. "Cut the crap Adam, you know exactly where I live and it's nowhere near Hawsby."

"Fair enough. I did hear you'd moved."

"Jimmy Munro?"

"He may have mentioned it."

"Please," I say, mildly irritated. "I just want to ask you a few questions and then I'll be on my way."

"What about lunch?" he says, "I'm starving." He's trying to soften me up because he knows what coming.

"Have you heard from Becca?"

"No. Have you managed to find her?"

"I said cut the crap."

"Hang about! That's not fair. I haven't heard from Becca, nor do I expect to."

"But you do know where she is."

"Okay. I know she's staying with you." *Jimmy Munro.* "What's the big deal? She had a problem and by all accounts you've dealt with it. I'm pleased for you and pleased for her. Pleased she's getting over the death of her aunt."

"Trouble is, she's only just beginning to find out the truth."

"Which is?"

"That you're her father."

335

Adam Cross drops the innocent, defensive manner and turns serious. "You don't know that."

"I have no irrefutable evidence, but it all points to you. I dare say you can't be certain either, but don't you want to find out?"

"To what end? It's water under the bridge. My life moved on years ago."

"Moved on? But you do stay in touch with your old pals in Domestic Counter Terrorism don't you?"

I take Adam's silence, the absence of denial, as confirmation. Grace made his life difficult when she found out who he really was. He'd exploited Fleur and fathered her children and she threatened to expose him, not because she was incensed by his duplicity, but because she could. I'm pretty certain she threatened to expose Parker too, so Adam went running to Parker who then got his flunkies to harass first Grace and then Becca. I know Jimmy had a role in trying to calm things down; I just hope he had Becca's interests at heart and not his own.

"What is it you want from me?"

"The truth."

He shrugs. "How should I know what the truth is?"

"You were an undercover cop. You and others abused the trust of those closest to you, pretending to be someone you weren't, cruelly exploiting their feelings and vulnerabilities for personal gratification. You knew exactly what you were doing and you never gave a second's thought about how your behaviour was going to screw up the lives of those women."

"I don't remember any of them complaining."

"Doesn't it weigh on your conscience, just a little?"

"Yeah, actually it does," he says angrily. "But we were doing a job. We had to integrate with these people, we had to be credible or we'd have been found out. It's not as if I had a choice about it. I couldn't just tell the head of DCT I was

336

uncomfortable making out I was a protestor. That's the whole point about undercover!"

"But you had a choice when it came to sleeping with the enemy."

"As I said, we had to be credible. What were we going to do? *'Sorry sweetie but I have a wife and two kids back home who I only get to see every now and then, so can you satisfy me in the meantime'*?"

"You didn't have a wife and two kids at the time. Or did you?"

"No! Yes!"

"Which is it?"

"I was in a relationship, yes, but I wasn't married, no."

"How convenient for you. Not so your mates. The point is you exploited and cruelly deceived people. That's what I find so disgusting. And you call *them* terrorists?"

"Those bloody hippies have no compunction about disrupting the lawful business of others and destroying property. They're extremists with extreme beliefs, convinced they and only they are right, have no respect for the democratic process or the rule of law. As far as they're concerned they can do anything to achieve their goals. Bloody anarchists! Same then, same now."

"Didn't bother you they were hippies and anarchists if it meant you got a free shag. Maybe you enjoyed it all the more because you despised them so much?"

"It wasn't like that."

"Fleur Harding loved you and as soon as she got pregnant you ran off."

"There's no proof it was me."

"Doesn't matter who the father was. You discarded her, left her traumatised, because you told her you cared for her, loved her even, when you didn't. Because you're a con man."

He dismisses this with a wave of his hand. "She got over it. She sloped off to New Zealand and probably forgot all about it. She obviously had no interest in bringing up her daughter either."

"Sorry Adam, but that's not the case. Fleur gave birth fully expecting you to return and when you didn't, she had a breakdown, she was sectioned and spent twenty years in a psychiatric hospital with a mental condition from which she's only now recovering."

He's shocked and confused. "But Grace said…"

"Grace lied."

He wasn't expecting it and he's not sure whether to believe me. There's no doubt Grace threatened him, not just for his undercover role in the police and the impact it had, but for his fathering Becca and his extra-marital affair. But all she wanted was money, not resolution or closure. She didn't need him to make amends.

"You can't blame me for that. There were other factors at play. And I'm not going to accept responsibility for a child without proof it's mine."

"You worked it out for yourself and came to the same conclusion. If it wasn't you, then who was it? You must have believed it was you because that's why you wouldn't sleep with Becca." He goes quiet, thinking, maybe even regretting, and I can't find it in me to hate him, even though I hate what he did. "You deserve some credit for that, at least."

"Heaven forfend I should earn a few fucking smartie points," he says, with heavy sarcasm.

"The irony is, you were telling me the truth when you denied having an affair with her. But what about Grace?"

"What about Grace? I admit it was a surprise when I saw her again. And things weren't going too well at home."

"Ah, yes! How are Annabel and the kids? I remember a speech you gave me denying your affair with Becca, telling me you'd never do that to your family."

"And it was true."

"But it didn't stop you having an affair with Grace did it? I mean you may draw the line at shagging your daughter but her aunt was obviously fair game."

"Grace and I were lovers before I ever met Annabel."

"Which makes it okay to carry on where you left off?"

"No!"

"You went looking for sex, Adam, and your old mate Jimmy Munro was the ideal man to help you get it. Annabel was right all along. You were having an affair, just not with the person she thought!"

A young waitress sidles over. She's nervous, not sure whether to interrupt. She caught the tail end of the conversation and looks uneasy. She lays down two menus. "Can I get you guys something to drink?"

"Water...please," I say.

"Large whisky."

He watches her scurry away out of earshot "We're getting a divorce."

"I'm sorry."

"Don't be. It is what it is. She's got a girlfriend," he says, with a wry smile. *Yes, I know she does.*

"You also told me you hadn't seen Becca for two years. What about the time in the pub when she caught you with Grace?"

"She just turned up! Anyway, it's none of your damn business!"

"Yes it is. You made it my business when you palmed her off onto me. What did you think would happen?"

"I don't know! I needed to get her off my back. She was banging on about Grace, demanding I do something. I had more than enough going on at the time. I needed time and space. I thought you might talk her out of it, make her see sense."

I can see straight through Adam Cross and my opinion of him hasn't changed from the first time we met; *'a decent*

339

*enough bloke'*, said Jimmy Munro and I probably agree. He's not proud of what he did in the past, but instead of confronting the problem he created, he ran away from it, beginning with abandoning Fleur while she was pregnant. He got away with it for twenty years until, because of problems in his own life and the choices he made, the past came back to haunt him. And still, he's in denial, still ducking and diving, expecting it to go away.

"You told Dave Parker didn't you?"

"How do you know him?" he says, looking alarmed for the first time.

"I'll take that as a yes. Grace told you she was going to sell her story to the papers and cause a load of trouble for you and Parker, both personally and professionally, unless you helped her out of her financial difficulties. Grace told Becca the bare bones of what she was up to which made Becca think her death was suspicious. Was it?"

"Of course not! Do you really think it was that important? Do you really think Grace was nothing other than a nuisance and an inconvenience. Jesus, the police are regularly accused of much worse than a bit of skulduggery. Parker wouldn't lose any sleep over it and neither would I."

"No, as it happens I don't. But it didn't stop Parker getting heavy with Becca chasing her around the country making threats. She's only a kid!"

"I know," he says, regret creeping into his voice. "He assured me they wouldn't hurt her. Just give her a warning and a bit of a fright."

I shake my head at him. It's pathetic. "You're supposed to serve the public, maintain their respect, be ready to offer individual sacrifice in order to preserve life, demonstrate absolute impartial observance of the law. I could go on. Do you recognise any of these principles?"

"What is it you actually want Kate?" he says interrupting, leaning across the table, going on the offensive. "Do you want

340

me to say sorry? Okay! I'm sorry! Do you want me to look after Fleur because that's what Grace wanted? Do you want me to pay her compensation for the inconvenience and trauma I caused? Say sorry to Becca for not being there for her, not watching her grow up, not supporting mother and her child? My beautiful child?" He's angry, but he's angry at himself, his emotions about to spill over.

I open my phone and turn the screen towards him. I took it this morning over breakfast. Arms around each other, happy, joyful, just like their mum and their aunt looked many years ago, full of life, excited about the future. They're stunningly attractive. Anyone would be proud.

He looks at it intently, eyes darting back and forth between the two faces, colour draining from his cheeks, and lets out a croak. "What's this?"

"There we are!" says the waitress bringing our drinks. "Are you ready to order?"

"Can we have a few minutes please?" I say sweetly and she scurries away again. "Pretty aren't they?"

"Fuck."

"Just like Emma and Josie."

"Fuck."

"Get it from their parents I reckon."

He lifts his glass and drains it in one. He looks around anxiously for the waitress so he can get a refill but she's disappeared.

"Wow," he says, running a hand through his hair.

"They're grown up now Adam. They're bright, beautiful and totally self-sufficient. They have lives of their own and they don't need you, me or anyone else. In fact, they're not even sure they want to meet you. There's certainly nothing you can give them they actually want. Apart from the truth that is." He nods in submission.

"What's her name?"

"Rebecca."

"No, the other one."

"Rebecca. Becca and Becky. Grace was having a laugh. They're now on the case."

"What do you mean?"

"They have all Grace's files, photos and evidence, I've put them in touch with Des Harding and together they are going to present it to anyone in the press who'll listen and force the police to answer for their behaviour. They don't want your money or Parker's money, they just want the truth to be told. Would you be willing to take a test?"

He spots the waitress and waves his empty glass in the air. It may be the whisky but his manner and appearance have changed. He's no longer harassed, defensive and in denial. Seeing the photo is a seminal moment for him.

"Yes. It's time we drew a line under it, whatever the consequences. Having Emma and Josie finally showed me what was important in life. I should count myself lucky I'm the father of such beautiful children. I always wanted them you know?"

"Annabel said you did."

"I need something to eat. Will you join me?"

"No thanks. I have to get back."

"I should thank you for doing such a thorough job. Tell me how much I owe you?"

"Nothing. I don't want money."

"You're going to carry on helping them?"

"If they want me to, but they're bright enough to handle it themselves."

"What are you going to do now you're finished?"

"I'm not finished."

The waitress brings him another whisky and he orders a sandwich. "I don't understand."

"You asked me what I want."

"Which is?"

"I know I gave you a hard time over this. What you and your mates did twenty years ago is shameful and deserves to be exposed, for everyone's benefit. But it's nothing compared to murder."

"C'mon. You don't still believe…"

"I'm not talking about Grace." I flick through the photos and show him one that makes him drain his glass again. "Remember? All best mates. Des Harding with Mal Devlin, Ged Connor and John Franklin. I've met you all, face to face. I know you and Des and I also know the other two: Dave Parker, head of the East Midlands NCS and his brother Jason, who now goes by the name of Palmer."

"How?"

"Does it matter?"

"I'd stay away from Jason Parker if I were you."

"Why?'

"Because he's a maniac. A real bad guy. He wouldn't have been there if it weren't for Dave."

"Go on."

"You don't want to know. Trust me."

"I already do. I've already been up close and personal, within an inch of my life. I don't know what he did back then, but I know what he does now and he's still doing it. And he's still doing it because his big brother looks after him."

"What are you saying Kate?"

"Jason Parker is a killer. I'm going after him and I'm going to take Dave Parker down too. Sorry if you get caught in the crossfire."

"You? Don't be stupid. Even if you're right, you can't do it by yourself. You need to go the police with evidence."

"I already did and Parker destroyed it. I can't trust them, any of them. So I'm going to get the evidence again and give it to the press."

"Why are you telling me this? I can't help you."

"Yes you can."

343

"Look I promise. If you think I'm going to run to Parker and warn him. I won't."

"That's exactly what I want you to do."

# CHAPTER 35

On the way back I call Becky who's still on a train somewhere enroute to Hampshire.

"I managed to get through to Charlotte Anders," she says. "She remembered Grace but didn't know she had died. It's sad, but it seems her death makes the story all the more interesting to them."

"That's the press for you."

"You should know," she says laughing.

"My journalistic career never reached the giddy heights of the national press, but I know how their minds work."

"I told her we had loads of material to handover and she said she'd put us on to their special investigations team. When I told her about me and Becca she couldn't contain her excitement."

"I'll bet. A top human interest angle to add to the mix. And she has two beautiful young women to put in front of her photographers."

"Stop it!" she says and can almost see her blushing down the phone.

"Seriously, though. Are you up for it?"

"Yeah!"

"Both of you?"

"I think so."

"Because it's going to take time before the story breaks, maybe months. And when it does you're going to come under attack regardless of how much support and sympathy you get. The trolls will smell an opportunity to throw all sorts of terrible stuff at you. You can't avoid it."

"I know. But we can't just walk away."

"What does Becca think?"

"She's gung-ho as you can imagine. She already experienced some of the pressure, and you know what she's like!"

"Let me know what I can do."

"Okay. By the way, we're going to Brighton next week to see Fleur. Would you like to come?"

"If that's okay with you two. Let me know you're home."

***

Becca's in a mood. I'd called her to give her my ETA but then got held up in roadworks. I kept her informed of my slow progress, but the main reason was to check she was okay. I couldn't keep the memory of her disappearance from the barn out of my mind, and now I've lit the fuse, the stakes just got higher. She greets me at the door, glass of wine in hand.

"Thank God! I was going crazy here watching daytime TV."

"No visitors in a black SUV then?"

She laughs nervously. "God no. But I kept the pepper-spray close by. I called Becky and we had a good chat. Wish she hadn't gone home, I'm missing her already."

"She's been gone six whole hours," I say mocking her gently. I give her a hug and reach for the bottle. "You must like sleeping on the sofa."

"Hey! She asked me to go there and meet her family."

"Great. When?"

"Er, tomorrow?" she says tentatively. She must have thought I'd be upset.

"That's an excellent idea. I'll take you to the station."

"You don't mind?"

"Of course not. I think it's wonderful. You two should spend time together while you can. You have twenty years to catch up on."

"Thanks Kate."

346

I'll miss having at least one of them in the house, but until I resolve my own issues, it's safer if they stay out of the way. It will be good for Becca to be exposed to the Saunders family. They sound almost normal, a world apart from everything she's ever known. It'll open her eyes to other possibilities. I catch her eye and notice she's grinning cheekily at me.

"She's got a thing about you," she says casually, but the smirk gives her away.

"Who?" *You know fine well who.*

"My sister. Just as well I saved you from Annabel."

"Becca!"

"Sorry! Just having a laugh."

"I love you both, just not in that way."

She flashes an eyebrow. "Too bad." She's unconvinced and with good reason. She was bored, had too much time to think and she's been on the wine. "No men in your life?"

I shake my head. "Not for a couple of years. Apart from an eighty-year-old peer of the realm with a magnificent Manor House in twenty acres."

"Wow! You're a dark horse!"

"It was purely platonic, I can assure you."

"What a waste!"

"He's dead now." I say, my thoughts filled with sadness. I sometimes think Edmund will make contact but he hasn't, not yet. I tell myself he's probably busy being besotted with Eleanor all over again.

"Aw, sorry."

"That what you're looking for?"

"What? Old guy with a fortune and a heart condition?" she laughs, but the humour dissipates quickly. "I don't know what I'm looking for Kate."

"You sound like Annabel."

"What? Fucked up?"

"I didn't mean it that way."

347

"I know what you mean. It's just that I don't have any goals or any idea where I'm going."

"Are you going back to Chevenham?"

"Don't know," she says, in a way that betrays genuine doubt. "It doesn't really fit in with what me and Becky are doing now and I want to see it through."

"It's not sustainable. Being an escort."

"I know."

"Jimmy said you could live here."

"Yeah. He called to find out how I was and then he offered me a job!" she says, excited by the attention, if nothing else.

"Did he? That's nice."

"I'm not sure I'm clever enough. Becky stole all the brains when we were in the womb. Bitch!" she says, laughing joyously. "Anyway, this is your place."

"I'll be moving on soon. Don't worry about me."

"Where?" she says with sudden concern, as if squaring up for an argument.

I shrug. "Somewhere." She doesn't pursue it. There's no life for me in Holburgh or anywhere else for that matter, but it doesn't mean I can't keep looking. "Becky said you were going to Brighton. I'll meet you there, if you don't mind my tagging along, that is."

"No! That would be great thanks. We could do with your support. We've no idea what to expect."

My phone pings. A text from a number I recognise.

*"Home safe and sound. See you soon. XX [Heart]."*

I stare at the screen and wrestle with my thoughts. A straightforward message, its underlying meaning as ambiguous as I want it to be.

"Problem?" asks Becca, seeing something in my eyes.

"Becky's home."

An object on the coffee table catches my eye for the first time. I hadn't noticed it before because it's neither unusual, nor out of place. "What's this?"

348

"Found it down the garden by the back gate. I was out there this afternoon topping up the tan and saw something glinting in the undergrowth."

I hold it and examine the tactile black shaft trimmed in chrome, the letters *S.T. Dupont* engraved around the collar. The cap comes away smoothly, revealing the nib with an engraved *'D'* and the symbol *'14k'*. I know something about fountain pens, especially those with a fourteen-carat gold nib.

"These are about five hundred quid new," I say, turning it to examine every exquisite angle.

"Grace bought something classy for once," says Becca. "Trust her to lose it."

*Classy indeed. I've seen one just like it.*

# CHAPTER 36

I take Becca to the station where we have an awkward and affecting farewell, culminating in a classic, waving-from-the-platform-at-a-departing-train, moment. The last time I'd seen Becca look this lost and lonely was when she emerged from hiding at a motorway service station.

"I don't want to leave you," she said, her eyes moist, lips pursed, holding back the tears. "You've done so much for me and I feel safe when you're around." The reality is that until I've resolved the issue of Palmer, she's much safer a hundred miles away in Hampshire.

"Don't be silly. I'll be seeing you both next week."

"It's just that you said you were moving."

"I'm not going to disappear overnight. We all have plans to make and I'm not leaving until I know what you've both decided to do. So give her a big hug from me. Call me when you get there."

I left with a heavy heart. Whatever the reason behind her sadness, she has a woman's intuition. I can't guarantee I won't disappear overnight, because I can't predict how my encounter with Palmer will play out. There has to be one if he's to be stopped. It's not that I'm afraid; if there's anything positive about my condition it's the absence of fear. That's not to say my brain doesn't play tricks like it does with everyone else, especially in the middle of the night. It's just I've been purged of my instinct to survive. It allows clarity of thought.

I don't know when to expect physical contact. I doubt he'll want to disrupt his family routine by coming all this way when his day job will bring him within striking distance. But I'm coming to the conclusion that I need to set the agenda. My phone has pinged twice since last night.

*"I know where you live. [Smiling face licking lips]."* It arrived around midnight, then at eight this morning:

*"Looking forward to a catch-up. [Face screaming]."*

Adam alerted Parker and Parker wasted no time alerting his homicidal brother that I wasn't giving up. But today, I have something else in mind.

"Hello Kate!" Nigel Webb sounds pleased to hear from me.

"Thought we might go for that walk today; you, me and Samson. I can bring a picnic?"

"You're an angel. Saturday is paperwork day; I don't need any persuading!"

***

Samson wasn't happy. He had to be dragged out of the house by his lead and once he'd finished barking, continued to snuffle and grunt until he got used to me being there. I came armed with some dog treats and after twenty minutes walking, stopped by a footbridge over a brook, crouched down and held out a hand. He barked and snarled, then greed got the better of him and he began to salivate. He let out a whimper before his ears went floppy and took the treats.

"You tart," I tell him, watching him lick his lips, looking for more. "I told him we'd be best mates," I say to Nigel, who's watching the exchange nervously.

"Looks like you've finally bonded."

"Yeah, well don't let him off the lead just yet."

We set off across a wheat field, chatting aimlessly about life in Holburgh, the pub and of course, the twins.

"I told you about Grace uncovering a scandal."

"You did."

"It happened twenty-five years ago and involved undercover police. It resulted in her sister Fleur, that's the twins' mother, being sectioned. Grace only recently discovered what really happened. She made a nuisance of herself, threatening to expose high powered individuals by going to the papers. That was what made Becca suspicious about the cause of death and afterwards, she herself was harassed by plain clothes police trying to keep a lid on it."

"These are the three guys Becky said needed to face justice?"

"More or less."

"You told me this, but I can't believe the police behave like that."

"Believe it. We have more than enough evidence and the twins have made contact with the press. They're very excited about the story."

"Thanks for clearing that up. After that evening in the pub I couldn't help feeling I was still under suspicion!" he says with a nervous laugh.

We reach a ridge with sweeping views across heaths to the coast, and stop to admire the vista.

"I love it here," he says. "Can't imagine ever going back to London."

"How long were you married?"

He takes a moment, as if considering whether or not to answer the question. I can tell he's uncomfortable, but he's clever enough to know that if he expects to get closer to me, he's going to have to open up. I made the first move by asking him to take a walk, so he needs to engage in some way.

"Twenty-four years," he announces with a hint of pride, tinged with regret. "We were already drifting apart. I just thought a change of scenery would provide a good basis to start again."

"No children, then?"

"I think that would have made a difference. My wife decided life was too short to devote exclusively to me; there was much more she wanted to do. It was all very amicable, and very sad."

"I'm sorry."

"Don't be. The good news is I'm now free to go for long walks with attractive young women. I knew there'd be compensations," he says, with sardonic humour. "No chaps in your life then?" He's getting confident now, emboldened by his openness, ready to dip a toe in the water.

"Not anymore. Why don't we have lunch?" I don't want to go there. I've given him the opportunity to pursue his interest in me, but I have other matters to discuss. I hand him a sandwich and we eat under the watchful eye of Samson sitting in front of us, staring intently, drooling.

"How well did you know Grace?"

"I'm not sure what you mean."

"You said she had a number of health problems, so you must have seen a lot of her."

"She was a regular visitor to the surgery, if that's what you mean."

"Did you see her socially?"

"No, of course not. Unless by accident, if we were both in the pub, for example."

"No dates then?"

"No! I told you. That would have been highly improper." I look out across the heath towards a sea that's a deep greenish-blue in the summer sunshine. "If she hadn't been a patient…" he goes on, "I mean… well she was certainly an attractive woman," he adds unnecessarily. *There's a little bit of truth in every lie.* He adjusts his position so he can look straight at me. "Why are you asking me this Kate? You don't still believe…?"

"No I don't Nigel, but there's something I'm not clear about."

"Go on."

"I understand Grace had a telephone appointment with you the day she died, but she didn't answer so you called Miriam and asked her to go next door and check up on her."

353

"I was worried. It seemed the obvious thing to do."

"Miriam found her and called you."

"Yes. I called the paramedics immediately and went straight round there."

"She died on a Monday."

"Did she? Yes, I think that's right."

"You don't do telephone appointments on a Monday."

It's a conversation stopper. There could be a simple explanation. The appointments regime could have been different then, or he may have made an exception because of her condition, or she may have asked for one especially to suit her diary. I'm sure Dr Webb would be accommodating to all patients if he could. But if the answer were simple, he'd say so.

"No, not usually."

I give him a moment to elaborate, but he seems reluctant. I fish around in my jacket pocket and hold up the Dupont. He looks at it without a word.

"I remember when I first met Becca, she told me Grace had been looking forward to spending the night with her new boyfriend. But it was all hush-hush. It was unlike Grace not to boast about her latest squeeze, she said."

"I knew this would happen one day," he says. "Where did you find it?"

"Bottom of the garden. Under a shrub by the back gate."

He lets out a hollow laugh. "Of course."

I give him a minute to compose himself. I hope he knows I'm not a threat to him. He may actually be relieved to get it off his chest.

"Grace Harding was quite a character. I got to know her because of her diabetes. She was larger than life, provocative and flirtatious, always one for a laugh. After my wife left, she came to see me but couldn't tell me what was wrong other than to say she'd been feeling unwell, and that just seeing me would make all the difference. She flirted shamelessly, always

354

asking if I wanted to examine her, whether she should take any clothes off. I did a few tests and she was lucky. I identified her heart condition, put her on medication and gave her regular check-ups. I admired her vivacity, and I admit, I found her attractive. I agreed to give her my mobile number in case of emergency. I told her it was because ambulance response times were getting worse, but I wasn't being totally honest and I think she knew that.

"One evening she called me complaining of severe chest pains. I rushed over to find miraculously, they'd subsided. She insisted I stay for a drink, as a 'thank you' for all my trouble and, well, I couldn't say no. We had a glass or two of wine, a good chat and a laugh and I said, *'before I go I'll check your blood pressure and listen to your heart'.* So I got my equipment out of my bag and she started to unbutton her blouse, but she did it very slowly and deliberately, keeping her eyes on me and I could see she had nothing on underneath."

He rubs his chin thoughtfully and takes a drink from the water bottle. He wipes his mouth then scratches the back of his head. He doesn't need to go on, but does anyway.

"Now, I've seen many naked people in my time. It's my job for goodness sake, so I shouldn't have been at all fazed by it. But this was different. It was the way she subtly moved her body, flaunted herself that did it. I was a free agent, I'd been discarded, so it felt good to have some attention and that, together with too much wine, tipped me over the edge."

"She seduced you?"

"I'm not complaining. I knew what I was doing and deep down I knew technically it was wrong, but I managed to convince myself it was right. I wasn't taking advantage, quite the opposite in fact, and I didn't mind. I knew it would end badly, but in that moment, there was no power on earth that would stop me. Afterwards, she asked me to stay, but I couldn't leave Samson at home alone. We decided I should leave by the back gate because I'd been there three hours or so and Miriam might see me. The subterfuge only added to the excitement."

"But it wasn't a one-off."

He shakes his head. "She said she liked dogs and I could bring Samson with me next time and so I stayed over a few times, but always left before dawn and always by the back door. It's a miracle no one found out."

Ordinarily, I would have no sympathy with a doctor who allowed his base instincts to overrule his professional obligations. But the way he describes Grace's behaviour, her character and personality are entirely consistent with everything I've learnt so far and there's plenty of evidence to support it. I have no regrets challenging him to get at the truth, but realise how difficult this is for him. If I have any regrets, it's that I never met the magnificent Grace Harding. She was a legend. But he still hasn't finished, not as far as I'm concerned, and this is going to be the hardest part. "Tell me what happened."

Samson is stretched out on the grass eyes closed, soaking up the warm sunshine, whimpering gently as he dreams of sniffing the bottom of a lady Staffie. I stroke his belly and he wriggles and snuffles in response.

"It was Sunday night, late. We'd had dinner and lots to drink and eventually dragged ourselves up to bed. Samson was asleep on the fireside rug, toasting himself on the dying embers. Honestly, I'd never been with a woman like Grace before. She knew what she was doing and what buttons to press and she wore me out. It was another hour or two before we were done and I was so exhausted I fell into a deep sleep. Samson's barking woke me up in the early hours and as I slowly came round I noticed Grace was gone and there was a commotion downstairs.

"I went down and found Samson chasing that bloody cat around the house. Grace was on the floor in a pool of blood, body twitching, in her death throes. I tried everything I could, but it was too late. She'd had a massive coronary and fallen."

The image is as clear to me as watching a scene from a film. "Smokey's scratching at the door, so she lets him in, forgetting, or possibly even ignoring the fact she has an aggressive dog inside. The two animals come face to face and attack each other, and in the ensuing panic, Grace suffers a massive heart attack, trips over Samson and hits the hearth."

"How can you be so sure?" he says, frowning.

"It's just one possibility." *I'm sure Doc. Even dogs have a conscience. Samson's attack on me wasn't just about what I am, it was about who I am and what he did.*

"I did all I could and then realising it was futile, I panicked, went into survival mode. It was a terrible accident and nothing would bring Grace back. There was no reason to sacrifice my career as well. So I removed all traces of my being there and left by the back gate. I waited until nine before ringing Miriam, and well, you know the rest. The reason I was so certain what happened was because I was there."

"And the police didn't look any further because you were on the scene, you knew her medical history, and were able to talk knowledgably about cause of death."

"There was nothing to find anyway," he says. "No one asked me where I'd been the previous night, there was no sign of a break-in or evidence of any weapon or violence. I lied by omission to protect myself, to prevent being struck off, but it didn't change any of the facts."

For what it's worth, I believe Nigel Webb and his tragic account of a doomed affair with the enigmatic Grace Harding. If he'd been guilty of something worse, he would have ended the conversation the moment I'd shown him the pen. He'd deny it was his, tell me it meant nothing and I could go and be damned. It's not for me to go running to the police demanding they look further into the circumstances of her death. I know enough about the way they work to realise how pointless it would be without providing any evidence other than Nigel's own testimony, which he could easily deny. Her cremation means there's no chance of a post mortem to confirm cause of death and even if there were, it would probably only prove what they already know. He made a mistake, an error of judgment driven by human weakness and natural desire, and he risks everything by admitting it. I take some comfort from the fact he's been honest enough to open up to me and I wonder if he feels better enough about it to confess to his superiors. The question for him is whether the alternative, living the rest of his life with a cloud hanging over him, is worse.

"That's why you offered to store Grace's things. You wanted to find the pen."

He nods sadly. "What are you going to do, Kate?"

"I'm going to explain to Becca and Becky what happened just as you told me, and I'm going to tell them I believe you. I can't guarantee they won't go running to the GMC, but I'll try to convince them that's a decision best left to you. It won't bring Grace back and it'll probably destroy the career of a good doctor."

"If I own up, they'll strike me off for sure."

"You'll know that better than me. But my guess is unless they receive a complaint from a third party, they'll probably slap your wrist, tell you to go away and not embarrass them. You will have cleared your conscience, at least in part."

\*\*\*

It's three by the time we arrive back at the surgery.

"I'm going to think about what you said. I think I need to come clean and take whatever they throw at me. Tell Becca and Becky I'm sorry."

"I'll do that, Nigel. Good luck."

358

"Case closed for PI Kate Duvall. I hope you're going to stick around," he says, and instantly, a look of horror appears on his face. "God! Don't take that the wrong way, please."

"I told the twins I'd be moving on at some point."

"I understand."

"There's a lot you don't understand Nigel, a lot I can't tell you. I have unfinished business here and soon as that's done I'll be heading for pastures new."

"I hope you find what you're looking for."

"I hope you do too."

***

Becca texts me to say she's arrived. Becky and her Dad met her at the station and the rest of the family, including grandchildren, is assembling at the Saunders residence, anxious to meet and greet the newest member.

The cottage seems eerily quiet now the twins have gone, strangely quieter than when I first moved in. Smokey comes for his treats and keeps me company for a while, letting me brush his coat for once. "So, it was you and that stroppy little mutt that caused havoc here a few weeks ago?" He's not bothered in the slightest. His only objectives are finding food and staying alive. There's no room in his minuscule brain to worry, feel guilt or bear grudges. Very laudable.

***

It's a sound I haven't heard for two years, but the months roll back and I'm asleep in the cottage in Oakdale. It comes to me as fresh and familiar as if it were yesterday. Short and sharp and high pitched, neither wind, nor wind induced. The cry of an animal, a fox or an owl or a cat and then it comes again, distant, muffled, two anguished syllables.

*"Jacob!"*

359

It's not the unwitting impersonation of a human by a dumb animal misinterpreted by a tired mind. It's a tormented soul, and she's back, invoking the spirit of a man she loved, a man for whom she paid the ultimate price and who rejected her nonetheless.

*"Jacob!"* she cries again. This time she's in my room, but only in my mind.

I feel her hand in mine and I'm looking down at someone in my bed, someone who looks like me, head tossing, limbs moving, disturbed, unconscious but engaged. For the first time in weeks, I've slept soundly and deeply, the pressure of fatigue and the comfort of solitude combining to finally quash my chronic insomnia. I try to grip her hand but when I look, it's gone. Through the aroma of coal fire and carbolic that fills my senses, I mumble her name.

"Edith?" I wait for a response or repetition, but seconds turn into minutes, silence prevails, the involuntary movements of the body in the bed slow and cease, returning to rest.

*"JASON!"* She screams. Not a cry for help. A warning.

The body in my bed jerks upwards, wide awake, a gasp of anguish in fear of the monster that will cut and stab and strangle, bludgeon it to death in a bloody orgy of violence.

I listen.

It's dark, the middle of the night, when imagination and fear undermine rational thought. An unusual noise woke me, a single snap like a gunshot. I listen. I detect random, almost indiscernible movement downstairs. A running tap, a cupboard door, crockery.

*"Someone's in the house,"* whispers someone in the bed.

I hear the kettle building a head of steam and the tinkle of metal on porcelain, a chair leg scraping the tiles.

A voice from below.

*"Everythin' will be fine me duck, once we've had a nice cuppa tea."*

360

# CHAPTER 37

It's a typical suburban road, lost in a maze of identical roads featuring fifties-built semi-detached houses with single garage, tiny front lawns mostly given up to hard standing, reflecting post-war planners' failure to predict the growth in car ownership. A once affluent, middle class estate on a downward spiral, left behind by the times. Kingsdown Road, situated to the west of Solihull, is long and straight, but the house I want is easy to find, sandwiched between two with *'For Sale'* signs poking out of their handkerchief lawns.

He knows where I live. I know where lives. He doesn't know I know. It's tempting to imagine a cackling, drooling monster holed up in a cave or a hovel, with no one but rats and cockroaches for company. A festering, loathsome pit of putrescence. The reality is far more prosaic; a normal life in semi-detached suburbia, his crimes a secret to all those around him, his neighbours unaware of the shock that awaits when eventually, the nice man next door is taken away.

I park the Mini a hundred yards away and walk back. I don't expect much of a reception at three in the afternoon. There's little sign of activity, and I'd be amazed if he answers the door, but I have one hand in a pocket clutching the pepper-spray, the other holding a bunch of carnations.

A surly teenager opens the door. A riot of brown curly hair that hasn't seen a brush for a decade, black, faded, doom-metal tee-shirt over baggy, low-slung jeans that have never seen the inside of a washing machine, and finally, the inevitable white trainers, brand new and pristine. *Priorities.* He's sixteen, slack jawed, indolent, and was busy watching porn or playing *Call of Duty* when the *'fucking'* doorbell rang.

"Hello there," says the smiley, fit bird at the door. I'm the essence of courteous stranger, unassuming, unthreatening,

361

neither lost, confused nor anxious and crucially, not clutching a clipboard or pile of brochures. "Is Mr Palmer at home?"

"Nah."

"How about Mrs Palmer?"

"Nah."

"And what's your name?" I must look like one of his teachers. He despises teachers, dreams of stabbing them or blowing them away with an assault rifle along with the entire class, but here, in the flesh, and caught off guard, instinct traduces him to a monosyllabic moron.

"Eeffan."

"Hi Ethan! I'm Kate. I'm a friend of your Dad's. Do you know when he'll be back?"

"Sat'day."

"What about your Mum?"

"Soon."

"Oh dear, I came all this way to see them and just my luck, they're out!" I give an exaggerated shrug. He puts both hands in his pockets. "You don't mind if I sit on your step and wait for your Mum?"

"Nah," he says, swallowing deeply. The cogs are whirring and his loins, stirring. An adolescent fantasy to be reinvented, embellished and bragged about to his mates. "You can wait…inside. If you like?"

"Aw. That's very sweet." I step into the porch and Ethan presses his back to the door, body rigid, desperate to avoid accidental body contact. "Jason told me all about you."

I move along the short hallway, stopping to tilt my head and cast a glance up the staircase, ignoring the sitting room on the right and heading for the kitchen.

"Very homely."

Ethan comes up from behind, squirming with embarrassment, wondering if I can tell what's going on in his head and simultaneously, down below.

"Do you want…water, or something?"

362

"Water would be nice, thank you. These are for your Mum." I lay the flowers on the counter.

Ethan does for me what he's never done for anyone in his life. He opens a kitchen cupboard, retrieves a glass, runs the tap until it's cold, then fills the glass, presenting it with a casual elegance, as if executing a master class in hospitality management.

I take a long, deliberate drink from the glass, and he watches me intently. I swallow deeply, ending with a satisfied grin. I look at him and he averts his gaze, twitching with hormonal anxiety. There's a sound from the front door. I put the glass down. Ethan's mum appears, carrying two shopping bags, tired and harassed, by the look on her face. She stops dead by the kitchen door.

"Hello! Mrs Palmer?"

She throws a glance at Ethan and then back at me, suspicion and fear uppermost in her mind, but anger gets there first. "Who's this?" she says to her son. "If you've been buggering around at school…"

"I haven't!" he says, flashing her a look of contempt.

"I'm not from the school Mrs Palmer," I add helpfully.

"Jesus. You a copper?" *Here we go.*

"No." *I'm not a hooker either.*

"Who are you then? What are you doing in my house?"

Whatever it is I've brought to her door it's not going to be good and she's certain it'll be one big problem for her alone to sort out. Her face is like thunder, but there's more to it than encountering an unwelcome, uninvited guest. She's slight, emaciated even, dry hair streaked with grey, colourless eyes sunken in pools of sallow skin. She has a scab on her lower lip and the stubborn remnants of a bruise above her cheekbone. And her posture is bent, a women carrying the weight of the world in two plastic bags.

"I'm sorry to intrude. I said I'd wait outside but your son very kindly offered me a glass of water. He said you'd be back

363

soon and he was right. I'm Kate," I say, smiling openly and extending a hand. She looks at it with suspicion, refusing to engage. "I met your husband a few weeks ago. He was very helpful and kind at the time and I wasn't able to thank him properly. So here I am!" I say breezily.

"Helpful? What did he do?" she says, not sure whether she's going to like it or not.

"It was late at night. I was being harassed by a man in a car park. I genuinely thought he was going to attack me, and I'm sure he would have if your husband hadn't intervened."

"Said nothing to me about it."

"Have you seen the papers?" She shakes her head. "Triple-M? Police have published a picture of the guy."

"I've seen it," says Ethan. "Big ugly bastard with tats…"

"Ethan!" snaps Mrs Palmer, still unsure what's going on.

"I suspect Mr Palmer… er, it's Jason isn't it?" She nods. "Jason wanted to stay out of the limelight. He was just doing his civic duty but actually he was a bit of a hero. At least he was to me. That's why I wanted to come here and say thanks properly and maybe, if you're free, take you all out for a pizza?"

"Wicked!" says Ethan suddenly enthused, unlike his Mum.

"He's not here. Won't be back 'til Saturday. He works away and only comes back weekends." She's clearly still not convinced. I would understand if she failed to recognise the picture I've painted of her husband. Her face creases into a frown. "How d'you get this address?"

"After he'd chased off the guy he called the police and we were just chatting and he said he came from Solihull. The police were there in a flash and they took down our details and I heard him say Kingsdown Avenue, but not the number. I had to ask around to find your house. Hope you don't mind."

Mrs Palmer realises she's still clutching her shopping and lifts her bags onto the counter. She hasn't once raised a smile and I don't expect her to. I think my story's quite good but I have no idea whether it's plausible and I'm not a mind-reader.

"She brought them flowers," says Ethan, going into bat for the fit bird.

"Well I'm sorry," she says, still grumpy and unsmiling. "Sorry I was a bit off. Wasn't sure who you were. Surprised Jase never mentioned it. Not usually modest about things."

"And I'm sorry I arrived unannounced. Honestly, it doesn't matter. I just wanted to say thanks, that's all."

"Want a cup of tea?" she says with little enthusiasm.

"No. Thanks very much, best I just head off. Maybe you can tell your husband Kate was here and give him my number if he wants to call me? But only if he wants to. I totally understand if he wants to forget all about it."

"I'll take it!" Ethan whips out his phone and adds my number.

"Why don't you take a photo? Just to remind him who I am. He shouldn't need it, but, you never know."

"Wicked!" I put on a flirty grin and he takes several shots, one for his Dad, one for his mates and one for himself, once he's Photoshopped my head onto the body of a porn star.

***

I wanted him to know that despite the threatening messages, I hadn't gone into hiding nor was I cowering in fear. He should already know as much from our original encounter but turning up at his house should confirm it. If it has the desired effect he'll be very angry indeed, but not worried; I'm just a weak and feeble girl and he's dealt with many of those before.

When he gets Ethan's message he'll probably make a beeline for Holburgh. I don't want a confrontation there. Not enough witnesses. I set the satnav, and before leaving, send him a message.

*"Heading for South Alston. Looking forward to meeting up and carrying on our conversation."*

He responds within a minute.

*"You just crossed a line, bitch. [Skull and crossbones]."*

***

In less than an hour, I'm booked into the hotel. I got a room on an upper floor overlooking the motorway services car park and take time to scan the area through mini binoculars. There are two white Sprinters in view but neither has black alloys and there are no Mercedes SUVs. It's only mid-afternoon and I don't expect anything to happen until it gets dark, or even whether it'll be today or tomorrow, but I planned for an extended stay and brought a change of clothes.

He's not by the bins, but a look inside the main building finds him perched on a stool in the games area, bags at his feet, playing blackjack on a machine. I assume he's used the facilities, as close up under artificial light he doesn't look like a dosser, nor does he smell like his mate Trevor. I watch him deftly pressing buttons and screen icons like a concert pianist, as the symbols spin and whirr and lights flash to a manic electronic soundtrack. He hasn't noticed me standing behind him. *Wrong again.*

"Watcha Kate?" he says without turning round.

"Are you winning?"

"Two quid up."

"Best quit then."

"Maybe," he says, engrossed in the task.

"Gambling's an addiction you know?"

"I know."

"They always win in the end."

Just as I say it, the machine goes berserk, cartoon music plays in celebration, all the lights flash and I watch with

366

fascination as his account balance spin up to a hundred pounds.

"Gotcha!" He slams a palm on a large black button and the vanquished console vomits a torrent of shiny coinage.

"I stand corrected. That'll keep you in socks for a while." He gathers up the coins and tips them into a plastic box. "Are you okay Eddie?"

"Tickety-boo," he says swinging around to face me. "Find your friend?"

"Yes I did thanks. She's fine and she's safe."

"What about you?"

I'm touched someone like Eddie has time to worry about others. "I'm fine, but I may need your help again."

"Always ready to assist a beautiful young lady."

"Let's get something to eat."

*****

I buy him a hot dinner and fill him in on the background while he devours it. I explain my plan and he nods without comment, focused on his food. I text Jimmy, telling him all about Eddie, where I am and why, and to stand by for his call. I text Parker as well, telling him to expect a call at some point from Eddie, my expert witness.

"Trev's coming by," he says.

"How is he?"

"Wouldn't recognise him."

Despite everything, I feel sorry for the hapless tub of lard, whatever reputation he may have had roundly trashed by the newspapers publishing his image and the tabloids screaming his guilt. It's no surprise he's taken steps to change his appearance.

Eddie looks up from his pie and mash. "Hello mate." I turn my head to look. He's right, I wouldn't have recognised him.

367

Smart jacket over a checked shirt and chinos, shiny shoes and a flat cap. Trevor has scrubbed up. He's also lost two stone.

"Hello mate," he says mimicking his friend. "Hello sweetheart."

"Hello Trevor." He's washed too. I can smell soap and fabric conditioner. "Come and join us."

"I want to apologise. For my behaviour. I was bang out of order," he says nervously, beady eyes darting around, avoiding mine.

"That's quite alright. I'm sorry for what happened."

"Kate got that geezer arrested but plod let him go. He stitched you up, he did."

"What you doing back here?"

"I'm going to try again, but I could do with your help."

"Kate's told me all about it," says Eddie. "You and me are going on a mission, Big Man."

***

Miriam is babbling incoherently. "Kate thank goodness! Where are you? They've been here looking for you. They smashed in the door. They've turned the placed upside down. I tried to stop them but one of told me to shut up and called me…an old slag…" she wails. "What on earth is going on?"

"Calm down Miriam. Did they say who they were?"

"Police of course!"

"Are you sure?"

"Of course I'm sure! Some were in uniform and wore helmets. They had one of those battering ram thingies. It was terrible."

"Did you get any names?"

"Names? No!"

"Are they still there?"

"Yes there's a big black car outside with two men in it."

368

I tell her not to worry and go to bed. I'll be back in a day or two. Adam did a good job. Parker lost patience and decided to carry out his threat to arrest me.

I wait an hour and send Parker a text.

*"Sorry I wasn't home. I've gone to South Alston to arrest a murderer. I know he's your brother and I know what you did. You either help me, or you help him. Your choice."*

# CHAPTER 38

Parker called three times but I ignored him and he left no messages. I watched from my window until eleven, then was overcome with fatigue and had to lie down. I set my phone alarm for an hour, but that's not what wakes me.

*'Ay up me duck, peeler's reet close. Mardy an' all. Utch up! Get yer skets on.'*

"Edith?" I shout out loud, sitting up abruptly, coal fire and carbolic filling my nostrils. I grab my binoculars and go to the window. A white Sprinter with black alloys cruises the sparsely populated car park at walking pace then proceeds to the service yard and disappears from view.

The phone pings. *"He's here. [Thumbs up]."*

I leave phone and keys behind in my bag together with my jacket. As I leave the room I hear a muffled ringtone. I go downstairs and head across the car park. It's almost midnight but it's dry and the night air is still warm. *What if he's not the guy, Kate?* I have no proof, it's true. The evidence, such as it is, came to me from someone long dead. I trust her more than I trust anyone living, but it's pure instinct and I may be about to make the biggest mistake of my life. *Life, Kate?* He needs to show me the bodies. I need to see for myself. For Palmer, it's the difference between life and death, if he only knew.

I spot a green Transit with registration B16 MAN and I have to smile. I carry on past the main entrance to the service yard. The Sprinter is parked where it was before. It's empty and there's no one by the bins. The hum of air conditioning vents is the only sound competing with the whoosh of traffic on the motorway. I lean casually against the warm bonnet of the Sprinter, and wait.

I haven't been murdered before. I have been killed. But that was an accident, a moment of carelessness, a split-second lapse of concentration that changed us forever. The tragedy is

370

my sister has to live with the consequences. The irony, is so do I. Later, I was left down a mine and died more than once before finding my way out. That was different. Those responsible knew what they were doing, relying on nature to take its course. That was murderous intent. But I've never been murdered. This is different.

There is no alternative for Palmer if he wants to remain a free man. I picture the image of mediocre domesticity I found at his home, the monster hiding in plain sight, living a double life. An abusive husband and father to a scruffy, indolent kid, exchanges pleasantries with his neighbours, goes to the pub with his mates, watches TV and eats his dinner. He spends the week away from home, cruising the country in a white van, preying on women for sex or murder or both. Jimmy called him a *'fuckin' lunatic'*, a judgment formed over twenty years ago. Adam called him a *'maniac'*, and warned me to stay away from him. And Des, *'a slimeball'*.

He must have a day job, his crimes, a hobby. Six in two years, the ones we know about. What about the previous twenty? The Triple-M crimes followed a pattern. Maybe giving away a few clues, building notoriety, adds some spice? It's of no relevance. He's coming to kill me and take my body to the same place as all the others and I'm going to let him.

He appears from around the building, scanning the yard left and right. He stops a yard or two away, hands on hips. The cheap smell of *Force* wafts in my direction. I turn my back on him and face the side of the van. He waits, suspicious it's another trap, but my arms hang loose by my side and I have no pockets in which to conceal a weapon.

"What am I going to do with you?" he says, in a hoarse whisper, inches from my head. I stay silent and wait.

It's swift and brutal. The flat of a hand on the back of my head, a violent push slamming my face into white sheet metal that reacts in protest with a loud retort and reverberates in my ears. A kick to the back of the knees. I crumple to the ground.

371

Despite giddiness and pain, I think. *He's trained to do that.* A hand gripping the waistband of jeans, half-lifting, half-dragging the semi-conscious, dead weight to the back. The bang and crash of doors, lifted up, tipped head-first onto coarse carpet, legs following behind, rolling over in a heap. Two hands gripping two wrists, dragged across the abrasive floor. Flipped over, face down, arms wrenched behind, ripping shoulder muscles, one hand gripping two, cold metal, click and ratchet. *Cuffs? Peeler's reet close. Copper?* Flipped over onto back, heavy weight straddling waist, cold reptilian eyes. Gaffer tape over bloody mouth. Heavy blow intensifies throbbing, and another. Pause, heavy breathing, not mine. Rustle of cloth… buckle release… slap of leather… zip. His. Cotton…tearing… ripping. Mine. Noise, diesel, rumble outside, idling, persistent. Pause. Lifted by torn cloth, fist, punch… head…black…

\*\*\*

I awake to a steady hum. No humps or bumps or sharp turns, just a faint whoosh of wind. I don't know how long I've been unconscious, but we're on a straight road without obstacle; a motorway. Muted, muffled music and sporadic words filter through the bulkhead.

My jaw aches badly. I rub my mouth on the rough fabric the covers the floor. It sends a rocket of pain through one ear and out of the other. I let it subside, then try again. An edge of tape has lifted, the glue compromised by blood. It clings to the carpet. I use small movements, abrading the flesh on both cheeks, teasing the tape loose to breathe more easily. The pain is diminishing, reconstruction underway. Now the tape hangs limply from one cheek and I breathe normally. Curled up like a foetus on its side, a hip aches, the cuffs cut into my wrists. I adjust position to alleviate the discomfort, stretching legs as far as they'll go. *Listen. "Man United… problem you got*

372

*Gary... Chelsea... lost another manager...look..."* Light filters through tiny gaps in door seals, enough to give shape to the space. Bench seating down each side, tools on racks, ropes hang from hooks, strapping, buckles, spades, shovels, picks, axe.

The van slows noticeably, swings to the left and up a long ramp. Then a roundabout, most of the way around, picking up speed again. More imperfections in the road, the thump of the occasional pothole or drain cover. Speed lessens, wind noise dwindles. We halt. It's temporary. Set off again, slower, left, right, left again, then deep ruts jar, rock me from side to side for ten minutes or more. Smoother surface, excess road noise, swing around in a half-circle. Engine cut. Door opens. Footsteps, then silence. Prison doors open wide. Moonlight floods the interior.

He climbs in and reaffixes tape. A punch knocks me almost senseless. Ankles gripped, body sliding along the floor, carpet chafing back, tumbling to the ground in a crumpled heap. Vision blurred, damp smell, woodland and compost. Echoing footsteps, clattering, metal on metal, adjacent thud. Flipped over, face down, taste soil, heavy weight on back, rope... neck... tight... can't breathe... vision fading... can't... breathe... can't ...

\*\*\*

She's holding my hand. She's next to me, watching, but I can't see her through the swirl of mist. The air is still and the silence absolute but the picture clears gradually and the faint rustle of the trees penetrates. She squeezes my hand and lets out a sigh. "Yer reet duck?"

The image clears; trees and bushes and ferns bathed in the light of a full moon. Down below us, there's a white van with black wheels, rear doors open, and on the ground behind it, a body lies motionless. Fifty feet away amongst the bushes, a

373

man digs, shovelling soft composted dirt methodically from here to there, creating a hole, making a pile. I watch transfixed. It's all familiar; the van, the man, the body, it's ripped clothing. Mine. I grip her fingers and extend a free arm and the image expands in size. I know the girl on the ground, I've seen her in a mirror. Her eyes are open, staring, her face bruised, bloodied, mouth gaping, arms and legs twisted.

"Nar then. Yer comin' wi' me duck?" she says.

Digging man stops for a moment, takes a rest, swigs water from a bottle. He'll finish soon.

"I'm not ready Edith."

"Wots up wi' thee?" she says. "Thee'll only get mardy ag'in, darn 'ere with 'im an 'is type."

Digging man resumes his task, with renewed vigour. I need to stay, but I need her permission.

"Please Edith?"

"Ah, well. Suit tha'sel, duck. I'll be waitin'." She loosens her grip and I stare at my hands but they begin to fade, dissolving in a cloud of mist that billows from nothing, the air swirling around my head, the sound fading to silence. The darkness descends, I can't see, can't breathe…can't… breathe….

***

The dirt is sandy and soft, filling fingernails with decomposed material. I flex fingers, then hands, feeling the earth around me, touching my body. The cuffs have gone, too valuable to bury. The wheel of a van, the exhaust pipe snaking out of sight, the sound of a shovel and the grunt of manual labour. I move legs and twist head and see white flashes amongst the ferns, bobbing up and down with each shovelful. Thoughts return, body recharges, strength slowly restores. Blinking eyes sharpen, hearing acute, senses revitalised, reinitialised.

His back is towards me, too busy to notice. I crawl around to the other side and get unsteadily to my feet. My jeans are covered in dirt, my ripped shirt too. It's mixed with my own blood; smears of it streak the side of the van. I touch my nose. It's intact. I'm intact.

*Where are they?*

I strain to hear, my hearing as keen and sensitive as any wild animal mandated by self-preservation. Smokey would be proud. It's faint, but there. It's only a matter of time before he hears it too. I traverse the front of the van where the driver's door remains open, keys still in place. I lean back against the side panel, fasten the one remaining button on my shirt, cross my arms and wait.

A tyre snaps a branch like a distant gunshot. He looks back along the track, the direction we came. No lights, just the rumble of diesel clatter, idling, unnatural, but unmistakeable. He tosses the shovel aside and turns, stumbling, falling, recovering, hands on the ground for support, looks up, sees me. His eyes are like saucers, his confusion about to be made complete. The energy returns. "Come on!"

I leap into the driver's seat and start the engine. "Get in!" He's paralysed with indecision. "Get in!" I shout again through the open door, before slamming it shut. He grabs the handle, but I've flicked the lock. He bangs on the glass. "There's no time!" I scream at him, ram the stick into gear and spin the wheels. The van lurches forward and I catch a glimpse of white shirt in the mirror, leaping onto the track, sprinting, running for its life. I slam on the brakes, and fasten the seatbelt. The passenger door is wrenched open and he throws himself in. I floor the pedal, the engine roars, the wheels spin, and he tumbles into the footwell, passenger door flapping madly, until it hammers into a tree trunk and slams shut.

He drags his body onto the bucking, bouncing passenger seat, rips open the glovebox and pulls out the Glock, stabbing it violently against my temple.

"What are you going to do Jase? They're right behind. Shoot me and you'll lose precious time. I can get you away."

He glances at the door mirror. Several sets of lights bob up and down in the door mirrors, the pursuers closing.

"I fucking killed you!" he shouts above the din of the engine and the banging and crashing of suspension bottoming out in the ruts, dense shrubbery slapping the sides.

"Typical bloke. Can't tell when a girl's faking it."

We hit sixty and the passenger seatbelt warning is flashing and bleeping but he's oblivious to it. We reach the end of the track. I wrench the wheel to the right without slowing and the van careers onto a gritted road, two wheels lifting off the ground, almost toppling over before crashing back to earth. The G-force sends him banging into the door.

"Jesus Christ. You fucking maniac!"

"That's what someone said about you Jase." I glance at the door mirror. I count three sets of headlights a distance behind plus blue flashes. "By the way, I loved the choking part. You certainly know what a girl wants."

"Who are you?"

"I just love that stuff. Can't you see?"

"What?"

"I came back for more, Jase. I came back so you could finish the job. Torture me, rape me and murder me. It's just the biggest thrill."

"Stop the van!"

"Is that where you bury them?"

"Stop the van!"

"They'll catch you! I don't want them to catch you, Jase. I want more!"

"You sick bitch!"

"Do you want to go to jail?"

"I won't go to jail," he laughs with ridicule and contempt.

"You think your brother will save you?"

"Don't need him. Fucking lightweight. Self-important fuck." The track seems to go on forever. It curves right and I hit seventy. "They won't arrest me."

We hit a pothole and it's like colliding with a rock, the impact sending a brutal shock wave through the seat, rendering me momentarily weightless. The Sprinter brushes it off. "You're a copper aren't you?" No reply. "You were undercover once and you still are." No reply. "What is it this time Jase?"

"Stop the van! He pokes the Glock at my thigh."

"Humour me Jase. What is it this time? Tell me and I'll pull over and you can take your chances."

"Everyone. Albanians, Serbs, Russians, you name it."

"Traffickers?" No reply. "You work for people traffickers? Awesome!"

"I gather intelligence."

Peripheral vision catches a glimpse of bulk approaching from the right, an animal running, heading for the track ahead, galloping into danger rather than away. I jerk the wheel but it's too late. "Fuck!" he screams, holding up an arm to protect his face. The deer hits side on and is catapulted out of sight, a crazed pattern and bowl-shaped, blood-spattered dent left in the windscreen. He drops the Glock which bounces into my footwell and I kick it under my seat

"Stop!"

"Tell me!"

"I transport them. Drop them off somewhere, anywhere."

We reach tarmac and I haul left, the tyres shrieking on tarmac. I drop two gears and floor the pedal again. The lights behind us are close and I can hear sirens.

"Them? Women?"

"Bitches."

"Rape and murder?"

377

"No! Not all!" he laughs manically. "One or two, no one knows who they are! They're not missed. They're nobodies."

"The Mini drivers aren't nobodies".

"Bit of fun. A hobby. Pull over!"

I veer right to overtake a lone car. He dives under my seat, feeling desperately for the gun and I pummel his neck with a fist but he's impervious to the blows so I grab a handful of hair and rip it out of his head. He bellows in pain and reaches up blindly towards my throat, his other hand under my seat and I dig a filthy thumb nail into his eye until I feel a pop and a spurt of sticky aqueous humour in my hand. He screams again and reaches up to grab my hair and uses animal strength to ram my head forward onto the steering wheel. I jab my elbow into his bleeding eye socket while blues flashes permeate the side window, sirens wailing. He goes for the gun again and this time finds it and presses it into my thigh. The noise is deafening, the pain extreme, the leg rendered useless. We approach a sharp curve, a black and white barrier looms. I push my right foot to the floor. He shoots again under my arm, but there's no pain And he's too late.

"WATCH......!"

The banshee wail of terror beside me is satisfyingly loud and continuous as we burst through the Armco, airbags exploding all around. The Sprinter takes flight, twists weightlessly in the air and comes to earth, the sickeningly violent impact shaking every bone in my body. Then I'm rolling over and over, arms flailing, legs kicking, as the Sprinter tears itself apart in a blizzard of shattered glass and tortured metal and vicious foliage reaches in, lacerates flesh, wraps its tendrils around the body next to me and sucks it out into oblivion. Down and down, over and over, tumbling and crashing...

Blackness...silence...

\*\*\*

I watch the chaos below me, the road closed to traffic in both directions, midnight motorists waved away by uniformed police ordering them back the way they came. Twelve vehicles are strewn across the road: three police cars, two fire appliances, two ambulances, four black SUVs and a green Transit. Uniformed policemen and women, men in plainclothes, loiter at the roadside near the ragged gap in the barrier, staring at the activity a hundred feet down, where frantic rescue workers clamber over the wreckage of a former white van, a smouldering pile of scrap metal now illuminated by multiple floodlights and torches.

I can see Eddie standing next to Trevor, who's fidgeting nervously with his cap. I can see Jimmy's driver Ryan in a huddle with three other guys in suits and in a separate group, I can see Parker and his best man, with four other plainclothes officers. I move closer and listen to the subdued chat.

"I can't believe it," says Eddie.

He and Trevor did a good job. I asked them to follow as discreetly as they could, on no account try to intervene, but call Dave Parker and Jimmy Munro along the way and let them know where they were. Jimmy sent Ryan with three burly doormen. They were told to avoid interception until the Sprinter had reached its destination, then decide themselves whether to move in, wait for the police or at least, witness what happened. "Warn them he's armed," I'd said.

Ryan's on the phone. "Sorry, boss. Nothing we could do."

Parker and his best man stand stony faced. "They're both dead, Dave."

"Should have put him away," says Parker, shaking his head. "I didn't even know the little shit. Haven't seen him for ten years."

"Wasn't your call, Dave."

"Should have been. I was leant on and I was weak. Should have been my call. Knew this would happen. Stupid bloody girl." I sense regret, not criticism, a first for Dave Parker. He

379

and his team came either to make sure I was stopped, or simply to do their jobs. I hope it was the latter.

A vignette of the wooded area where I was strangled, the mass burial ground, is projected in the dark sky. It's ten miles away, yet the image is clear. Police cars, forensics vans, ambulances arriving one by one, a growing crowd of professionals in uniform and hazmat suits moving carefully amongst the ferns. They mark out a large area with illuminated posts and striped tape, ready to find Jason Palmer's DNA on the bodies.

Down below, four paramedics are climbing up the slope, carrying a stretcher aloft, a black body bag strapped on top. They reach the road where four more take over and walk it to an ambulance. Parker and his best man follow them.

"That the girl?"

"Yes sir. Dead sir, but at least she's in one piece."

"What about the guy?"

"We got a torso. Still looking for a head."

I watch them slide stretcher and body bag into the ambulance and close the doors. No need for anyone else inside.

I feel her hand in mine. "Nar then. Yer comin' wi' me duck?" I watch the ambulance take me away and as it rounds the bend and disappears from view, the scene below begins to dissolve.

# CHAPTER 39

They're already in the carpark waiting. Becca leaps out of a white Mini and races towards me, almost smothering me in a bear hug. "Missed you!" Becky wanders up and watches us with a wry smile.

"Is this a private hug or can anyone join in?"

Becca releases me and I take her sister in my arms. She holds on and when eventually, I see her eyes, they're moist, but happy.

"Okay lovebirds, that's enough of that," says Becca.

"Becs?" says Becky in mock outrage, the pink rapidly spreading across her cheeks.

"You two have been apart three whole days," says Becca. "You hadn't seen me for twenty years and all I get is a peck on the cheek and a list of instructions," she says, mocking her sister gently. "Hey Kate, can you believe I'm this good looking?" she says, presenting her twin with a flourish. "And her brothers are hot. Too bad they're spoken for. I like Ben though, he's so cute."

"He's gay Becs."

"So? Couple of hours alone with me will straighten him out. I'd call that a challenge."

"You," says Becky, pointing a finger at her sister, "are outrageous."

"Thanks!" says Becca, delighted with the compliment. "They were all lovely Kate. Made me feel like family."

"You *are* family." Becky sounds careful and restrained, but there's an underlying tension I know only too well, a nervous anticipation of what's to come. "Thanks for coming."

"Not at all, but if you want to go in by yourselves, I'm fine with that."

"No way!" says Becca. "We need you to carry the box of tissues!" Typical of Becca to make light of a difficult situation. The best jokes always grounded in truth.

They join hands and I follow them to the main entrance. Greenacres reminds me of Chevenham on a smaller scale. Surrounded by parkland and set amongst trees, the Victorian building is imposing, yet peaceful, a tranquil and benign environment for people suffering mental illness. Inside though, the familiar smell of hospital is a stark reminder of its main purpose.

Dad is a resident of somewhere like this and Mum, not far behind. My sister, still struggling with her chronic pain and disability, left to cope alone. People there, as here, lives mostly spent, being gently managed out of existence. I'm one of the lucky ones, most would say. What would any of them give to be me?

I let them lead. The girls chat to a receptionist and then take a seat in a small waiting area. They sit nervously on the edge of their seats looking at the constant traffic of nurses and assistants fetching and carrying, pushing the dazed in their wheelchairs, supporting the walking wounded as they shuffle along.

I move my head around in a circle, stretching muscles that still ache.

"Do you have a sore neck?" asks Becky, looking concerned.

"Pulled something," I answer with a suitable grimace.

"Let me." She stands behind, massaging my shoulder blades, pressing her thumbs into my neck. Becca looks on, amused.

The ambulance was in no hurry to get to the hospital, but the crew needed to offload the corpse in case they received another call. By the time we'd arrived, I'd managed to poke a finger through a hole at the top of the zip and work it down far enough to get my hand out. It was hot and sweaty inside and I stank. I was also covered in my own blood. I decided my injuries needed at least a few hours to repair and I didn't want to unduly freak the paramedics, so I waited until the doors opened before making any noise. A groan and some heavy breathing greeted the young paramedic whose name badge told me she was Sonia.

"Oh my God!" she said, jumping in and kneeling beside me, grasping a hand. "They said you was dead, sweetheart. Krish! Krish!" she yelled, rubbing my hand as if to restore circulation. "Krish!" A young chap appeared. "She's alive, Krish!"

"They said you had a broken neck, broken back, broken… everything. They said you were shot. I'm so sorry."

"Quick, get her inside," Krish had said, and within minutes I was being propelled down the corridor on a high-speed gurney. Nurses cut off my clothes, washed me and dressed me, a junior doctor checked me over, put a sticking plaster on my forehead and made me stay there overnight. In the morning, I still had a few bruises, but they could see no reason to keep me in and took me back to South Alston, still in my hospital gown. The hotel receptionist was very sympathetic, sorry to hear about my fainting episode last night and let me into my room.

"I heard Palmer killed himself," says Becky, resuming her seat.

"It's all over. They found the bodies."

The girls look haunted, thinking of the horror. Becca suddenly brightens.

"Hey! I took the job!"

"Really? That's great!"

I already know this. I called him on my way home.

"Am I tae understand reports of yer death have been exaggerated," he said without emotion. "For some reason I'm not surprised. Why would that be Kate?"

"I have a guardian angel."

"Becca's comin tae work for me."

"That's nice."

"That offer's still open."

"I'm moving on Jimmy."

"Yeah!" says Becca, excited. "Assistant to the marketing director in the entertainments division." She looks happy. "Can I come and stay for a bit, until I get settled somewhere?"

"Of course you can. When are you coming home?"

"Friday."

"I'll be out all day." I hand her my house key. "Here. Miriam's got a spare. She can let me in."

"Are you sure?"

"Sure."

"Becs and I are going to meet Charlotte Anders and her investigations team tomorrow," says Becky. "Do you want to come with us?"

"Thanks, but I'll let you two lead this one. You're more than capable."

I met Anders yesterday. I gave her the background and my involvement with the twins starting with my introduction to Becca by former undercover cop Adam Cross. I also told her the Triple-M murderer Jason Palmer, aka Jason Parker, aka John Franklin had been an undercover cop for over twenty years, that he'd been arrested a few weeks ago but released on the say so of Dave Parker, his brother, aka Ged Connor, former undercover cop and now a high ranking NCS officer. When she stopped salivating, she asked me to repeat the entire story to her editor.

"It's a serious scoop Kate," he'd said. "But you're a journalist, so why give it away? Why not write it up yourself?"

"I don't exist," I'd said unhelpfully. "I'm just a source, and I have other things to do."

A nurse in a dark blue tunic approaches.

"Rebecca?"

"Yes," say the twins together, standing to attention.

"We're both Rebecca," says Becky.

"I'm Sharon, one of the senior duty managers."

"This is our friend Kate," says Becca. "Is it okay for her to come with us?"

"Of course. I thought we should have a quick chat first."

She leads us down a long corridor and into a meeting room. It's largely original, with marble fireplace, high ceilings and cornicing, ceiling rose and sash windows that look out onto a lawn. We sit around a polished mahogany table.

"I understand you've come to see Fleur?" The twins nod nervously. "We like to welcome visitors, but first may I ask what your relationship is?" The twins exchange glances and Becca nods to her sister.

"We're sisters, you can probably tell. And we believe Fleur is our mum, although we never knew her. We actually have no evidence other than anecdotal, and that's through our Aunt Grace, who recently passed away."

"How long have you known?"

"Only a few weeks. After Grace died we were dealing with her affairs and saw the correspondence about Fleur and her being discharged."

"We've also been digging around," says Becca, "talking to people who knew her twenty years ago and we've got some pictures." Becky moves closer to nurse Sharon and flicks through a selection of images on her phone. Nurse Sharon smiles benignly.

Since Becky told me they were coming to visit, I'd been mulling it over. I was reluctant to raise it with them but if the experience of the last few months is anything to go by, there is every chance this is just another lie. There is no evidence Fleur is their mum nor Adam their dad. DNA tests could prove it, but if they didn't, if they were negative, the alternatives could be worse. In the end, I judged them to be mature and sensible enough to deal with whatever they found out, regardless of the consequences. They've embarked on a journey to discover the truth and this is just part of it. It's really none of my business.

"She'll be pleased to receive visitors," says Sharon. "I don't think anyone has ever come to see her." It fills my heart with sadness. I wish I knew why Grace abandoned her sister. She may not have made the decision to have her sectioned, but cutting all contact suggests more than just cruel self-interest. I hope the girls find the answer in Grace's diaries. "I'll bring her in, if you're ready?" The twins look nervously at one another and take each other's hand.

We listen in silence to a ticking clock. Two agonising minutes later, she's back, holding the arm of a bewildered, forty-something who's eyes scan the three people in the room, then settle on the twins. *Time to go.*

"I'm going to leave you to it. I'll wait in reception." I turn to the fragile woman and extend a hand. "Nice to meet you Fleur. My name's Kate."

She takes my hand and I'm surprised to find her skin is warm and her grip, firm. "Kate?" she says brightening. "Edith said you'd come."

\*\*\*

I get straight in the car and drive away. I feel wretched leaving the girls behind without an explanation, but they have enough emotional baggage to deal with and anyway, I wouldn't be dissuaded; it would only postpone the inevitable. I packed all my stuff in the Mini before I left the cottage and given Becca the key. She'll be able to start her new life in her own place, with a new job and I hope, spend many happy years with her sister and her new family. Becky will take it hard, but she'll get over it. I became terribly fond of her. More than fond.

I head north and pick up the M23 and then go west on the M25. I've heard Herefordshire is pretty and I've never been there. The radio mutes and the centre console lights up, indicating an incoming call.

"Kate honey! Where have you been?" bellows an ebullient voice from Noo Yawk. Gloria Sherman, my agent, over the top as ever. I finally got round to texting her my new number.

"Busy Gloria. Very busy."

"Wanted to let you know you *The Cottage* broke into the top fifty last month."

"That's nice."

"Publisher's asking when they'll get the new one that's overdue?" she says. It's a mild reprimand.

"Working on it."

"Got a title?"

"*Twice Shy*."

"Okaaayyy," she says, unconvinced. "We can work on that."

"I'm driving. Let me get back to you."

"Make sure you do honey. You have a nice day, now."

I'll change the names, and no one over here is ever likely to read it, but the American market loves charming, quintessentially English crime capers. If only they knew. There's another call.

"Annabel?"

"Hi Kate. Sounds like you're on the move?"

"Yes I am."

"I wanted to let you know. Adam has told me everything. He's told me about the twins and all about his earlier life. I haven't quite forgiven him yet, but I've said I'll stand by him and I'm going to give it a try. I can't wait to meet them," she says, excited.

"I'm very happy for you. Happy for you all."

"You did a pretty good job for a non-expert. Maybe we can get together for a drink sometime?"

I want to set her straight but I don't have it in me to hurt her anymore, and I can already imagine the quivering lip.

387

"That would be nice." I know it's a lie, but it's best to fade away. She doesn't know this is the last call and very soon, I'll have a new number. "Tell me something."

"Yes?"

"Why did you and Adam pick Hawsby to take the kids on holiday?"

"We didn't. It was Josie."

"Josie?"

"Adam spread this map out on the table and said we were all going on an adventure far away, but each of us had to pick a place and we'd decide which was best. I picked the Maldives, just to be awkward, which of course he vetoed because it wasn't on the map. Emma picked Disneyland, but I told her the ghastly place wasn't on the map either and vetoed that too. So while we're all arguing, Josie's been quiet, and then, out of the blue, at the top of her voice she shouts 'HAWSBY!' and points at the Wolds. No idea where she got that from. We had to look it up!"

Printed in Great Britain
by Amazon